The Infamous Duchess

Giving her a swift examination, Henry admired the loose strands of hair curling almost seductively next to her temples. He wanted to run them between his fingers. He also wanted to run the pad of his thumb across the bridge of her nose and trace the freckles cascading onto her cheeks. He wanted to do a lot of things. Most of which she wouldn't allow just yet.

But there was almost something reassuring about that—about knowing that when he finally kissed her, it would be because he'd truly earned it.

Because if there was one thing he could say with certainty, it was that Viola Cartwright was not the sort of woman to take kissing lightly. When he kissed her, it would mean something to her, which meant that *he* would mean something to her. And that piece of knowledge was like a comforting balm surrounding his heart.

By Sophie Barnes

Novels

THE INFAMOUS DUCHESS
THE ILLEGITIMATE DUKE
THE DUKE OF HER DESIRE
A MOST UNLIKELY DUKE
HIS SCANDALOUS KISS
THE EARL'S COMPLETE SURRENDER
LADY SARAH'S SINFUL DESIRES
THE DANGER IN TEMPTING AN EARL
THE SCANDAL IN KISSING AN HEIR
THE TROUBLE WITH BEING A DUKE
THE SECRET LIFE OF LADY LUCINDA
THERE'S SOMETHING ABOUT LADY MARY
LADY ALEXANDRA'S EXCELLENT ADVENTURE
HOW MISS RUTHERFORD GOT HER GROOVE BACK

Novellas

MISTLETOE MAGIC
(FROM FIVE GOLDEN RINGS:
A CHRISTMAS COLLECTION)

SOPHIE BARNES

Diamonds
in the Rough

The Infamous Duchess

AVONBOOKS
An Imprint of HarperCollins*Publishers*

THE INFAMOUS DUCHESS. Copyright © 2019 by Sophie Barnes. All rights reserved. Printed in the United States of America. No part of this book may be used or reproduced in any manner whatsoever without written permission except in the case of brief quotations embodied in critical articles and reviews. For information, address HarperCollins Publishers, 195 Broadway, New York, NY 10007.

First Avon Books mass market printing: April 2019

Print Edition ISBN: 978-0-06-284974-8
Digital Edition ISBN: 978-0-06-284975-5

Cover design by Guido Caroti
Cover illustration by Paul Stinson
Cover photo: Michael Frost (couple); theancienthome.com (chair)

Avon, Avon & logo, and Avon Books & logo are registered trademarks of HarperCollins Publishers in the United States of America and other countries.
HarperCollins is a registered trademark of HarperCollins Publishers in the United States of America and other countries.

FIRST EDITION

19 20 21 22 23 QGM 10 9 8 7 6 5 4 3 2 1

*To all of my lovely readers
with many thanks for your incredible support*

Chapter 1

St. Agatha's Hospital
London, 1820

Viola Cartwright, Duchess of Tremaine, stared down at the crisp piece of paper balanced between her fingers. Since she'd read the words written thereon, her heart had run off, leaving her chest with a painful knot in its place. She expelled a long breath in an effort to calm her riotous nerves and perhaps ease the churning in her belly. It was to no avail. Even though she'd known this moment would eventually come, she hadn't been prepared for the news of her stepson's homecoming.

Hoping against all odds that she might find a different message if she read the letter again, she adjusted her spectacles and considered the bold script for a second time.

>Findlay,
>Please be advised that it is time for me to come home. My ship sails from New York harbor

*on the fifteenth of March with expected arrival
in Portsmouth no more than thirty days later.
I hope I can count on you to greet me upon my
return.*

> *Robert Cartwright,*
> *Duke of Tremaine*

No request for the loyal butler to inform Viola. No
mention of her at all.

Setting the letter aside on her desk, she raised her
gaze to Findlay, who stood near the door of her office waiting. "Thank you for showing me this." She
couldn't imagine what she would have done if he
hadn't warned her.

Findlay nodded. "I felt it my duty to do so."

He took his leave, and Viola forced herself to relax. She didn't owe Robert anything. The decision
to marry his father had been hers and hers alone.
Robert should have no say in the matter. Especially
not since he'd chosen to marry the Earl of Clarendon's daughter right before departing for his father's
coffee plantation in the West Indies. He'd been away
ever since and had written only once to inform his
father that his wife was dead and that he'd sold the
plantation. There had been no word from him since.
Worse than that, when Viola had written to inform
Robert of his father's passing, her letter had been returned. It had taken two years to track him down
somewhere in India—a task she could finally claim
to have accomplished satisfactorily.

And yet, the pricking of skin at the nape of Viola's
neck made her wary. She and Robert had not parted
on the best of terms and she worried how he would
react to her now, knowing she'd married his father.

A quick rap at the door brought a nurse into Viola's office. "You're needed in the operating room.

Florian is already there," she said in reference to one of the best physicians Viola employed at St. Agatha's Hospital. His full name was Jonathan Florian Lowell, but he chose to go by his middle name because he claimed it helped people differentiate between him and his older brother Henry. This had not changed since he'd inherited his uncle's title and become the Duke of Redding. He still insisted his colleagues call him Florian.

Viola blinked. Florian was supposed to be on his way to Paris with his wife, the Duke of Huntley's sister Juliette. They'd planned everything so they would be back again in time for Juliette's expected due date. So if Florian was still here, then . . .

She was on her feet in an instant and hurrying after the nurse. "What can you tell me, Emily?" she asked as they half walked, half ran through a series of corridors and down a long flight of stairs.

"A man, roughly thirty years of age by my estimation, has been shot. Florian brought him in himself."

"Any idea who the man might be?"

"No. If Florian knows him he gave no indication."

Of course not, Viola thought. Why would he? Issuing orders and acting with haste would have been his top priority. They pushed through a pair of double doors and turned down another hallway, entering the first room on their right.

"Help me," Florian said as soon as he spotted Viola. His expression was tight and professional, but his eyes revealed a crack in his otherwise serious demeanor.

Viola rushed forward while Florian continued speaking. "I am going to give you some morphine for the pain," Florian told the patient concisely. "It should put you to sleep."

Locating a bowl of hot water, Viola reached for

the nearby soap, soaked her hands and proceeded to scrub them clean. Florian was adamant about cleanliness. He adhered to William Buchan's notion of poor hygiene spreading disease and infection. He also believed in considering new developments in medicine. So when a German colleague of his had managed to isolate morphine from opium years ago and had written to Florian of its improved effect over laudanum, Florian had started his own study into the new medication. He'd been so pleased with the results that it had become his preferred opiate even though it was not yet commercially available anywhere.

Emily handed Viola a towel, and once her hands were dry, Viola picked up another bowl containing gin-soaked surgical tools.

"I am going to get you through this," Florian added to the patient, his rough voice piercing Viola's heart. "You are not going to die today. Do you hear? Now drink this."

Fishing out a scalpel, a probe, a pair of forceps and a needle, Viola placed the surgical tools side by side on a silver tray and handed Florian a wad of antiseptically treated linen. The patient's jacket, vest, cravat and shirt had all been removed and were lying in a heap on the floor.

"Thank you," Florian muttered. He proceeded to clean the discolored wound in the patient's left shoulder. The man was pale, his body trembling slightly beneath Florian's touch, until the morphine's effect caused him to relax in a state of gradual unconsciousness.

Reaching for a sponge, Viola helped dab away excess blood. "I take it you know him," Viola said as she watched Florian probe the wound carefully with his finger.

"Locator," he replied while presenting her with the palm of his hand.

She picked up the tool and gave it to him, then helped hold open the wound for better access. Florian slid the locator in, probing for the lead ball and other foreign matter lodged beneath the patient's skin. She'd seen the procedure performed a dozen times before.

"He's my brother," Florian suddenly said, answering her question. He knit his brow and closed his eyes, allowing his sense of touch to guide him. "There! It's not too deep, thank God, but there might be some fabric as well. Let me have the forceps."

Viola handed the tool over and sponged the wound clean once more. She wasn't too surprised to discover that the man lying outstretched on the operating table was Henry Lowell. His reputation as a notorious rake was such that even a nonsocial woman like herself could not avoid hearing of some of his exploits, like the affair the Earl of Elmwood had accused him of having with his wife.

"Please check this against his shirt," Florian said. He dropped a piece of bloodied linen into a small empty bowl.

Grabbing the garment, Viola stretched the front of it out on a nearby counter and tried to match the piece of fabric to the part of the shirt that was missing. "I think there might be a little bit more," she told Florian.

He bowed his head again and probed deeper. Seconds ticked by with infernal slowness until, with a long exhale, he pulled the tiniest fabric piece free. Getting the lead ball out after that was fairly simple, after which the only remaining task was to trim the dead skin around the wound with a scalpel and suture it.

"I'm sorry he got shot," Viola said, not because she had much sympathy for a renowned libertine, but because it was clear to her that Florian was upset. She threaded a needle with waxed silk and handed it to him as soon as he'd finished using the scalpel.

He snorted and proceeded to stitch up the wound. "He's a wonderful brother and I love him dearly, but he can also be a bloody idiot at times. In this case, he chose to offer a young dandy advice on his clothing."

Viola pressed her lips together to refrain from smiling. This was, after all, a serious matter. She was fairly sure Florian wouldn't approve of her being amused by it. She cleared her throat and began preparing a compress. "Which poultice do you prefer to use?"

"I'll have the one with the crushed onion and honey."

Spreading the mixture out on a thin piece of linen, Viola placed it carefully over the wound while Florian went to clean his hands. She then added a thicker wad of clean linen on top and asked Emily to help her secure it with a bandage.

It wasn't until she was finished that she allowed herself to consider Mr. Lowell's appearance. Until now, she'd been methodical in her work and professionally detached. With her task completed, however, she became aware of Mr. Lowell's size and, more to the point, his stunning physique.

This was not a man of leisure but one who exercised frequently. His belly was flat, his abdomen tight and his arms well-defined by muscles. As far as she could tell, he was broader than Florian, but this was not the only thing that set the brothers apart. While Florian's hair was vibrant with varying shades of copper, Lowell's was raven black. His jaw was also more angular and his lower lip slightly fuller. Staring down at him, Viola fleetingly wondered about the color of his eyes, now hidden from view beneath a pair of lids that were fringed with thick, dark lashes.

"It's surprising no one ever suspected us of being only half brothers," Florian murmured, startling Viola from her quiet perusal.

"People often believe what they're told as long as the story's convincing enough. In your case there was no reason for anyone to think you weren't Armswell's son."

Not even Florian's brother had known until Florian had told him last year that their fathers weren't one and the same. While Mr. Lowell shared Armswell's blood, Florian had been sired by Bartholomew, one of England's most infamous criminals. The scandal when the news had broken had almost destroyed Florian's career.

"I suppose so," Florian said. He touched his knuckles briefly to his brother's arm before saying, "We should get him upstairs so this room can be cleaned."

"Of course." Viola turned for the door with the intention of calling a couple of orderlies to assist. She paused and glanced back at Florian. "How come you're here, by the way, and not on your way to Paris with Juliette?"

Florian shrugged. "Henry came to see me last night, told me about the duel and asked if I might be able to delay my trip." He glanced at his brother. "I'm glad I did."

"Of course. It was the right decision to make." She considered his weary expression for a second before saying, "He'll be all right now and there's a team of well-trained staff to help with his recuperation. So if you want to catch the next ship, I see no reason why you shouldn't. You and Juliette deserve your adventure. Once the baby arrives, there'll be no time."

Wincing, Florian removed his surgical apron, tossed it in a basket for laundering and rolled down his shirtsleeves. "There's not enough time as it is. My work is demanding, Viola, which is why we weren't able to get away sooner."

"Then for heaven's sake go on your trip with Juliette while you still can and entrust me with your brother's care."

"You're taking on a lot of tasks, Viola. Between running the hospital, readying the rejuvenation center for its grand opening and now this . . . I really ought to be staying."

"We've discussed this, Florian. Running the hospital is second nature to me now and the rejuvenation center is coming along splendidly." Intended to offer the rich a spa-like experience without going to Bath, the center would provide the hospital with additional funds. For although St. Agatha's still ran smoothly thanks to donations, it could not continue to do so for long. Due to the free care it provided to the poor, its popularity continued to increase, which meant it would soon require expanding. For this to be possible, Viola would need to ensure a steady income, and her plan was to use the center's profits to do so. "Last I checked, the artists were about to get started on the murals, and that was already a few days ago. Besides, we both know I'm more likely to draw a crowd for the grand opening than you are. It won't matter what Society thinks of me, Florian. People will come for the sole purpose of sating their curiosity if I send out the invitations. They'll want to catch a glimpse of the woman who snagged a duke one day and inherited his fortune the next."

Because of her brief marriage and her lack of interest in mingling with a social class to which she did not feel she belonged, she'd kept a low profile by moving into a modest house after her husband's death, focusing on her work and maintaining what would probably be described as an unremarkable appearance.

"As for your brother," she added, "he'll undoubt-edly sleep most of the time, I should think."

Florian hesitated. "He will wake up eventually, and when he does, he'll want to be entertained. He doesn't like being bored."

"I don't think anyone does. Do they?"

Florian watched her with his typically inscrutable expression. But Viola knew him well enough by now to know he was carefully weighing the options she'd laid out before him. "My servants can help with the grand opening. You'll need someone there to wel-come the guests and to offer them drinks and some sort of food."

"I'll meet with your manservant and cook to make the necessary arrangements."

He hesitated briefly, then grabbed his jacket from a hook on the wall and shoved his arms into the sleeves. "Very well. I shall agree to think about it."

Happy with that assurance, Viola smiled to hide her concerns and continued out into the hallway. Be-cause although Florian deserved a reprieve and she'd pushed for it, his absence would mean she'd some-how have to deal with Robert's arrival alone, not to mention Florian's handsome rake of a brother. And the truth of the matter was she had no idea how to handle either.

When Henry Atticus Lowell awoke, the first thing he became aware of was the gentle tread of someone moving carefully about. He flexed his fingers and felt the soft cotton of a sheet draped over his body. Well, it would seem he was still alive, thanks to his broth-er's miraculous efforts. And the pain . . . it was more of an ache now, which was a definite improvement.

Hesitantly, he opened his eyes just enough to let a

bit of light in. It was blinding, the sunshine spilling in from a nearby window with unforgiving brightness. He winced and immediately closed his eyes again.

"Mr. Lowell?" The voice that spoke was feminine, soft and soothing, a mere whisper almost. Henry grunted his response and sensed the woman come nearer. "I hope I did not disturb you." A soft hand settled upon his brow for no more than a fleeting second. "You do not seem to have a fever, which is excellent news."

He drew a deep breath, focused on the tightening effect it had on his chest, and gradually expelled it. "No." Again he tried to open his eyes, to see the nurse who'd come to attend him. She sounded lovely and . . . The light was no longer as bright as it had been. It shone at the woman's back, surrounding her in a halo of gold. She was fair, with dark blond tresses catching the sun and tossing it back. Her face, however, was perfection itself, a pair of pale blue eyes and full lips portraying the deepest shade of rose he'd ever seen.

Perhaps he had died after all.

Henry closed his eyes on that thought and allowed himself to drift off again, certain he'd just caught a glimpse of heaven and one of its prettiest angels. But the matter of leaving his earthly state was quickly dismissed when he woke again later to find his brother sitting nearby. The room was now cast in shadows, alerting Henry to the late time of day.

He tried to speak but wheezed instead and was grateful for the glass of water Florian swiftly pressed to his lips. "Thank you," he managed after savoring the cool liquid flowing down his parched throat.

Florian eyed him with stalwart gravity. "I was worried about you for a moment."

Henry grinned and shifted, immediately regretting

doing so when his wound stretched uncomfortably in response. He winced and grew serious, making every effort to relax. "Is that really all I deserve? A mere moment of concern?"

"Humph! I've enough faith in my own skills to know when more is unnecessary. That's the moment I'm talking about. The second it took to assure myself that I wouldn't have to convey the news of your death to our parents." He paused for a second, and then, "What the devil were you thinking, antagonizing a cocky lad who's barely quit his leading strings? You know someone like that is going to fight before he thinks."

"You're lucky he isn't here to witness your insult or I daresay he'd call you out next. All I did was tell him his orange jacket looked ghastly and that his tailor ought to give better advice."

"Christ, Henry."

"What? Would you not prefer for someone to tell you that you look ridiculous instead of continuing to parade about as if you're presenting high fashion?"

"Of course I would, but that's hardly . . ." Florian let the words fade and placed his hand on Henry's arm instead. "I'm glad you're all right and that you're still here. The alternative would be unthinkable."

Henry allowed a faint smile. "I made you miss your ship." He felt terrible about upsetting his brother's plans, but he'd also been more afraid than he'd let on and had wanted his brother's medical expertise to be available.

"Yes. You did."

"Can you forgive me?"

"After everything you've done for me? How could I not?"

Grateful, Henry sank further back against his pillow. And yet . . . "I haven't done so much."

Florian held his gaze. "No. Of course you haven't. You only helped me fight Bartholomew after discovering I'd lied to you about him for fourteen years."

"Telling me he was your father was not a simple thing."

"No. It was not. But that doesn't change the fact that perhaps it is I who should ask for your forgiveness?"

Henry sighed. "You're my brother, no matter what. Forgiving you was easy."

"Thank you."

Florian shifted as if discomforted by the intimacy of their conversation, so Henry decided to change the subject. "There was a nurse here earlier, or at least I believe she must have been a nurse."

The edge of Florian's mouth lifted. "And?"

"Well, I was merely thinking that if she's been assigned to my care, it would be nice to know her name."

"Hmm . . ." Florian didn't look convinced by this explanation, as evidenced when he said, "I don't want you flirting with the staff, Henry. You need to recuperate and they need to do their jobs without you ta—"

"For God's sake. I only want her name. You needn't make it sound as though I have questionable intentions."

Florian sighed. "Fine. If you can describe her to me, I might be able to help."

Pleased, Henry couldn't stop from smiling. Especially not when he thought of the woman he'd seen. "She's fair with golden hair and eyes the loveliest shade of blue I have ever seen."

"Ah. I believe you must be referring to Emily."

Henry frowned. It was almost as if his brother sounded relieved. "Emily . . ." What a lovely name.

"Thank you, Florian. I promise not to flirt with her too much." Florian gave him a quelling look to which Henry laughed and immediately flinched in response to the pain it caused. "You should go. Your ability to amuse me today is not helping with my recovery."

"Are you sure you'll be all right?" Florian asked, ignoring his comment. "Perhaps—"

"No." He shook his head adamantly. "Take the next ship to France, Florian. Enjoy your holiday in Paris with Juliette. I shall be perfectly fine until you get back."

Florian stared down at him for a lengthy moment and finally nodded. "Very well then. I will see you in roughly one month." He moved as if considering an embrace but froze and, pulling back, simply reached for Henry's hand and gave it a squeeze. "Take care of yourself, brother. And please, do try to stay out of trouble."

Henry smiled with deliberate mischief. "Of course, Florian. You can count on me to do precisely that."

With a soft scoff and a shake of his head, Florian strode from the room, leaving Henry to think about what to say the next time he saw Emily.

Chapter 2

Tucking a loose strand of hair behind her ear, Viola considered her reflection in the mirror and gave herself a firm nod. She looked acceptable. Not pretty by any means, but then again, who needed prettiness in a place where cleanliness, precision and expediency were of the highest value?

With one final look at herself, she picked up her spectacles and placed them in the pocket of her skirt before leaving her office. It was time for her to make her rounds, and with Florian's departure the day before and the promise she'd made to look after his brother, she would need to check up on Mr. Lowell. According to Emily, he'd slept since yesterday afternoon, which meant he'd gotten a good sixteen hours of rest at least.

Passing a room shared by four female patients, Viola stepped inside and saw that Mrs. Richardson was awake.

"How are you this morning?" Viola asked the older woman, who'd fallen from a ladder and broken her leg two days earlier.

Mrs. Richardson pulled back the cover and wiggled her toes. "Feeling better already," she said with a cheerful smile, and Viola saw that the bandages wrapped around her leg to hold the splints in place had been painted in bright displays of color.

"Who's the artist?" Viola asked in a whisper so as not to wake the other women who still slept.

"Yours truly," Mrs. Richardson replied. "My daughter brought me my watercolors the day before yesterday. She said she heard something about Viscount Armswell's son, Mr. Lowell, being brought in around the time she arrived—mentioned him having been shot?"

"Hmm . . . You know I cannot discuss other patients with you, do you not?" She'd have to find out which of her staff members had betrayed Mr. Lowell's identity loud enough for others to hear.

"So that would be a yes to my question," Mrs. Richardson said with a satisfied smile. "Doesn't really surprise me, all things considered."

Unable to stop her curiosity, Viola took a step closer to Mrs. Richardson's bed. "You know him then?"

"No. Of course not. His family's much too high in the instep for the likes of me."

That was what Viola had suspected. Mrs. Richardson didn't seem particularly well off, even if she was able to afford watercolors.

"One does hear things, however," Mrs. Richardson went on. "From what I have learned, Mr. Lowell is a proper scoundrel. I've a friend who's employed by the Dowager Marchioness of Wentworth as her companion and she claims to have seen Mr. Lowell at various social gatherings. According to her, he's always flirting with one woman or another. Says she even thinks he may have intended to proposition the Duchess of Coventry before she married the duke. Saw him sticking a bit too closely to her side a couple of Seasons ago. Claims it was all rather distasteful, seeing as

Her Grace had just come from the slums and all that. Lowell was like a tiger just waiting to pounce."

Viola didn't like anything about that description. "Perhaps he genuinely liked her," she suggested, "and was simply trying to be friendly without any ulterior motive." Her loyalty toward Florian prompted her to defend his brother in spite of her own opinion of him, which wasn't much different from Mrs. Richardson's.

Mrs. Richardson gave her a dubious look. "He took up with Viscount Blithe's widow after that, and the viscount had only been dead one week. Not to mention his affair with Lady Elmwood last year."

Mrs. Richardson pressed her lips together as if intending to stop from saying anything more. But then she quickly continued. "My friend says Mr. Lowell has two extra houses in London—one where he keeps his mistress and the other where he conducts his affairs with unassuming young women."

Viola bit her lip to stop from laughing. She leaned toward the older woman in a conspiratorial way. "You make it sound as if he's a predator luring the innocent into his lair."

"Suffice it to say that I have it on good authority Mr. Lowell enjoys the company of women excessively. So much in fact, it's likely to get him killed one day if he doesn't start being more careful."

Refraining from mentioning the real cause of his most recent duel, Viola promised Mrs. Richardson she'd have some breakfast delivered soon and went to continue her rounds.

She arrived in Mr. Lowell's room twenty minutes later to find the man in question propped up against a pile of pillows and with the *Mayfair Chronicle* in his lap. He didn't notice her right away, his concentration fixed on whatever it was he was reading, which allowed her a moment to study him discreetly.

When she'd last seen him, he'd been hovering between sleep and wakefulness. She'd checked to see if he had a fever and he'd stared at her for a long moment before slipping back into unconsciousness. Now, his eyes were focused with great intensity on what he was reading while a stray lock of black hair fell carelessly across his brow. It afforded him with a touch of untidiness that she found oddly charming and perhaps even a little attractive. If she was being completely honest. Until she reminded herself of the sort of man he was and instantly warned herself not to fall under his spell.

So she stiffened her spine and strode forward with purpose. He looked up and their eyes met. Viola's heart stuttered and her belly turned over without any warning, prompting her to look away.

"Good morning, Mr. Lowell," she forced herself to say. He was only a man. And she'd dealt with plenty of those in the past. Though none quite as handsome as this fine specimen.

Stop it!

Somehow she managed to offer a smile and remain upright. She made herself meet his gaze once more, her breath catching slightly the moment she did in response to the interest she saw there. Unnerved yet determined to avoid showing weakness, she concentrated on doing her job by asking, "How are you feeling today?"

"Rather well, now that you are here," he murmured. His voice was like silk slipping over her skin.

Oh, he was good. *Too good.* She clasped her hands together and squared her shoulders, intent on resisting his charm. Which became infinitely easier when he quirked an eyebrow and added, in the most seductive tone she'd ever heard, "Emily."

Viola felt her lips twitch at first. And then she

laughed. "Emily?" She laughed a bit more while he began frowning. And then a thought struck her and she turned immediately serious. They were in a hospital, after all, and he was looking very confused. So she went to the side of the bed, bowed over his head and stared down into his right eye while prying it slightly more open with her fingers. "Do you know if you hit your head when you were shot?"

"No." He allowed her to look in his left eye as well. "Why?"

She leaned back. His pupils appeared to be responding normally. "Because you think I'm Emily and the two of us look nothing alike."

He shifted a little higher against his pillows while she proceeded to pour him a glass of water. "That's odd. When I asked my brother about you and gave a description, he told me your name was Emily."

Setting the glass to his lips, Viola helped him drink. "Well, I cannot imagine what you told him, but I am Viola. Viola Cartwright, to be exact." She rarely gave her title, preferring to avoid unnecessary attention in favor of being treated like the rest of her staff.

A charming smile brightened his features. "Then your name is even lovelier than I initially thought."

A surge of warmth swept through her, pricking her skin. Disliking the effect he was having on her and feeling unmoored by the rare attempt at flattery, she said nothing and went to disinfect her hands. "I need to take a look at your wound, Mr. Lowell."

"You may call me Henry, if you like."

Her stomach bounced in a most uncomfortable way. "I'd rather not."

"But if I am to call you Viola, then—"

"You are a patient, Mr. Lowell, and therefore free to address all the nurses by their given names. Just as you would address a maid." Putting up barriers between them now was both vital and wise. Especially if she was to resist him.

"That hardly seems fair." He was practically pouting now, and God help her if the expression didn't make him look totally adorable.

"These are the hospital rules," she said, deliberately turning away so he wouldn't see her smile. She made sure to compose herself completely before turning back to face him. "If our inequality disturbs you, you are free to call me Mrs. Cartwright." There. She'd effectively made herself quite unavailable.

His smile fell a little. "A pity when your given name is so very pretty."

She arched a brow. "I realize I've put you in something of a bind, for which I do apologize."

He was the one to laugh this time. "Why, Mrs. Cartwright. Are you always this delightful?"

"Only where you are concerned, it would seem," Viola muttered, and then immediately chastised herself for allowing him to engage her. Amusement sparkled in his dark brown eyes, stirring her senses in ways to which she'd thought herself immune.

Giving herself a mental shake, Viola removed Mr. Lowell's newspaper from the bed, pushed down his sheet and began tackling his shirt. It was what she did, what she'd done more times than she could count, and yet for the first time ever, she felt her fingers tremble as she fumbled with the fabric.

Pull yourself together, she chided herself. But then her fingers made contact with his skin and he sucked in a breath. Without thinking, she raised her gaze to his and immediately regretted doing so. Because he was watching her closely and with the sort of look . . .

Her pulse beat faster and her mouth went instantly dry. She forced her attention back to her work, clinging to the methodical familiarity it offered.

When she'd finally changed his compress and bandaged the wound again, she took a step back and breathed a sigh of relief. As she reached for the newspaper with the intention of returning it to her patient, her eye caught the section he'd been reading, which prompted her to pause.

She shook her head and looked at him in amazement. "You like the puzzles?" It didn't seem to square with his rakish reputation.

He smiled, not the flirtatious sort of smile he'd given her before, but a more playful variety. A shrug followed. "I find them entertaining."

"So do I," she admitted, and for a long second after, it was impossible for her to look away. It was as if his gaze was pulling her to him.

Feeling a wave of heat creep over her skin, she returned her attention to the newspaper in her hand with the intention of reading one of the puzzles herself. Her hand instinctively went to her skirt pocket and paused. She knit her brow, attempting against all hope to make out the blurry words without using her spectacles.

Failing, she returned the newspaper to Mr. Lowell's lap. She was plain enough as she was. No need to add to her undesirability by showing off her long-sightedness as well. Not that she wanted Mr. Lowell to find her desirable, because she most definitely didn't, but Robert had always laughed when he'd seen her wearing her spectacles, which was why she only ever put them on when it was absolutely necessary.

Mr. Lowell gave her a curious look, but rather than broach her unwillingness to attempt the puzzle, he settled back against his pillows and yawned. "I do apologize, Mrs. Cartwright, but I seem to require more rest than usual at the moment."

She chuckled lightly and with a strange appreciation for his consideration toward her. "Let's not forget you were recently shot and underwent surgery. It would be strange if you weren't feeling somewhat put out."

The edge of his mouth lifted. "Beautiful and amusing," he murmured. "Remind me to send my dueling opponent a thank-you note. Had it not been for him, you and I might never have met."

She pursed her lips before saying, "Something tells me you would have arrived here sooner or later." Determined not to let him detain her any longer, Viola picked up the bowl containing the old compress and bandage and strode to the door.

"One moment," Mr. Lowell spoke to her back.

Muttering a curse, Viola paused on the threshold and turned. "Yes?"

He smiled beatifically, which not only put Viola's nerves on edge but also made butterflies soar in her belly. "Might I request a bath after my nap? And if so, will you be good enough to assist me with it?"

A rush of heat swept through Viola, so intense she feared she might catch fire. Of all the things he might have asked, she had not expected this. It proved he was more of a scoundrel than she'd imagined, because heaven above, the man was shamelessly staring at her with a wolfish gleam to his eyes and a smirk on his handsome face.

"I . . . um . . ." *Oh, for God's sake!* Viola straightened her spine and pressed the bowl she held to her chest like a shield. "Considering the immobile state of most patients, bathing tends to require a great deal of heavy lifting. Consequently, the nurses are all exempt from this duty." She smiled back at him and told him gently, "I'll ask the strongest orderlies I can find to come and help you as soon as possible. And since you're not allowed to make any movements that might put a strain on the wound, I hope you'll allow them to clean the more hard-to-reach places for you."

Mr. Lowell's smile evaporated completely.

Offering no more than a nod, Viola used his dumbfounded silence to make her escape. It wasn't until she was well out of sight and hearing that she allowed herself the grin that threatened. She'd gotten the best of Mr. Lowell just now and she found she rather enjoyed it.

Henry stared at the vacant doorway, his mind still occupied by the woman who'd turned the tables on him only seconds earlier. She was stunningly beautiful, not in the classical sense, but in a way that set her apart from the rest. He'd been wrong, he realized, to tell his brother her eyes were blue and her hair golden. No wonder he'd thought he was speaking of the other nurse, Emily, instead of Viola, whose eyes were an interesting shade of gray. They were the eyes of a sharp and intelligent woman—the sort of woman whom he suspected capable of holding his interest for infinite lengths of time. Her hair, on the other hand, was perhaps a bit duller than Emily's, but it was thicker and longer, as judged by the volume of her tight chignon. He'd longed to unpin it and watch it fall over her shoulders ever since he'd first seen her.

But it wasn't just her eyes or her hair that was fascinating. It was also the shape of her mouth, the perfectly plump lower lip and the dimples at either side. And then there were the freckles . . . Lord help him, he'd never thought he'd find tiny little dots of brown so attractive, but they somehow seemed to suit her personality, which clearly leaned toward the teasing side.

Sighing, he decided he had to encourage more of the same. Because her ability to get the better of him had provoked him in ways nothing had in recent years. Which was why it was such a pity she was only a nurse.

It didn't matter how smart or feisty she was, because when it came to doing his duty, he would have to choose a respectable lady from amid the peerage. This was the only way to improve his reputation and prevent further scandal from befalling his family.

Of course, he would also have to consider a woman who wasn't already married.

What an unfortunate shame that was.

Henry picked up the paper and stared at the puzzle. Mrs. Cartwright had said she enjoyed them and yet she'd clearly avoided attempting to solve it. He wondered over that for a while and when he failed to arrive at a plausible explanation, he decided to get some more rest. Not that he was particularly tired. He'd affected the yawn for Mrs. Cartwright's benefit so she'd have an excuse to leave his side. For although he regretted letting her go, he sensed she wasn't the sort of woman who responded well to a man's blatant interest. Her constant attempts to school her features and refrain from smiling, along with the way her hand shook when she returned the newspaper to him, were telling. She was loyal to her husband and refused to be charmed by another man, which only made him like her more.

Thankfully, when he woke again later in the day and requested the bath he craved, he was able to convince the orderlies who brought the small tub to his room that he was perfectly capable of managing on his own. Initially they insisted they help, but when he showed he could stand on his own two feet by himself without falling over, they relented.

"I understand you have chosen to ignore my advice and refused to listen to the orderlies when they asked to stay in the room with you while you bathed," Mrs. Cartwright said when she came to see him in the evening. She was holding a tray on which Henry spied a plate of food and a glass of something he hoped might be wine. "Your wound is serious, Mr. Lowell and the cause of some restriction. What if you slipped in the tub while reaching for the soap? What should I tell your brother then after promising him I'd ensure your complete recuperation?"

Henry did his best to hide the smile that threatened. And failed. "Forgive me, but I do think you're overreacting."

She stared at him, and for a moment he feared she might toss the tray and all of its contents directly at his head. Instead, she took a step closer and narrowed her eyes in a way he found both alarming and strangely arousing. "I work in a hospital, Mr. Lowell. I see what happens when people aren't careful enough. The last man I met who slipped in his tub arrived here with two broken wrists *and* a concussion."

It was clearly time to accept her point of view and do the right thing. "I apologize, Mrs. Cartwright. From now on I'll heed your advice. You have my word and my full cooperation."

Her shoulders dropped as her jaw went slack, and it occurred to Henry that she was dismayed by his willingness to cede the argument. A frown followed. She pursed her lips as if in speculation. "Really?"

"I swear it." He smiled brightly. "And if I break my promise, I'll . . ." He considered his options for a moment while regarding her carefully. "I'll work in your employ for a week after I recover."

Her lips twitched. "Why do I feel like this is a trick?" Moving around the bed, she approached the table next to it and set the tray down. The delicious smell of spiced meat and vegetables wafted toward him from a covered plate and made his mouth water. The glass of wine standing beside it had him straightening his posture in anticipation of his meal.

"You think I might deliberately misbehave in order to spend more time in your company?" he asked. Shifting his gaze away from the tempting contents of the tray, he looked up at her and felt his heartbeats echoing through him. Christ, she was lovely. "Even though doing so would involve submitting myself to your will?"

A choked sound rose from her throat. "Of course not." Her cheeks were turning a fascinating shade of pink. "That would be ridiculous."

"Would it?" He stared at her boldly, appreciating the small gasp she made and how the air seemed to crackle between them. A pity she wasn't a possible choice when it came to his future wife. Because although he placed little weight on titles and rank since he'd rather consider character first, he wasn't free to marry whomever he pleased. Not as an earl's heir and not when he was trying to restore his own reputation. Indeed, the woman he chose to marry would have to be as respectable as they came and of good social standing. It would also help a great deal if she wasn't already married.

He laughed when he realized how shocked she looked. "I jest, Mrs. Cartwright."

Relief swept over her features. "Of course you do." She took a step back.

"I've never enjoyed eating alone. It would give me great pleasure if you would remain here with me for a while and keep me company." Surely there was no harm in that. She glanced at the door as if salvation waited beyond it. Henry took a deep breath and then spoke the one word he hoped might sway her. "Please?"

Her eyes met his and he saw in them her struggle with indecision. When she eventually slid her gaze across to the vacant chair beside his bed and nodded, joy fizzed through his veins like rich champagne.

"I cannot stay long, Mr. Lowell. I am expected home for dinner."

"I see." The joy turned to flat disappointment. Her husband was probably waiting for her to join him. Attempting a smile to hide his true feelings, yet determined to do the right thing, he said, "Now that I know this, it would be thoughtless of me to desire your company. If you would rather—"

"No. It is quite all right." She picked the tray up again and waited for him to reposition himself before placing it in his lap. Lifting the lid off the plate, she set it aside and lowered herself to the chair. "It must be dull to remain abed all day, so I can appreciate your need for conversation."

What he appreciated was she, but he refrained from saying as much. Instead Henry took a bite of his food. It wasn't the best pork roast he'd ever had, but it was certainly good enough. Why, it was almost as if the flavor was diminishing the ache from his wound as he chewed. He washed the meat down with a sip of his wine.

"Your husband is a lucky fellow, Mrs. Cartwright." He proceeded to cut a potato, once lengthwise and then across, before dipping each piece in the gravy and making a very deliberate effort not to look directly at her. Her silence was pulling his muscles and tendons together in tight knots of tension.

"I'm not married," she finally said.

Henry's entire body relaxed. This new information shouldn't make a difference to him since he'd already determined that there were other reasons for him not to pursue her. Yet knowing she was available flooded his mind with extreme satisfaction, even though he knew it was wrong, considering what her words meant.

"You're a widow."

"Yes."

Carefully, he raised his gaze and was slightly surprised to find her studying him. A wave of heat washed over his skin even as she glanced away in an obvious effort to hide her interest. "Then who's waiting for you with dinner?" he asked, and proceeded to eat some more meat.

She cleared her throat and shifted in her seat. "A couple of friends with whom I share my home." A soft smile pulled at her lips. "Life can be hard for a woman with no prospects. I felt compelled to take them in when they told me of their troubles."

Henry frowned. "As kind as that makes you, it also suggests you were living alone for a while before these friends of yours came to join you."

"I was," she confirmed. "For almost a year."

Henry set his fork down and stared at her. "That is most unusual, Mrs. Cartwright, not to mention unsafe. Especially when considering your young age and your beauty." Had she no family who cared what people might think of an unmarried woman living alone without a companion? Was there nobody to offer her some protection?

"Perhaps I am not as young as you think, Mr. Lowell. As for my beauty . . ." She took a deep breath while allowing her fingers to toy with the fabric of her gown. When they stilled, she said, "I thank you for the compliment, but I know I am not the sort to turn heads. You may rest assured that I have been perfectly safe from harm until now."

"But what of your reputation? Even if you are older than twenty, which is what I imagine your age to be, a respectable young woman does not live alone, no matter what." He realized he was suddenly angry, not at her but on her behalf. She'd obviously been neglected by those who ought to have her best interests at heart or . . .

"You do not know my circumstances well enough to place judgment, nor are you entitled to do so." She spoke calmly but with an edge of authority to her voice. "As you are my patient, it is my duty to care for you and ensure your recovery, but my personal life outside this hospital is none of your concern. Unless, of course, you wish for me to reproach you for your affairs."

Damn the tabloids and damn his stupid attempt at ruining his own reputation. He'd done it so successfully that Mrs. Cartwright had labeled him a reprobate scoundrel right from the start. "None of the rumors you've heard about me are true," he told her, even though he doubted she would believe him.

"What about your affair with Lady Elmwood?"

He blew out a breath. "The earl is jealous of any man who talks to his wife. It was a misunderstanding."

"And I suppose all of your other exploits described in the newspapers over the years are false as well and that you are instead a saint?" She stood, collected the tray from his lap and set it aside on the table. "I am not a fool, Mr. Lowell. The fact that even I am aware of your poor reputation can only mean one thing."

He dared not ask and yet he had to know. "And what is that?"

Flattening her lips, she looked at him with eyes that held little hope for his salvation. "You are notorious and probably far more dangerous than I would ever have imagined possible before I met you."

Rendered dumb by her statement, Henry failed to voice a defense and was forced to watch as Mrs. Cartwright turned away and strode from the room, leaving him utterly alone with his thoughts. Never in his life had he met a woman with that much backbone or such ability to make him feel small and undeserving of her attention. It made him want to prove himself to her, to show her that he was nothing like the man she believed him to be but rather the sort who deserved her respect.

Returning home to the modest town house she inhabited on Gerrard Street, Viola shut the door and paused to listen. A loud thud was followed by a rapid drumming sound. She turned toward the stairs, waited expectantly and smiled broadly when a large, dark brown beast skidded across the top of the landing and proceeded to bound down the steps. His tongue flapped from the corner of his mouth as he flew toward her, barely managing to slide to a panting halt on the slippery marble floor.

Viola crouched down and scratched her Rottweiler lovingly behind his ear. "Good boy, Rex." His tail wagged furiously from side to side as he nuzzled deeper into her hand, begging for more affection. She laughed, allowing him the pleasure while reaching into her skirt pocket and retrieving a small piece of meat.

Rising, she stood over him and commanded him to sit, rewarding him with the tasty morsel and another scratch of his head.

"Oh, Viola," Diana, one of Viola's two housemates, said as she entered the hallway from the stairs leading down to the kitchen. "I thought I heard you come in."

Viola removed her gloves and placed them on a narrow table next to the wall. "I suppose it's hard not to with Rex making such a commotion every time."

"He's a loyal dog and misses you tremendously when you're not here," Diana replied. Younger than Viola, she'd been sold by her uncle to a bawd and was one of the two runaways Viola had rescued after relocating from Tremaine House. The other was Harriet, who'd fled a brothel after taking a beating. Viola had offered both women shelter and food, and in return they carried out some of the chores Viola didn't have time for. They also ran a support group every Monday at the hospital to help and advise other women in similar situations. All in all, it was an arrangement that had become increasingly permanent over time.

"Thank you," Viola said. She gave Diana a pleading look. "I don't suppose dinner's ready?"

Diana smiled. "Of course it is. Harriet has made the tastiest pork pie and vegetable soup."

"I still wonder at her culinary skills," Viola said.

"We're very lucky to have her." Diana went to the door through which she'd recently come and called for Harriet to come upstairs and join them.

"How was work today?" Harriet asked Viola when they were all sitting at the dining room table eating their soup.

Viola took another spoonful of the tasty broth and savored the soothing warmth it provided as it slid down her throat. She glanced at her friends. "Mrs. Richardson was in a fine mood and Emily proved very helpful in cheering up an eight-year-old boy who was brought in with a fever. It looks like influenza, but I'm not too worried since he appears to be a strong and otherwise healthy child."

Diana and Harriet responded with appropriate sounds of interest while Viola continued relating the highlights of her day. As an afterthought, she told them, "I also finished the invitations for the grand opening of the rejuvenation center so they can be sent out tomorrow."

"How many people have you invited?" Diana asked.

"One hundred."

Harriet's eyes widened. "Do you think they'll all show up?"

"I expect so, if for no other reason than curiosity." They finished their soup. Viola helped Harriet and Diana remove their bowls and put clean plates on the table.

"And Mr. Lowell?" Diana asked while serving herself a piece of roast meat.

Viola felt her stomach contract. Of course she'd mentioned his arrival and had voiced her concerns about being responsible for his care because of the added interaction this would require. She had, however, hoped to avoid discussing him further. But apparently that wasn't possible.

"I quarreled with him this evening." She took the dish with the roast from Diana and selected a piece of meat for herself before offering it to Harriet. When neither woman commented, she said, "He refused to heed my advice on bathing and later suggested that some might think me a loose woman when he discovered I'd once lived completely alone." Grabbing the bowl with potatoes and carrots, she spooned several onto her plate while recalling Lowell's horrified expression. His reaction had struck a sensitive nerve.

"You shared such personal detail with him?" Diana was staring at her with a quizzical expression while Harriet looked equally stumped. "How unlike you, Viola."

"He said my husband was lucky to have me and when I told him I didn't have a husband, one comment led to another until I eventually told him he had no right to judge me considering *his* reputation."

Harriet smiled. "Bravo, Viola."

"Indeed," Diana murmured. "But in spite of the set-down you gave him, I must urge you to be careful where Mr. Lowell is concerned. Men like him do not bring up a woman's husband unless they hope to discover whether or not she has one."

Viola nodded. "I am aware but I also despise lying, so when he told me my husband was fortunate to have me, I could not allow myself to deceive him."

Harriet leaned forward and peered at Viola. "You like him."

"I most certainly do not." To suppose such a thing was silly in light of what she knew about him.

"Your cheeks are turning pink," Diana remarked. "For someone who claims to despise lying, you really ought to make more of an effort at being honest with us and with yourself."

Frowning, Viola stabbed a piece of meat with her fork. "Very well. I will admit that I find him charming and that I enjoy sparring with him. I mean, you know how well I enjoy a good challenge and—"

"Oh dear," Harriet murmured.

Diana shook her head slowly.

"What?" Viola asked. She ate the piece of meat on her fork.

Harriet and Diana exchanged a look before Diana took a deep breath and said, "You have accepted his invitation to flirt with you, Viola, which essentially means you've admitted an interest."

Viola stared at her friend and suddenly laughed. "That is ridiculous. I talk to all my patients, Diana. You know that. Everyone does. So for Mr. Lowell to presume there might be more to it than professional courtesy would be utterly mad."

"Except for the fact that you readily took his bait regarding the husband remark, gave him the answer he needed and chose to attack his reputation when he said something offensive to you." Harriet took a sip of her wine before adding, "Essentially, this proves you care, even if only a little, about all of his past indiscretions. A woman without any interest at all would not do so, Viola."

Concern pricked at Viola's skin. She reached for her wine and took a long sip. "How can you be so certain about this?"

Both women raised their eyebrows. "We have some experience with men," Diana said while Harriet returned her attention to her food. "Trust us when we tell you, Mr. Lowell has designs on you, Viola, which is hardly surprising, given what we know about him. As your friend, I advise you to be cautious where he is concerned."

"Of course," Viola assured her. "That goes without saying since I have no interest in encouraging any man's attention."

"Perhaps not," Harriet agreed. She'd set her fork aside and was giving Viola her full attention. "But a rake of Mr. Lowell's renown is more dangerous than you can imagine. He will know precisely what to say in order to seduce the most defiant woman straight into his bed."

Chapter 3

When Emily stopped by Viola's office the following day to inform her that Mr. Lowell would allow only *her* to tend to his wound, she bristled. After her conversation with Harriet and Diana the previous evening, she'd gone about her day with the intention of letting others check up on his well-being and then report back to her. This had worked until now, but could go on no longer. Which was rather unsettling since it would mean having to see him again. The mere idea of it released a swarm of butterflies in her belly. Because if his comments and smiles had proved anything to her thus far, it was that in spite of her very best efforts, she wasn't immune to his good looks or charm.

Quite the opposite.

But, she was first and foremost a caregiver who'd made a promise to Florian. So, with the same degree of trepidation most people would feel if forced to jump from a cliff, she marched into Mr. Lowell's room and ignored the furious pounding of her heart.

"Why must you disrupt things?" she asked, speaking before she had time to think.

"Is that what I'm doing?" His dark brown eyes followed her as she went to the chest of drawers by the wall and collected a few supplies.

"Emily is perfectly capable of changing your compress and bandage."

"I'm sure she is," Mr. Lowell said, "but I want you."

The words were softly spoken. A verbal caress meant to break Viola's defenses. She turned to face him. "Why?"

He smiled then, disarming her completely. One second ago, she'd been ready for battle. Now, however, her legs had grown weak while her brain seemed to sigh with pleasure.

"Because of this." He gestured between them. "You challenge me, Viola." He paused for a second as if considering, then chuckled lightly and added, "You're also lovely to look at."

She glared at him, which made him frown. And then he said, "You disagree." He shook his head as if such a concept was inconceivable to him.

Instead of engaging, Viola rolled her eyes and brought the materials she needed closer to the bed. "Come on then," she said, resigning herself to the task at hand. "Let's get this over with."

He eyed her coyly while she pulled back his sheet and proceeded to lift up his shirt. Her hands made contact with his skin, and just as before, she felt herself tremble.

"I like it when you touch me like that," he murmured as if his voice alone could entice her to do the wickedest things.

She cleared her throat and met his gaze as frankly as she could muster. "Perhaps you would like the orderlies to give you another bath, Mr. Lowell?"

He started to laugh, then winced with pain and fell silent. The tension between them was effectively dispelled, allowing Viola to focus. She worked quickly, intent on going to check on Mrs. Richardson again as soon as she was finished.

"There. That ought to do it," she said, satisfied with her work. She began pulling down Mr. Lowell's shirt but froze when he caught her wrist.

To her chagrin, her entire body came alive beneath his touch, her skin warming precisely where his fingers made contact. "I'm sorry if I have made you feel uncomfortable." He released his hold on her slowly, as if preparing to grab her again if she tried to flee. "This wasn't my intention. I just . . . I like having fun, Viola, and flirting with a woman who's able to respond in kind is vastly entertaining. It is also the only source of amusement available to me at the moment."

To Viola's surprise, Mr. Lowell looked utterly sincere. The mischievousness from earlier was gone from his eyes. In fact, he appeared to be truly concerned he might have offended her somehow.

Against her better judgment, she chose to take pity on him. "It's all right," she said. "I suppose the days can be rather long when all you're doing is lying in bed." She recalled the paper he'd been reading yesterday. "Did you at least manage to solve all the puzzles?"

"All except one. It was mathematical in nature and I simply couldn't figure out the missing numbers." He reached for the paper and held it toward her. "Here. Why don't you give it a try?"

Taking a step back, Viola deliberately started tidying away her supplies. "You can read it to me while I work. It's more efficient that way."

He frowned but refrained from protesting, for which she was grateful. "If two plus one is thirteen, and five plus three is twenty-eight, and seven plus five is two hundred and twelve, then how much is nine plus two?"

"Oh, it's one of those." Viola poured a glass of water for Mr. Lowell and handed it to him. "Here, it's important for you to drink."

He did so and winced. "Perhaps I can have some more red wine later?"

She laughed. "Maybe. If you promise to stay on your best behavior." She considered the problem. "I think I need to see this written down."

"That's what I thought, but you said I should read it out loud so—"

"No, I mean like actual numerals. Spotting the pattern is difficult when the numbers are spelled out. It doesn't make the same sort of sense."

"Oh. Right. Do you have a pencil?"

She picked one from her pocket along with the small notebook she carried with her, placing the paper at just the right distance so she could see what she was writing. She jotted the numbers down from memory and studied them for a moment. "Ah!"

"Ah?"

She cut a glance at Mr. Lowell and smiled. "The answer is seven hundred and eleven. You have to subtract first and add afterward. So take two away from nine, which gives you seven and then add nine to two in order to get eleven."

He knit his brow and considered the sums she'd written down. "I really hate it when mathematics doesn't make any sense. This is ridiculous."

"I agree, but it was listed as a puzzle, which I suppose it is. Even if the numbers don't add up as they should."

"Well, at least you have put my mind at ease. That problem would have kept me up at night otherwise."

"I seriously doubt that, Mr. Lowell."

He grinned. "How well you know me already."

A moment of silence settled between them and it occurred to Viola that she was reluctant to leave.

Which was curious. He was a rake and she had no interest in that sort of man. Or in any man, for that matter. She'd gained her independence and was loath to part with it—to relinquish her freedom and submit to another's will.

No thank you.

And yet, she wasn't eager to go and check on Mrs. Richardson either. So she lingered, unsure of what to do next. To her relief, Mr. Lowell came to her rescue.

"Would it be presumptuous of me to ask you if you would like to play a game of cards with me?"

She hesitated. Her friends' warnings echoed through her head. They were right to be worried on her behalf. But her acquaintance with Mr. Lowell would be temporary. He would recover and leave, and when he did, he'd give his attentions to someone else.

Consequently, she shook her head. "Not at all. It's been a while since the last time I played so I would enjoy that, though I do have a few other tasks to attend to first."

"In that case, I shall rest awhile and gather my strength," he said. "If you play as well as you care for a man you would rather avoid, I believe it will be a challenging game."

It took longer than Henry expected before Viola returned to his bedside. During her absence, he contemplated the conversations they'd had over the last two days. They'd been refreshing and full of quick rejoinders. Which made him wonder about her upbringing and her education. Certainly, she would have to be middle class to hold the position she did within the hospital. From what little he'd seen, it appeared as though Emily was her subordinate, which placed Viola in a position of some authority, making Henry all the more curious about her background.

"Does vingt-et-un suit?" Viola presently asked, positioning the table next to his bed in a way that allowed for their card play. Opening a small box, she poured a pile of counters onto the table surface and distributed them equally between the two of them.

"It is one of my favorite games," he said, even though he generally preferred playing it against more people because of the increased challenge.

Pulling up a nearby chair, Viola took a seat. "Shall we draw to see who's the banker?" she asked, producing a deck of cards and spreading it into a fan. He picked a card and so did she, beating him with a king to his ten. She smiled. "I'll deal then."

He watched her do so with the skill and fluidity of someone accustomed to handling cards. "Who taught you to play?"

Her expression grew wistful. "My father. It was his favorite diversion after work." She proceeded to deal the first card and he checked it, happy to find an ace.

He selected five counters and pushed them toward the middle of the table. "And what was your father's profession, if you don't mind my asking?"

She dealt the second card. "He was a physician." She checked her cards without a hint of what it contained.

Henry did the same, frustrated to see a five. "I'll split my hand," he said, placing his cards face down on the table and adding an additional five counters. She gave him two more cards and he was happy to discover that one was a queen. "It makes sense then, that you would become a nurse."

She added five counters as well and dealt herself another card. "My father taught me everything he knew. He was not of the opinion that women should be restricted on account of their sex. Had it been up to him, I would likely have gone to university to study medicine."

He presented her with his vingt-et-un before collecting his winnings. "Does it bother you that you couldn't?"

She gathered up the cards and handed the deck over to him. "I have been blessed with incredibly good fortune, Mr. Lowell. In some ways I believe I may have been able to accomplish more than most physicians do in their lifetimes."

Well, that was a pretty boastful statement. And yet she didn't sound as if she was trying to show off, although he was of the opinion that she gave her profession more credit than it deserved if she honestly believed that being a nurse was a greater accomplishment than being a physician. The difference was, a nurse wasn't trained to do a physician's work, while a physician could easily do what a nurse was trained to do, if necessary.

But perhaps Viola viewed herself differently. If her father really had taught her everything he knew, then perhaps she was able to set a broken limb and maybe even perform minor surgery. He considered this while shuffling the cards and dealing, watching her closely as he did so.

"Does Florian let you help in the operating room sometimes?" he asked.

She gave her card a quick look and pushed a few counters forward. A swift nod followed. "I often assist." She raised her gaze and met his across the short distance between them. A fire burned there, and in that moment Henry wished she would feel such passion for him. "I was there when he operated on you. It was I who cleaned your wound and handed your brother the necessary tools." The smile she gave him next was conspiratorial in nature. "I have seen inside you, Mr. Lowell."

He held his breath, aware only of her stormy eyes and the pounding of his own heart. "And what did you find?" Were they even talking about his wound anymore?

She paused for so long he was almost tempted to reach out and shake her. But then she chuckled and leaned back, relaxing against her chair. "A bloody mess." And with that final statement, she placed her cards face up to reveal two kings and an ace.

Damnation! He'd been so mesmerized by her he hadn't even known he'd continued to deal. "I think I'd like a brandy," he muttered.

She grinned openly, and for a second he knew he saw her. The true Viola. The one she hid from the world with her serious façade. To his stupefaction, it occurred to Henry that what he wanted most in the world was to make her laugh like this daily. He wanted to be the man who made her happy.

The realization quieted his mind in a way few things had in recent years. He'd been so busy turning The Red Rose into the successful club it now was and helping his father with his financial difficulties, he'd had no time to reflect on what really mattered. For the past year he'd thought it was getting married, and perhaps that was true if his bride-to-be was a woman of Viola Cartwright's dedication and intellect. He didn't like knowing that the most he could hope to have with her was a brief acquaintance destined to end the moment he left the hospital.

"The best I can offer is a glass of wine. And only if you are ailing."

He ignored the melancholy trying to grasp him and asked her as seriously as he could manage, "Would it help if I told you I feel a fever coming on?"

The palm of her hand went swiftly to his forehead,

cool and soothing and oh so wonderful. "Hmmm . . . Perhaps a small glass of wine would do you some good," she said, and went to fetch one.

"I was hoping you would join me," he said when she returned with only one glass in her hand.

"I am working, Mr. Lowell. To imbibe even a little would be irresponsible." She handed him the glass and resumed her seat by his bed while he drank.

Henry savored the spicy liquid even though it wasn't the best he'd ever had. But he supposed the wine they kept here was for medicinal purposes and not for the sake of enjoyment. Still, it soothed and comforted and made him feel wonderfully relaxed. "Thank you." He eyed the cards still on the table. "Shall we play some more?"

"If you like."

They finished five more rounds before Henry was forced to name Viola the overall winner. He helped put the counters back in the box where they belonged while she collected the cards.

"My brother says the Duchess of Tremaine is the hospital's protector," Henry said in the hope of encouraging more conversation and making her stay. Viola stilled, and Henry proceeded with the question he wanted to ask. "I was wondering if I might be able to meet her while I am here."

Viola slowly tied the cards together with a ribbon and placed the deck and the box of counters in a small drawstring pouch. "Why the interest?"

He shrugged. "I suppose I find the notion of any woman building a business and running it successfully a fascinating one."

Viola crossed her arms and tilted her head. "Really?"

"It cannot have been easy, is what I mean. I am simply impressed, that is all." When Viola raised an eyebrow, he sighed. "Very well, I am also a little bit curious to see what she looks like, considering she never sets foot in Society."

"But you must have heard rumors?" She toyed with the skirt of her gown as if transfixed by the way the fabric moved.

Henry watched her with interest. It wasn't jealousy he sensed in the tone of her voice but something else altogether. Unable to put his finger on it, he answered her question. "They say she's a social climber but I know from Florian's accounts that this cannot be true."

The edge of her mouth lifted. Silence expanded between them until she finally spoke. "Did it ever occur to you that you might have met her already?"

He tried to think, his mind shuffling through the faces he'd seen since arriving at St. Agatha's. It couldn't be Emily or any of the other nurses he'd encountered, which meant . . . His eyes locked with Viola's, surprise hitting him square in the chest. "You?"

The secretive smile she'd been wearing widened, and she dipped her head as if in greeting. "A pleasure to make your acquaintance, Mr. Lowell."

Viola hadn't planned on revealing her true identity to Mr. Lowell because she knew he would see her differently the moment she did. But after enjoying their card play together this afternoon, she couldn't be dishonest either. They had, after all, become friends of sorts, if only in the loosest of terms. But it was enough for her to know she'd feel guilty about lying to him.

A rake of Mr. Lowell's renown is more dangerous than you can imagine.

Harriet's words rushed to the front of her mind,

but it was too late to regret her moment of honesty now. Aware of the risk she took by divulging her title to Mr. Lowell, Viola waited for his reaction, which would be either disbelief or admiration. She knew this from experience—from the peers she'd dealt with on the committee in charge of securing funds for the hospital. Most had initially found it hard to accept that she was St. Agatha's patroness. Her age and her sex had both worked against her, which was yet another reason why she appreciated Florian's support. She'd needed him, if only to make people listen.

But as Mr. Lowell's eyes widened, she saw that they also gleamed. Not with disbelief or admiration, but with something else entirely, namely a mixture of relief and opportunity. Viola instinctively schooled her features in response.

"I can assure you the pleasure is all mine," he said. "My brother has said such wonderful things about you, Your Grace, I confess I became intrigued and hoped to one day make your acquaintance."

Viola considered him. Perhaps she'd misjudged his initial response to her confession? "You needn't address me so formally. In fact, I prefer if you don't." Seeing the question in his eyes, she explained, "My parents were not nobility and . . . Well, suffice it to say that I have never felt comfortable with my title. Viola will do, or Mrs. Cartwright, if you prefer."

"Then Viola it is," he said with a grin while studying her as though seeing her for the very first time.

Feeling a blush coming on, she deliberately dropped her gaze to her lap. The comfortable companionship they'd shared earlier had somehow been lost and replaced by extreme self-awareness on her part. She shifted slightly in her seat and considered taking her leave so she could return to her duties.

"Your . . ." He hesitated briefly, and she glanced

up to find him looking slightly perplexed. An odd sense of bafflement played across his face, and then he blinked and caught her gaze. "I suppose he must be your stepson, even if he is older than you."

A chill snaked its way along Viola's spine. She clutched her hands together in her lap. "You refer to the new Duke of Tremaine. The former Marquess of Bremferrol?"

"Precisely." He watched her closely. Pensively. "He and I have known each other since adolescence."

Oh God!

"Really?" She spoke as if her voice was disconnected from her body. Florian had never mentioned any connection to Robert, but then again, he might not have known all of his brother's acquaintances. Or maybe he'd decided not to share the information with her because he didn't want to give her additional reason not to like Henry.

"We were school friends. Attended both Eton and Cambridge together."

"Mmm-hmm . . ." What else could she possibly say to that? As it was, she was trying not to judge herself too harshly for enjoying Mr. Lowell's company when the truth was she ought to have known better. His reputation alone should have warned her he'd be the sort of man with whom Robert had likely caroused before leaving England. Every article she'd read about him in the papers over the years ought to have done so as well, not to mention Mrs. Richardson's comment about his notoriety and her friends' words of warning. And yet Viola had ignored it all in favor of playing cards. And in so doing, she'd let down her guard and allowed herself to *like* the scoundrel.

"Tell me," he was saying, "how on earth did you manage to build a hospital?"

The change in subject startled her slightly. "I, um . . . My husband left me a generous inheritance." She did her best to focus on what she was saying and ignore the fear creeping over her skin. "When he died, I spent most of it on purchasing this building, renovating it and employing competent people, like your brother."

"An impressive feat, to be sure. The people of London are indebted to you, Viola."

While the compliment sounded sincere, Viola could not ignore the softness with which he spoke it. There was an element of enticement present, perhaps unintentionally, but there all the same.

He will know precisely what to say in order to seduce the most defiant woman straight into his bed.

Viola stood so quickly the movement pushed back her chair with such jarring force that it squeaked against the floor. She'd known to be careful and yet somehow he'd breached her defenses. How on earth could she have let that happen?

Mr. Lowell stared up at her while she stared back down at him. "All the more reason for me to remember my duty." There was a slight quiver as she spoke, which couldn't be helped.

"Viola." His voice implored her to stay even as she walked to the door.

Viola continued out into the hallway without looking back, acutely aware she was being a coward but also knowing she had no choice but to flee.

Chapter 4

Henry's thoughts lingered on Viola as the day wore on. He pondered the way she'd reacted when he'd revealed how well he knew Robert. Panic had flickered in her eyes and her entire body had seemed to retreat as if he suddenly posed a threat. It had been curious to watch and equally alarming. It had also resulted in Emily coming to tend to his wound that evening, and when he'd inquired about Viola, he'd been told she had other patients to see to.

He did not encounter her the next day either, at which point he grew concerned. Because if he was correct and it was his connection to Robert that had put her off, he feared discovering what his friend might have done to distress her so.

He knit his brow and considered the possibilities. As lads, Robert had been the wilder one—the one who snuck brandy and cheroots into the dorm at Eton and bravely took the blame the one time when they'd gotten caught.

Later, at Cambridge, Robert had started a private group that selected its members based on position and wealth. Joining had been a natural thing for Henry considering his longstanding friendship with

Robert by then. And it had been fun for a while. He'd enjoyed the parties and the women Robert had managed to procure. Until he started becoming aware of Robert's temper. Henry had witnessed it on a few occasions, like when Robert refused to pay for a woman he'd bedded because she'd failed to meet his expectations. A fight had ensued in the brothel they'd visited, and eventually they'd both been tossed out with a warning to never return.

Two days later, Henry had happened upon the demimondaine at the heart of the conflict. She'd been begging for coin when he'd gone into town. Bruised and with her lip cut, she'd screamed accusations at Henry as soon as she'd seen him, pointing to her beaten face and claiming his friend was to blame for her losing her job.

Shocked and embarrassed by the unwanted attention she'd drawn to him, Henry had fled. When he'd mentioned the incident later to Robert, Robert had said that such lies were what one could expect from a whore such as her. He'd denied ever laying a hand on the woman, but something in his eyes had made Henry wonder. It was part of the reason why they'd drifted apart in the years that had followed. Because somewhere deep down inside, Henry had known that his friend had returned to that brothel and taken revenge. He just hadn't wanted to believe it.

Regardless of his wishes, Viola didn't return until the following morning. Even though she'd pulled her hair back in the tightest knot he'd ever seen and her face conveyed nothing but the utmost professionalism, he still thought her stunning. A curious alertness pulled at his gut the moment her eyes found his. For although her expression was guarded and she seemed intent on refusing to smile, warmth emanated from her gaze—a testament to how she truly felt about him.

"You look well today, Mr. Lowell. According to what Emily tells me, you have continued to improve since I saw you. Having discussed your progress with her, I have concluded that you are ready to be discharged the day after tomorrow."

Henry's heart fell. He didn't want to go home. He wanted to stay here and talk to her. He wanted to watch her gray eyes come alive with mischief, shrewdness and irritation. It didn't matter which emotion she emitted, as long as it was directed at him.

"Perhaps you should check her prognosis yourself," he suggested.

She shook her head. "No need. I trust Emily completely."

"But . . ." He knew he was grasping for excuses now. Any would do. "My brother left me in your care. Surely you owe it to him to ensure my health is as sound as Emily claims."

Viola's jaw tightened and he could see her struggling with her decision. Eventually she sighed and went to clean her hands. "I do not like having the competence of my staff questioned, Mr. Lowell."

"Forgive me. It is just, I believed we were getting along rather well, you and I, and then all of a sudden you were gone and refrained from coming to check on me for one full day and—"

"Running a hospital keeps me busy." She set her supplies on the table next to the bed. "Socializing with my patients is a luxury I do not always have."

"And yet you took the time to play cards with me."

When she didn't respond, he resolved to change the subject. Perhaps if they could discuss something else, something less personal and of greater interest to her, he could lure her conversational side back out again. It was worth a try.

"Florian says you're building a rejuvenation center."

She pulled at his sheet and tugged on his shirt, wrestling the fabric into the desired position with mechanical movements. "Yes." She began untying his bandage while carefully avoiding making contact with his skin in a way she'd never bothered to do before.

Interesting.

"So how is it coming along? Is it almost finished?"

She glanced at him briefly and quickly averted her gaze once more. "It is."

So much for encouraging her conversational side. He sighed and determined to try again with a different sort of question. "What prompted you to consider such a project?"

The bandage came off and she carefully pulled back the compress to study the wound. "It wasn't my idea. The duchesses of Huntley and Redding came up with it when they learned the hospital needed a steadier income." She explained why this was important, changing the compress to a clean one as she did so.

"From what I understand, this center will offer saunas, the relief of muscular aches through hand pressure, invigorating tonics, herbal compresses and other such things. Is that correct?"

She tied the fresh bandage she'd used to hold the compress in place and proceeded to pull down his shirt. "It is supposed to provide an alternative to going to Bath."

Henry said the first thing that popped into his head. "I think it's genius."

Her face turned more fully toward him, just enough for him to see she was smiling. Not a lot, but enough to convey her appreciation. He tried to think of what to say next and settled on "What else are you planning?"

She straightened her posture and studied him for a brief moment as if unsure whether to encourage more conversation. Holding himself completely still, Henry gazed straight up at her with what he hoped would be construed as innocent curiosity rather than a deliberate attempt at increased contact.

To his relief, it worked after what felt like the longest pause he'd ever had to endure.

"I am thinking of having enriched spring water bottled and brought to London so we can serve it to our customers as an added exclusivity."

"That would certainly encourage people to come through your door." Henry regretted seeing her clean away her supplies and wash her hands once more because he knew this meant she would soon depart. "Location is important as well, of course. I trust you've found a good one?"

She spoke while she worked. "I managed to acquire a reasonably sized building on Swallow Street."

Henry stared at her while doing his damnedest not to smile too broadly. "Really?" He hesitated, aware that she'd turned in response to his comment and that she now watched him expectantly. Ah well, she'd discover the truth soon enough, so he might as well tell her. "That's the same street my own place of business is on."

She shook her head with incomprehension.

"The Red Rose?" he prompted. She continued to look like she had no clue what he was referring to. "I opened it a few years ago with the intention of creating a social club for ladies and gentlemen alike. It offers meals and entertainment."

"I wasn't aware." Her words were pensive.

"It's at the Piccadilly end of Swallow Street. I expect your rejuvenation center is at the Oxford Street end?" She nodded mutely. "Then we are practically neighbors."

He was thrilled, while she was clearly a bit uncertain about this new development. Which made him all the more eager to understand her. Because he sensed there was more to her sudden reluctance to socialize with him than his reputation alone. She'd gotten over that enough to keep him company, after all. But when he'd brought up Robert . . . There was definitely a complicated past there, and while Henry generally refrained from interfering in his friends' past indiscretions, he liked Viola too much to ignore any possible wrongdoing on Robert's part.

"I would not go quite that far, considering there must be at least a hundred yards between our properties," she said.

He rolled his eyes. "Must you ruin my enjoyment with such a minor detail?"

To his immense satisfaction, the edge of Viola's lips quirked. "Have you not realized yet that my greatest pleasure is ruining yours?"

Recognizing a playful lilt to her voice, Henry pushed up onto his elbows and gave her the cheekiest smile he could muster. "That does not bode well for our future together."

The blush flooding her cheeks was delightful. "Mr. Lowell." And her voice, while reprimanding, was equally breathless.

A spark of intense awareness raced through him. Now they were making progress. "Fear not, however," he murmured, "for although my pleasure may not be your highest priority yet, Viola, I can assure you that I intend to take yours most seriously. Now, how about we go outside for a bit. Is that possible? The sun is shining, so it looks like a glorious day, and being confined to this bed is starting to wear on my nerves."

She stared at him as if he'd just dropped from the

ceiling. "I, er . . ." Her eyes darted around the room looking at anything else but him, which only proved the flustered state he'd put her in, which further proved the effect he was having on her. She was far from immune to his suggestion that they were destined to be more than friends.

"Is there a garden for us to visit?" he asked when he saw she was having some trouble composing herself.

She blinked. "Yes. There's a small one." Her words were quieter than usual. Clearing her throat, she clasped her hands together before her and glanced at the door. "I will ask one of the other nurses to escort—"

"No, Viola. I would like for it to be you."

"But—"

"I am leaving soon, but before I do, I would like to have the honor of getting to know you better."

Uncertainty puckered her brow, but her eyes warmed with the wish to accept. To Henry's immense satisfaction, temptation won. "Very well, Mr. Lowell. I will agree to accompany you, but I cannot stay more than half an hour."

"Then I shall cherish every minute all the more."

Her lips quirked. "You really are a scoundrel."

"In some ways, yes," he agreed, "but I'm not nearly as bad as you may believe."

She nodded as if in agreement, or was it understanding? Henry wasn't entirely sure. He was just pleased to have won her over, if only for a brief moment. For it meant that in spite of all the rumors she'd heard and her obvious displeasure at him calling Robert a friend, she instinctively trusted him somehow.

And if this proved anything at all, it was that the wall she'd built around her heart could be scaled.

Henry rose from the bed and dressed while she waited for him in the hallway. After a year of searching ballrooms and social events for the perfect woman to woo, he'd found her at his sickbed. No doubt about it. Viola was smart and had a good head on her shoulders. She ran a business, for heaven's sake, which meant she would understand the meaning of money. She was not the sort of woman who was going to squander a fortune on unnecessary things the way his father had done. Rather, she would be more inclined to advise Henry on how to administer his own funds sensibly.

Of course there was also the added benefit of her status. As a duke's widow, she was more than an excellent match for a future earl. And since a physical attraction existed between them, Henry was hopeful that their relationship would also be filled with passion.

One thing was certain. He wanted her more than he'd ever wanted another woman before, and by God, he meant to have her, no matter what he had to say or do to convince her that this was the best way forward for both of them.

What on earth was she thinking, agreeing to accompany Mr. Lowell outside? After everything she'd learned about him, how could she have surrendered to his suggestion?

Because she wasn't thinking, she reminded herself. She was feeling and wanting and, oh . . . she should have been stronger and told him no. Except she'd swiftly dismissed that option and told herself that if his health started to fail and something happened to him, Florian would blame her and she would never forgive herself for the neglect.

Which was rubbish, of course. Mr. Lowell's wound

was healing nicely. There was zero chance of him suddenly collapsing and taking a turn for the worse. It was all an excuse to allow herself a bit of indulgence. Because in spite of all that she knew, including his friendship with Robert, she genuinely liked him. More than that, she liked how she felt when she was around him, as if she was more than the cogs and wheels that kept St. Agatha's going.

Mr. Lowell's attention toward her made her feel special, which was probably ridiculous considering the length of their acquaintance and all the women who probably waited for him to be discharged. But they weren't here right now. She was. And she craved the way he looked at her, as if she was all he'd ever wanted, even though she knew that couldn't possibly be true.

As he walked beside her she realized how tall he was. She hadn't noticed when he'd been lying in bed, but there was at least a head's difference between them. And he was close, so close she could feel his heat pushing against her right shoulder and arm. When they reached the door leading out to the garden, he opened it for her, and as she passed through it, the touch of his hand at the base of her spine made her insides quiver.

It was fleeting, a simple gesture to guide her forward, yet the heat of it lingered for long moments after, provoking a yearning within her for more. God help her, this man was leading her straight into madness and she had agreed to willingly follow.

"An extraordinary sanctuary," he murmured, scattering her thoughts. "I never expected to find so much color out here. The flowers, hedges and fountains are all incredible."

"The idea was to create a soothing atmosphere to hasten recovery in our patients. The fountains were quite an expense, but I think they're pretty and I love the sound that they make."

He glanced down at her and she looked up. The afternoon sun was behind him, casting its golden rays upon his dark hair and making it shimmer. "I quite agree," he said, and offered his arm. "Shall we take a turn of the garden?"

Viola hesitated only the second it took her to realize that while there were other patients and a couple of nurses about, none seemed to have much interest in them. So she nodded and placed her hand on his arm and tried not to think of how firm it felt or how well matched they seemed as they started to walk. Impossible, of course, since every cell in her body was keenly tuned to his masculine presence.

"If you will permit, I would love to come back here one day with my sketch pad," he said when they'd walked a few paces in silence. "The scenery is superb. I especially like that climbing plant over there. And the patients themselves would be interesting models, I think."

His comment surprised her somewhat. "I would not have taken you for an artist." She'd rather envisioned him gambling away in a smoky room or lounging in bed with one of his paramours.

"Does the image not suit your preconceived notion of me, Viola?" He met her gaze and immediately chuckled, proving to her that he'd judged her correctly. "I developed a fondness for drawing when I was a boy. Florian would bring all sorts of plants into the house and I would sketch them for him, since he had no talent with that at all. Together we catalogued all of the plants available at our country estate in a notebook. After I drew them, Florian wrote down their names and medicinal properties."

"Do you still have it?" Viola asked in the hope of seeing the journal one day.

"Florian does. I believe he keeps it locked away somewhere at his home." They turned toward a corner where a pair of benches had been placed beneath a rose-covered pergola. "He told me once that it is his most prized possession."

"And so it should be considering the time and effort the two of you put into it."

The smile he gave her forced her to hold on more tightly to his arm. "It is more than that, Viola. That journal forged an unbreakable bond between us. It taught us to work together and support each other while creating something for us to be proud of."

"You care for him deeply, don't you?" She wasn't sure why she asked the question except perhaps to have his sensitive side confirmed.

"I love him fiercely."

His pronouncement was more than what she'd expected. It startled her because of how rare it was to hear a man speak so openly of his feelings. Her father had of course told her that he loved her, but it was not the sort of thing he would ever have blurted to anyone. Perhaps because it meant being vulnerable, which wasn't at all what she would have expected from a man she'd only recently met, let alone from a rake.

"Does that surprise you?" he asked. They had reached the benches, and when she removed her hand from his arm, he gestured toward the nearest one.

Viola sat and waited for him to join her before saying, "No. Not really. I know you have done a lot for each other in ways of offering support. When you learned of his true parentage last year and that the two of you don't share the same father, you didn't allow it to change things between you. I know he was grateful for that."

Mr. Lowell glanced across the garden while sunlight spilled across his cheeks. It allowed Viola to catch a glimpse of stubble he'd yet to shave, and for an odd reason she could not explain, she found she liked him looking slightly unkempt.

"Florian is a remarkable man. I have always held him in the highest regard, so it makes no difference to me if his father was England's worst criminal. I only regret that he felt unable to confide in me sooner."

Sympathizing, Viola allowed for a bit of silence to pass between them while watching a couple of sparrows hopping along the path. "Do you have any pets?" she asked with some strange intention to further confirm that he wasn't as bad as she'd thought. Indeed, she was starting to think that she might have misjudged him completely—that the entire world might be wrong about who Mr. Lowell actually was.

"I have a cat named Newton."

"Really?" She tried to picture him with the creature and decided it suited him rather well.

Lips quirking, he dropped his gaze to hers. "He shares his namesake's solitary and untrusting nature." A frown emerged upon his brow. "It makes one wonder if names can shape a personality."

He stretched out his legs and crossed them at the ankles, alerting Viola to their length and the sturdy outline of his thighs beneath his trousers. "I have two horses as well. A pair of Scottish Clydesdales."

Viola stared at him blankly. She knew absolutely nothing about horses. At least not enough to know what a Clydesdale was.

"I know they're not the customary choice for a London gentleman to ride," Mr. Lowell went on, "but they're extremely strong and energetic. In truth, I don't think they get enough credit. And I absolutely love the feathering around their lower legs. It gives them character, if you ask me."

"They sound very handsome."

"Oh indeed, they are." He held her gaze. "Perhaps

I will have the chance to show them to you one day." Before she was able to agree or object, he asked, "What about you, Viola? Do you have any pets?"

"I have a dog," she said. "My late husband gave him to me as an engagement present."

"I see. And does this pup of yours have a name?"

"Rex." It was her turn to smile at him with the knowledge that she was about to say the unexpected. "He's a Rottweiler."

Mr. Lowell's eyes widened just enough to convey his surprise. "Really?" He studied her a moment, until her skin heated beneath the intensity of his gaze. "I ought to have known, oughtn't I? A strong woman should own a strong dog. Now I think of it, I imagine you and Rex are well suited for each other and that he is quite an effective protector."

A charge filled the air between them, born from the deep awareness of how well he already seemed to know her. It was slightly terrifying in a way. Most of all because she sensed that she also saw a part of him that he attempted to hide from the world. Not the rake, but a man with feeling and empathy for others. Her pulse quickened and panic took over. To like him too much would be far too dangerous, since she could not afford to become emotionally entangled with any man. Her past experiences wouldn't allow it, and neither would her dedication to the hospital or her appreciation for independence. So she stood, forcing him to rise as well.

They started back toward the door leading to the wing where Mr. Lowell's room was located. "I think my late husband had the same thing in mind. But I do not need Rex to protect me. I'm perfectly capable of doing so myself."

"Indeed?" He eyed her with interest.

Heat flared in her cheeks but the urge to astound

him was far too tempting to be denied. "My father taught me to use a pistol most effectively. I carry one with me wherever I go. Just in case."

Mr. Lowell grinned the way a child might do when discovering the secret to a magical trick. "Of course you do."

"I have no husband or male relations to offer protection," she explained.

"I see I was wrong to think you were foolish for living alone for a while. On the contrary, you're a smart woman, Viola, and your father was wise to teach you."

"To be honest, those hours of practice we spent together when there was time to do so are among the most precious memories of my childhood."

"I gather he was a busy man."

"As busy as most physicians, I suspect. Just consider your brother."

Mr. Lowell nodded. "It is part of the reason why I insisted he take the trip he'd been planning with his wife. I'm glad he did, for no one deserves some time off more than him. Except maybe you."

They reached the door and went back inside. "My work means the world to me, Mr. Lowell. I do not wish to take a break from it for any reason." When he looked ready to argue, she added, "It fills my days completely and gives me immense satisfaction. I do not have time for anything else in my life."

He didn't respond for a long while after. Not until they reached his room and prepared to part ways. Turning to face her, he spoke with feeling. "You may not think so, but I intend to change your mind on that score. I mean to prove to you that making time for me will benefit you greatly, not only professionally, but"—he dipped his chin and whispered close to her ear—"privately too."

His breath stroked her cheek, and Viola's stomach contracted in response. Before she could get her brain working again and voice an answer, however, he was gone, leaving her more rattled than ever before. Because in spite of her efforts to stop him from trying to pursue her, it seemed she'd achieved the opposite.

Irritating man!

The effect he had on her was so distracting she could scarcely concentrate on her work for the rest of the day. Doing so was impossible when his words continued to chase her wherever she went.

It wasn't until she arrived home later that she was able to find the reprieve she required, though not at all in the way she had hoped.

"The table's already set so I'll just have everything brought up to the dining room," Diana said after greeting her in the hallway. She turned to go but paused to add, "I almost forgot. A letter arrived for you earlier today. I put it on the desk in your study."

Viola thanked her and went to see who the letter was from. It had not been posted but hand delivered. Apprehension nipped at her skin, turning to full-fledged anxiety the moment she tore the seal and read the bold script.

Viola,

    I must confess I was both surprised and relieved to find you absent from Tremaine House upon my arrival. Still, there are matters between us that must be settled, which is why I propose we meet at my home tomorrow afternoon.

      In anticipation of your response,
      Robert Cartwright, Duke of Tremaine

Inhaling deeply, Viola read the words three more times before dropping the letter onto her desk. She didn't want to see the man who'd lost his inheritance to her. Not to mention the fact that she'd once been in love with him and that he'd broken her heart. But the most important reason of all was perhaps her decision to marry his father as he lay dying. The act still made her feel guilty, because she knew in her heart she was undeserving of the title she'd gained.

A heavy sigh pushed its way through her. As much as she wished it, she couldn't avoid Robert forever. So maybe it was best to get it over with. Perhaps she'd even discover that there was no reason for her to be concerned about seeing him again. He'd only promised her the world, after all. But that had been a long time ago, and they'd both married different people since.

She'd also changed in the years between, she reminded herself.

You're stronger now than you were before. Show him that.

Determining to do so, however, proved harder than she'd imagined when she found herself seated in his parlor the following day. She was familiar with the space—had spent countless hours here when accompanying her father on visits to the late duke; the man who'd ensured she would want for nothing when he'd given her his name and fortune.

As she ought to have expected, Robert made her wait almost half an hour before he finally deigned to put in an appearance. The moment he did, Viola's heart lurched and her stomach flipped over. It was as if no time had passed at all since the day he'd declared her unfit to be his bride. She was once again reminded of the naïve young girl she'd been, ready to trust and believe that the happily-ever-after she'd always dreamed of could be hers, as long as she did what Robert asked.

Instead he'd destroyed her faith in men by showing her how easy it had been for him to fool her. As long as he'd tempted her with the one thing she'd wanted the most.

Love.

Concealing her distress beneath a façade she hoped looked as calm as it felt, Viola stood with as much dignity as she could muster. "Welcome home, Robert." She dipped her head in greeting. "It is good to see you again after all this time."

He was closer now, having crossed the room while she'd spoken. His hair was the same brown shade she remembered, albeit with a little less luster, his eyes as blue as they'd been the first time he'd kissed her, though fresh creases at the corners suggested that life had not been easy for him while he'd been away. "I am the Duke of Tremaine now," he told her. "Please remember that when you address me in the future."

Viola blinked, recalling how she'd instinctively used his given name. Because they'd been intimate once. Friends even. But all of that was now in the past.

"Forgive me." And then she forced herself to say it. "Your Grace."

He smiled as smugly as when he'd presented her to his fiancée five years earlier. It had happened in this very parlor the same day she'd given her body to him. Her father had been dead for almost a year by then, and she had been invited to live at Tremaine House under the old duke's protection. When Robert had asked her to come and join him shortly after their lovemaking, she'd thought he meant to propose. Instead he'd announced his betrothal to Lady Beatrice. The introductions that had followed had been swift and jarring. Viola had felt it like a stab to her chest. She'd felt like a spectator in a nightmare, her body completely numb while the world crashed down around her.

"But you declared your love for me," she'd stupidly insisted later that day when she'd managed to find Robert alone.

He'd looked at her with the sort of pity she'd since determined never to inspire in anyone ever again. "You are a sweet girl, Viola, but you cannot seriously have thought I would ever consider marrying you."

She'd stared at him as if seeing him for the very first time. "Of course not."

"We belong to different social classes. It would never work."

"So you built an illusion for me out of lies?"

He'd winced ever so slightly before hardening his gaze and saying, "You cannot lay all the blame at my feet alone when we both know you were more than eager to let me have you."

She'd done something then that she would not have thought herself capable of. She'd stepped forward and slapped him. And then she'd quit Tremaine House and hadn't seen Robert again. Until now.

"I cannot believe you married my father," he said, spitting the words with disgust. He shoved his hands in his pockets and went to the window to look out over the garden. "And to think I almost felt bad for you after announcing my betrothal to Beatrice." He snorted. "You seemed genuinely distressed, but instead you were only sorry to lose the ladder you hoped I'd provide."

"No." She shook her head as he turned to face her. His jaw was more pronounced than it had been when she'd last seen him, and lines of hardship marked his brow. There was even a scar on his left cheekbone, she saw now, reminding her their lives had diverged in their years apart.

"Liar!" His shoulders bunched angrily beneath his well-tailored jacket, puckering the superfine fabric. "You are a social climber, Viola, and when you couldn't have me, you launched yourself at my father. Isn't that right?"

She shook her head, horrified that this was how he saw her—how anyone might see her—and yet she'd heard the rumors and had long since been forced to acknowledge how things looked.

"Your father was a kind and generous man." She sank down onto a nearby chair. "My father saved your life when you were an infant, Robert, and your father always believed he owed him a debt of gratitude for that. Marrying me and ensuring my continued well-being was his way of paying that debt."

Robert stared back at her for a long moment before saying, "No. It was your way of robbing me of my rightful inheritance." He glared. "Somehow you managed to convince him to leave everything to you."

"That is not true." She hadn't even known the extent of the wealth Tremaine had willed her until after the funeral. "And he didn't leave everything. There are still the entailed properties and—"

"Much good that will do me besides incurring debt." He started pacing, hands clutched behind his back. "You ought to know I intend to contest it."

"What?"

He stopped and faced her, the planes of his face pronounced by hard shadows cast in relief on account of the afternoon light spilling in through the windows. "I've hired a barrister." His eyes gleamed with the promise of vengeance. "He believes it will be fairly simple to prove that you took advantage of an old man on his deathbed. Especially since Findlay happened to mention that my father was prone to moments of confusion before he passed."

Viola's stomach began to churn. "But . . ." She

shook her head. "Most of the funds your father left me have been spent. I have little to give you."

His lips curled, deforming his features with anger. "That is not the point, Viola. It is no longer about the amount of money I hope to get out of this. It is about watching you suffer the same kind of loss you have forced me to endure."

A bleak chill swept over her, blanketing her in despair.

"If I win," he continued in the calmest voice he'd used until now, "you shall have to return the funds my father left you to the best of your abilities. Even if that means parting with your precious hospital." He smiled the sort of smile that declared his hate for her. "I'm sure the building itself will fetch a pretty penny when I sell it. So prepare yourself, Viola, because I have every intention of taking what's rightfully mine."

Chapter 5

Crossing the street, Henry clutched his most recent purchase under his arm and tipped his hat in greeting while passing another gentleman on the pavement. He felt much improved today and had therefore decided to go for a walk. Hell, he could use the exercise after spending the last several days in bed. When his valet had offered to spoon-feed him this morning, Henry had finally had enough. He would not be treated like an invalid when all he'd sustained was a shot to the shoulder.

Quickening his steps, he appreciated the exertion, the strain the brisk walk put on his body and the way it pushed his muscles and tendons to perform. Up ahead, a woman turned the corner and began coming toward him with what appeared to be a massive dog by her side.

Henry smiled. He'd know that particular silhouette anywhere. It was without a doubt Viola, strolling along with a hound the size of a small pony.

Approaching her, he noticed the exact moment when she recognized his identity. Because she actually stumbled slightly and drew to a halt. Intent on discouraging her from pretending she hadn't seen him, from crossing the street as if meaning to call on one of the houses opposite, or attempting some other ridiculous ploy to avoid his company, he called out her name like a common street vendor selling his wares.

"Viola!"

She stared at him and looked about, as if trying to decide whether she was willing to draw attention by admitting that she was the woman he'd called to.

He grinned, enjoying her discomfort and her silly way of thinking because the only other person in the street besides them was the man he'd greeted earlier. Henry obviously wasn't calling to him.

"Good afternoon," Henry said when he was finally within speaking distance. He glanced at the dog, who was panting so much that drool was dripping from each side of his oversized mouth. "Fine day for a walk."

"Yes," Viola agreed. She seemed to wait for him to say something more. When he didn't, she added, "I am glad to see you up and about. You look well, Mr. Lowell. Better than when I last saw you."

He nodded. "I feel much improved, which I'm sure must be thanks to your excellent care." He was pleased to see a flicker of pleasure in the depths of her lovely gray eyes. Responding with a debonair look, he said, "Will you introduce me to your companion?"

A smile tugged at the edge of her lips, producing a pair of enticing dimples. She coughed slightly as if to hide her reaction, cleared her throat a little, and finally gestured toward the massive creature. "This is Rex."

Henry considered the dog, who looked more like a big furry bundle of affection than an actual threat. Reaching out, he scratched him roughly behind one ear and smiled when Rex leaned into his fingers with greater insistence.

"Traitor," Viola muttered, albeit with a hint of amusement.

Henry glanced at her, still stroking the dog. "I wouldn't worry too much if I were you. Most people won't dare approach you as long as you have him with you, but I know the sort of woman you are, so I also know the sort of dog you would raise."

"How can you possibly know me so well after only a few interactions?" Her voice held a note of wonder that squeezed at Henry's heart.

"I'm very observant," he said. "Especially when the subject of my observation is of great interest to me." Noting how her blush deepened and the way she deliberately broke eye contact, he decided to change the subject and save her from too much discomfort. "Where are you heading?" Because he knew the hospital lay in the opposite direction.

"Home." The word was forcefully spoken. She followed it with a sigh. "Today has been a trying day, Mr. Lowell. I hope you will excuse my tone, which has absolutely nothing to do with you."

Henry glanced in the direction from which he had come and said, "Perhaps my wonderful company will help improve your spirits. I'll happily escort you, if you like." When she looked as if she might decline, he deliberately waggled his eyebrows, which earned him a chuckle.

"You are incorrigible."

"I cannot deny it."

She grinned this time and appeared to relax. "Very well then. If you do not mind taking a detour."

"Not at all," he assured her. "I take tremendous pleasure in sharing your company."

She frowned at him and gave Rex a tug on his leash. "You ought to know that I am not especially fond of flattery or over-embellished compliments."

They started walking while Henry wondered about this peculiarity of hers. Most women loved being told how pretty and desirable they were, but for reasons he couldn't understand, it seemed to bother Viola whenever he said something nice about her. It was as if she believed he was being insincere, which could only mean that some event in her past must have crushed her self-esteem. He wondered what it could be.

"What did you purchase?" she asked a few seconds later, drawing his attention to the parcel under his arm.

He assumed the gravest expression he could muster. "*The New Principles of Gardening.*"

She gave him a sideways glance. "You must be joking."

"Why?"

"Because . . ." She waved her free hand as if searching for an explanation. A frown puckered her brow. "Are you really serious? *The New Principles of Gardening?*"

"I can show you, if you like." He pulled the parcel from under his arm.

"No, no, Mr. Lowell. I shall take your word for it." And then she laughed and shook her head, and Henry's heart soared in response to the lyrical sound. "Of all the things I would have expected, from cigar boxes to a new game of chess . . . I never would have taken you for a botanist."

"Oh, I'm not, I assure you, which is why I purchased the book." They turned a street corner and the pavement grew narrower, forcing them closer together. His shoulder brushed hers, producing a thrilling hum along the length of his arm. "I need something with which to pass the time until I'm fully recovered and I've always marveled over the beauty of a well-kept garden. After seeing the one at the hospital, I had a moment of inspiration."

"It sounds as though you have plans to renovate."

"I'd like to. As with most gardens here in London, mine is not particularly large. My gardener insists I keep it simple, but I do not see why simple must equal dull. I want color and vibrancy, Viola. I want a garden that's just like . . ."

You.

In his excitement he'd almost let his tongue run away with him. For although she wasn't outwardly colorful, her personality definitely was, and it was this, he realized now with startling clarity, that he'd missed since leaving the hospital. Indeed he'd longed for it so much he'd finally resorted to looking at pictures of flowers in a book while dreaming of recreating something of what Viola imparted with her beauty and vigor.

"What?" she asked, curiosity clinging to that single word.

Henry reached for an explanation that wouldn't serve as an unwanted compliment. The last thing he wished was to push her away now that they were getting along so well. "Like the gardens you see in the villages with roses climbing up cottage walls and marigolds brightening the flowerbeds. I want peonies and . . . and . . . those bell-shaped flowers on the long stalks."

"Foxgloves?"

"Yes!" He glanced at her and saw she was smiling with a trace of wonder in her eyes. "And since I know next to nothing about growing flowers, I thought I'd do some reading and learn what I can. At least then I'll be able to advise my gardener on what to plant."

"You are not at all what I first expected," she mused.

"I hope that's a good thing."

She grew pensive, then said, "I have yet to figure that out."

The comment seemed to jostle the positive mood she'd acquired while they'd walked, reminding him of her earlier comment. *Today has been a trying day.*

Placing one hand on her forearm, he drew her to a halt. "Viola, you should know that although I plan to pursue you romantically, I first and foremost wish to be your friend." He spoke plainly, hoping to convey how serious he was about this. "If you ever need my help or simply someone to talk to, you can count on me to listen and offer advice."

She stared back up at him, and for a long moment he believed she might tell him her troubles. But then she turned away and resumed walking. "I thank you," she said when he fell into step beside her. "Truly I do." And then, more hesitantly, "But I fear associating with you would be unwise, not only because of your interest in me, which I still mean to try and dissuade, but because of your reputation. I cannot risk a connection with you because of the negative effect it might have on my reputation and possibly on my businesses as a result. I am sorry."

Convincing her that every word she'd ever heard was utter nonsense would be no easy task. Pulling her to another halt, he kept his hand on her arm this time, holding her in place and meeting her gaze with extreme determination. "During the time you have known my brother, he must have mentioned his family."

She tilted her head as if to consider. "Occasionally."

Henry leaned in a little. Just enough to make her avert her gaze. There was an almost imperceptible shift in her breathing as another flush rose to her cheeks. He smiled, liking the extent to which he affected her. "Did he ever talk about me?"

She blinked and gave a quick nod. "Of course. He

is exceedingly fond of you, Mr. Lowell." She recommenced walking, pulling away from his grasp in the process.

Following her, Henry made no further attempt to touch her. Instead, he said, "Then he must have told you that none of the rumors about me are true."

"To be honest, we never really discussed it."

Henry frowned. He would not be able to rely on Florian to help him out this time. Apparently winning Viola's trust would be far more difficult than he had ever imagined. Unless he told her the absolute truth. Now there was an idea worth trying. "What if I were to tell you that every affair I've ever had and every scandalous thing I have done was a product of fiction?"

She looked at him. Her eyes widened and her lips parted as if in surprise, but rather than follow her astounded expression with one of complete understanding and tell him that what he said made perfect sense, she laughed. "Come now, Mr. Lowell. You cannot think me dimwitted enough to believe such a tale. A respectable gentleman would never allow the world to think less of him on purpose." She knit her brow. "Frankly, I am a little offended by your attempt to fool me in such a ridiculous way, though I do admire your determination."

"Viola."

"I will allow that your reputation may not be as bad as the gossip suggests, for if it were I would not have enjoyed your company as thoroughly as I have, nor do I think it likely that you would have a cat named Newton or that you would speak of your brother with the sort of affection you showed a couple of days ago in the hospital garden. But to think it completely unblemished would be unwise on my part, I believe." She slowed her pace and moved toward the steps leading up to the narrowest house on the street. "This is unfortunately where we must part, Mr. Lowell." She reached inside her pocket and produced a key. "Thank you for your escort and for brightening my day."

He touched the brim of his hat and smiled, happy to have offered her some small reprieve from whatever concerns were pressing on her mind, even if their recent discussion had not produced the result he hoped for. "I am always at your service, Viola."

Her eyes flashed with a hint of appreciation before she turned away, pulling Rex up the steps behind her. Henry waited until she was safely inside and he heard the lock click into place before starting back the way they had come.

Deciding to take a quieter route instead of the quicker one Piccadilly offered, he turned north on Princess Street. He was just about to cross to Brewer Street when he caught a flash of scarlet out of the corner of his eye. Instinctively glancing toward it, Henry froze. What the devil was Carlton Guthrie doing strolling about in the middle of Mayfair?

Henry stared at the man whose flamboyant attire was as well renowned as the crimes he'd committed. The Scoundrel of St. Giles, the papers often called him—a moniker fit for the sort of man he was known to be, even if the authorities had never managed to find him guilty of anything.

In his younger days, when Henry had been hell-bent on tarnishing his own good name, he'd deliberately visited a few establishments in St. Giles, where he'd gambled on boxing matches and played high-stakes dice. He'd even seen the Duke of Huntley fight once when he was just an ordinary man. Before his inheritance changed his life and brought him and his sisters out of the slums. Guthrie had been there too. He'd stood out in the crowd like a splash of bright paint on an otherwise gray façade, so Henry had eventually inquired about him.

Curious to know Guthrie's errand and worried it might be nefarious, Henry waited for him to turn onto Compton Street before following at a discreet distance. It didn't take long to realize he was heading toward Soho Square. Henry kept his pace casual and far enough from Guthrie to prevent him from hearing his footsteps. Too far, perhaps, with Frith Street being so short that when Henry turned onto it, Guthrie was already out of sight. Henry hurried out into Soho Square and looked quickly about. Large homes marked the perimeter, among them Tremaine House, whose front door was presently closing.

Henry frowned. It had to be a coincidence. Guthrie would not be sitting down to tea with Robert, who was much too high in the instep to ever admit the Scoundrel of St. Giles into his home. No. Guthrie must have gone off in a different direction. Most likely to Broad Street and onward to his own neighborhood.

Abandoning the idea of pursuing him further, Henry set his course for Swallow Street. He arrived at The Red Rose ten minutes later and made straight for his office. Setting his newly purchased book on his desk, he called for his steward, Mr. Faulkner, to come join him.

"You mentioned an issue with the roof yesterday." As soon as Henry had returned home from St. Agatha's, he'd sent a missive to Mr. Faulkner, asking him to join Henry for dinner. Over the course of a couple of hours, the loyal employee had apprised Henry of everything that had happened at The Red Rose during his absence. "Have you found someone to fix the leak?"

"Yes. A couple of roofers were hired this morning. I expect them to start work tomorrow."

"Excellent." Henry glanced at a file he'd found

waiting for him on his desk. "Do we have samples as usual of the wines being offered by Berry's?" The grocer specializing in importing wines and spirits of the finest quality was one of Henry's most cherished suppliers.

"Right over there," Mr. Faulkner said. He gestured toward a crate on the floor next to the side table.

Henry stood and went to take a closer look. He picked up the first bottle and read the label before comparing it to the wine's description in the file he'd been provided. "Let us get started on the tasting, then, so we can decide which wine to promote next month."

It was an idea he'd been developing during the past year and one that had proved quite effective, since his taste in wine was apparently one that agreed with most people. By pushing a monthly wine, he encouraged many of his customers to come back regularly so they could learn which wine he'd selected next.

The process took time as usual. Each sample had to be enjoyed individually. He had to discover the character and consider the combination of flavors. It reminded him a bit of Viola. She too was a luxury to indulge in slowly. As with the wine, he would savor each of her many nuances. Until she eventually surrendered and agreed to be his. No matter how challenging such an accomplishment was proving to be.

The following morning, after enjoying a hearty breakfast, Henry decided to pass a couple of hours in the library. Lowering himself into his favorite chair in front of the fireplace, he propped his feet up on the accompanying footstool. With a pot of coffee on the table beside him and a couple of Cook's shortbread biscuits for him to savor, he settled in for a relaxing morning.

"Sir," his butler, Mr. Andrews, announced an hour later when he stepped into the room, "Lord and Lady Armswell have come to call. They are accompanied by the Earl and Countess of Scranton. Shall I show them into the parlor?"

Henry closed the book he'd been reading and set it aside, abandoning his intention to learn about proper soil preparation for the moment. "I will do so myself." He stood and followed Mr. Andrews out into the hallway. "Please instruct one of the maids to bring up a tray. Remember to remind her of my grandmother's strawberry allergy."

"Of course, sir."

Mr. Andrews headed for the servant stairs while Henry continued toward the foyer, arriving there in a few quick strides. "What a lovely surprise," he declared even though he could think of a dozen things he'd rather do right now than sit down to tea with his parents and grandparents. All they ever wanted to discuss with him these days was potential brides.

"I am so relieved to see you looking well," his mother said once he'd shown them all into the parlor and gestured for them to sit. He took the remaining chair—a spindly one that he generally avoided. Newton prowled toward him, pressing himself against Henry's leg, so he slid his hand along the cat's supple coat. "We rushed back from Bath as soon as we heard you'd been shot."

At last. A new conversation subject.

"What on earth were you thinking?" Armswell asked. "You gave your poor mother a fit of the vapors and your grandmama almost suffered an apoplectic incident!"

"I did no such thing," Lady Scranton declared with a scowl, "though to say you did not give us all a mighty fright would be something of an understatement." She punctuated her remark with a firm nod and directed a sharp look at Henry. "It is a relief to see you are still alive."

"Did the papers not mention that I survived the duel?" Henry asked. He was genuinely curious to know how the journalists had painted his most recent brush with death in order to sell their papers.

"Your condition was declared uncertain," Lord Scranton said gruffly while adjusting his bulky size to the delicate sofa on which he was sitting.

"And we all know what that means," Lady Armswell announced. "They might as well have written that funeral preparations were forthcoming!"

Henry groaned and reached for his mother's hand. "As you can see, that will not be necessary just yet, Mama."

"I should hope not." She sniffed. "But you would do us all a tremendous favor by avoiding unnecessary threats to your life in future."

"One doesn't avoid a duel when one is called out, Mama."

"Certainly not," Lady Scranton agreed. "What one does is avoid the situation leading up to a challenge."

"Your grandmother is right," Scranton said. "I can think of no other man who's been called out as often as you have, Henry. The fact that you are still among the living is something of a miracle if you ask me."

Everyone nodded in unified agreement while Henry hoped Mr. Andrews would soon appear with news of some dire emergency requiring his immediate departure from this accusation-riddled conversation. Instead the parlor door opened to admit two maids bringing tea, porcelain teacups and a plate stacked with blueberry tarts.

"Which is all the more reason for you to marry with haste," Lady Armswell insisted once the maids had gone and the tea had been served.

Henry froze with his teacup en route to his mouth. What the devil had he been thinking when he'd told them of his intention to hang up his rakish mantle in favor of reformation? He looked at his guests and saw that they watched him with keen expectation. His father raised an eyebrow and his grandmother leaned forward in her seat and tilted her head. "Well?" she finally inquired when nobody else spoke.

"Well what?" Henry asked, still hoping to extricate himself somehow from the mire of promises and duty his life had become.

"What," Lady Scranton asked with exacting words, "are you doing about your marriageable prospects?"

"Ah." She couldn't have been any clearer. Henry thought of Viola and swiftly banished her from his mind. Because although he had every intention of pursuing her, he would not allow his family to know it. One hint of his intentions and there was no doubt in his mind he'd lose his chance—which was slim enough as it was. "I will set my mind to it once again when I'm fully recuperated."

"And when do you suppose that will be?" Armswell demanded to know.

Henry gave him a cavalier shrug. "I honestly cannot say." He needed time. Time to plot and plan and discover the best course of action where Viola was concerned. Courting her would be no simple matter since she never attended social events. He'd been fortunate to happen upon her today when she'd been out walking. "Recuperation takes as long as it takes. I shall inform you when I am ready to continue hunting for a bride."

"You needn't make it sound so unpleasant, Henry," Lady Scranton chided.

He raised a challenging brow at her. "Your collective urgency with this matter is what makes it so. If it were up to me, I would take my time with finding the right woman. But ever since I told you of my plan to one day marry, you've been pushing me toward the altar with increased vigor."

"We only want what is best for you," Lady Armswell said.

"Which is for you to secure an heir before your next duel," Scranton muttered with censorious force.

Henry snatched up a tart and stood. He stared down at his family's upturned faces. The continuation of their titles was his responsibility. He knew this, which was why he'd decided it was time for him to secure his progeny almost a year ago. He just hadn't found the right woman until now.

So far, everything had gone according to plan, except for the duel. But oh, if it had not been for his getting shot, he might not have met Viola, and that would have been a terrible pity. Biting into his tart, Henry absently wondered if she would enjoy receiving flowers.

Probably not, considering how she refused to be complimented in any way. She would not allow the use of her title, to which she had the right; she did not appreciate being told she was pretty or that her company was favored. Indeed, she would probably hate him for sending her flowers, which meant he obviously had no choice but to do so, if only to be the thorn in her side. Until she would let him be more.

"Let us remember that finding a wife was my idea," Henry said. "I will do so at my own pace and only if you agree to stop interfering."

"Fine," Armswell said. "But I expect to see you trying."

"And so I shall," Henry assured them all. "As soon as my shoulder no longer pains me." He shoved his blueberry tart into his mouth and turned away to admire his fireplace while the conversation behind him turned to other things. Another fifteen minutes passed before his family finally left, leaving Henry emotionally exhausted and with a headache that made him want to go outside and do something. So he went in search of some discarded clothes and stepped out into the mess his garden had become now that he'd asked his gardener to uproot almost everything.

Grabbing a fistful of some unlucky plant, he gave it a yank and tossed it aside. It came loose easily enough with a spray of dirt to go with it. Henry grinned and moved on to the next. It was simple work, easy enough on his right shoulder as long as he used his left arm, and immensely satisfying.

He slept well that night and felt better when he woke the next morning. Better still after eating a hearty breakfast. Most of all, after visiting a local hothouse and picking out the perfect bouquet.

He could not wait to hear Viola's response to it.

Chapter 6

Viola looked up from the hospital ledger she was going over and carefully pulled off her spectacles when she saw what could only be defined as a piece of garden maneuvering its way into her office.

Good Lord!

"Viola?" Emily's voice spoke from somewhere behind the bucketful of roses, gladiola, carnations, green leafy bits and whatever else had been combined to create what appeared to be an eclectic piece of shrubbery. "Have you seen this?"

Viola shot out of her seat and rushed to help Emily with the flowers. "Where did they come from?" Viola asked as soon as they'd found an appropriate spot for them in a corner.

"I'm not sure. The card was addressed to you."

Viola took the card Emily gave her while eyeing a long leafy stem. "Is that . . ." She leaned forward and sniffed to be sure. "Rosemary?"

"Mmm-hmm. And it is not the only herb either. There's lavender over here, a touch of coriander there, some thyme, chamomile and what looks like a piece of licorice root."

Viola put her spectacles back on and tore open the card.

I know you do not want the attention a bundle of flowers this size will ensure, but I could think of no other way to convey my thanks for the recent care you provided me during my stay at St. Agatha's Hospital. According to The New Principles of Gardening, each plant has a medicinal purpose which I hope you will find of some use to your work. If not, please see fit to divide it up and redistribute. I am sure there are patients who would at the very least appreciate the scent.

Sincerely,
H.A.L

Viola stared at the sprouting foliage. "It is from Mr. Lowell," she murmured. Florian's brother had elected to give her the most ridiculous display of gratitude she'd ever seen. And yet, she had to admit it was also the most thoughtful, because he intended for it to serve a purpose beyond adding color and beauty to a room. He wanted her to get some use out of it.

Emily turned to look at her with dismay. "Is he cracked in the head?"

Viola chuckled. "Perhaps, but in the best way possible." She could not help but appreciate the gesture for what it was, even if she refused to fall prey to whatever ulterior motive lay behind the elaborate offering. For now, however, she would put that aside. "Come on. Let us remove the herbs and send them down to Mr. Owens." As the hospital's apothecary, he would surely appreciate fresh supplies. "We will divide the rest into smaller bouquets. I think we can make enough for most of the patient rooms."

"I'll go and collect some empty bottles to use as vases," Emily suggested. She left to do so, leaving Viola to pick the various herbs from between the flowers.

"Heavens!" a familiar voice declared about five minutes later. Viola looked up from her crouched position to see Amelia Heathmore, Duchess of Coventry, and Gabriella Matthews, Duchess of Huntley, enter the room. "It smells like a perfume shop in here!"

Viola stood and greeted both women. "It is from a former patient." Although she'd considered Amelia and Gabriella friends since Florian had become related to both of them through marriage to Amelia and Huntley's sister, Juliette, she did not want to share the identity of the man who'd chosen to single her out with a bucketful of flowers.

Gabriella chuckled. "He must have been very happy with whatever it is you did for him, Viola."

"What makes you think it's from a man?" Viola asked while crossing her arms and attempting to arch a brow.

Both women cut her a look of obvious disbelief. "A woman would never have something like that delivered," Amelia said.

"If you ask me," Gabriella added, "I'd say you've acquired quite the admirer, Viola."

Oh God!

Turning to her desk, Viola discreetly opened a drawer and slipped the accompanying note from Mr. Lowell inside. "Even if that were true, I wouldn't be interested."

"So then you know who the flowers are from?" Amelia asked her curiously.

"No," Viola lied. "I cannot imagine who it can be."

Gabriella and Amelia shared a conspiratorial look before Gabriella said, "I am sure we can deduce it if we set our minds to it. All we have to do is look at the patients you've had here during the past week. It would not take long for us to figure out which of the men would be able to afford a bouquet this size, for I can assure you it was not cheap."

"No need," Viola said, shuffling papers together and rearranging her ledgers. "As I said, I'm not interested."

There was a pause—a silent void—and then, "But why?" both women asked in unison.

"You are still young," Gabriella said. "Especially when considering you have been married before."

"And aren't young widows all the rage?" Amelia asked.

"Oh yes," Gabriella said. "The gentlemen will fawn over you, Viola, if you would only put in the occasional appearance at some of this Season's events."

Setting her palms down onto her desk, Viola braced herself on her arms and stared at her friends. "I do not want to be fawned over or flirted with or chased by any man." Seeing their shocked expressions, she expelled a breath and leaned back. "I have endured enough of that to last me a lifetime, I assure you. From now on the only thing that matters to me is ensuring the future of this hospital and the new rejuvenation center." *While doing my best to keep both out of Robert's clutches.*

"Right." Gabriella shared a look with Amelia and then asked, "How is the rejuvenation center coming along? When Florian came to call on me before leaving for Paris, he said it was almost finished."

Viola blinked. "Florian came to call on you?"

"He came to call on both of us," Amelia said. "He worried about his extended leave of absence and asked us to check up on you occasionally."

"In other words, you wish to see if I'm managing well enough without him?" Viola regarded the women who looked like princesses when compared to her own drab nurse's attire.

Gabriella nodded. "I believe we were right to do so too." She took a step forward and peered at Viola. "There are shadows beneath your eyes. Are you sure you are getting enough sleep?"

"As much as I can afford," Viola assured her.

"I think you need a reprieve," Amelia said. "You are obviously exhausted, and with Florian away I can only imagine how trying it must be for you to run a hospital *and* complete the renovations on the rejuvenation center all by yourself."

"There is much to be done," Viola confessed before she could think better of it.

"And we are here to help," Gabriella said.

Amelia smiled. "Which is why we propose an outing."

Viola shook her head. "I have to finish tallying the numbers in the ledger." It was vital she knew the financial state she was in before she heard from Robert again.

"Bring it with you. We'll drop it off at my house and ask Thomas's secretary to handle it," Amelia suggested.

"And then we'll go and check on the rejuvenation center together," Gabriella added. "I'm extremely curious to know how it is coming along."

Viola considered their offer. She had been neglecting the rejuvenation center lately. She'd actually meant to go and visit the building later today to check up on the progress the workers were making. Feeling the weight of the world slide away just a little, she welcomed the relief she felt in response to the prospect of receiving some assistance.

"Thank you. Both of you."

Gabriella smiled. "And when we are finished, we shall have an ice at Gunther's. My treat."

Viola prepared to leave, only to catch sight of

the flowers. She paused in the middle of putting on gloves. "What about those?" she asked just as Emily returned to the room followed by three orderlies carrying bottles and buckets of water.

"I think they're in good hands," Amelia said. She turned to Emily. She was carrying two baskets full of additional glass bottles. "We intend to take Viola out for a couple of hours. Do you think you can manage without her until she returns?"

"Absolutely," Emily declared with a cheerful smile. "The orderlies here will help me distribute the vases once I've prepared them."

Amelia caught Viola's eye. "See?"

"Just grab the ledger," Gabriella said, "and let us be off. The sooner we leave, the sooner you'll be back."

Giving the room one last look, Viola was forced to acknowledge that Emily had everything well in hand. So she did as Gabriella suggested and followed both her and Amelia out of the room.

"This is incredible," Gabriella said as she took a turn of the rejuvenation center's foyer half an hour later. "Just look at that ceiling!"

Viola looked up and immediately caught her breath. When she'd instructed the artist her foreman had hired on how to paint the ceiling, she'd simply said she wanted the overall atmosphere to be exotic. Never in a million years would she have envisioned the intricate swirls of gold leaf combined with bright shades of purples and reds. It matched the selection of accent tiles running between the plainer beige marble slabs on the floor.

"Is it coming together as you envisioned?" Viola asked Gabriella. Even though this project was hers, the idea for it had been Gabriella's. She'd suggested it more than a year ago when Florian had mentioned a need to ensure stable funds for the hospital.

"Oh, it exceeds every expectation I could have had," Gabriella said. She left Viola's side to take a turn of the gorgeous space while Amelia studied a pair of intricately chiseled columns supporting an archway at the back of the foyer.

"Ah, Mrs. Cartwright," Mr. Tibbs, the foreman declared by way of greeting as he entered through an arched doorway on the right. "I thought I heard voices." He greeted Amelia and Gabriella politely before asking, "So what do you think?"

"It is perfect," Viola told him sincerely. "Exactly what I was hoping for. Better, even."

Mr. Tibbs grinned, his broad shoulders and large frame vibrating heartily as he did so. "I'm so pleased to hear it. Especially since I've asked the painter to create borders to match in the other rooms. Come on, I'll show you." He led the way through a series of rooms, each slightly different from the last but similar enough to create a unified theme.

Elaborate borders ran along walls, edged the ceilings and framed the doorways. Most were still works in progress with apprentices marking the patterns in pencil so the artist himself could come in and paint.

"How long do you think it will take for all of this to be finished?" Viola asked, noting that there was still a lot left to be done, including the laying of tiles in one of the indoor pools and the installation of a large stained-glass window that had yet to be delivered.

"Another week, I expect." They returned to the foyer, where a couple of workers were now in the process of installing a large, elaborately carved door at the opposite end. "Most of it is cosmetic from this point on since all of the structural issues have been taken care of."

"So it will be ready for the grand opening on the twenty-fifth?"

"I see no reason for it not to be," Mr. Tibbs said. "In fact—"

"Oh my God!"

Startled by the loud exclamation, Viola turned to find Mr. Lowell standing behind her and staring up.

"Impressive, isn't it?" Gabriella asked as she went to greet him.

He lowered his gaze and addressed Gabriella. "Without a doubt." His eyes scanned the room, settling on Amelia next, whose presence he acknowledged with a tip of his head, before finally honing in on Viola. His lips tilted and then he smiled, jolting her heart and producing a flutter in the pit of her belly.

Lord, he was handsome! She'd allowed herself to forget the extent of his good looks. But the effort proved impossible when he was standing there in front of her with a roguish gleam in his dark brown eyes and a few stray locks falling haphazardly across his brow.

"Mr. Lowell." Why on earth did she sound so breathless?

He leaned slightly forward, expectantly waiting for her to continue. Which was difficult when he'd turned her brain to mush. Collecting herself was no easy task, but she was determined to try since the alternative was to surrender and risk getting hurt. So she straightened her spine and squared her shoulders, intent on banishing the effect he was having on her, and asked the only question that seemed to matter right now. "What are you doing here?"

Although she'd managed to bank all emotion beneath a bland expression, Henry had not missed the momentary look of deep appreciation in Viola's eyes when he'd given her his full attention. She could pretend indifference as much as she liked, but Henry knew she was anything but. He even suspected she was glad to see him, though she'd never admit it. At least not to him.

"I was on my way over to The Red Rose when I spotted the Coventry carriage and decided to look in." He smiled broadly. "I hope my decision to do so isn't too much of a bother."

"Not at all," Viola told him after a small but noticeable pause. "You are very welcome."

He doubted that was completely true but refused to argue the point. Instead, he addressed the burly man still standing by Viola's side. "Are you the man responsible for this incredible display of craftsmanship?"

"I . . . um . . ." the man hedged.

"This is Mr. Tibbs, my foreman," Viola explained.

Henry tipped his hat in Tibbs's direction. "Sir, I salute you. Your vision is exemplary!"

Tibbs looked visibly pleased with the compliment. "Thank you. I appreciate that, sir." He gave a quick nod and promptly left with the excuse of having *something* to see to.

As soon as he was gone, Henry took Viola boldly by the arm and led her farther away from Amelia and Gabriella under the pretext of wanting a closer look at the door a group of workers was securing with large brass hinges. "Did you receive the flowers?"

"Yes. Thank you. It was much too much."

Pleased by her softer tone, he allowed himself to lean slightly closer—so close he could smell the dry scent of starch from her clothes with a hint of something else clinging to her hair. He inhaled again and froze, appreciating the fresh aroma of citrus combined with rich hints of honey and ginger. It was like a tea he wanted to drink or perhaps a cake he would like to sink his teeth into. His skin heated and desire threatened to overwhelm with such force it took every bit of restraint he possessed not to pull her against him and enjoy a small taste.

But to do so would ruin everything. So he tightened his jaw, expelled a deep breath and pulled himself back, adding distance. "As my note explained, the flowers were for the hospital." He'd known it was the only way he could give them without her refusing the gesture.

"Nevertheless," she said, still trying to fight him on it. When he raised an eyebrow, challenging her to continue, she relented and eventually smiled. "It was actually very thoughtful of you. I know my apothecary will be especially grateful."

"I'm glad to hear it." And then, to add a bit more amusement, he told her slyly, "The alternative was a basket filled with colorful bandages and hand-blown bottles for tincture."

She laughed and covered her mouth to stifle the sound, her bright eyes peeking out from behind the tips of her fingers. Lowering them slowly, she dared to ask, "Really?"

Henry nodded and grinned while savoring how pretty she was when happiness shone in her eyes. If only there was a way to make this moment last forever. But then his gaze dropped to her lips and his chest contracted, leaving him short of breath and tightly strung with the uncanny need to claim her.

She must have noticed, because she turned away quickly and went to join her friends, whose expressions were marked by frank curiosity. Chastising himself for allowing desire to show when he knew it would work to his disadvantage, Henry muttered a curse before schooling his features.

"Ladies," he said, crossing the floor with the purpose of a man who refused to give up. "I would like to invite you and your husbands to dine with me tomorrow evening at my club." To ensure there was no misunderstanding, he addressed Viola directly, "You are welcome as well, Duchess. Indeed, I fervently hope you accept."

Before too much weight could be placed on this remark, he gave his attention to Amelia and Gabriella as if their attendance was just as important to him as Viola's. He held his breath and waited expectantly for them to reply, hoping it would be in the affirmative. If he was going to stand the smallest chance of securing Viola's attendance, he would need their agreement.

"I think that sounds like a wonderful idea," Gabriella said. Henry exhaled a sigh of relief. "Raphe has been talking about visiting your club for a while now. Tomorrow is as good an opportunity as any."

"Thomas and I have no other plans. Dining out at The Red Rose sounds like a lovely diversion," Amelia added.

Everyone looked at Viola in anticipation of her response. She hesitated, and Henry's heart proceeded to pound. *Say yes. Please say yes.* He needed this—some way to see her in a more intimate setting—the means by which to romance her.

"I'm sorry," she began, "but I—"

"Oh, come on, Viola," Amelia said. "All you ever do is work, which can't be very healthy."

"Amelia's right," Gabriella said. "You never go anywhere or do anything."

"That's not true," Viola told them. "I take Rex for a walk once a day."

"That doesn't count," Gabriella said. "And what do we tell Florian if he returns to find you've collapsed from overexertion? He wouldn't forgive us."

"That would never happen," Viola told her friends with a frown.

"Not as long as we prevent it," Amelia agreed.

"But I . . . I . . ." Viola looked at them each in turn and finally said, "I have nothing to wear!"

"Oh. Is that all that's troubling you." Amelia came up on Viola's other side. "Gabriella and I have plenty of gowns between us. We'll have a selection of dresses delivered in the morning and you can take your pick."

"I don't know." Viola glanced at Henry.

She appeared to be struggling with her decision so he decided to make one last attempt at winning her over before allowing her to decline. "We can play billiards after dinner."

Interest sparked to life in her eyes just as he'd hoped it would. "I don't know how to play," she hedged, still unsure, it would seem.

Henry met her gaze and held it while aiming for the friendliest smile he could muster. "I can teach you. It will be fun, Viola. I promise."

To his immense satisfaction she refrained from looking away, her eyes locked with his while she made her decision. Henry could scarcely breathe on account of the pure intensity of the moment, for he knew how defining it was. She would either trust him or she wouldn't.

Eventually, after what felt like a torturous eternity, she nodded. Her lips slowly lifted to form an enthusiastic smile. "Very well. I shall join you."

Henry's heart soared while his body sagged with relief. It did not matter that she wasn't looking at him anymore but rather discussing tomorrow's dinner plans with the duchesses. All that mattered was she would be there, and he would be ready for the next phase of his courtship.

Chapter 7

Giving himself one last look in the wide mirror that hung above the chest of drawers beside his desk, Henry straightened his jacket, gave the sleeves a slight tug and faced his steward.

"Is everything ready, Mr. Faulkner?"

"Yes, sir. Four bottles of the 1811 Veuve Clicquot, Comet vintage have been put on ice as per your instructions. Your favorite violinist has also arrived and is prepared to commence momentarily."

"And Monsieur Renarde?" Henry asked, referring to the French pastry chef he'd hired before the club had even opened—when The Red Rose had been but a dream.

"He has created the most delectable confections I have ever seen." Mr. Faulkner smiled broadly. "Your guests will be most impressed."

A knock sounded and Mr. Faulkner opened the door, admitting one of the waiters. "Mr. Lowell, sir. The Earl of Yates is asking to see you. Shall I show him in?"

"Right away," Henry said. "Thank you."

The waiter left to convey the message. "I should return to my duties," Faulkner said. He paused in the doorway to look back at Henry. "Don't worry. We have done this hundreds of times before. Whoever it is you're trying to impress will be dazzled this evening. Mark my word."

And then he was gone, replaced seconds later by Yates and denying Henry the chance to consider his nerves. Which was just as well. He could do with a distraction from his concerns about whether Viola would have a nice evening.

"I came to see if you're still in one piece," Yates said as he crossed the floor to shake Henry's hand. "You look remarkably well, all things considered."

"My brother stitched me up before leaving for Paris. After that, I received excellent care from one of the nurses."

Yates responded with a wide grin. "One of the pretty ones, I hope?"

"The prettiest of all," Henry assured him. He gestured toward a chair, offering Yates a seat. "I hear you've been rather busy lately. Are the rumors about you courting a young lady true?"

Yates sat and stretched out his legs. "To some degree. That is, I have been spending a fair amount of time with my sister's friend, Miss Evelyn Harlow. The fact that I have plans to marry her, however, is entirely false."

"Oh?"

"The idea is to get other gentlemen to take notice. If they wonder what an earl might see in an untitled woman like her with seemingly few prospects, they may be eager to console her when I break things off."

Henry raised an eyebrow. "I take it your sister invented this scheme?"

Yates grinned. "She is indeed the creative one."

"You're a good man, Yates. One of the best, in fact, which is why I'll even share my best brandy with you while we talk."

"The 1776?"

Henry poured them each a glass. "Precisely." He offered one to his friend, who took it with thanks. "I would advise you to take care regarding Miss Harlow, however. It would be a pity were she to get hurt."

Yates looked a bit perplexed. "Hurt? Why on earth would she get hurt?"

Henry gave him the frankest look he could manage. "Because you are romancing her. It may not be real, but it is certainly real enough for the papers to wonder when you will officially announce your betrothal."

"That is the point," Yates said, and took a sip of his drink.

"I realize that, but what if she gets carried away with the allure of marrying an earl."

Concern flickered in Yates's eyes. "I had not considered it, Lowell." He frowned. "She is an agreeable woman with whom I enjoy spending time or this would not have worked at all, but I can't really marry her."

"Why not?"

Yates stared back at Henry with eyes the size of saucers. "I—"

A hard knock interrupted their conversation. "Enter!" Henry shouted.

The door opened and Mr. Faulkner looked in. "The Duke of Tremaine would like to see you, sir. Shall I show him in or would you rather I ask him to wait?"

Uncertainty born from Viola's reaction to Robert surfaced for a second. He buried it quickly, however, intent on making his own assessment of the man he'd once called a friend. "By all means, show him in," Henry said. He met Yates's gaze while Faulkner went to fetch the duke. "It will give us a chance to make up for lost time."

"I wasn't even aware he was back," Yates murmured right before the door opened again and Robert entered the room.

He looked weatherworn, Henry decided. As if too much salty sea air had dimmed his luster. And flecks of gray were now starting to show on both sides of his dark brown hair. "Gentlemen," he announced, striding to shake first Yates's hand and then Henry's. "It is good to see the two of you again." He glanced around. "I have to say I'm surprised, Lowell. When I went to call on you at your house, your butler said I'd find you here instead. From what I gather, you own this place?"

"Bought the building three years ago and opened it to the public eight months later. I've been running it ever since." Henry snatched up an empty glass and tilted it slightly. "Brandy?"

"Don't mind if I do," Robert said. He lowered himself to the last remaining chair. "It's impressive, Lowell. I'm glad to see one of us has had some success." He glanced at Yates. "Though I'm sure you've had your fair share as well. You always were the lucky one."

"I'm afraid my luck may have run its course," Yates said. Henry handed Robert his drink. "Debutantes flocked to my side when I wasn't interested, and now that I'm thinking of finding a wife there's hardly any to be found. Everyone's getting married in quick succession."

"Surely not," Robert said.

"Well, Lady Gabriella is off the market and so are her husband's sisters, Lady Amelia and Lady Juliette."

Robert frowned. "They don't sound familiar. Do I know them?"

"You wouldn't. They entered Society two years ago when their brother inherited the title after the old Duke of Huntley and his sons all died." Yates expelled a tired breath and leaned back further in his seat. "It's a long story, which I'll happily share with you some other time."

"How intriguing," Robert muttered. "According to what I read in the gossip column this morning, you're supposed to be off to the altar soon with a certain Miss Harlow?"

"That's just what people are supposed to think," Yates muttered. "I'm only helping her get noticed while I wait for the woman I intend to marry. It's taking longer than I would have hoped, however."

Cradling his glass between his hands, Robert tilted his head as if in contemplation. "You shouldn't feel too disheartened, Yates. Marriage isn't all it's cracked up to be. In fact, it can be a bloody nuisance. Especially when you have the sort of wife for whom the world is ending if she can't have her afternoon tea. Lord help me, I don't know what I was thinking, getting myself leg-shackled to a woman who refused to eat from a plate that wasn't made from bone china. She didn't even leave the house for a year after arriving in Anguilla because she found the road too bumpy for comfortable travel."

"It doesn't sound as though she was cut out for life in the Colonies," Henry said.

Robert grunted and took a large gulp of his brandy. "That's putting it mildly."

"Must be nice for her to be back in England," Yates said.

"Oh, she died a few days after agreeing to leave the house," Robert said. "Stepped on a snake in our driveway." He snorted. "Bloody ironic if you ask me."

Shocked by his friend's blasé manner, Henry shared a brief look with Yates, who appeared equally dumbfounded. "I take it you don't mourn the loss of her," Henry muttered.

Robert stilled. His brow puckered. "Ours was a marriage of convenience. I didn't know when I'd be coming back, so I wanted to settle my future before I left. Meanwhile, I believe the idea of leaving England excited Beatrice. She called it her grand adventure. But then she ended up seasick for most of the journey, and her romanticized view of traveling fell apart quickly. After that, there was nothing Anguilla could offer to make her happy."

"You make an excellent argument for pursuing a love match, Tremaine," Yates said. His voice was pensive. "Had you and your wife cared for each other, I believe the experience would have been altogether different."

Robert snorted. "You're too idealistic for your own good. True love is almost impossible to find. Especially amid the aristocracy."

"I'll grant you it won't be easy," Yates said, "but I am determined to try."

"Then I wish you luck," Robert said, "for I can assure you that you will need it."

"Have you always been this cynical?" Henry asked. The man who'd returned from Anguilla bore little resemblance to the boy Henry had known in his youth. His character had hardened during his absence. The heartless manner in which he'd conveyed the details of his wife's death made Henry very aware of this fact. Or perhaps he'd always been like this, and Henry just hadn't wanted to face it. Like at Cambridge when the rumors about Robert's violent tendencies started to spread. What if they'd all been true?

Robert shrugged one shoulder. "Experience has opened my eyes and shown me how cold, calculating and selfish women can be." His expression cooled. "Take my stepmother, for instance." Henry straightened in his seat while apprehension thickened in his veins. "She had the gall to marry an ailing man more than fifty years her senior."

"Perhaps she cared for him," Henry suggested. Having met Viola, he couldn't imagine her being the scheming sort.

Yates made a strangled sound while Robert glared. "Don't be an idiot," he said. "That woman was nothing before she married my father. She's still nothing as far as I am concerned, but now she's a nothing with a bloody title to her name. *My* title!"

"You're clearly distraught over this," Yates said, stating the obvious while looking increasingly uncomfortable with the negative turn of their conversation.

"Of course I am, and why shouldn't I be?" Robert's chest rose and fell with increased agitation. His mouth twisted and his eyes hardened. "That little conniving harlot stole from me!"

"What?" Henry couldn't believe it. "You *are* speaking of Viola Cartwright, are you not?"

"Have you met her?" Robert asked. He grinned without humor. "Don't be fooled by her plain appearance or by her pleasant demeanor. She took advantage of the confused state my father was in before he died."

"You're saying she tricked him?" Henry asked.

Robert nodded. "She made him rewrite his will the same day they married. He left everything to her—his entire fortune, save the entailed properties which weren't his to give."

"Bloody hell," Yates murmured.

Henry seconded that notion without comment. What had happened to Robert was incredibly unfair. And yet he still couldn't imagine Viola had plotted to claim a title and steal Robert's rightful inheritance on purpose. There had to be another explanation.

"I don't intend to let her get away with it, though," Robert said after a brief moment of silence. He looked at his friends in turn. "I'm contesting the will. By the time I'm done, Viola will have to seek refuge in the poorhouse."

"Have you informed her of this?" Henry asked as casually as he could manage.

"I took the pleasure of doing so a few days ago. As soon as I hired a barrister and confirmed I have a case I can win."

Henry drummed his fingers lightly against his armrest. "You do realize this can drag on for years. The court loves nothing better than to grease its wheels with a client's money. Your barrister won't be in any hurry to close this case, Tremaine, and by the time he does, you could find yourself in debt."

"Maybe. But letting the matter rest isn't an option." Robert stood and went to the sideboard, where he poured himself another measure of brandy. He downed it swiftly and set his glass aside. "There's a lesson to be taught and an example to be made. Once I'm through, hell will freeze over before another woman dares to do something similar."

"Then we owe you a debt of gratitude," Yates remarked. He tilted his glass to salute Robert before finishing off his own brandy. He stood. "I have to go now. Wilmington and Hawthorne expect me to join them at White's."

"I'll come with you, if you don't mind," Robert said.

"If you expect them to be the rakish fellows they were before you left, you'll be sorely disappointed," Yates said. "Both have married and settled down into domestic lifestyles."

Robert sighed. "I swear, women have no purpose in this world but to destroy us." He went to shake Henry's hand. "Thank you for the drink, Lowell. I hope to see you again soon."

Yates said his farewells too, and then both men were off, their conversation fading as they rounded a corner at the end of the hallway. Henry rubbed the palm of his hand across his jaw. He and Robert had always gotten along in the past, even if his personality had slowly started to clash with Henry's.

But then Robert's father had elected to send him away to the Colonies and everything had changed. With Robert gone, the chaos that had once been Henry's life had gradually settled. He'd slowly begun examining his own future, and after taking one look at his father's ledgers, he'd realized he needed to act. Debts had to be paid and an income secured. The Red Rose had been born from a need to do both and was now one of the most popular venues in London.

Henry sighed. Experience shaped a person's character. While pushing himself toward success had been hard at times, he'd had his family and friends to support him. Robert, on the other hand, had been stuck halfway around the world with a wife he hadn't cared for and who hadn't cared for him. It couldn't have been easy. But to come back and accuse Viola of dishonesty, to drag her before a judge in an effort to void the will his father had written, seemed a bit much. Especially since Henry couldn't for the life of him align the woman he knew with the one Robert described.

Which could only mean there was more to this rift between Robert and Viola than Robert had revealed. The sort of bitterness lacing his words as he'd spoken had to be rooted in longstanding conflict. And that made sense when Henry considered the way Viola had reacted when Henry had told her Robert was his friend. She'd clenched her hands together while molding her mouth into firm disapproval.

Whatever had happened between them went beyond her marrying his father and securing the Tremaine fortune for herself. Henry was certain of it and decided to investigate further. Because if there was one thing he knew without any doubt whatsoever, it was that trouble had landed on Viola's doorstep and that she would soon need all the help she could get.

Chapter 8

The six gowns Gabriella and Amelia had sent to Viola's home for her to pick from were the most exquisite she'd ever seen. Unfortunately, none of them fit, and by the time Viola had gotten around to trying them on, it was too late to make alterations. Which meant she was stuck wearing cotton instead of silk.

At least the hem had a ruffle, but as she stood in front of the mirror studying herself, she wasn't sure it would help counterbalance the mundane color of beech-tree gray. A sigh escaped her. She hadn't been planning to venture out into Society when she'd ordered it. She'd been imagining an event that would require equal parts practicality and respectability.

"We could try pinning one of the other gowns instead of actually sewing it," Harriet suggested when she came to check on Viola's progress. "It might look quite nice if we do it discreetly."

"There isn't time," Viola said with a quick glance at the clock. The Huntleys were due to arrive in five minutes to pick her up.

"I have a colorful bead necklace you're welcome to borrow," Diana said as she came to join them. "It's not very costly but it's pleasing to the eye."

"Thank you," Viola told her friend. She grabbed a burgundy shawl, which at least added some degree of color, and wrapped it around her shoulders. "But the truth is I do not mind what I'm wearing so terribly much." She gave a shrug. "I feel comfortable in it."

"Being comfortable and looking good aren't always the same thing," Harriet argued. "One must occasionally sacrifice one in favor of the other."

"That shouldn't be necessary," Viola told her. She exited her room with her friends close behind her and began descending the stairs.

"It often is when one is trying to attract a man's interest," Diana said at her back.

"Then it is a good thing I'm not doing any such thing." Arriving in the foyer, Viola turned to smile at Diana and Harriet. Neither looked even remotely convinced.

"So then you intend to heed our advice and avoid Mr. Lowell's attentions?" Diana asked.

"By having dinner with him," Harriet added.

Viola glanced at the door and hoped the Huntleys would soon arrive to save her from this conversation. "I am having dinner with a few acquaintances of mine. The fact that Mr. Lowell happens to own the club where we shall be dining is inconsequential."

A knock at the door announced that the carriage had arrived.

"I think she's delusional," Viola heard Harriet saying as she exited her home.

"Without a doubt," was Diana's response as the door closed firmly behind her.

Perhaps they were right, but Viola was starting to think they'd misjudged Mr. Lowell's character as poorly as she and the rest of Society. Especially if what he said was true and he had indeed fabricated every salacious rumor himself. It seemed unfathomable, but so did the prospect of him turning out to be every bit the dangerous rake he was purported to be.

The problem was, he was simply too nice.

"**W**hat happened to the gowns we sent you?" Gabriella whispered close to Viola's ear as they walked toward The Red Rose's entrance later.

"Apparently you and Amelia are not the same size or shape as me," Viola whispered back while deliberately lifting her chin and straightening her spine. She would not be pitied by anyone—least of all by Mr. Lowell. "So I am wearing the only good dress I have, even though I am perfectly aware that it's not very fashionable or appropriate for an evening such as this."

At least the neckline was a little bit lower than the ones on the nurse's gowns she wore most days. The hint of skin it revealed made her feel less frumpy than if it had reached all the way to her neck.

"The truth is you do not need extravagant gowns to look pretty, Viola. I actually think the cut you're wearing suits you exceedingly well," Gabriella told her.

"You don't consider the color too bland?"

"It agrees with your complexion and fails to distract from your natural beauty."

And then they were walking through the arched doorway to the club, where a man who introduced himself as Mr. Faulkner stood ready to greet them. He sent a servant to inform Mr. Lowell of their arrival before helping the ladies off with their cloaks and taking the gentlemen's hats.

"Good evening, ladies and gentlemen!"

The masculine voice speaking with confidence at her back announced Mr. Lowell's arrival. Tearing her gaze away from the stunning decor of the dining room she could glimpse from the foyer, Viola turned to face him. And almost lost her balance when the tip of her slipper caught the hem of her dress.

Lowell rushed forward and caught her by the elbow, steadying her with a friendly laugh. "I'm glad to see my establishment still has the power to shock people into losing their footing."

Viola's cheeks heated, though not from embarrassment. On the contrary, her sudden state of disconcertment had everything to do with Lowell's appearance and the touch of his hand. Because as handsome as he'd been while confined to his cot at the hospital and the two times she'd happened upon him since, nothing could have prepared her for how dashing he looked tonight in his evening attire. It clung to his broad shoulders and tall frame, matching the shade of his hair to perfection.

"Your Grace," he murmured, removing his hand from her elbow to leave a cool spot in its place.

He smiled with boyish amusement, eyes gleaming with pure excitement. And then his gaze lowered ever so slightly to the bare expanse of skin above her neckline. It lasted but a second, so quick no one else would notice. But when he raised his eyes to her face once more, Viola's breath caught in her throat, for there was no denying this man had scandalous thoughts where she was concerned.

Thoughts he hid very well by calmly adding, "It is lovely to see you again."

Turning away, he greeted the rest of the party while Viola tried to gather her wits. Her body tingled in anticipation of spending the rest of the evening with him. This was madness! How could her common sense let her crave this man's attention so, in spite of her every intention to resist it?

Yet here she was with him now offering her his arm. As the only unattached woman, she could not refuse. Nor did she want to. So she placed her hand carefully where it belonged, acknowledged the flutter in the pit of her belly for what it was, and allowed him to lead her into the restaurant.

"You look incredible, by the way," Mr. Lowell murmured while steering her between a few tables. "Utterly delectable."

His voice was warm and smooth—seductive in its softness. A flare of heat rushed over her skin. "Thank you," she managed, even though she was sure he was just being polite. "You look quite dashing yourself."

"Why, Mrs. Cartwright. I do believe you may be warming toward me." His voice was light with amusement, yet filled with immeasurable pleasure.

"Don't get ahead of yourself just yet," she warned in a tone meant to tease, for the truth of the matter was, she had yet to see any evidence of a man who did not deserve her friendship or respect.

They reached their table and he pulled out a chair so she could take her seat while Amelia and Gabriella took theirs. And then Lowell sat down beside her. His shoulder brushed hers as he shifted, sending a dart of heat straight down her middle. Viola sucked in a breath and held it, determined to regain her composure. But doing so was difficult when the heavenliest scent of sandalwood emanated from his person.

Thankfully, Mr. Faulkner distracted her by handing out menus. Viola accepted hers with thanks and the gratitude she felt at being able to ignore Mr. Lowell for the time it took her to study it. Except it occurred to her, as she opened the leather-bound folio, that she wouldn't be able to read what it said without the use of her spectacles. And she'd deliberately left those at home with no intention of embodying the long-sighted bluestocking this evening. Which left her with a bit of a predicament.

Considering her options, she decided she had only

one, which was to ask for help. She glanced at Coventry first. He sat to her right, but was turned slightly away while he spoke to Amelia.

Bracing herself, Viola drew a deep breath and addressed Mr. Lowell. "Is there anything particular you can recommend?"

He leaned slightly closer and held his menu up higher, offering them a little seclusion from the rest of the group. Viola's pulse quickened. "The oysters are especially tasty if you are in the mood for an appetizer." His breath caressed her cheek in a way that caused tiny embers to dance across her shoulders. "Or perhaps the onion soup?"

Viola drew a deep breath. "I'm afraid I am not very fond of oysters. Or onion soup." She hesitated briefly before asking, "What else is there?"

He paused before saying, "There's pickled herring and caviar. Smoked salmon if you prefer."

She gave her own menu a quick glance. It appeared as if there was much more than that, only she could not read it.

Biting her lip, she made some pretense of considering her options before asking, "How about the meats?"

"The roast pork is one of my favorites. Either that or the lamb."

She stared at the blurry writing before her. "Hmm . . . don't you have any fowl?" She froze, realizing her mistake the second the words left her mouth.

"Well yes," he said as if nothing was amiss. "Right there." He ran his finger down part of the page.

Viola tried not to squint. Instead she nodded as if she was perfectly aware of what he was showing her. "Those are some very appealing options," she said, hoping to stop him from suspecting a thing.

"This oven-baked chicken with glazed carrots and mushroom sauce is really good," he said. "You see it? It's right there." He pointed to a specific spot on the page.

Viola nodded. "Yes, I see it." She stared at the menu as if studying it more closely. "Chicken is perfect. Thank you, Mr. Lowell."

"You're very welcome, aside from the fact that we do not serve chicken. The dish you just agreed to order is pheasant." He raised one hand and gestured for Mr. Faulkner to approach. Then, in a very low whisper, he said, "Please bring me my spectacles. They're on top of my desk."

He'd seen right through her. Viola stared down at the edge of the table while coming to terms with the fact that her secret was out. She wasn't sure how she felt about it exactly, for although she thought spectacles ruined her appearance, she rather liked knowing that Mr. Lowell needed them too.

"I hope you're not troubling your steward on my account, Mr. Lowell," she said, needing to fill the ensuing silence between them.

"On the contrary, I did it for myself." He moved his head even closer to hers and quietly murmured. "I imagine a pair of spectacles will suit you tremendously, Viola."

For reasons she couldn't explain, his tone painted an image of her wearing nothing else. It was most provocative and inappropriate and not at all what she wanted. And yet her bodice grew suddenly tight, reminding her of a similar experience she'd had five years earlier. She'd surrendered to desire back then and it had been a terrible mistake.

"Then you would be wrong, Mr. Lowell." The way Robert had made her feel once—small and insignificant—echoed through her. "Spectacles draw attention to my eyes."

"And what's wrong with that?" he asked while a

waiter poured wine in their glasses. "You have lovely eyes, Viola. They remind me of raindrops on a windowpane."

"On a dull day," she added.

Mr. Faulkner returned at that moment and discreetly handed the spectacles to Mr. Lowell. "Why must it be dull?" he asked after thanking Mr. Faulkner. "I think it is a matter of perspective, don't you?"

She wasn't so sure. A rainy day with clouds blocking out the sun was not the most uplifting. To have her eyes compared to such a thing did not make her feel particularly pretty or eager to don a pair of spectacles.

And yet, as much as she tried to avoid asking the question, she couldn't resist for long. "How do you mean?"

He positioned the menu before them just so, and held the spectacles in front of her eyes. "There is nothing more invigorating than striding through the rain and feeling the cool splash of water against my skin. There is also nothing more soothing than listening to the pitter-patter of raindrops as they fall against the windows. While some might find it dreary, it reminds me that even though most days are calm and unremarkable, nature is filled with powerful emotion."

Although the spectacles allowed her to see, Viola hadn't been able to concentrate on what was written on the page in front of her. Mr. Lowell's words had distracted her completely. "You're right, I suppose. Rain does have its merits even though I have always preferred when it's sunny. It brings out the color in the world and makes everything so much brighter."

He chuckled low, the rich timbre whirling around her and heating her skin. "I will agree that such days are pleasing in a different way."

Alerted by the pointedness with which he spoke,

she instinctively darted a look in his direction. Their eyes met, and her heart shuddered while a gust of awareness blew over her skin.

"You might not like the color of your eyes, Viola, but to me they're perfect because they're different. What you may consider uninteresting, I see as filled with intelligence and mystery. Your eyes are those of a woman whose mind intrigues me—a woman I wish to spend time with. Which is why I asked you to join me this evening."

Undone by his words, Viola's every apprehension about keeping his company melted away. She liked him too well—so well she was already wondering when she might see him again. "I did not want to come," she told him honestly. She'd been afraid. Afraid of how he would make her feel—afraid of wanting more than what was wise and afraid of eventually getting hurt. "But I am glad I did. Your club is beautiful, Mr. Lowell, and you are proving to be more than I ever expected."

"I trust that's a good thing?" Hope shimmered in the depths of his coffee-colored eyes.

She could not stop the heat creeping into her cheeks or the flurry of nerves squeezing her belly, but she could provide him with an honest answer. "I believe it's a very good thing, Mr. Lowell."

Appreciation warmed his features and made him look even more handsome than seconds before, which was something Viola would not have thought possible.

"Are you ready to place your orders?" Mr. Faulkner asked. He'd returned to their table without Viola noticing, his words scattering her thoughts like autumn leaves carried away on a breeze.

Mr. Lowell lowered the menu and closed it, reminding Viola that they weren't alone but that they were seated together with four other people. How on earth could she have forgotten that? Slightly dazed, she listened while Mr. Lowell inquired about everyone's preferences, advised on a few different options and conveyed the final choices to Mr. Faulkner. He ordered smoked salmon and pheasant on Viola's behalf and then the menus were handed back to Mr. Faulkner, who quickly vanished once more.

"Thank you for inviting us here this evening," Huntley said as he raised his glass and saluted Mr. Lowell. "It was an excellent idea."

"I've been trying to convince him to come here for a while," Coventry said. He lifted his own glass while the rest of the party followed suit, cheering the fine establishment and wishing Mr. Lowell continued success with it.

"I regret to admit that it hasn't been a priority," Huntley said. "There have been a lot of other things for me to see to for the past couple of years."

Viola could well imagine. He'd risen from poverty when he'd inherited his title. Moving from St. Giles to Mayfair with his two sisters and having to learn how to navigate high society must have been an extraordinary challenge.

"You needn't explain," Mr. Lowell said. "I completely understand." He gave his attention to Amelia. "You've been at least as busy as your brother. Tell me, how is your school doing these days?"

"It is thriving," Amelia said. Wanting to help the poor children of St. Giles receive a proper education, she'd bought a house on the edge of the slum and turned it into a place of learning. "We did have a bit of a setback last year with the typhus outbreak, but we've since made up for the time we lost when we were forced to close."

"You made the right decision," Viola said. "Typhus is a terrible disease. Many people died, but more would have done so had it not been for Florian and Juliette. His immunity and dedication served us well, as did her idea to quarantine those with symptoms on a ship."

"But you did your part as well, I'm sure," Mr. Lowell said.

Viola took a sip of her wine. "I kept the hospital running."

"Which is no small feat," Coventry said.

The rest of the group nodded. "It is unusual for a woman to involve herself with medicine," Huntley said. "At an administrative level, I mean."

"What are you implying?" Gabriella asked with raised eyebrows while Amelia gave her brother an equally expectant look—the sort that ought to warn the duke to tread carefully at the moment.

"Merely that I have only heard of women being nurses. Viola is the only female physician I have ever met."

Viola almost choked on the wine she was drinking. "I am not a physician, Huntley. I am merely St. Agatha's patroness."

"I think we can all agree that you're far more than that," Mr. Lowell said.

Feeling a flush spread across her cheeks, Viola willed herself to regain her equanimity. The effect he was having on her could not be denied, and she wasn't the least bit sure what to do about it. "All I have done is provide a building."

Silence ensued for a length of time before Gabriella remarked, "But you renovated that building."

"And you see to the daily running of it," Amelia added.

"From what I have been able to gather, you even assist with the surgeries," Coventry said.

"Which must require some medical training," Huntley told her.

Viola glanced at them each in turn. "Renovating the

building was not as complicated as you might think. I merely hired a foreman who handled everything on my behalf."

"Having renovated a building of my own," Amelia said, "I know it is not as simple as that. There are always decisions to be made and work to check up on."

"Well yes, I suppose that is true," Viola agreed. "I just never really thought much of it." She flattened her lips and knit her brow while thinking back on the project she'd undertaken right after her husband's death. It had been staggering in its magnitude, but the distraction had been a welcome one. It had given her something else to focus on besides her husband's relations, who'd made no effort to hide their dislike of her when they'd shown up for the funeral.

A waiter arrived, setting down plates before them. Viola's mouth watered as she looked at her salmon, perfectly pink and decorated with a light drizzle of mustard sauce, a curled lemon slice and dill. Picking up her cutlery, she cut a piece and popped it in her mouth, the buttery texture and zesty flavor a decadent treat for her taste buds.

"Good?" Mr. Lowell queried so low only she would be able to hear.

Viola nodded. "Mmm-hmm." She washed down the bite with some wine and stabbed the salmon with her fork while saying, "My father believed in gender equality, so he taught me everything he knew." She shrugged a little on that thought. "The fact that he had no sons is probably also worth mentioning at this point."

"It is a minor detail," Mr. Lowell said. "What matters is the opportunity you were granted."

"I agree," Gabriella said. "Women are just as capable of learning things as men. Limiting us to playing instruments, doing needlework and looking pretty is a waste."

Coventry tilted his head. "While I agree—especially

after witnessing my own wife's ability to run a business—I do think many would argue that keeping a home in order is no simple feat."

"You're right," Gabriella said. "It isn't. Especially not when there are servants to manage and parties to host. It can be something of a logistical problem at times. But"—she dipped her chin and served her brother-in-law a very frank stare—"I will still encourage my daughter to follow her dreams. Whatever they may be."

"Let us not forget that if you'd been allowed to follow yours, my dear," Huntley said, "you and I might never have met because you would have been off chasing insects in some exotic location."

Gabriella blushed. "I'm ever so glad I wasn't." Her eyes met her husband's and her blush deepened, inciting a twinge of envy deep inside Viola's chest.

She'd fulfilled her dream, Viola reminded herself. What need had she for anything more? The question prompted her to glance in Mr. Lowell's direction, and for a second, she could not help but be caught up in the way his jaw worked as he chewed his food.

Ridiculous.

She returned her gaze to her own plate before he could notice her perusal, worried he might believe she was falling for him if he caught her looking. And then he'd probably flirt with her even more, which would not be the least bit helpful. For if there was one thing she really didn't need, it was to give another man the power to crush her heart, no matter how tempting it was to do so.

Chapter 9

When Henry felt the heat of her gaze against his skin, it took every bit of willpower he possessed to stop himself from turning toward her and meeting those silver eyes that sparkled like moonbeam-kissed puddles. How she was able to dismiss them as dull was beyond him, for in truth, they were more unusual than any he'd ever seen and thus more intriguing.

But it wasn't just her eyes that were different, it was Viola herself. Her uniqueness made him want to understand her, to pick apart her brain and figure out why it worked the way it did. It also made him realize that treating her the way he'd treated other women in the past would get him nowhere. So he allowed her curious regard of him while feigning ignorance.

She was dedicated to her work and didn't flaunt the position. In fact, considering he'd never seen her make a public appearance, she either valued her privacy or did not care for Society. Possibly both. Or maybe she did not want to face gossip, which was something she probably would when considering her age, her looks, and the fact that she'd married a man old enough to be her grandfather and gained an impressive title in the process.

Thinking back on his recent conversation with Robert, Henry couldn't for the life of him align the selfish woman his friend had described with the one sitting beside him. She didn't seem to have a single malicious bone in her body. But on the other hand, he couldn't understand her reason for wanting to marry an old man unless it had been to acquire his title and fortune. And the fact that she came from few means was not exactly a point in her favor, so he could understand why Robert would assume the worst of her. Still, Henry was sure he was missing something. The facts didn't quite add up.

He reached for his glass and took a sip, aware that she'd given her attention back to her own plate. To his left, Gabriella was telling her husband about the latest spider she'd caught. An impressive find, apparently. Henry shuddered. He'd never cared for insects and was of the opinion that they didn't belong in the City. So he allowed himself to continue his contemplations instead while enjoying his close proximity to Viola.

She'd tried to hide the fact that she could not read without spectacles, which was silly, even though he did understand her. Because the only people who ever ventured out in public with such an accessory tended to be well into their dotage and beyond the point of caring what others might think. Viola, however, definitely cared. She had not wanted him or anyone else to know she had an impairment. She also hadn't wanted them to see what she looked like wearing spectacles, which was why he'd tried to ease her mind a little by suggesting he rather fancied the idea of seeing her like that.

In response, her cheeks had turned a delightful shade of pink, the color sweeping down her neck and out of sight since he'd sworn not to glance at her décolletage again. Doing so when she'd first arrived had been enough. A series of dastardly thoughts had followed, like the idea of kissing his way across that wide expanse of creamy perfection, of licking the swells of her breasts, of dipping his finger beneath the taut fabric and . . .

He'd forced a laugh and led his guests toward their table in the hope of concealing his inappropriate reaction.

Coventry grinned at something Amelia was saying and Henry smiled, reminded of the happiness his own brother had found with his wife, Juliette. He hoped they were both enjoying their travels. His smile broadened and he popped the last bite of food into his mouth. Of course they were, because they had each other. In spite of scandal, they'd found the sort of companionship and love Henry dreamed of.

Sipping his wine, he gave Viola a cautious look as she dabbed her mouth with her napkin. For now, there was no denying his desire to court her and wed her was based on everything other than love, like physical attraction and admiration. It was too soon for it not to be, but surely with time love could bloom, could it not? After all, his reasons for choosing to pursue her weren't based on attraction alone. It also had to do with her drive, her kindness toward others and her obvious determination to resist his charms, which only made him want her more. He genuinely enjoyed her company, was thrilled when he'd witnessed the pleasure she found in card play and was pleased by her fondness for puzzles. He could already picture them working out riddles together in the Sunday paper and trying to best each other at games.

And she had the meanest-looking dog he'd ever seen. He wasn't sure why he found that so endearing, but there was just something charming about the unexpectedness of it. Add to that the various layers of her personality, of which he suspected there were many, most of which he'd yet to discover. And since he also had a penchant for puzzles, it only made sense that he wanted to solve her.

"The way I choose to decorate the space is extremely important," she was telling Gabriella. Henry's ears perked up. He listened with greater attention while the waiters cleared their plates. "I want it to be different from anything else people are used to, which is why I decided to aim for a Persian theme."

"Are you talking about the rejuvenation center?" he asked, recalling the intricately carved wooden door he'd seen there, the impressive mosaic floor and the elaborate mural artwork adorning the walls. It had brought to mind every story he'd read in his well-used copy of *The Arabian Night's Entertainment*.

Viola nodded. "Yes. It's time for me to start purchasing furniture and decor. Unfortunately I haven't had time yet, and with the grand opening coming up, I really must get started on it. The only problem is, I'm not sure where to look for Persian-looking things, which worries me a little."

"I wish I could help," Gabriella said, "but the only foreign design elements I've seen in recent years have been Greek, Roman and Egyptian."

"Those have been quite the rage," Coventry said, joining the conversation. "My aunt redid her entire home in the Greek style a couple of years ago. Cost her husband a fortune!"

Henry considered the problem carefully before saying, "Perhaps I can help." Viola's eyes brightened to a shade that revealed a hint of blue. *Fascinating*. "There's a large market in Woolwich where vendors sell a hodgepodge of furniture and knickknacks from all over the world—things merchants have picked up and can't get rid of in any other way. I've always enjoyed taking a stroll there to see the things they put on display. Picked up an automaton from there last year for next to nothing. When I had it evaluated I was told it was made by Pierre Jaquet-Droz or possibly by one of his sons."

"I've never heard of him," Coventry said. The waiters, who'd now arrived with the main courses, set the plates before them.

"Neither had I," Henry said, "but it turns out he was a late eighteenth-century watchmaker who designed and built these animated dolls to advertise his business, which also specialized in mechanical birds." He proceeded to cut his pork.

"How intriguing," Viola said with the sort of interest Henry wished he could hold in the palm of his hand and admire forever. "So what can yours do?"

He smiled, pleased to have piqued her curiosity. "He can write." And with that statement, Henry stuck a piece of meat in his mouth.

"He?" all three ladies asked in unison.

Knowing he had them—and most especially, Viola—riveted, Henry swallowed his bite and grinned. "My automaton is a boy. Looks like he's about five years old." He reached for his glass and paused with his fingers around the stem. "He can pen a custom text up to forty letters in length."

Silence. And then, "But how?" Viola asked.

Henry set his glass to his lips and drank while savoring this moment. His heart beat a steady rhythm, aligning itself completely with her advancing curiosity, which was like an army whose march he'd redirected.

"A crank winds the mainsprings and then there are stacks of gears that determine the text. When he writes, he dips his quill in ink and even follows the nib with his eyes. It's really quite astounding." Deliberately, Henry chose not to offer a viewing of it.

If Viola desired to see the automaton, he wanted her to ask. So he ate a bit more food while the rest of the party did the same and then he said, "So, considering my own find, it wouldn't surprise me in the least if the sort of decor you require can be located at the Woolwich market."

"Perhaps we ought to ride out there tomorrow and take a look," Gabriella suggested.

Viola beamed. "Oh, indeed, I would love that. Thank you, Gabriella."

"Can you spare the morning, Lowell?" Amelia asked.

"I have no other plans," he said.

"Are you sure it's no inconvenience?" Viola asked him softly, as if she felt obliged to do so while secretly hoping he wouldn't say that it was.

"Not at all," he assured her. "I believe it will be most diverting."

"We'll need two carriages," Coventry said.

"We can pick up Viola at, say . . . nine o'clock?" Huntley suggested.

"I look forward to it already," Viola said with a smile so radiant it made Henry's chest swell with deep satisfaction.

He allowed himself an inward cheer. Acquiring her friendship, earning her trust and finally wooing her required perseverance and time. Fortunately for him, he had these traits in ample supply, because building a business required both. And now that he'd done so and met with success, he had no doubt about his abilities where Viola was concerned.

When dinner ended, punctuated by a marvelous selection of cream cakes and champagne, the gentlemen stood and helped the ladies rise. Since Gabriella and

Amelia were already paired off with their husbands, it came as no surprise that it was Mr. Lowell who pulled back Viola's chair and offered her his arm.

She accepted, even though the butterflies flapping around in her belly were warning her not to. After all, she had no desire to like him as well as she already did or to find him amusing. She did not want to acknowledge that she invariably ended up enjoying his company in spite of her best efforts not to. Because doing so was bound to lead to trouble.

Especially since she had no intention of ever remarrying. Freedom was not an easy thing for a woman to come by and yet she'd managed to gain it. To give it up would be foolhardy. She was used to keeping her own schedule, to managing her own accounts and engaging in proper work. Having a husband tell her she ought to stay home and mind the children was not the sort of life she aspired toward.

So then the only remaining option if she were to allow a man's attentions—and there was still a very big *if*—would involve becoming a mistress, and that was absolutely out of the question. Although she supposed she could consider a brief affair, if the need arose, but if anyone were to find out about it her reputation would suffer and her businesses along with it. Which was something she absolutely could not allow.

"Are you ready for the game of billiards I promised?" Mr. Lowell inquired as they left the restaurant. "I find a bit of competitive sport invigorating after a tasty meal." He led them all down a corridor and into a large room where five felt-covered billiard tables stood side by side, one of which was already being used. At the far end of the room was a comfortable seating arrangement, and at the other a counter where visitors could request drinks from a waiter.

Viola's nerves thrummed with sudden excitement. Her enthusiasm over the prospect of learning this game had been growing ever since Mr. Lowell had made the suggestion the previous day and peaked upon seeing one of the players at the first table shoot a white ball toward a colored one. It made a satisfying *clunk* before propelling the second ball into a corner pocket.

Mr. Lowell leaned closer, bringing a waft of sandalwood with him. "It isn't hard. I will teach you the basics in no time at all."

Although she knew she was being unwise when his scent alone was doing peculiar things to her insides, Viola could not say no.

"Thank you," she murmured, her skin tightening in response to the slow slide of his arm against hers as he released her.

"I think you'll love it," he said with a smile, eyes dancing with pure exhilaration before he turned away and went to select a cue stick.

Viola's heart thudded against her chest. He was unbelievably attractive, and for reasons she still couldn't fathom, he was interested in her.

"Ready?" Mr. Lowell asked as he came to stand beside her, cue stick in hand.

Huntley and Coventry were already playing against their wives at other tables, and for a few seconds their game had distracted Viola. She sucked in a breath in response to Mr. Lowell's sudden proximity. He wasn't touching her at all, and yet, for reasons she could not explain, it felt as though he was.

"Yes," she managed to say. The word came out breathy, causing her to wince.

If he noticed, he showed no sign of it. Instead, he indicated the three balls waiting to be put into play. "As you can see, there is one white, one yellow and one red. The white and the yellow are cue balls and each player has his"—he flashed a smile—"or *her* own. You can be white and I shall be yellow. The aim of the game is for each of us to use our cue balls to knock the red ball into one of the pockets."

"That sounds fairly straightforward," she said.

"It is." He explained the point system next, which wasn't too complicated. "That's it." Lifting the cue stick, he put his hand on the table, fingers outstretched and thumb slightly raised. He then placed the tip of the cue stick on his thumb's proximal phalanx. With the other hand, he gripped the back of the cue stick. "You want to hold the cue stick at your hip with your dominant hand and create a bridge with the other the way I've done. Bridges vary, so you may want to try a few different positions, but the one I'm showing you right now is the most basic." He repositioned his legs and leaned forward. "Then lower yourself to the table so you're looking along the line of the shot you plan on taking. Line up the tip of your cue stick with the cue ball, the red ball and one of the pockets, if at all possible."

His arm moved the cue stick gently back and forth, sliding the tip across his thumb. Viola stared, her mouth going dry in response to the elegant yet somehow powerful image he portrayed with his jacket drawn tight across his back and fierce concentration straining his features. And then his cue stick shot forward with swift precision, hitting the cue ball and sending the red ball smoothly toward a corner pocket. It landed with a dull thud and the moment it did, Viola cheered.

"Oh, well done!" She couldn't help but marvel at the skill with which Mr. Lowell had just accomplished his goal. "You make it look so easy."

Straightening, he grinned, eyes bright with amusement. "Thank you, Viola, but as you must know from learning to shoot a pistol, it just takes practice. Since I practically live here, I've played my fair share of games in recent years." He went to collect the red ball from the pocket. Returning it to the table, he approached Viola and held the cue stick toward her. "Your turn to try."

Taking the unfamiliar object from him, Viola weighed it in her hand. It was light, so it shouldn't be difficult for her to hold it as easily as he had done. Recalling how he'd positioned himself, she gripped the end and leaned over the table, placing her hand just so . . .

Something touched her thigh and her heart seized. Fingers curled around hers, and forming coherent thoughts became an impossible task. She swallowed, realizing Mr. Lowell had moved in beside her, his thigh flush against hers as he worked to reposition her hold on the cue stick.

"There," he said with a husky voice that did awkward things to her insides. "Grip it firmly, but not too tight." *Dear God, that sounded shockingly suggestive!* "Now relax your posture. Easy does it . . . Yes, just like that."

Viola drew a shuddering breath. She could scarcely concentrate on account of the fiery heat coursing through her. His nearness was simply too much. Too . . .

He shifted slightly. His fingers brushed hers on the table as he carefully and with aching slowness rearranged the position of her thumb. Viola's heart pounded, blood roaring through her veins as she struggled between the urge to run and her desire to stay. It was as if he surrounded her, crowding her with his potent masculinity to the point where she feared her legs might give way.

"Now focus, Viola," he said so close to her ear she could feel his breath tickle her skin. "Keep your eyes on your target and take your shot when you're ready."

Focusing proved a slight problem considering the state Mr. Lowell had put her in. She wondered if he suspected the inappropriate way she'd responded to his words. A sudden flush swept over her body. The man was said to be a seducer of women, so there was a good chance he'd done it on purpose.

She closed her eyes briefly and took a deep breath. She was Viola Cartwright, for heaven's sake; a woman capable of wielding a pistol and scalpel with equal skill. For the past two years, she'd proved herself capable of achieving more than most men ever did in their lifetimes because of her focus.

Tapping into that resource now honed her concentration and allowed her to send the red ball into the nearest pocket by knocking the white cue ball against it.

Relief and immense satisfaction filled her. "I did it!"

"Well done." Mr. Lowell collected the red ball from the pocket, placed it on the table and drew the cue stick out of her hand and smiled. "My turn now."

He didn't touch her again for the remainder of the game, allowing her to find the positions that worked best for her on her own. Keeping his distance from her by continuously taking his shots from the opposite side of the table, Mr. Lowell remained on his best behavior for the rest of the evening.

"You're a natural at this," he told her encouragingly the next time she managed to sink the correct ball in one of the pockets.

"I had an excellent teacher," she replied with a smile.

"If you are referring to me, then I'm flattered," he said with a wink right before taking his turn. The yellow ball rolled smoothly across the green felt and clanged against the red ball, which bounced against the side of the table, missing the pocket by a hair's width. He muttered something beneath his breath and straightened his posture. "Looks like it's all up to you. If you sink that red ball now, you win the game, Viola."

She met his gaze, which was warm even though it lacked the sensuality from earlier. Instead she found the same kind of thrilling excitement she felt when competing against someone else. Except in this instance, it wasn't for himself but for her. He wanted her to succeed, and that piece of knowledge completely undid her.

Averting her gaze from his, Viola gave her attention to the balls on the table. She considered the best angle for the shot and positioned herself accordingly. It wasn't complicated. The balls were lined up perfectly. But she could feel Mr. Lowell's eyes on her, and this made her hands tremble. She glanced up at him briefly and relaxed in response to his serious expression.

Shifting her weight for better balance, she honed in on her target and slid the cue stick forward with just the right amount of force to carefully place the red ball in the pocket.

"Brilliant!" Mr. Lowell cheered.

Viola straightened herself and grinned while turning to face him. "What an exhilarating game." She was thrilled with the progress she'd made in only one evening and with beating a man who'd played so many times before.

"I'm glad you enjoyed it." He approached her for the first time since the beginning of the game and held out his hand to accept her cue stick.

As she handed it to him, a pulse went through her in anticipation of his touch. But unlike earlier, he made no attempt to brush his fingers discreetly against hers. In fact, he made sure to keep his hand far enough away from hers on the cue stick to avoid any contact at all.

"Thank you for the game," Viola muttered. She could not explain the strange sense of loss now filling her body. It was as if an invisible hand had reached inside her and pulled away half of her joy.

When it was finally time for her to take her leave, Mr. Lowell did nothing more than offer a smile before saying, "Thank you for a lovely evening. I look forward to our outing tomorrow." But he spoke not only to her, but to Huntley, Coventry, Gabriella and Amelia as well, and as proper as that was, Viola was forced to acknowledge a twinge of disappointment when he failed to single her out.

Chapter 10

Viola was finishing her breakfast the following morning when Diana brought her a letter. "This just arrived," her friend said. She and Harriet had both been up by the time Viola had come downstairs. After giving them a brief account of the previous evening, which had ended later than Viola was used to, her friends had left her to enjoy the morning paper while she ate.

"Shall I start clearing the table?" Diana asked.

"If you don't mind, I would really appreciate that," Viola told her. "Huntley and his wife will be here any moment to pick me up." She tore open the unfamiliar seal and scanned the contents, her pulse accelerating with every word she read.

Dear Madam,
I wish to inform you that His Grace, the Duke of Tremaine has hired me to oversee the case he wishes to make against you. It is imperative that we meet to discuss the matter at your earliest convenience. I therefore ask that you respond to this letter promptly and apprise me of your availability.
Sincerely,
Michael B. Hayes, Barrister-at-Law

She'd known this would arrive eventually, but she'd allowed herself to forget about the trouble Robert threatened to cause. Instead she'd concentrated on work and enjoying time with friends. Her shoulders sagged and she dropped the letter on top of the table. The prospect of spending the day at Woolwich no longer appealed. The knowledge that she was now officially pitched against Robert in a battle over money had put a sour taste in her mouth.

Briefly, she closed her eyes and envisioned the catastrophe this could turn into. Even if she won, the news of the case would likely be snatched up by some hungry journalist. Her rise to wealth would be stirred up again, reminding the *ton* that she was an upstart who did not belong.

And if she lost . . .

She shook her head, unable to conceive of such an option.

So she took a sip of her tea. First order of business would be acquiring a barrister of her own. The solicitor who'd helped her with her inheritance and the legalities involved in setting up the hospital, had been older than her husband and had recently died, so he could no longer recommend anyone. Pondering this predicament for a moment, she decided to ask Huntley and Gabriella if they could. With new resolve, she took the letter to her study and placed it on her desk. She then went to put on her spencer, bonnet and gloves, and was ready the moment the knocker sounded at the front door.

"I'll get it," Viola called to stop Diana and Harriet from dropping whatever they were doing.

"Have a great time," she heard them both call from the back of the house.

Collecting her key, she opened the door and sucked in a breath the moment her eyes met Mr. Lowell's.

"Good morning," he said, and stepped slightly aside so she could exit her home. "I trust you slept well?"

Viola nodded. "Yes. Thank you." She shut the door behind her. Hands trembling on account of her silly nerves, she fumbled with the key for a second before she managed to slip it into the lock and turn it. "And you?" she then asked, recalling her manners.

"Oh yes," he said. Offering her his arm, he escorted her down the steps and toward the first carriage, where Huntley and Gabriella waited. The Coventrys were in the second carriage with the window open, so Viola waved and wished them both a good morning while Mr. Lowell led her forward. "Had a little trouble falling asleep, but once I did, I had the most blessed dream."

Viola could not for the life of her understand why such a statement would prick at her skin, but there was something about the way he spoke—a suggestiveness that alerted her senses. Of course, it only got worse when his hand clasped her waist in order to help her up into the conveyance. The heat of his touch seemed to linger, reminding her of the danger Mr. Lowell posed to the orderly life she valued.

Greeting the Huntleys, Viola lowered herself to the opposite bench. Mr. Lowell sat down beside her and closed the door, then Huntley knocked on the roof and the carriage rolled forward. Viola clasped her hands in her lap. She could not ignore the feel of Mr. Lowell's thigh pressing up against hers on account of the narrow space or how solid it seemed.

"It will be fun to get out of London for a bit," she said in an effort to force her brain to think of something besides Mr. Lowell's physique. "I have not left the City since I was a child and I accompanied my father to some of his lectures."

"There is a lot to see outside of London," Gabriella said. "Have you ever considered traveling?"

Viola thought back on a dream she'd had right after her father died, of running away and not looking back. In it, she invariably ended up in the same place. "I would like to visit the seaside."

Huntley smiled. "I saw the ocean for the first time myself last summer. The endless expanse of water is definitely impressive."

"I've seen paintings," Viola said, "but I'm sure it's not the same thing."

"It gives an idea, but it does not stir all your senses," Mr. Lowell said. "When you walk on a beach there are so many sounds and smells to experience. There are the waves rolling toward the shore and the wind tugging at grassy dunes. It's so much bigger than a painting can possibly convey."

Intrigued, Viola allowed the description to lure her into a daydream for a while. She lost herself in it until a bump in the road made her thoughts return to the letter she'd received from Mr. Hayes and what her response to it ought to be. She supposed she should try and meet with him as soon as possible—tomorrow even, if that was an option. Because as much as she wanted to ignore the entire debacle and toss the letter into an open fire, she knew that wasn't possible.

"Are you all right?" Gabriella asked her when they arrived at Woolwich. The carriages had been parked and they were now waiting for Amelia and Coventry to alight from theirs.

"Perfectly," Viola said. She forced a smile.

"You've been awfully quiet for the last half of our journey." Gabriella eyed her carefully. "If there's anything you would like to talk about . . ."

Viola glanced toward the Coventry carriage where the duke was assisting his wife, and then toward Huntley and Mr. Lowell, who were now discussing an upcoming boxing match.

Cupping Gabriella's elbow, Viola gently maneuvered

her friend farther away and said, "As a matter of fact, I mean to ask if you or your husband are able to recommend a good barrister."

Gabriella's eyes widened. "Heavens, Viola! You're not in some sort of trouble I hope?"

Viola bit her lip and scrunched her nose. "I might very well be. Robert—the Duke of Tremaine, that is—wants to oppose my husband's will. He . . ." Her heart suddenly lurched with suppressed panic. "He plans to take back the money Peter left me by whatever means necessary."

"Good Lord!" Gabriella's face blanched.

"What is it?" Huntley asked, noting his wife's distress.

Viola shook her head. She did not want her problems to be aired like this and she didn't want to ruin what promised to be a fun outing for the rest of the group.

"It's, um . . . I . . ." Gabriella gave Viola an apologetic look. "You did ask me if I or my husband can help, so I have to ask."

"Ask about what?" Mr. Lowell said, stepping right into the middle of the conversation.

Viola groaned. "It is nothing. Forget I said anything, Gabriella, and let us simply enjoy the market. We can talk about this later." And then, to stop any further discussion, she deliberately pasted a smile on her face and went to greet Amelia and Coventry, who were now approaching.

Henry studied Viola as they walked between the stalls. She'd grown distant after mentioning her desire to visit the seaside. It was as if a matter of tremendous weight pressed upon her mind. She'd also looked anxious when Huntley had wanted to know what she and Gabriella were discussing. More so when *he'd* inquired, leaving no doubt in his mind that she did not want him involved with whatever it was that was bothering her.

Gabriella of course gave nothing away. She'd simply told Huntley that they would discuss this—whatever *this* was—later, no doubt upon their return to London when there was no one else around to overhear.

And that bothered Henry, because he really liked Viola now that he'd gotten to know her. There was a playful side to her that she often suppressed, but he'd managed to bring it out a few times already. Watching her find amusement in pastime activities, to smile for a while and abandon her serious demeanor, thrilled him. Her happiness had started to matter to him, so if something or someone was threatening her peace of mind, he wanted to help. But how could he when she'd deliberately placed a wall between them the moment he'd asked?

He continued to ponder this while watching her stroll along. Her thoughts were clearly not engaged with the task she was supposed to be performing because she kept missing items that he was sure would fit perfectly with the Persian look she was aiming for.

Intent on drawing her attention to this, he came up beside her and caught her by the arm. The gasp she emitted was a welcome change from the solemn mood she'd been in so far, as was the light sparking in her eyes when she saw it was he.

Appreciating her response, he casually looped his arm with hers. "I want you to see something special," he said as he pulled her around and guided her back to a stall they'd passed a few minutes earlier.

She looked briefly uncertain. "But what about everyone else? We can't simply—"

"We'll catch up with you," Henry called to the rest of their group. "If we lose you, we'll meet you back at the carriages!"

"Mr. Lowell, I—"

"Will you still not call me Henry?" he asked.

"Please don't take offense, but I'm not sure that would be wise." Her words were quietly spoken amid the din of the crowd.

He drew her to a halt and waited until she looked up into his face before saying, "Because you fear the intimacy of such informality?"

Her throat worked as if she tried to form words but failed. A dark pink hue flushed her cheeks but she didn't look away. Indeed, Viola was too brave to do so—too strong to give up when challenged.

"You know my intentions where you are concerned, for I have been honest about them right from the start," he added. "I want you, Viola, in ways I can't even begin to describe."

"You should not say such things." Her voice was breathless, and although her words attempted to push him away, her eyes told a different story of longing and deep desire.

"Then you must forgive me, for I cannot seem to help it." He dropped his gaze to her lips and felt every muscle inside him strain at the sight of her tongue darting out to moisten the soft piece of flesh. "Christ, Viola." The things she did to him. "All I ask is to hear you say Henry."

His request seemed to vanquish the effect he'd been having on her, for she turned her attention to the stalls and started walking again. "I do not call Huntley or Coventry by their given names and I know them better than I know you."

Well, that was a bit of a blow to his ego. Rallying, he argued, "Only because you are not friends with them but with their wives, whom I address as Gabriella and Amelia, in case you hadn't noticed."

"Of course I have, but you are family now that Florian and Juliette have wed."

"Fair point," he conceded, and decided to let the subject rest. There were other battles to be fought today and this was probably the least important one of them.

"Now here's what I wanted to show you," he said, indicating a tall wood cabinet with lacework carvings balancing across the top. "I believe you missed it."

"You're absolutely right." She moved toward the piece of furniture as if in a trance. "This is perfect!"

Her amazement made his heart swell with pleasure. And then she glanced at him briefly with endless gratitude, and he found himself reduced to a green lad incapable of forming words.

So he simply smiled and stuck his hands in his pockets to stop from reaching for her again. Because all he could think of right now was how he wanted to pull her into his arms and bask in her radiance.

"How much is this?" she asked the vendor, an older man with bushy eyebrows and a portly belly.

"Eight pounds, luv. Brought it all the way from Morocco." The man smiled and smoothed his hand over the side of the cabinet. "Nothing else like it in these parts."

Viola's brow knit, producing a row of furrows. Henry prepared to step forward and inform the man he was out of his mind to demand such a sum.

But then Viola said, "I'll give you one."

Henry whistled low and rocked back on his heels with a grin. The lady was clearly accustomed to haggling.

The vendor's eyes narrowed. He straightened his posture. "Are you deliberately trying to insult me?"

Henry stiffened and prepared once again to come to Viola's aid. As it turned out, she had the situation well in hand.

Crossing her arms, she stared the vendor down. "Not at all, sir. I am merely telling you what I am willing to pay. But since it's too little . . ." She turned to leave.

The vendor glanced at Henry, who merely shrugged and said, "She's the one who wants it. I'll just as happily let you keep it."

He prepared to follow Viola, who was already several feet away.

"Hold on," the vendor called, halting Viola and bringing her back with what appeared to be great reluctance. "How about six?"

She shook her head. "Two."

"You've got to do better than that," the vendor told her. "Let's make it five?"

"I'm sorry, but that's too much." Viola started to turn away once again as if she meant to leave.

The vendor threw up his hands in surrender. "Four pounds. That's the best I can do. Final offer."

She seemed to consider while the vendor appeared to hold his breath. Slowly, she nodded. "If you include those glass lanterns over there and ensure delivery, you have yourself a deal."

The vendor flattened his lips, hesitated briefly, and finally gave a curt nod. He stuck out a grubby hand, and to Henry's amazement, Viola shook it. She then reached inside her reticule and produced the money she owed.

"Pleasure doing business with you," she told the vendor after writing down the rejuvenation center's address and handing it to him. "I'll expect these items no later than tomorrow afternoon."

Or you'll have me to answer to, Henry wanted to

add. Instead he merely implied the fact with a direct glare and a slightly raised eyebrow.

"What fun that was," Viola told Henry as they continued on their way. She was more animated now than when they'd initially arrived, her eyes sparkling with the thrill of her achievement.

Mesmerized, Henry took a second to respond. When he did, it was to give her the compliment she deserved. "I must say, you bargained with impressive skill, Viola. I confess I did not expect it."

She moved toward another stand. "Why? Because I'm a woman or because I'm a duchess?"

"Neither." He already knew he'd be a fool to underestimate her grit on account of her title. "It's because you're so . . . and I hope you don't take this the wrong way . . . but I was going to say unassuming."

She pursed her lips and studied a selection of fabrics that Henry guessed came from India. "When I started work on the hospital, I had no idea what I was doing." She moved on to a pair of brass vases, picking them up and turning them over in her hands before returning them to the table on which they stood. "Many people took advantage of this." She turned to face him more fully. "When I learned of my mistakes, I decided that in the future I would determine the value of something before beginning a negotiation and that I would always be prepared to walk away empty-handed instead of overpaying."

Henry stared at her as she moved on to a large chest with elephants and roses carved into the side. He watched as the vendor came to talk price, and for the second time that day he admired Viola's ability to strike an incredible bargain.

In a way, it was yet another thing they had in common, this awareness of money and the value of it. While most women in her position would have spent their fortune on pretty gowns and accessories without second thought, it appeared as though Viola spent hers sparingly.

Unless of course she was choosing to be cautious for a different reason. Henry thought on this as they recommenced walking. Last night, Robert had said that he planned on contesting his father's will. Was it possible he'd started the process already? It would certainly have put a damper on Viola's mood if he had.

Following her to another stand, he considered his options, and, after weighing the pros and cons, settled on complete transparency. "Viola." His hand caught her arm, drawing her back toward him. Her eyes met his, wide and inquisitive. "I want to ask you something." He took a fortifying breath. "Did your conversation with Gabriella earlier have something to do with Tremaine contesting your husband's will?"

Viola almost tripped over her own feet. And then she froze, her breath stuck in her throat. Was it possible she might have misheard him? She didn't think so. Tremaine was his friend. It wasn't unlikely that he'd called on Mr. Lowell in recent days after his return and spoken of his intention to destroy her. It made perfect sense the more she considered it, which made her wonder if spending time with Mr. Lowell was wise, since his loyalty would probably be toward Robert, whom he'd known for much longer.

Heart banging against her ribs, she turned to face the man whose companionship she'd come to enjoy. "When did he tell you?"

"Last night. Shortly before you arrived at the club."

She winced and dropped her gaze. God! How stupid of her! Instinct had warned her to keep her distance from him and yet she'd allowed temptation to win. "You hid the knowledge well," she told him bitterly.

"It wasn't exactly the sort of thing I could bring up over dinner. And besides, I didn't want to ruin the evening by questioning you on a subject you clearly don't want to discuss."

Raising her chin, she studied his face and was stunned to find sympathy rather than censure there. "You're right. I don't want to discuss it. Least of all with one of Tremaine's friends."

A nerve at the edge of his jaw twitched. "It's been years since he and I saw each other last. A lot has changed since then." His eyes pinned her, holding her captive. "Having gotten to know you, I do believe I have a good sense of who you are as a person."

"Really?" She failed to keep the trace of disappointment she felt from her voice.

Jaw tightening, he pulled her close to his side and spoke to her in low tones while leading her along. "Whatever your reason for marrying Tremaine's father, I don't think you took advantage of the old man and I don't believe you deserve Tremaine's wrath."

Viola sucked in a mouthful of air and gulped it down. "But—"

"On the contrary, I believe you should have just as good a chance of winning this case as he has." They strolled slowly, his grip on her firm yet soothing. It was lovely—the sort of closeness she could get used to if only she'd conquer her fears and allow it. "So if you agree and you haven't already acquired a barrister, I would like to introduce you to one I happen to know. He's a very competent fellow who's helped me and my family with legal advice on countless occasions."

Viola could scarcely think of what to say besides, "Thank you." He was trusting her without demanding an explanation. Her eyes grew uncomfortably moist and she suddenly feared she might cry. The kindness he was showing toward her when she'd initially thought the worst of him was simply too much.

"Is that a yes then?" he asked.

She nodded. "Tremaine wants to take everything away from me. He says he plans on selling the hospital once it is his, which is something I cannot allow." Her hand gripped at his arm with a sudden need to steady herself. "After receiving a letter from his barrister this morning, I knew I needed my own representation." She cut a look in Mr. Lowell's direction and saw that he was listening with a grave expression. "That is in fact what I was discussing with Gabriella earlier. I just . . ."

"You didn't want me to know."

Embarrassed, she gave her attention to the stalls they were passing. "It is a sensitive issue for me, and to be honest, I wasn't sure if I could trust you."

"I see." He cleared his throat and said, "Few people would be so blunt. It does you credit."

Appreciating the compliment, she couldn't help but smile a little. "You did say that he was your friend, and you and I have only known each other for just over a week. It made sense that you would choose to take his side over mine."

Dropping a look at her, he told her seriously, "Not when it is clear to me that he's in the wrong."

They walked a few steps in silence before she said, "It means a great deal to me that you're willing to help me with this, Mr. Lowell."

"And it means a lot to me that you're willing to trust me to do so. Considering my reputation, I wouldn't blame you for thinking I have an ulterior motive in helping you."

"Do you?" she asked.

He shook his head. "No. I want to help because I care about you, Viola, though I will admit that it pleases me to know we'll be spending more time together."

She made a satisfied sound but said nothing further. They reached a cross in their path and he steered them to the left, toward a stall where ornate screens, rugs and tables seemed to fit the style she was looking for. "Let's finish your purchases so we can meet up with the rest of our group. When we return home you can respond to Tremaine's barrister and we'll make plans for you to meet with mine."

Chapter 11

Seated behind her desk in the office she used at St. Agatha's Hospital, Viola added yesterday's purchases to her ledger, tallied the expenses and calculated her remaining funds. She then double-checked her work for good measure and blew out a breath. There was still a good sum of money left—money she'd have to give to Robert if he won the case.

A knock sounded at the door and Emily entered the room. "Mr. Lowell and Mr. Steadford are here to see you."

"Thank you, Emily. Please show them in." Rising, Viola smoothed her skirt in a vain attempt to steady the sudden trembling of her hands. For some silly reason, Mr. Lowell's opinion of her had started to matter a great deal, and when she'd dressed this morning, she'd dearly wished she had something cheerful and possibly even alluring to wear.

But since she hadn't, she'd asked Diana to set her hair instead, which allowed for a prettier style than the tight knot she usually wore at the nape of her neck. Her pulse quickened and her nerves jumped as she became increasingly wary of Mr. Lowell's opinion. Would he even notice or . . .

"Good morning, Your Grace," he said, entering her office with the confidence of a man who knew his purpose.

The "Your Grace" threw her a little, but she supposed he did it for the benefit of the gentleman who followed him into the room.

A second of silence ensued, and Viola realized Mr. Lowell was staring at her with bemused interest. His lips quirked, tilting slightly to the right. And then he said, "I like what you've done with your hair." Her stomach flipped over. "And those spectacles do suit you remarkably well."

Viola sucked in a breath. Her hands flew to her face, ridding herself of the spindly metal frames perched upon her nose and setting them on her desk. She needed them for work and had forgotten all about them when she'd asked Emily to show her guests in.

Mr. Lowell grinned. The annoying man was clearly savoring her discomfiture. She frowned at him and he immediately sobered. "May I present Mr. Dorian P. Steadford? I've apprised him of your situation to the best of my ability, but perhaps you can offer further explanation and insight into your marriage and your relationship with Tremaine."

Viola stiffened and reached for the edge of her desk, clutching it for support. If there was one thing she did not wish to delve into, it was this. But she could hardly expect not to, all things considered. Not if Mr. Steadford was going to help her.

So she squared her shoulders and gestured toward a pair of chairs facing her own. "Please have a seat, gentlemen. May I offer you some refreshments?"

Both declined. "I think it best if we get on with this," Mr. Steadford said. He eyed his pocket watch. "We're due to meet Tremaine and his barrister in just over an hour." Steadford pulled a notebook from a satchel he'd brought along with him. "Can you tell me the name of the man Tremaine has hired?"

Viola returned to her seat, claiming it so the men could sit as well. "Mr. Hayes." She looked at Mr. Steadford to gauge his response to that name.

His face, however, remained inscrutable as he produced a pencil from his jacket pocket and proceeded to jot something down in his notebook. "He has a good team of clerks," Mr. Steadford said. "If you've something to hide, I can guarantee you they'll find it." He raised his gaze to Viola, who'd begun to feel slightly faint. "So my advice to you is to tell me everything. From the beginning."

A wave of tiny shivers assailed her. She stared back at Mr. Steadford and Mr. Lowell. Perhaps this had been a mistake. It was at the very least a terrible bind, because she knew she needed the help and yet she was very uncertain about telling these men everything. Especially where her mother was concerned, since her identity could potentially influence their opinion of her, if they didn't approve. But she *would* tell them what could easily be discovered by Mr. Hayes so as not to put Mr. Steadford at an awkward disadvantage.

"My father's name was Jonathan Marsh and he was the Duke of Tremaine's physician," she began. "Over the course of their decades-long acquaintance, the two became friends. Peter—my late husband, that is—valued my father's advice and sought his counsel often. They also met to play chess and to simply talk about all manner of things between heaven and earth. After my grandmother died, I accompanied my father on all of his visits to Tremaine House. I was five when I first met Robert and his father."

"What about your mother?" Mr. Steadford asked. "Was she not able to take care of you during these visits?"

"She died when I was born," Viola quickly told him.

"So you knew the former duke very well," Mr. Steadford noted.

She nodded. "Yes. He became something of an affectionate uncle to me." Seeing Mr. Lowell's eyes go wide, she realized her mistake and hastened to add, "He didn't take advantage of me if that is what you think. The duke was kind to me. He and I never . . ." She closed her eyes briefly and fought for strength, then forced the necessary words past her lips. "We never consummated the marriage."

"Because he was too infirm?"

"Well yes, he was. The poor man was dying and drew his last breath the day after our nuptials, but even if that hadn't been the case, he would not have made such a demand of me."

Silence followed, interrupted swiftly by the scratch of Mr. Steadford's pencil. Unable to look at either gentleman, Viola kept her gaze firmly on the surface of her desk. Her cheeks had grown unbearably warm and her dress had started to itch.

"When my father got sick," she said when Mr. Steadford prompted her to continue, "he went to Tremaine and asked for a favor, even though I never knew about this until later." She pulled a shuddering breath into her lungs and released it, then carefully raised her gaze to the two men sitting before her. "I was fifteen when my father died. After the funeral, I learned that Tremaine had promised him he'd always look out for me because I had nobody else left in the world who would care enough to do so."

Tears pricked the corners of her eyes but she forced them back. "Four years later when Tremaine caught a serious case of influenza and it became clear he would not live much longer, he suggested we marry." She could still recall his pained expression and the fear he'd had of failing her and her father by not fulfilling his promise. "I was against the idea at first because I knew the rest of his family would resent me."

"But he convinced you?" Mr. Steadford asked.

"He believed a powerful title would open up doors for me, and the more he talked about it, the more I started believing it might be true. And then when he told me of the idea he and my father had once discussed, of creating a well-run hospital with free care, and that I was the only one able to fulfill this dream, I felt I had no choice but to accept."

Mr. Steadford frowned. "Do you remember if his will specified what the money he left you was meant to be used for?"

"Yes." Viola recalled every detail. "The majority was set aside for the hospital. The rest was willed directly to me, to spend as I saw fit."

"The rest?" Steadford asked.

Viola nodded. "My husband left his entire fortune to me—a total of twenty-three thousand pounds, of which eighteen thousand was spent on the hospital; acquiring the building, renovating it, buying equipment and hiring staff. He left nothing to anyone else."

The solicitor looked stumped while Mr. Lowell . . .

To Viola's surprise, he looked as though he'd already been made aware of this fact. By Robert, no doubt.

"If you'll forgive me for saying so, Your Grace," Mr. Steadford muttered, "I begin to comprehend Tremaine's desire to fight you."

"Ordinarily, I would happily give him the money he feels entitled to." She didn't know if they believed her, but it was the truth. She didn't need much for herself to get by on. "The problem is I've spent almost all of it."

"On the hospital?"

This question came from Mr. Lowell, and Viola couldn't help but scoff. "Well, it certainly wasn't wasted on an extravagant lifestyle." He knit his brow, as did Mr. Steadford. Viola sighed. "A small part of it went toward the house I purchased for myself. It's not very grand, in case you're wondering, but it's good enough for me."

"Seems like it may have been an unnecessary expense," Mr. Steadford said. "Why not remain at Tremaine House?"

"Because I did not wish to." Irritated by the line of questioning, Viola stared straight back at Mr. Steadford. "The money was mine to do with as I pleased."

"Yes," Mr. Steadford agreed. "But I still need all the facts. For example, if you had been turned out of Tremaine House upon your husband's death, I might have been able to use that to our advantage."

"It wouldn't change anything. I will be painted a fortune huntress by Tremaine no matter what, so even if he had turned me out, I doubt I'd get much sympathy from anyone."

"You would from me," Mr. Lowell said without even blinking.

His unwavering support undid a knot behind her breastbone. It mattered that he saw her for who she was instead of the scheming opportunist Society had turned her into.

"As nice as that may be," Mr. Steadford said, bringing Viola's focus back to the subject at hand, "it is not very helpful." He leaned forward ever so slightly and pierced her with his sharp blue eyes. "Tell me, what was your husband's state of mind like in the days leading up to his death?"

Viola's thoughts started tumbling through her head, collapsing like a house of cards blown over by a puff of air. As much as she wished it, she could not run from the truth. Not when it was one of Robert's strongest arguments against her.

"Viola?" Mr. Lowell prompted.

She met his gaze, silently wishing they could leave the subject alone. Peter didn't deserve to have his kindness repaid by her divulging such information. He deserved to be remembered for the intelligent man he'd once been.

"Your Grace," Mr. Steadford said, snapping his notebook shut. "In order to win, Mr. Hayes's best course of action will be to prove that you took advantage of an ailing man who didn't have all of his wits about him. So I ask you again, was your husband in perfect mental health?"

"There were episodes," Viola confessed, and then hastily added, "but nothing unusual, considering his age."

"He was how old?" Mr. Lowell quietly asked.

Viola dropped her gaze and fidgeted with the skirt of her gown. "Seventy."

"Right," Mr. Steadford muttered. "And who was his physician after your father's passing?"

Viola swallowed. This conversation was going from bad to worse. "Mr. Blaire," she said, speaking as if from outside her own body. She felt as though she was falling into a bottomless well from which she'd never find a way out.

"I'll need to take his professional assessment into consideration," Mr. Steadford said.

That brought Viola's attention back to the solicitor's face. "No." She shifted in her seat. "Mr. Blaire was the first physician I hired when I opened the hospital, but I was forced to press charges against him last year for negligence and the endangering of others. He has spent eight months in prison and is not due for release for another six weeks."

"Very well," Mr. Steadford conceded. "What about the solicitor who drew up your husband's will? Perhaps he can offer some insight."

"His name was Mr. Porter, but I'm afraid he's no longer alive," Viola muttered.

Mr. Steadford nodded but made no further comment about Mr. Porter's passing. Instead he said, "I take it the will was altered the day before your husband died? Right after you were married?" Viola nodded. "In that case I may be able to argue that Mr. Porter would not have facilitated this unless he was certain your husband knew exactly what he was doing."

He made a note and raised his gaze to Viola's once more. "Since he is dead, however, I'll have to make do with witness accounts from your late husband's servants."

Viola bit her lip. "You should know that I let almost all of them go in order to save on the expense of keeping Tremaine House running. Only the butler and housekeeper remained."

Mr. Steadford's brow puckered with concern. "I get the sense that this case is becoming increasingly difficult by the second."

"I am sure I could locate a few of them," Viola hastened to say. "Mrs. Starling, the cook, went to work for Baron Hawthorne, so questioning her will be easy."

"And did Mrs. Starling interact with your husband on a regular basis? Enough for her to be able to vouch for his ability to make rational decisions at the time when he chose to marry you?"

"Not really."

Mr. Steadford held his position for a second and then leaned back against his seat. "In that case, it would be useful if you can think of something we might be able to use against Tremaine. Anything at all that would encourage a judge to sympathize with you rather than him."

"If I may," Mr. Lowell said with a quick glance at her before focusing more directly on Mr. Steadford, "I would suggest looking into Tremaine's behavior. While I will agree that people can change and that he might be different now that he's older, he developed a quick temper during our time together at Cambridge." He paused briefly before quietly adding, "I suspect he once beat a demimondaine after she failed to please him."

Viola gasped. "Surely not."

"Do you have any evidence of this?" Mr. Steadford asked. "A reliable witness, perhaps?"

"No, but—"

"Then I'm afraid we cannot use it. Especially since some would argue that the woman probably got what she deserved."

Viola frowned. "That's rather harsh. I'm sure she chose her profession out of desperation, but even if she didn't, a man has no right to hit a woman for any reason and if he did so, then—"

"Yes. I agree with you," Mr. Steadford told her soothingly, "but it doesn't change the facts. Society will favor a duke over a harlot any day of the week, no matter what, and even if they didn't, the lack of proof makes it difficult to argue. Tremaine will simply deny it."

Feeling defeated before the case had barely begun, Viola swallowed and managed an absent nod. "Of course. I will try to think of something else that may be of use."

"Good." Mr. Steadford eyed his pocket watch again. "In the meantime, we should probably head over to Tremaine House for our meeting there. Perhaps our path to victory will be clearer after we hear what the duke has to say."

"**A**re you absolutely certain you still want to get involved with this?" Steadford asked Henry while Viola exchanged a few words with one of the physicians they passed on their way toward the hospital's front door.

"I think I have to," Henry said with a quick glance in Viola's direction. Her attention was completely focused on the man with whom she was speaking, instilling a strange combination of envy and admiration in the pit of his stomach. Shaking it off, he told Steadford, "Florian has dedicated his career and an ample amount of his recently acquired fortune to this hospital. If he were here, he would offer the duchess his unwavering support." Henry would not share the additional fact that he wanted to hold on tight to every excuse he could find to spend time with Viola. Not only because he needed a wife and he thought her to be the best option, but because he liked her and cared about her well-being. She mattered to him more and more with each passing second, which meant he could not stand idly by and watch her lose everything she held dear.

Steadford's gaze sharpened. "Do you know how much he has invested?"

"No." Henry felt his brow pucker beneath a curious frown. "Why do you ask?"

"Because there could be something there that we ought to investigate further."

Steadford had no chance to elaborate because Viola joined them at that exact second. The way her lips tilted the moment her eyes met his made Henry suck in a breath. Hell, involving himself in Viola's affairs and offering to help had just as much to do with his clandestine courtship of her as it did with the duty he felt toward safeguarding Florian's interests. More so, if he was being perfectly honest.

"Allow me to assist you," he said when they reached his carriage. Her hand settled neatly in his palm, sending a frisson of energy straight up his arm. Heat arced through him, jolting his heart and leaving him momentarily out of sorts.

Behind him, Steadford cleared his throat, and when Henry turned to glance at him, he realized that the barrister saw straight through him, his one eyebrow raised with mocking censure.

"What?" Henry asked in challenge.

Steadford studied him for a second, then leaned a bit closer and said, "Be careful, Lowell. She doesn't strike me as the sort of woman who wants a man to come to her rescue."

Bristling, Henry merely responded with a curt nod before climbing up into the carriage and dropping down onto the bench across from Viola. She was the very embodiment of true independence, living in her own house, running her own business and going about her own routine. Convincing her to give that up for a husband with legal authority over her would not be easy. And yet, the more time Henry spent in her company and the more he got to know her, the more certain he was that she was the woman he wanted to marry.

Caught up in the challenge he faced, he drummed his fingers restlessly against his thigh. What he'd felt before as he'd handed her up into the carriage went both ways. He was certain of it, considering the numerous times she'd blushed in his presence and the trouble she'd taken with her hair today. It couldn't be for Steadford's benefit or for Robert's, which had to mean she'd thought of him when she'd chosen to style it so prettily.

Giving her a swift examination, he admired the loose strands of hair curling almost seductively next to her temples. He wanted to run them between his fingers. He also wanted to run the pad of his thumb across the bridge of her nose and trace the freckles cascading onto her cheeks. He wanted to do a lot of things. Most of which she wouldn't allow just yet.

But there was almost something reassuring about that—about knowing that when he finally kissed her, it would be because he'd truly earned it.

Because if there was one thing he could say with certainty, it was that Viola Cartwright was not the sort of woman to take kissing lightly. When he kissed her, it would mean something to her, which meant that *he* would mean something to her. And that piece of knowledge was like a comforting balm surrounding his heart.

It did not, however, help in the slightest when Henry entered Robert's study fifteen minutes later and informed him that he would be helping her.

"I never expected you to be my Brutus, Lowell," Robert said with an unmistakable note of contempt. "It surprises me to discover that our friendship means so little to you that you would knowingly support that"—he swiped a hand in Viola's direction—"lying charlatan in her effort to steal what is rightfully mine, when you ought to be backing me up."

"I regret you see it that way," Henry replied, affecting the calmest tone he could muster. "In truth, this has nothing to do with our friendship or my acquaintanceship with Her Grace. It relates to the fact that I believe you are in the wrong."

"Shall we sit?" Mr. Hayes interjected as if Robert did not look as though he might have an apoplectic fit. A vein pulsed dangerously next to his left eye and his jaw was clenched as if holding back a torrent of expletives. It reminded Henry of how easy it was to enrage him and made him wonder for the first time if

Robert's account of his wife's passing was accurate. It sounded more like a fabricated tale than fact.

He managed a curt nod and gestured toward the available chairs. "Please."

Henry waited for Viola to sit and then claimed the seat directly beside her. "Just remember," he whispered while leaning slightly toward her, "there is an end to this. It will not last forever."

Her eyes, filled with worry, met his. "Thank you, Mr. Lowell. I will try not to forget that."

Looking down at her hands neatly folded in her lap, he wished he could cover them with his own and offer additional reassurance. But to do so would not be appropriate or helpful since it would reveal the true reason for his involvement to Robert. And since Henry still didn't know the specifics regarding Viola's history with him, he preferred not to agitate the situation any further.

"Let us first address the purpose of my client's legal action against Her Grace, the Duchess of Tremaine, so there is no confusion," Hayes said. He regarded Viola with an assessing look as if sizing her up. "She was the daughter of the late duke's physician, a young woman fifty-one years her husband's junior and without the sort of pedigree one might expect from a duchess." He droned on, outlining all the facts in the most monotonous way possible, before asking, "What seventy-year-old gentleman would not happily encourage the attentions of a young, energetic woman? And when one considers the benefits marriage will give a man, I daresay the former duke might have been too tempted to resist."

Before Henry could leap to Viola's defense, she was on her feet, forcing the men to rise as well. Henry desperately wanted to soothe her but wasn't sure how to do so without pulling her into his arms.

"Viola," he tried, but she seemed not to hear him.

Her entire focus was on Hayes, who stood like a pillar of supreme stubbornness, with no hint of offering any apology for what he'd just said. "You overstep," she finally managed, her voice trembling just enough to convey how upsetting Hayes's words had been.

She raised her chin and then stepped toward Robert. "How can you imply that I married your father for selfish reasons?" She leaned back, and suddenly there was only deep sorrow clinging to her slender form. "You've known me most of my life. You know the sort of person I am and that I would never do such a thing." Her voice lowered and she quietly murmured, so softly Henry had to strain in order to hear, "Considering what was once between us—"

"There was nothing," Robert hissed, and Viola retreated, sinking back onto her seat in painful defeat.

Henry's heart struggled to keep on beating. *Considering what was once between us.* The words kept playing in his mind, taunting him until his muscles grew tight and he realized he was clutching the armrest so hard his knuckles had whitened. It was a whole new experience, this unpleasant wave of possessiveness coursing through him. He'd never felt like this on account of any other woman before, and he decided he did not like it in the least. He also didn't care for the ease with which Robert had reduced Viola to a shadow of the woman she'd been one minute earlier. Or how the many questions and concerns now flooding his brain prevented him from offering her the comfort she surely needed.

"Since Tremaine hired me, I have taken the liberty of doing some research," Hayes said, as if everyone was getting along splendidly. "It appears you are also funding a new project." He peered at Viola, whose face had turned ashen.

"No," she breathed.

"Are you saying that I am mistaken?"

She blinked, shook her head, inhaled deeply. "No, but . . . the rejuvenation center is a joint project between myself and the Duke of Redding. You cannot go after that."

"We can if you've used a portion of your inheritance on it. Or is Redding the sole proprietor?"

"We're partners," she said, as if struggling to speak. "He owns the majority but—"

"You've made a handsome contribution."

"Well yes. I could not in good conscience allow him to—"

"And the rest of the funds?" Hayes asked, interrupting her once again.

Henry bristled. The man's rudeness was becoming intolerable.

"I've some left."

Hayes stared at her. "We'll need to determine how much."

"Do you mean to strip her of all her belongings?" Henry asked Hayes in anger.

"I am merely looking out for my client's best interests," Hayes said in a manner indicative of great ambition. All he cared about was winning, no matter who got hurt in the process.

"And the coin you are bound to receive if you win," Henry argued, with every intention of bringing the man's despicable character into focus.

"To support our case," Hayes said as if Henry hadn't spoken, "I present the medical journals of the late duke's physician, Mr. Blaire." He picked up one of five leather-bound books stacked on Robert's desk and flipped it open. "This entry, for instance, dated November 1817, months prior to the duke's death, reads: 'His Grace shows increased signs of memory loss. When I mentioned the picture I showed him last week, he failed to recall the color of the flowers or that the sea could be glimpsed in the background.'"

"That can be easily dismissed," Steadford said, speaking up for the very first time. "You would have to prove that the duke paid enough attention to that particular picture to register such detail. And besides," he added, "Blaire is currently serving time for medical misconduct. I doubt his opinion will be well received in court."

"There are numerous notes of a similar nature," Hayes said, apparently choosing to ignore Steadford's argument. "But I doubt we'll even need them." Hayes's eyes hardened, and Henry straightened his back, preparing himself for whatever else the solicitor had up his sleeve. "I rather think Her Grace's inferior background offers an excellent foundation on which to build an indisputable case."

"You forget she was legally married to the previous Duke of Tremaine and that he amended his will so it would include her," Mr. Steadford said.

"I forget no such thing," Mr. Hayes insisted. "Indeed, I am counting on a good judge to be just as appalled as I am by Her Grace's ability to snatch up a fortune that ought to have gone to the duke's son and his relatives. So prepare yourself," he added, pinning Viola with a glare. "I will pick your character apart until every aspect of it has been thoroughly scrutinized." He paused for a second as if considering, then suddenly asked, "Who was your mother, by the way?" He leafed through some notes. "I don't recall any mention of her identity during my discussions with Tremaine." He glanced at the duke, who merely shrugged.

Noting the sudden stiffness in Viola's posture, Henry said, "I hardly see how that is of any concern to you. As you yourself have said, you want to contest the late duke's will on the basis that his wife took advantage of him. To this end, questioning Her Grace about her mother is hardly going to supply the evidence you need." He stood, eager to quit this room and this house. "If that is all, I will wish you both a good day."

"But—"

"Come, Duchess." He held out his hand to Viola and waited. She blinked, gazed up into his face with wide-eyed surprise and slowly placed her hand in his. Once again, a hum of energy flew up his arm the moment her palm touched his. Swallowing, he closed his fingers around her hand and helped her rise, acutely aware of the blush coloring her cheeks and the bashful look she gave him from beneath her long lashes.

She was his. Regardless of what had transpired between her and Robert, Henry would make damn sure of it.

Chapter 12

Feeling as though the floor was tilting beneath her feet, Viola held on tight to Mr. Lowell's arm and allowed him to escort her out of Tremaine's study, through the familiar hallway beyond, past a vase that still stood where she'd placed it two years earlier, and into the street.

"This must have been terribly distressing for you," Mr. Lowell said. He released her arm, which made her feel oddly unmoored. "I'm sorry it didn't go better."

"It's all right," Viola said, even though she didn't feel like anything would ever be all right again. "I didn't expect this to be easy."

"I need to be clear with you, Your Grace," Steadford said when he caught up to them. "Your response to Mr. Hayes's inquiry about your mother was telling. You're obviously hiding something, and I promise you that whatever it was, Mr. Hayes will find it even if he has to hire a hundred people in order to do so." He stared Viola down, increasing the sense of dread already coursing through her. "Your only recourse right now is to confide in us so we can defend you against the attack that is coming."

Glancing aside, Viola searched for an appropriate

response. "My mother was poor and uneducated, but that never mattered to me or to my father. According to what he has told me, she loved me very much. Her greatest concern as she lay dying was for me and my future."

"As reassuring as that may be, it doesn't provide me with the information I need," Mr. Steadford said. His brows dipped until they met in the middle of his forehead. "Mr. Hayes is going to start selecting his weapons. He is going to dig deep in order to find them, so what I need to be completely sure of is that you have been as forthcoming with me as possible. The last thing we want is for that man to find some damning piece of information you neglected to share with me."

Even though her stomach had tied itself into knots, Viola managed to stand up straight and meet Mr. Steadford's stern expression with resolve. "There is nothing damning for anyone to find." No records remained.

"Good." Mr. Steadford touched the brim of his hat. "In that case I'll begin working on your defense right away. We'll be in touch." He gave Mr. Lowell a nod and walked away, leaving them standing beside Lowell's carriage.

"He's a good barrister," Mr. Lowell said, "and he is on your side, even though I realize his manner might make it seem as if he's not at times."

"I know."

He glanced at his carriage and then at Viola. "If I may, I would like to suggest a drink at my club. You look as though you could do with a little fortification."

As tempting as the invitation was, she knew she ought to resist. "Thank you, but—"

"Viola." His voice was calm. "I am asking you as a concerned friend who cares about your well-being. There is no ulterior motive," he said, and suddenly smiled. Lowering his voice, he spoke with a hint of humor. "I am not trying to lure you into my secret lair of debauchery."

She couldn't help the grin that followed or the flare of heat fanning out across her shoulders. "Does such a place truly exist?" And why on earth was she curious to know if it did?

"Maybe." He reached for the carriage door and opened it wide. "Maybe not." Holding out his free hand, he waited for her to accept his invitation. "It does not signify since all I am offering you right now is companionship."

Hesitating, Viola stared into the depths of his dark brown eyes. He made her feel attractive, even though she knew she wasn't. Somehow, against all odds, Mr. Lowell had turned her world upside down. For the first time since Robert had broken her heart, Mr. Lowell had made her look forward to spending time in another man's company.

"Truly?" Recalling his touch as he'd taught her how to play billiards, the mischief shining in his eyes when he'd beat her at cards and the kindness with which he'd offered his assistance the moment she'd required it, she suddenly knew that she wanted a whole lot more. She wanted him. And as frightening as that prospect was and as much as she knew she could never risk a romantic liaison with anyone, it seemed to right her lopsided world. "You will not attempt to seduce me?"

He inhaled deeply, nostrils flaring while he stared back at her with dark intensity. "Not today," he murmured.

Disappointment raced through her, which was of course ridiculous since she wasn't really looking to have an affair. She was a reasonable woman who prided herself on her respectability, and that respectability had to be maintained at all cost if she was to stand a chance of winning in court. One wrong move would give Mr. Hayes additional ammunition to use against her. But she would be lying if she said she didn't want to feel desirable.

She'd spent the last two years dedicating herself to her goals, to making an old man happy and then to saving the sick. And she'd told herself that this was enough, that she never wanted to fall prey to passion again. Now, placing her hand in Mr. Lowell's, she realized she'd been wrong.

His fingers closed around hers, and Viola's breath caught.

"But that doesn't mean I won't try tomorrow," he murmured, his silky voice following her up into the carriage, instilling in her a sense of excitement, the likes of which she'd never experienced before. This was a game, she realized—a very complicated one in which the players would either surrender or walk away unfulfilled. It occurred to her that they'd been playing it for a while already, ever since he'd woken up at St. Agatha's Hospital after undergoing surgery, and she'd been the nurse who'd tended to him.

Climbing into the carriage, he shut the door, lowered himself to the opposite bench and knocked on the roof so the driver would know they were ready. Lounging against the corner directly across from where she sat, he stretched his legs out at an angle. His large body shrank the interior and made her feel smaller than usual.

"Will you tell me what's really between you and Robert?"

In spite of his leisurely tone, a chill curled around Viola's spine and a knot formed in her throat as her eyes began to sting. Of all the things they might discuss on their way to The Red Rose, this was the one that appealed the least. And yet, Mr. Lowell's searching gaze was inviting her to be honest. He cared about her answer, and as upsetting as she feared it might be to him, she knew it would be a mistake not to tell him the truth when he was so boldly asking to hear it.

"I made a terrible mistake where Robert was concerned," she quietly murmured. The knot in her throat tightened. Blinking rapidly, she tried to stop the tears from falling, but it was pointless. They spilled from the corners of her eyes, dampening her cheeks. "He was such a fixed part of my life growing up. Whenever my father and I would visit Peter, Robert was there, except when he was away at Eton and later at university." When Henry said nothing, she continued as if her voice was detached from her body. "In the years that followed, I grew up, from a girl into a young woman. And then my father died and the world as I knew it crumbled around me. But Robert was there. He acted as though he cared, as though I mattered to him, and I gradually fancied myself in love with him, even though I have later realized it wasn't love at all, but merely a childish infatuation."

"How young were you when you realized you'd developed a *tendre* for him?"

"Sixteen." She dropped her gaze to her lap as she thought back to who she'd once been. "When I asked him if he loved me in return, he told me he did." An indelicate sob tore its way past her lips, embarrassing her so completely she wished she could flee. But that was not an option. Not when she was confined to a carriage and not when she had to face this and put it to rest. "It's the reason why he so easily manipulated me into doing what I did, because he told me that's how men and women prove their affection for one another. He said, 'If you love me like you say you do, you'll enjoy this.' And then he . . ." She laughed as if the world was coming apart at the seams, with raw despair and anguish. "He hurt me, but I told myself over and over again that this was the price to pay in order to win him."

"Jesus, Viola."

"When it was over," she gasped, her body shaking in the aftermath of her revelation, "he told me he'd had better. And then he walked away and left me." She drew a deep breath and held it, counted to three and quietly exhaled. "That's when I realized that every kindness he'd shown me had been a trick—a deliberate effort to use my vulnerability against me. Later that day, I learned that he was engaged to Lady Beatrice. It wasn't until I married Peter that I discovered he'd been made aware of what Robert had done to me. I'm not sure how he found out, but I do know it's why he sent Robert away, and I also suspect it's the reason he left as much as he could to me instead of to his son."

"I hardly know what to say."

Viola winced. "I expected as much." She swiped at her eyes.

"No." He was suddenly beside her, enfolding her fingers with his. "You misunderstand me." Raising her hands to his lips, he kissed her knuckles. "I don't know what to say because I'm afraid I will frighten you with my anger, not at you but at him, Viola. *He* wronged you most grievously, took advantage of a girl who was barely more than a child. He used your love for him as a weapon to make you submit and to steal from you in the worst possible way."

"So you . . . you do not resent me for what I allowed him to do?" She could scarcely believe it.

Without hesitation, he pulled her into his arms. "You are still the kind, generous woman I know and you did what you did because your heart was pure— because you believed the best of a man who wasn't to be trusted." He kissed the top of her head while she pressed her face to his chest, taking comfort in the wonderfully familiar scent of sandalwood and bergamot.

"Over the years, I have realized how lonely I was back then. My beloved father was gone, Peter was old and I had little company besides Robert. I suppose what I really wanted was proof that I mattered." She tilted her head back and looked up into his steady gaze. "Instead I got the opposite."

"If only we'd known each other then, Viola. How different your life might have been if I'd been there to give you the love and protection you needed." His throat worked as if he was having some trouble getting the words out. "But I'm here now, and I am not leaving your side."

She scarcely knew what to say besides "Thank you." But that seemed so insufficient when compared to his kindness and support. So she chose to say nothing at all and just hold him as he held her while savoring the comfort of his embrace.

He released her before she was ready. But rather than return to his side of the carriage, he stayed beside her, simply holding her hand.

A companionable silence filled the carriage until Mr. Lowell suddenly asked, "Who's your favorite poet?"

Viola blinked, momentarily thrown off balance, but then she gathered her wits and said, "To be honest, I've never really enjoyed poetry. I prefer a good novel—a story with an exciting plot and compelling characters."

"Why?" He sounded genuinely curious.

She shrugged one shoulder. "I suppose I like all the wonderful experiences available to me in a pile of bound paper."

Allowing herself to look at him, she found his eyes illuminated with equal parts curiosity and wonder.

When he spoke again, it was with the utmost softness. "Then allow me to ask a different question." The edge of his mouth lifted. "Who is your favorite author?"

"Jane Austen, but I also enjoy the occasional Daniel Defoe and Henry Fielding."

"I think Jane Austen matches your personality best." His eyes narrowed and he pressed his lips together before adding, "There's softness inside you and playfulness too. You seek to help people, which means you have tremendous kindness and love in your heart. I can see you reading something romantically uplifting with a touch of wit."

His smile settled more firmly into place. "Which of her novels do you favor?"

Heat warmed her cheeks as she gazed back into his eyes. "I would have to say *Mansfield Park*."

"Of course." There was no doubt in his mind that she would identify with Fanny Price and her ability to rise above her inferior birth. "It is a lovely story."

"You know it?"

"Is that so shocking?" He could see that it was because of the charming way her bottom lip dipped in the middle and the inquisitiveness with which her brow rose. "I have also read *Emma*, *Pride and Prejudice* and *Northanger Abbey*."

Expelling a breath, Viola sank back against the squabs. "I confess I would not have thought it."

"Because I'm a man?"

Her mouth hitched a little at one corner and her eyelids lowered ever so slightly. It was enough to convey some small measure of discomfort. "I suppose so."

He grinned, pleased by her honesty. "That's fairly biased in light of your own involvement with medicine, a field dominated entirely by men." The carriage turned a corner and slowed. "Not that I disapprove," he said when he saw she was getting ready to argue, "for indeed I believe what you have done and what you continue to do is really quite splendid."

The carriage halted and Henry opened the door, alighting in one swift movement so he could offer Viola his assistance. She placed her hand carefully in his, sparking a flame where both their palms met.

"You have a peculiar interest in curiosities, Mr. Lowell." Her gaze met his, and he saw in the depths of her eyes a desperate need to be understood and accepted for who she was. "Am I like your automaton? An oddity for you to marvel at? Is that the reason for your sudden interest in me?"

"No." He knew he had to tell her the truth even if she wouldn't believe it. "You are someone I greatly admire, a woman whose company I do not take for granted but seek because you are more than most people aspire to be."

She stared at him, her hand still resting in his. And then she licked her lips and Henry applauded his restraint, since every cell in his body now screamed for him to pull her into his arms and kiss her.

"I had advantages, first because of my father's profession and then by meeting Florian. His open-mindedness has allowed me to involve myself in St. Agatha in a way no other physician would."

Henry released her hand and offered his arm so he could lead her inside The Red Rose and toward his office. "You said you helped him extract the lead ball from my shoulder. Does he also allow you to operate on your own?"

"Sometimes, with his supervision and when no one else is there to see. But mostly I assist him and finish up with the sutures." She suddenly smiled. "He says mine are neater."

Henry's chest tightened. Although his brother was now happily married and had never implied he'd been involved with Viola, he had to ask, "Is there any truth to the rumors about you two?"

Having arrived in his office, Henry gestured toward a chair and crossed to the sideboard.

"You mean the ones about us being lovers?" She gave him a look that seemed to say he was cracked in the head for asking. "Don't be ridiculous."

"It is common knowledge that you have a close working relationship, and with you being a widow, it would not have been a preposterous idea while Florian was still a bachelor."

She laughed quite suddenly and shook her head. "Why on earth would your brother have an affair with me when he could have had any woman he wished for? It makes no sense."

Her inability to see her own beauty was heartbreaking. Knowing that altering her perception would not be accomplished in the space of five minutes or even in a day, he gestured toward the selection of decanters he kept at the ready. "Do you prefer brandy, sherry or claret?"

"Sherry, please."

He handed it to her while reveling in the knowledge that she and his brother had never been intimate.

As for Robert . . .

Henry's muscles tightened as he recalled what that scoundrel had done. He'd take savage pleasure in ruining Robert's face with his fists right now.

"I was wrong to think the worst of you when we first met," Viola said. "I just assumed . . ."

"You thought there had to be some truth to what you'd heard?"

"Well yes." She pressed her lips together. "I'm sorry, I—"

"Don't be. You only believed what I wanted you and the rest of the world to believe."

"I still don't understand."

Opening a desk drawer, he retrieved a deck of cards and proceeded to shuffle it. "When I returned from university and made my first appearance at a ball after three years of absence, I was pursued by every mama looking to get her daughter settled. So I let it be known that I was not appropriate company for any young lady to be keeping." He dealt a few cards and leaned back in his seat. "Of course, it didn't deter the widows or the married women from looking for a bit of fun, but it helped me avoid marriage until I was ready for it."

She picked up her cards and shook her head. "How peculiar." And then she laughed. "It's quite the ruse, the most notorious scoundrel no more of a threat to a young woman's virtue than any other honorable gentleman she might encounter. What are we playing?"

He smiled because she amused him and because he enjoyed their effortless conversation, and also because she was so damn lovely. He placed four additional cards face up on the table. "Cassino. Are you familiar with it?"

Her lips tilted. "Of course." She took the five and the two with her seven.

"The items you purchased for the rejuvenation center should be arriving this afternoon." He added a three to the two on the table and she added an ace.

"Yes." She puffed out a breath as he took the next trick with a six. "I'm thinking of heading over to the center after I leave here in order to have a look."

"Perhaps you'll allow me to escort you?"

She raised her chin and her eyes met his. "Thank you, Mr. Lowell." A soft smile pulled at her lips. "I think I'd like that."

Pleasure filled him from top to toe on account of her quick acceptance. He was clearly making progress with her and loving every minute.

Chapter 13

Seeing how perfectly the cabinet she'd bought fit the space she'd intended for it distracted Viola a little from the butterflies Mr. Lowell invariably caused to flutter about in her belly. He wasn't just charming and incredibly attractive. He was also exceedingly kind, helpful and amusing, not to mention understanding when it came to her past. She really enjoyed being around him. Not only because of the constant distraction he offered from the lawsuit and the pressing concern of possibly losing everything she'd worked so hard to build these past two years, but because she was growing increasingly fond of his company.

She still couldn't believe he'd beaten her at cards before escorting her up the street to the rejuvenation center. And when she'd asked for a rematch, he'd declined, scoundrel that he was. A smile tugged at her lips as she wiped the cabinet door with a cloth. It was a bittersweet chore when she wasn't sure if she'd lose it and everything else she'd purchased for the center to Robert. Still, she wasn't about to concede defeat until forced to do so. The whole unit was dirty from standing outside at the market and had to be thoroughly cleaned no matter what.

"I checked the various rooms and believe this

rug will fit really well in the upstairs one with the terracotta-colored walls."

Viola turned to face Mr. Lowell, who, to her surprise, was standing a few feet behind her, legs braced in a solid stance and with the rolled-up rug resting firmly on his shoulder. Gone was his jacket, discarded Lord knew where. His shirtsleeves had been rolled up past his elbows to reveal a pair of strikingly handsome forearms.

Viola blinked. Strikingly handsome forearms? She had to be losing her mind. Especially since she'd seen those arms before at the hospital. Indeed, she'd seen a lot more than that while helping Florian operate on his brother, but she'd been preoccupied by the gravity of the situation, by the job she'd been required to do and other things she couldn't recall at the moment because her mind was going blank.

"Um . . ." she managed in the most articulate way possible, because really, who was she kidding? The man was a truly extraordinary specimen of pure masculinity. And she ought to know because he wasn't the first man she'd seen in a state of undress. Far from it.

He raised an eyebrow. "Yes?"

"I'm sure you're right."

Grinning as though he found her response incredibly amusing, he swung toward the stairs. "Come on then. Let's go and see if I am correct."

"You want me to come with you?" She wasn't so sure that was wise. Least of all now that he was presenting her with a marvelous view of what appeared to be a very fine backside indeed. Her mouth began to water. If only she didn't want him as much as she did.

"Of course," he called as he started up the stairs, his breeches stretching across his thighs as he went. "This is your place of business, Viola. I believe you will want to make sure it is decorated according to your wishes."

Certainly, but did that really have to involve a flutter

in the pit of her belly or an endless series of hot little shivers caressing her skin? With a sigh, she followed him, resigning herself to the all-too-familiar state he was putting her in. For years she'd endeavored to avoid falling prey to desire again, to save herself from the type of heartache Robert had once caused her. And yet within a week and a half, Mr. Lowell had awakened a hunger inside her—a craving that only grew with each passing second. Worst of all, she felt increasingly powerless to stop it.

Did that make her wanton? Perhaps, but if that were the case then surely she would have had similar responses to other men, like Florian, for instance. Yet she'd never felt anything but friendship toward him even though she was able to acknowledge his handsomeness. And if she were perfectly honest, her feelings for Robert had been entirely different from the ones she now experienced toward Mr. Lowell. With Robert, she'd known the infatuation of a young girl whose heart had been free and ready to love. With Mr. Lowell, she felt the restraint of that misplaced trust while desperately hoping she might one day be brave enough to accept the secret yearnings of her mind, body and soul. Yearnings she'd thought long dead until Mr. Lowell had awakened them with his cheeky smiles and sparkling eyes.

Entering the room he'd mentioned earlier, she found him crouched on the floor as he rolled out the rug. He raised his gaze to her only briefly before continuing with his task. A dazzling pattern of cobalt blue intertwined with gold graced the dark wood floor, complementing the wall color beautifully.

"What do you think?" Mr. Lowell asked. Straightening himself, he stood and took a step back to admire the piece.

Viola could only tell him the truth. "It is perfect."

"I quite agree." His voice had softened and when she looked up, she saw he was watching her closely.

But then he spun away as if surveying the space, and she was left to wonder if she'd imagined the gleam of desire in his eyes. Her heart told her it was real but her brain insisted she must be deluding herself, because if there was one thing she knew for certain, it was that she was far from perfect and that a man as handsome as Mr. Lowell couldn't possibly think otherwise, in spite of his words to the contrary.

"This seems a bit out of place," he said, indicating a narrow table that was shoved up against one wall. "And there's a hole in it."

Crossing to where he stood, Viola looked at the spot to which he pointed. "That's intentional." Her heart sped up a little for some absurd reason. "This table will be in the center of the room. It's intended for a client to lie on while having hand pressure applied to their backs and shoulders. I've actually hired a Chinese couple who specialize in this technique. The wife will tend to the women and the husband to the men. The hole is there so the client's face won't be pressed into the mattress—so they can breathe more freely."

"I see." Mr. Lowell nodded as if her explanation made perfect sense. "Shall we move it into position then?" Grabbing one end of the table, Mr. Lowell lifted it slightly, testing the weight. "It's not too heavy. We can easily manage without disturbing the workers."

His inclination to do the job himself instead of being one of those pompous aristocrats who stood about barking orders for servants to follow made the wall Viola had built around her heart dissolve even further. He wasn't just a handsome face or a bit of fun company. He was also useful and unassuming, and as Viola picked up the other end of the table and helped him maneuver it into the middle of the room, she decided that she not only liked him but respected him. A lot.

"There. That wasn't too difficult." He gave her a wink, and happiness curled her toes. "Let's test it." Before she could think to protest, he'd climbed up onto the table and placed himself face down so his mouth and nose aligned with the hole. "Hmm."

She knit her brow in question. "What is it?"

Rising up a little on one of those distractingly handsome forearms, he offered a lopsided smile. "This is really comfortable."

"You didn't expect it to be?"

"I'm not sure what I expected, to be honest." He lowered himself again, and when he spoke once more, it was with a muffled mumble. "Let's see how this works then, shall we?"

Viola's ribs clamped tightly around her heart. "What do you mean?" She knew exactly what he meant.

He flung one arm out and swatted toward his back. "Do the hand pressure thing."

"Mr. Lowell, I'm really not educated in that sort of technique so it would probably be best if—"

"It doesn't have to be perfect, Viola. I'm just curious to see what it's like."

"It's not appropriate," she felt compelled to say.

He sighed and rose back up again, this time with the sort of expression that seemed to say, *I thought you had more sense than to let such a trifling matter ruffle your feathers.* Instead he said, "The door is wide open and the place is full of workers. Look, here's one right now." He nodded a greeting to the man who entered the room.

"Forgive the intrusion," the man said, "but I thought I'd come and hang the mirror we spoke about earlier." He gave Mr. Lowell a funny look before returning his attention to Viola.

"Of course," she said. "Please go right ahead."

"And don't mind us," Mr. Lowell told him from his position on the table. "We're just testing the equipment and making sure it works to Her Grace's satisfaction." He tilted his chin at Viola. "Come on then," he said, and dropped his head once more.

Viola gave the worker a hesitant look and saw he was already busy taking measurements and marking the wall behind her. Inhaling deeply, she took a small step toward the table on which Mr. Lowell was waiting. He seemed so relaxed, and considering the riotous state he'd put her nerves in, that was incredibly irritating.

I'm a professional, she told herself. She'd nursed an endless number of men since opening St. Agatha's Hospital two years earlier. But this was different. This was intimate, even if Mr. Lowell made it seem like the most normal thing in the world. It wasn't. She knew it in the way her hands trembled with the prospect of touching him so directly. Shockingly, it occurred to her that she might even covet the chance to do so, as evidenced by how easily her resistance had wavered and crumbled.

A more resilient woman would have quit the room and returned downstairs to continue cleaning the cabinet. She, on the other hand, placed her palm upon his shoulder and squeezed. His only response was a languid sigh, encouraging her to continue. So she added her other hand too and pressed deep, pushing her thumbs against the tense muscle in the way she'd seen Mrs. Zhang do when she'd demonstrated her technique to Viola during her interview.

Bolstered by the fact that Mr. Lowell showed little response besides lying there, she allowed her hands to knead along the sides of his back, then up the center and again to his shoulders.

He expelled what sounded like an involuntary groan and Viola's hands stilled. "Are you all right?"

"Mmm-hmm."

She increased the pressure, more slowly this time. His shoulders were broad and his hair . . .

Silky black locks tickled her knuckles as she worked close to his neck. Leaning forward, she put her weight into the movement, and when she inhaled, the enticing combination of sandalwood and bergamot lured her closer.

"Your Grace?"

Viola straightened her spine and took a step back, her pulse leaping lightly at her wrist as she turned to face the worker who'd addressed her. "Yes?" Her breath came heavily, and to her dismay, she could feel heat burning her cheeks.

"Will this do?" The worker pointed to the mirror, which now hung exactly where Viola intended it to.

"Yes. Thank you." She swallowed and reached for the table to steady herself.

"I think this place will be a marvelous success," Mr. Lowell said as he hopped off the table. "That felt really good." He rotated his shoulders and strode to the door, pausing there as if to wait for her. "Come with me. There's something I want to show you."

Viola stood in stupefied wonderment as he disappeared round the corner. Was she really the only one affected by what they'd just done together? She drew a sharp breath to calm her nerves, aware there was nothing wrong with it per se. She was after all a widow, and they hadn't been behind a locked door. Indeed, they hadn't even been alone! And yet somehow, she felt as though she'd just been slightly seduced. Although bearing in mind their positions, maybe she'd been the one doing the seducing?

Shaking her head, she forced one foot in front of

the other, intent on following Mr. Lowell wherever he intended to take her. She was keenly aware that the path on which they were traveling was far more dangerous than she'd ever dared to imagine.

Henry was incredibly grateful for the extra bit of time it took Viola to join him in the next room. Her delay allowed him to hide the effect of her touch behind his jacket, which he now held strategically in front of himself. Having discarded it here earlier when he'd climbed a ladder to hang one of the lanterns she'd bought, he'd hurried to retrieve it.

Christ!

It had been impossible not to respond as he had with her long, slender fingers working upon him in ways that produced all manner of inappropriate contemplations, all of which involved fewer clothes and privacy. Hoping his face wouldn't give him away, he attempted a bland expression and allowed for the barest hint of a smile when she entered.

A frown creased her forehead, making him wonder ...

"You wanted to show me something?" she asked.

He shook himself into motion and went to collect the tinderbox he'd left on a small built-in ledge to one side. "I borrowed this from the foreman. Close the door, will you?"

"Mr. Lowell."

Her voice was stern and censorious and, to Henry's amusement, did little to quash his desire. Least of all when he imagined her using that voice on him while wearing a pair of spectacles. By God, he really had to get his depraved mind sorted.

So he thought of the cod-liver oil he'd been forced to consume as a boy and the wasp sting he'd suffered one summer and how that would feel right there where . . . Yes, that did it. He breathed a sigh of relief and dropped his jacket back onto a vacant chair that must have been brought in on a whim because it didn't match anything.

"I just want to show you what I've done." When she looked at him as though he must think she'd fallen off a wagon, he added, "The effect won't be as good if the room is flooded by light from the hallway." Still, she hesitated, so he blew out a breath and gave her the most imploring look he could muster. "Please?"

Her nostrils flared a little and her eyes seemed to brighten. And then . . . "Very well, but please be quick about it."

He grabbed the ladder leaning against the wall while she closed the door until it stood only slightly ajar. Climbing the rungs, he reached the desired height and balanced himself against the rails.

"Do be careful," Viola told him.

He smiled as he handled the tinderbox. "It warms my heart to know you're worried about my safety."

She snorted while he struck a flint, sparking a flame. "An accident would be bad for business."

He laughed and held the flame to the candle inside the lantern. A glow emerged, reddened by the colorful glass casing and shining a pattern of rectangles onto the walls, ceiling and floor. Carefully, Henry descended the ladder and set the tinderbox back in its place. He glanced at Viola, who stood as if dazed.

"It's so beautiful."

Her words were mere whispers reaching across the distance between them and pulling him closer. But he resisted the lure in order to simply admire her wonder. "I agree." And then, to dissuade her from discerning his true meaning so she wouldn't think him too forward, he cleared his throat and quickly added, "I'm not sure what your intention is with this particular room, but the atmosphere is very pleasing."

A smile lit her eyes as she turned to him. "This will be where the women can enjoy a cup of tea and relax. It is where they will wait to be taken through to the room we were just in or to the sauna or bath or one of the other treatment areas we offer."

"When do you intend to open for business?"

"As soon as possible." She allowed her gaze to collide with his, the effect so powerful he almost felt the need to sit. "I'm planning to host the grand opening on the twenty-fifth."

"That doesn't leave much time to prepare." She was only allowing herself four days in which to add the final touches.

"I know, but I don't want to wait any longer than that." She bit her lip, studied him for a second before saying, "The hospital needs the extra income in order to grow. With patient numbers increasing each month, we'll soon have to turn people away, which is something I don't want to do. So I'm thinking of acquiring additional buildings to serve as specialized branches. I even made a list of the physicians and surgeons I'd like to hire, but they're all the finest at what they do so they won't come cheap. "

Henry pondered that for a moment. "Aren't Florian and Juliette helping you with funds?"

"Well yes. Florian has donated an impressive sum, and Juliette's charity events have, as you probably know, become incredibly popular, what with all the imaginative prizes she continues to auction off. But it isn't sustainable and it won't be enough for what I have in mind. Besides, I don't want to always rely on donations or for me to have to ask Florian for help when required."

"I know he's happy to offer. The hospital means a great deal to him."

"Yes, but it's time for St. Agatha's to become self-sufficient." She expelled a weary breath. "And depending on how things turn out with Robert, I believe having an extra supply of money at the ready will be wise. I won't ask Florian or anyone else to pay back the sum of my inheritance."

She was proud and unwilling to be a burden to others. Henry admired her for that—for choosing the harder path instead of falling on her friends' good graces. "That's only if you lose, which I doubt you will with Mr. Steadford by your side."

"I hope you're right." Her voice wavered.

Henry strolled toward her until they were only a foot apart. "Then let us plan a party." Her breath quivered upon her lips as she exhaled, and he couldn't stop from taking her hand in his to offer reassurance. "I have a wonderful social network. If you agree, I will be happy to send out additional invitations on your behalf if you give me a list of the people you've already invited."

"But there's so little time left. I cannot possibly ask you to take on such an enormous task."

He let her hand go. "Of course you can. We are friends, are we not? And friends help each other." He grinned to ease the tightness inside his chest. "Besides, it is my duty to look after my brother's best interests while he is away."

Her face lit with tremendous appreciation and for a second, he believed she might throw herself into his arms to convey her gratitude. *Please do.* He held his breath and the moment passed. She turned away and went to the door, opening it wide.

Pausing there, she glanced back at him. "Thank you for all your help, Mr. Lowell. Returning to Society after all this time is really rather nerve-wracking."

"You needn't—"

"I know what people think of me." She raised her chin a notch. A gesture he'd come to recognize as a valiant effort to hide any lack of confidence. "It is not so different from what Robert believes, and having to face that is not something I look forward to."

"Then don't." He could think of no other way in which to help but to offer her a way out. "Let Gabriella and Amelia do the hosting if you don't want to."

She dropped her gaze for a moment before meeting his once again. "No. This is my project. Mine and Florian's." Her eyes shone with determination. "Without him here, I must put in an appearance. It means a lot, knowing you'll be there to support me."

A flare of heat darted through Henry's body. His skin tightened around his muscles. "I care for you a great deal, Viola. You should know that by now."

"Yes," she murmured, her lips slightly parted on that final word, and for some bizarre reason he sensed that she was agreeing to something else entirely—like the need to surrender to their mutual attraction.

But before he could analyze her response further, she spun away and disappeared into the hallway beyond, leaving him to wonder how much longer it was going to take before Viola Cartwright would finally be his.

Viola's heart pounded hard against her chest as she fled the room. There was really no other way to describe the haste with which she hurried back downstairs and frantically searched for her foreman. She needed to look busy—too busy to keep on talking with a man whose shoulders and back would be forever imprinted in the tips of her fingers.

Breathing heavily, she leaned against a doorway

to steady herself. He tempted her in ways that were making her lose her mind.

"Your Grace," her foreman said, startling her so much she flinched. Good heavens, what was happening to her? "We're doing well with the schedule." He came a bit closer. "The artists should be done in another couple of days and then we'll just need one more day to clean up."

"That's wonderful news. Thank you!" He grinned and returned to his work, allowing Viola to take a moment for herself. She closed her eyes and inhaled the strong scent of plaster, paint and wood shavings.

"You look exhausted," Mr. Lowell said, his voice creeping over her skin and doing delicious things to her insides.

Opening her eyes, she saw he was closer than she had expected. A smile pulled at his lips. "In a good way," she admitted.

He leaned toward her, and for the first time in five years, she felt no aversion to the idea of being kissed. In fact, she believed it might be rather pleasant, if Mr. Lowell were the one to kiss her, that was.

Warning bells started sounding in her head, and she instantly straightened herself and moved past him. "I should get back to the hospital."

"Then inviting you for dinner is not an option?" he asked, catching up with her in a few easy strides.

She glanced up at him and drew to a halt in the foyer. "I'm afraid not, but thank you for asking."

Looking past her, he seemed to consider the traffic out in the street, visible through the open door. "Perhaps you'll allow me to escort you to the grand opening on Friday instead?" He looked at her with warmth in his eyes, and her breath caught.

"As much as I'd like to accept, I worry it might give people the wrong impression."

He nodded and stuck his hands in his pockets. "You worry they'll think we're involved."

"I'm sorry, but I need to make the best impression possible." Oh dear. That came out horribly wrong. "You know my own reputation concerns me. I have to put my best foot forward on Friday in order to encourage people to purchase a membership. If they think you and I—"

"It has always bothered me, how much we care about the opinion of strangers." He breathed a heavy sigh. "I understand your reasoning, Viola, as sorry as I am that it can't be different."

Unable to speak, she gave a nod of thanks accompanied by a small smile. If only he was the reprobate he made himself out to be so turning him down wouldn't be so horribly hard. Instead, he was quite possibly the nicest man she'd ever met, and as she said good-bye and walked away, it occurred to her that she'd been wrong about everything right from the start. It wasn't that he wasn't good enough for her, but rather that he was perfect in every way. If she could only overcome her own fears in order to give him the chance he deserved.

Chapter 14

Deciding to send his carriage ahead without him, Henry started walking back to his house. Moving was vital right now, the need for exercise overwhelming. Damn, but he wished he'd been wiser in his youth. But he'd thought himself smart, and the future had always been something he'd worry about later. Well, later was here now, and because of the rumors he'd deliberately created and spread, he'd wrecked his chance of forming an attachment to the most incredible woman he'd ever met.

Bloody hell!

Increasing his pace, he listened to the click of his heels against the pavement while reflecting on the day he and Viola had spent together. He'd enjoyed her company immensely and missed her now that she was no longer with him. Aware of her reluctance to form an attachment, he'd known he might be pushing his luck by suggesting she join him for dinner, but he'd been reluctant for their time together to end.

As he ought to have expected, she'd refused the invitation, along with his offer to escort her on Friday. Clenching his fists, he expelled an agitated breath. He'd ruined his own reputation in an effort to push women away only to find that the one he actually wanted did not want him in return.

A humorless smile pulled at his lips. Not true. She did want him. He could see it in her stormy eyes whenever she looked his way, but there was a struggle going on inside her—a tug of wills that held her back. Perhaps if he could acquire just an ounce of respectability, this would change?

He hoped so, but doing so took time. Changing Society's opinion of a person from bad to good was not as easy as changing it from good to bad. For now he resolved to continue as he had by being Viola's friend, listening to her, helping her and letting her come to him.

So he set his course for The Red Rose. There was work to be done there. The advertisements he meant to place in the *Mayfair Chronicle* next week would not design themselves. But his intention to be productive was briefly disrupted when he arrived and saw Yates coming toward him in the foyer.

"Where have you been?" Grinning, Yates gave him a quick once-over. "I'm guessing that's either confectioner's sugar from the bakery down the street or dust from only God knows where."

"It's from Viola Cartwright's new place of business." Henry stepped aside to let a few guests pass. "She needed a bit of help arranging a few things."

"I bet she did," Yates said with a smile too wide for his face.

Henry frowned. "It's not like that. There was a lamp."

"Mmm-hmm."

Muttering an oath, Henry brushed past his friend and continued toward his office. When he sensed Yates was following him, he added, "She's a respectable woman. There's nothing going on between us."

"Is that because she knows you're a scoundrel?"

"I believe so," Henry said with resignation. He led Yates into his office and poured them each a drink. He handed one to his friend.

"You could reform, you know," Yates suggested, and took a sip of his brandy.

"I don't really need to, truth is."

"What do you mean?"

Henry went to sit behind his desk. He waited for Yates to claim one of the chairs opposite before saying. "I'm not really a rake."

Yates snorted. "You know I've never judged you for your affairs. You're good company and an excellent friend. How you choose to divert yourself is your business."

"But it's all lies." Christ, if it was this hard convincing his friend of the truth, Society would never believe him. "A deception I crafted to keep the debutantes away."

Yates went utterly still. He raised an eyebrow and slowly leaned forward. "Are you telling me you're a virgin?"

"God no!"

Yates looked only marginally apologetic. "It is a logical question considering what you just said." He took another sip of his drink. "Are you really being serious?"

"Absolutely." Henry glanced at the amber liquid in his glass. "Problem is, it's ruining my chances with Viola Cartwright."

"I knew it!" Shifting his gaze, Yates stared at his friend. "I knew you were interested in her."

"Very well," Henry agreed, "you've found me out. The problem is I don't know what to do about it."

"As a member of St. Agatha's committee, I've had the pleasure of getting to know her since the hospital opened." When Henry scowled, Yates raised one hand in surrender. "As colleagues, Lowell. Nothing more." He lowered his hand and proceeded to drum his fingers slowly against the armrest. "Her dedication toward the hospital cannot be denied. Are you sure you're up for competing with that?"

"My hope is to marry her, Yates, so that would be a yes."

"I see." Yates seemed to consider. "Then why not let the world know that this is your intention?"

"That I mean to marry Viola Cartwright?" Henry scoffed at the idea. "She values privacy and discretion, Yates. I don't think she would appreciate me placing her squarely in the gossipmongers' line of fire."

"I didn't mean for you to name your intended, just merely to let it be known that you're looking to marry, settle down, set up a nursery and so forth."

Henry frowned. "I'd have every desperate young woman and her mama banging my door down." Which was why he'd refrained from making a public announcement about his intentions. He'd seen first-hand how all the debutantes had reacted last year when his brother, Florian, had become a duke. But when Uncle George, the Marquess of Riverton, had lain dying, he'd asked the king to elevate him to duke. The request had been granted and since George had no children, he'd been able to add a Special Remainder to the new letters patent, naming Florian his heir.

An ordinary physician one day, capable of walking down the street without anyone taking notice, chased and fawned over the next. Henry shuddered at the very idea of encouraging such attention.

"Looks like you have a choice to make then, Lowell." Yates tilted his head and allowed a smile to slide into place. "You can either continue guarding your secrets and keep your duchess at arm's length forever, or you can take the risk of making yourself available for marriage by announcing your new eligible state to the world."

Yates's words made Henry contemplate everything that mattered to him long after his friend had gone. He wanted Viola to be his, and in order to do so, he would have to be the man she knew him to be, not just to her, but to everyone else as well. He would have to make it clear that his days as a rake were over.

With this in mind, he finished writing up the advertisement for his club and slipped it into an envelope along with a longer letter to the *Mayfair Chronicle*'s editors. Handing the missive over to one of his club's errand boys, Henry departed with a new sense of accomplishment. The days ahead would probably be difficult, but he also knew they'd be worth it if it meant convincing Viola to have him.

Reaching his house, Henry unlocked the door briskly and stepped inside. His manservant, Mr. Andrews, came to greet him. "I require a change of clothes," Henry told him while peeling off his gloves. Helping Viola decorate had left him feeling a little dusty.

"Yes, sir." Mr. Andrews took the gloves. "But first, you ought to know that Carlton Guthrie is waiting for you in your parlor."

"What?" Henry couldn't hide his surprise or his curiosity. What the hell was the crime lord of St. Giles doing here in his home and what the devil could the man possibly want with him?

Mr. Andrews's expression grew increasingly apprehensive. "I hope you'll forgive me for admitting him, sir. I honestly wanted to turn him away but he insisted the matter he wished to discuss with you was of great importance and urgency."

Henry glanced toward the parlor door. "You did the right thing then." He turned back to Mr. Andrews. "Did you serve him any refreshments?"

"No, sir. Not yet."

"Very well then. Please ask one of the maids to bring up some coffee and I'll go see what my unexpected guest wants." Henry crossed to the parlor door without another moment's hesitation. Opening it, he found the flamboyant man that was Carlton Guthrie reclining in an armchair.

He stood as soon as he saw Henry, his purple velvet coattails falling back into place as he did so. At his neck he wore an extravagant cravat from which an amethyst-tipped pin protruded. His vest was silver damask, his trousers cut from black and gray plaid with purple accent lines woven into the pattern. Close by, on an adjacent chair, sat the top hat that matched his jacket.

"Good afternoon, Mr. Lowell." Guthrie applied a firm tone that brooked no nonsense. "I 'ope ye'll forgive the intrusion."

Still apprehensive about the purpose of Guthrie's visit, Henry eyed him carefully. Guthrie's gaze was steady, his lips a rigid line beneath his curling mustache. If Henry were to wager, he'd bet the man was younger than his choice of clothing and grooming made him appear.

Henry produced a smile. "In truth, I cannot wait to learn why you have come to call." He gestured toward the chair Guthrie had risen from. "Please, have a seat and enlighten me."

Guthrie sat and waited for Henry to do the same before saying, "It's about Tremaine."

Henry's interest increased several notches. "What about him?"

"I thought ye should know that I asked 'im to call on me about a week ago at me place of business. In St. Giles."

Taken aback, Henry stared at him for a moment before asking the obvious question. "Why?"

Guthrie's mustache twitched and his eyes brightened. "Turns out 'e's lookin' to settle a business transaction quickly and I figured I might be able to 'elp."

Henry leaned forward in his seat and met Guthrie's gaze directly. "What sort of business transaction?"

"The sort that involves a buildin' he 'opes to acquire—a 'ospital as a matter of fact."

Henry's insides clenched and his hand gripped the armrest. "A hospital."

"Tremaine's already lookin' fer a buyer."

Henry recalled seeing Guthrie in Mayfair a few days earlier. He must have been meeting with Robert after all. "Is that why you went to see him last week at his home? To discuss the logistics?"

"That's precisely it."

Henry's cravat felt too tight all of a sudden, his lungs constricted by his vest and his jacket, even as he struggled to maintain a calm demeanor.

A knock at the door brought a maid into the room. She set the tray she was carrying on the table between Henry and Guthrie, poured two cups of coffee and departed. The door closed with a click. Henry reached for his cup without bothering to add the milk he generally used. He took a sip and set it aside.

If Robert was already looking for buyers, it meant he was confident about the case. Far more than Henry was comfortable with.

"Why are you telling me this?"

Guthrie shrugged. "Because I believe you and I can help each other take Tremaine down."

"I beg your pardon?"

"Have another sip of yer coffee, Lowell, and try not to be so shocked."

Henry raised his eyebrows but did as Guthrie suggested. How could he not be shocked when Carlton Guthrie, the Scoundrel of St. Giles and London's most notorious crime lord, was presently suggesting a collaboration between them.

"I don't follow. What do you stand to gain?"

Guthrie sighed as if bored with the notion of having to explain. "Suffice it to say that I feel indebted to ye and yer brother. Ye took out my greatest rival last year. With Bartholomew gone, I can finally rule St. Giles in peace."

"You fancy yourself the king of sin, do you?"

"If ye like," Guthrie said with a grin. "But that's besides the point, I believe. Thing is, Tremaine's a right bastard who deserves to rot in hell fer the rest of his days, and *ye*, Mr. Lowell, can make sure that 'appens."

Astonishment was too mild a word to describe what Henry was presently feeling in response to Guthrie's words. "What are you talking about?"

"Well, 'e's a murderer, ye know. The coldest sort there is."

"What?"

Leaning back in his seat, Guthrie shifted his weight as if trying to make himself more comfortable. His face conveyed no hint of the morbid subject he'd just addressed. Instead, he looked like a man about to embark on a great adventure.

"Five years ago," Guthrie began, "I was doin' me nightly rounds of St. Giles, makin' sure all was in order an' such, when I 'eard a scream. I ran in the direction from which it came to discover a young woman lyin' in the street. She'd been stabbed, an' the man who'd done it 'ad taken off. Probably because 'e heard me comin'."

A chill swept the length of Henry's spine. He dreaded where this was going because he already knew.

"The job was sloppy, accomplished in 'aste," Guthrie

said. "The woman was still alive when I reached 'er, though barely. Before she died, she did manage to tell me 'er name, though, as well as that of the man who attacked 'er." Guthrie took a sip of his coffee and set it aside with infuriating slowness. "Olivia Jones was killed that night by Tremaine, but 'e left the country before I could figure out 'ow to bring charges against 'im."

"Because he was a duke's son and you are Carlton Guthrie. It would have been your word against his, and with a good barrister on his side, you never would have succeeded."

"Quite the contrary, I imagine."

Henry nodded. "What makes you think this information will bring him down now?"

"I don't," Guthrie said. "I'm just tryin' to explain my reason fer wantin' to 'elp ye. So if there's anythin' ye need, do let me know."

"I'll keep that in mind," Henry said, even though he had no plan of taking Guthrie up on his offer. After all, Henry was trying to save his own reputation, not make it worse by taking the risk of being associated with Carlton Guthrie. As it was, Henry could only hope that no one had seen Guthrie arrive at his home.

"Thank ye fer the coffee, Mr. Lowell." Guthrie stood and put on his hat.

Henry stood as well and followed his guest to the door. "You're most welcome. In fact, it is I who ought to be thanking you. The information you've given me this evening may prove more useful than you think."

The edge of Guthrie's mouth lifted. "I 'ope so, Lowell."

As soon as he was gone, Henry went to his office, took a seat behind his desk and pulled out a piece of crisp white paper. He then dipped his quill in the inkwell and started to write, because if what Guthrie said was true, then there was a chance Henry might be right about Beatrice Cartwright. If Robert had killed her as well, then surely there must be some evidence of it, even if it meant Henry had to post a letter to the West Indies in order to find it.

Chapter 15

The next three days went by in a blur. Viola saw nothing of Mr. Lowell during this time. But that didn't stop her from hearing about him. Not after an article he'd written appeared in the *Mayfair Chronicle* Wednesday morning announcing his intention to marry. The headline read, "London's Most Notorious Rake Reforms." The piece claimed he had every intention of being faithful to his future bride and that his youthful days of carousing were officially over.

Viola wasn't entirely sure what to make of the news. Perhaps she'd made a mistake when she'd refused his escort. Perhaps doing so had made him abandon all hope of eventually winning her. Perhaps he'd deliberately had the article published because she'd hurt him and he was now looking to find someone else to marry. Announcing his intentions to the world was certainly an effective way of hastening the process.

She spent the rest of the day regretting the way they'd last parted and hoping he might come to call. When he didn't, she sent him a note Wednesday afternoon asking him if there was any news from Mr. Steadford. He responded by note as well, informing her that the barrister had located and interviewed some of Viola's former servants and that the result was encouraging.

The missive contained no other information. No personal comment to suggest he had any interest in what she was doing. It left her feeling more alone than ever before. Because the truth was, she missed him, and she had no one besides herself to blame for the emptiness now consuming her chest.

Not knowing how to handle this unpleasant state of being, Viola busied herself with her work. One of her best physicians, Mr. Haines, proved tremendously helpful, advising her as Florian so often did about the treatment options for the newly admitted patients.

"Are you feeling all right?" Diana asked when Viola returned home Thursday evening. "You look horribly pale and there are dark circles under your eyes."

"You're clearly not getting enough rest," Harriet said. "And you're obviously working too hard as well."

"I'm fine," Viola said as she pulled off her bonnet and shucked her spencer. Both were returned to the hook on the wall were she usually kept them.

Neither woman looked convinced.

"I recommend a hot cup of tea followed by a hearty meal and a good night's sleep." Harriet was already heading toward the kitchen door. "I'll bring everything upstairs and join you in a minute."

Resigning herself to her friends' care, Viola followed Diana into the parlor, where a cozy fire burned brightly in the grate. Rex, who'd come to greet her as usual, stayed close to Viola's side. He curled up on the floor next to her feet as soon as she'd taken her seat on the sofa.

"We're worried about you," Diana said while they waited for Harriet. "You're facing too many problems alone."

"That's not really true. I have Haines helping me out at the hospital and Lowell offering assistance with Robert." Viola sank back against the sofa and offered Diana a smile. "It could be worse."

"I suppose it always can be," Diana said. She tilted her head and considered Viola. "He still hasn't come to see you, has he?"

"Who?"

Diana rolled her eyes. "Lowell, of course. Because we've seen you exhausted before Viola, but this is different. You look . . . heartbroken."

Tears burned Viola's eyes as they pressed against them. She would not cry. And yet she could already feel a wet trickle against her cheek. Swiping it away, she straightened her posture and faced her friend. "I think I've lost my chance with him."

The door opened and Harriet stepped in. She was carrying a tray containing a teapot and cups. After closing the door behind her, she took one look at Viola and paused. "Heavens. What on earth did you say to her, Diana?"

"I merely inquired about Mr. Lowell."

"Ah." Harriet placed the tray on the table and handed out cups, which she then proceeded to fill. "I suppose that explains the miserable expression you're wearing."

"I should have said yes when he offered to escort me tomorrow. I should have . . ." She wasn't sure what she should have done anymore and it didn't really matter anyway, did it? "He'll find someone else to court now."

"Maybe he will and maybe he won't," Diana said. "But I'm inclined to believe he's still attempting to win you."

Viola stared at her. "How?"

"Because of the article he wrote." Diana looked at her as if the point she was making was crystal clear.

It just wasn't to Viola. "He's obviously hoping to attract other eligible young ladies."

"Or he's trying to repair his reputation so people will know he has honorable intentions where you are concerned." Harriet sipped her tea while Viola tried to absorb this idea. "You told him yourself that you feared being seen in his company—that it might reflect poorly on you at a time when you cannot afford any negative gossip."

"Yes," Viola muttered. "Yes I did." Was it really possible that he'd done this for her? "But if this is his reasoning, why not come to see me? Why stay away?"

"We could ask the same of you," Diana said. "A relationship is not a one-sided endeavor, and since you did deny him the pleasure of his escort, he might be sitting at home just as you are right now, hoping you'll change your mind."

"I can't do that," Viola said even as she wished she could. "It would give him the wrong impression. He'd think I'm willing to be his wife."

"Aren't you?"

The question, posed by Harriet, resulted in a long moment of silence during which Viola reflected on her life, the dream she'd had as a little girl of marrying for love and living happily ever after, and the reality she'd been dealt instead.

"I don't know, but I do have to be completely sure before I allow him to think that I might be." She looked at her friends. "Few women achieve independence. Most are subject to their husband's wills. I'm not sure I want that for myself."

"It's certainly a big decision and one you shouldn't make lightly," Diana told her. "But while you think on it, I suggest Harriet and I try to cheer you up. After all, there is a party for you to attend tomorrow evening. Are you still nervous about it?"

"A little, but only because I want it to be a success."

"At least Florian's family will be there to support you," Harriet said. "As long as you stay by their side no one will dare say a word against you."

"Right now I think most of the people attending are simply looking to catch a glimpse of the infamous duchess," Viola said. She'd used their curiosity to lure them, and although she loathed the idea of socializing with people who'd gossiped about her over the years, she needed to secure them as her clients. And who knew, perhaps when she met them all in person, they'd see what Lowell and Florian and her other friends saw—that she wasn't the scheming social climber they thought her to be.

"I say we give them something to remember, then," Harriet said. She smiled broadly. "After you've eaten, you'll try on the gown you ordered."

It was a beautiful creation fashioned from emerald green silk. Viola had hung it on her wardrobe door so she could look at it every time she entered her bedchamber.

"And tomorrow we'll style your hair," Diana added. "When you arrive at the rejuvenation center in the evening, heads will turn and every gentleman present will flock to your side, including Mr. Lowell."

Liking the idea of drawing his attention, Viola smiled. She did not care if anyone else found her pretty or remotely attractive, but she wanted him to. Even though she wasn't sure if they'd share a future together, it mattered to her that he, the most wonderful man she'd ever known, wanted her.

Chapter 16

Viola had not intended to be late to her own party, but she'd never been to a ball before, or any other social functions for that matter. As a result, it had taken a great deal longer than she'd expected to get ready. Her hair alone had taken an hour, shaping it and pinning it in just the right places. What Diana and Harriet had accomplished was almost magical. They'd added volume where none had existed before and framed her face with the softest curls.

When Viola had finally looked at herself in the cheval glass after donning her gown, she'd been surprised. Not only because her friends had lowered the bodice enough to reveal the tops of her breasts, or because they'd trimmed the edge of her décolletage with shimmering beads intended to draw attention, but because, for the very first time, she looked both wealthy and fashionable, like the duchess she was supposed to be.

"Perfect," Diana murmured beside her. Harriet nodded, and the two women escorted Viola downstairs, where a hired carriage awaited.

"We hope you have a wonderful evening," Harriet told her, and gave her a hug.

Diana helped her into the carriage. "Good luck." She closed the door and the carriage took off at an even pace. The rejuvenation center wasn't too far and Viola arrived there within ten minutes.

Taking a deep breath, Viola opened the carriage door and stepped down onto the pavement, where she was instantly greeted by Coventry and Huntley who both appeared as if out of nowhere.

"We were watching for you," Huntley said with a smile and a look in his eyes that conveyed a great deal of surprise. "May I say you look absolutely stunning, Your Grace."

"A diamond of the first water," Coventry added. He offered his arm. "Our wives insisted we escort you inside."

"Thank you." Viola placed her hand on Coventry's arm and allowed him to guide her toward the front door.

They arrived in the foyer, and Florian's manservant, Mr. Dunhurst, was there, his voice loudly announcing her arrival. Silence settled, curious stares followed and then came the whispers, whirling around her like autumn leaves rustling in the wind.

Viola straightened her spine. "Thank you for coming," she said, as loudly as she could manage. "I hope you enjoy your evening." Unable to stop herself, she searched the room for the only person whose presence truly mattered. He was standing some distance away, his gaze sharp with interest and something else she could not define.

Pleasure flooded her insides as Viola acknowledged the effect she was having on Mr. Lowell. Until a subtle movement at his side caught her notice and she became aware of the woman who clung to his arm. She was young, with hair spun from copper and gold. Her lips were a bright shade of pink, her eyes a dazzling blue. Incredibly stunning, she rose up onto her toes and whispered something in Mr. Lowell's ear.

He immediately smiled in response, and the pleasure Viola had felt seconds earlier turned to ice. This was not how her evening was meant to proceed. Mr. Lowell was supposed to come greet her, flirt with her and make her blush in that way she'd come to crave. Instead he was with someone else—a debutante, she presumed, who'd be more than willing to accept any offer of marriage he made.

Viola took a shaky breath. It was too late. She'd been too indecisive, too unwelcoming of Mr. Lowell's advances, and now he'd moved on to someone else.

"Viola." She heard Gabriella before she saw her. The duchess slipped past a couple of men, bringing Amelia with her. "Oh my goodness. It's quite the crush already and I don't believe all the guests have arrived yet."

Relieved with the distraction her friends offered, Viola smiled in greeting. "I must say I'm impressed with the turnout." She cast a fleeting glance in Mr. Lowell's direction and saw he was starting to come toward them. Having to greet him right now, to have him introduce her to whoever the young woman was and possibly declare her his fiancée, would be much too difficult. "Perhaps we ought to move into the next room so we're not blocking the entrance."

Agreeing with her, they proceeded toward an arched doorway on the right, pausing occasionally so Viola could greet people individually and exchange a few words. To her relief, everyone was polite and eager to compliment the center. Not a single word of censure was spoken.

"You have truly outdone yourself, Viola," Amelia said when she saw how the lounge area had been decorated with divans upholstered in mauve damask silk.

The rich color was further accentuated by matching veil curtains adorning a series of windows set in an ochre-colored wall.

"Just look at the detail on that mirror over there," Gabriella said. "And that counter you've placed beneath it is simply fantastic. An incredible piece of craftsmanship."

"I'm still not entirely sure what purpose it ought to serve," Viola said. "Florian found it in the attic of Redding House after his uncle died. He suggested we use it here because of the intricate floral carvings."

"It's most unusual," Huntley said. "I've never seen anything like it."

"Looks like a display shelf," Coventry supplied, "except longer and wider."

"You could use it for that," Gabriella said. Her eyes seemed to brighten with renewed excitement. "You could place little boxes or baskets filled with soaps, lotions and perfumes on it. By offering the same products your employees use on the clients for sale, you might add some extra income."

Viola stared at the duchess. "That's a marvelous suggestion." A thought began taking shape in her head. She considered it a moment before saying, "Since this center was your idea to begin with and keeping in mind how good you are at coming up with ways in which to improve it, I wonder if you would like to be more involved with the day-to-day running."

Gabriella beamed. "I should like that a great deal, Viola." She looked up at Huntley. "If you agree."

Her husband placed his arm around her waist and quietly murmured, "If it makes you happy, my love, I agree wholeheartedly."

Ignoring the swift pang of envy piercing her heart, Viola addressed the practical issues of such an arrangement. "Your time would have to be donated."

"But of course! I would not dream of demanding compensation, Viola. Not when I do not need it and certainly not when I know the income is meant for St. Agatha's," Gabriella said at the exact same moment Mr. Lowell appeared.

Viola's heart began thumping more loudly. A series of hot little embers proceeded to dance across her skin as he took her in. When he reached for her hand and raised it to his lips, her body began to tremble with a need for added closeness, the likes of which she'd never experienced before.

"Mesmerizing," he murmured, his voice brushing her knuckles the second before his lips touched her gloved skin.

Sparks shot up her arm and across her shoulders before diving straight down her middle. Viola's bodice tightened and continued to do so as Mr. Lowell's gaze dropped to the swell of her breasts. He dropped her hand and straightened his posture, and for several seconds Viola could not recall why she'd tried to avoid him earlier.

Ah yes. The diamond of the first water.

The reminder cooled her response to him most effectively. She raised her chin and met his gaze boldly. "Good evening, Mr. Lowell. I wasn't aware you'd arrived yet."

He gave her an odd look before giving his attention to the rest of the group. "Have you tried the salmon bites with dill yet? They're incredibly delicious."

"I don't think I've ever experienced such tiny meals before," Coventry said. "It's most ingenious really, since one can eat while continuing to stand about chatting."

"A necessity since I lack the space for a supper room large enough to accommodate everyone," Viola said. "When I met with Florian's chef to discuss our options, he said he'd craft tiny portions that could be consumed without the need for cutlery."

"I believe he's French," Mr. Lowell said. "They're renowned for their innovative cuisine, are they not?"

"I really have no idea," Viola remarked.

Mr. Lowell's gaze deepened. "Please excuse us," he said without taking his eyes off hers. And then, to her shock and dismay, he grabbed her hand and drew her away from her friends without saying another word.

"What are you doing?" she asked.

"Spiriting you away." He pulled her along at a purposeful stride, through a doorway, down a corridor and into a vacant room. Shutting the door, he turned to her, and expelled a series of heavy breaths.

Viola's stomach started to twist itself into several knots when she saw the look in his eyes: stormy, desperate, half mad with need. He looked like a man who'd been starved for a month and was in dire need of finding a meal. It was unlike anything she'd ever witnessed before, and she wasn't entirely sure how to respond. So she just stood there saying nothing and waited for him to explain.

He stared back at her in silence, until she thought he might not say a word. But then he raked his fingers through his hair, disturbing the neatly combed locks and causing a few to spill over his brow. He started to pace while muttering something she could not hear. Pausing, he seemed to consider what to do next before taking a step toward her. His jaw was tight, his eyes holding her captive with deep intensity.

"Viola." Her name was hoarsely spoken. It drifted between them like a prayer and a promise. His fingers touched her hand, slowly as if to test her reaction. When she failed to pull away, they wove between hers, binding them together.

"What are you doing?" Her voice wasn't nearly as strong as she'd hoped. It matched her weak knees and the butterflies soaring about in her belly.

"Trying to understand." His throat worked with rough little movements. "You saw me when you arrived, Viola, but rather than come to greet me, you turned away and then pretended not to know I was here."

"I believed you were fully occupied." In spite of her effort to sound nonchalant, hardness curled around each word.

Realization flashed in his eyes and the agitated expression he'd been wearing since entering this room was replaced by profound interest. He took a step closer—so close she could feel the warmth of his body against her own.

"You saw me with the Earl of Hedgewick's daughter, Lady Regina, and imagined the worst." A smile pulled at the edge of his mouth and his eyes suddenly brightened. "You're jealous."

"I most certainly am not."

Mr. Lowell, damn him, grinned. "You absolutely are. It's evident the way your eyes narrowed when I mentioned her name."

Deciding she did not have time for this, what with guests to attend to, Viola took a step back, intent on pulling away and adding some distance between them before quitting his company. But the moment she tugged on her hand, he tightened his hold and pulled her flush up against him.

A whoosh of air escaped her lungs when her softness made contact with his solid chest. Instinctively, her free hand rose to clasp at his shoulder in a desperate attempt to steady herself. A brief moment of surprise followed until she managed to come to terms with what had happened and the fact that she now found herself embraced by a strong wall of muscle.

God help her.

Somehow in the midst of it all, he'd released her hand and wound both arms around her, encasing her in his warmth and infusing her with his scent. Viola dared not move. Least of all when she felt the press of his palm against the small of her back. It slid slightly lower, and to her dismay she found that she did not want it to stop. Rather, she longed for him to explore her more fully, to touch her in ways she'd not wanted to be touched in years.

"I want to make something abundantly clear," he murmured close to her ear while his other hand traced a lazy path along the length of her spine. "You are the only woman I want, Viola. There is no other, no reason for you to worry I might have lost interest, for I can assure you that interest in you is the last thing I'm lacking."

She wanted to believe him. "How do I know you're not toying with me?"

He leaned back, and when he met her gaze, his expression was grave. "Because you've gotten to know me." The words were spoken honestly, without any hint of pretense. "Search your heart, Viola, and ask yourself if you trust me."

She didn't need long to consider. "I trust you completely." The realization steadied her soul and quieted the riotous emotions she'd experienced earlier.

His nostrils flared. "Since announcing my intention to wed, I've been visited by numerous parents hoping to secure a match for their daughters. Lord Hedgewick is no different. He insisted I keep Lady Regina company while he went to converse with a friend. As transparent as it was, I could hardly abandon the poor woman. She's only recently made her debut."

"How anyone ever believed you to be a scoundrel is unfathomable."

"You did."

"That was before I got to know you."

"And now that you have?"

She paused as if caught at the edge of a precipice. "I don't know. I think I need time to untangle my emotions and figure out what I truly want."

He was quiet for a moment and then he nodded. "Take as long as you need, Viola. I'll wait."

She swallowed, a little undone by his understanding. "I probably ought to get back to my guests."

"Very well." He pressed his lips to her forehead and kissed her fondly. As if he had not just toppled the last of her barriers. He squeezed her shoulder, released her and added distance. The edge of his mouth lifted and he was suddenly smiling. "You are right. There's a party for us to attend, and if you are not otherwise engaged, I would like to invite you to dance with me, Duchess." He winked and Viola laughed, unsure of how he managed to ease her concerns with such seemingly little effort.

"I would love that," she said, a little surprised by how drastically her opinion of him had been changed in recent weeks and by how *she* had changed from a woman intent on avoiding his company to one who longed to share it.

Perhaps it was because he did not push her or make demands or take her for granted. Instead he listened, inquired about her interests and shared his own with her. He offered help and support when they were needed without asking for anything in return, even after she'd said they could never be more than friends.

Enjoying the familiar feel of his arm against hers as he guided her back to the party, she decided that never was a really long time. Especially since she was already half in love with the rogue who'd revealed himself to be quite the gentleman.

Chapter 17

With Viola's arm tucked snugly against his side, Henry escorted her through the crowd and directly toward the musicians. For the purpose of the evening's event, a salon adjoining the foyer had been allocated for dancing.

"I would like to request a waltz," he said, addressing one of the violinists when the previous set ended.

Viola sucked in a breath and he turned to her with a smile, loving the shade of pink now blanketing her cheeks. His chest tightened with the awareness of how things had changed between them in the last half hour. Or perhaps they'd been gradually changing all along? Whatever the case, the important thing was they'd been honest with each other. Wasn't that the most solid foundation for a lasting relationship? Truth and communication?

The next tune started and he pushed this thought to the back of his mind while leading Viola onto the dance floor. It was time for him to show off the Duchess of Tremaine and for the world to see how incredible she was.

"Nervous?" he asked.

She gave him a wary look. "I do not know how to waltz."

He smiled to offer reassurance. "Don't worry. It is fairly simple and I know the steps so you will be perfectly fine. Allow me to guide you."

Uncertainty creased her brow, but whereas a less courageous woman would have made an excuse and retreated, Viola stayed, determined to prove her worth to Society.

All Henry could do was stare at her while his heart expanded with pride. She was brave and smart and utterly magnificent. And when she placed her hand in his and his palm settled firmly against her lower back, he felt like a prince upon whom the sun had decided to shine.

"I'm going to step forward in a second," he told her gently, "and you will step back. With your right foot."

She nodded, and then the musical prelude settled into a steady rhythm that compelled them to move. Keeping time with the beat, Henry guided Viola smoothly around the dance floor. Concentration was apparent in the sharpness of her eyes, but she caught on quickly and, to his surprise, avoided stepping on his toes.

"You see," he told her when they'd made two rotations of the dance floor. "It is not so difficult. Now try to relax a bit more. Your shoulders are very tense."

"I am trying, but it is easier said than done."

"Perhaps this will help?" He whirled her around and she suddenly laughed, the sound so pleasing he wished he could capture it in a box and listen to it whenever he wished.

A hint of mischief touched her lips. "You are very good at this, Mr. Lowell, and I have to confess, it is a lot of fun."

"Will you not call me Henry?" It was, he realized, his most fervent wish at this point, more urgent than that of kissing her, though that was without a doubt a close second.

Her smile stayed on her lips, her eyes locked with his. "Very well."

His breath caught and held. He pressed his fingertips into her back and savored the gasp that blew past her lips. He dipped his gaze, admiring the perfect shape of that dark pink flesh. "I need to hear you say it, Viola." He knew he was probably pushing his luck, but it couldn't be helped. He was even willing to beg. "Please."

Her tongue swept over her lower lip, moistening it. And then she spoke with soft deliberation. "Henry."

A shudder rolled through him, tightening his muscles and heating his skin with unparalleled need. *Christ!* He was going to play this marvelous moment over in his head later on when he got back home and climbed into bed. How many times had he imagined this? More than he could count, and yet reality was so much better.

"Thank you," he murmured, because he knew he had to say something before she discovered how ready he was to carry her out to the nearest carriage and take her somewhere—anywhere, really—where he could show her how desperate she made him.

A blush rose to her cheeks and he wondered if she knew what he was thinking—the effect she had on him and if . . . if perhaps she might be more willing to consider such a path now than she had been before. He dared not ask. It was much too early for that, but having her say his name was a start.

"Would you like some champagne?" he asked when the dance was over and he guided her back toward the foyer. He was not unaware of the interest with which most of those present watched them, nor was he surprised. After all, he had the most beautiful woman in the world on his arm.

"Yes please," she said, and he instantly flagged down a man with a tray full of glasses. Grabbing two, he handed one to her and took the other.

"Henry!"

Turning toward the familiar voice, he found his grandparents coming toward them. "I thought I saw you earlier," his grandmother said, "but then you disappeared and . . ." Her gaze went to Viola. "Will you introduce us?"

"Of course." He moved a little to one side and said, "Viola Cartwright, Duchess of Tremaine, I would like for you to meet my grandparents, the Earl and Countess of Scranton."

"A pleasure to make your acquaintances," Viola said.

"Indeed, the pleasure is entirely ours," Lord Scranton told her. "We've been admiring this new rejuvenation center of yours and are both quite eager to acquire memberships to it. As are many of our friends. I have to say, what you have created here is truly impressive. Takes me back to my visit to Turkey."

"Oh!" Viola's eyes glowed. "Ottoman and Arabic design have been my inspiration, though I must confess I have only ever seen it illustrated in books."

"Well, you have recreated the atmosphere perfectly," Lord Scranton said.

Viola beamed. "Thank you." She glanced at Henry. "Your grandson was actually tremendously helpful with that. He showed me the market in Woolwich where some of the pieces I used to decorate the center were purchased."

"I love that place," Lady Scranton said. "One can find the most surprising things there."

"So I've been told," Viola said with a knowing smile directed at Henry.

His chest expanded with pure adoration. When he glanced at his grandmother, he saw that she'd noticed, because a flicker of amusement danced in the old woman's eyes. She turned to Viola. "Would you like to take a turn of the room with me? I find the need to exercise my legs."

"Brilliant idea," Lord Scranton said. "I have a few things I need to discuss with my grandson, and my wife is eager to see some of the other rooms. Perhaps you'd be kind enough to show them to her, Your Grace?"

"I would be delighted," Viola said. She looked at Henry, her eyes fully focused on him and nothing else. "I will see you a little bit later." And then she was walking away with his grandmother, and Henry had to force his feet to remain where they were.

"She's different from how I imagined," his grandfather said with a thoughtful touch to his voice.

Henry turned to face him. "How so?"

"Well . . . with all the gossip about her when she married Tremaine, I expected a cold and calculating sort of woman, but she doesn't strike me as such at all."

"She's anything but," Henry said. "And people ought to realize that, considering she founded a hospital that doesn't charge patients for care and the fact that she has always kept to herself. She certainly didn't marry to improve her status or she would have been out in Society more."

Scranton sipped his champagne. "I agree." He paused as if muddling something over. "She doesn't really look the part either, does she?"

Henry stiffened. "What do you mean?"

"Considering the other duchesses we know, like

Huntley's and Coventry's wives, who are strikingly beautiful, the Duchess of Tremaine fades into the background a bit. I mean, she's plainer than one would expect when considering her impressive title."

Shoulders straight and posture stiff, Henry stared at Scranton while trying to decrease the pressure now building inside his head. He glanced across the room to where his parents were chatting with a group of friends and briefly considered excusing himself to go join them. "Viola is the most beautiful woman here." It was so obvious to him he could not understand how anyone else might feel differently.

Scranton's eyebrows rose. "I meant no offense, my boy. It was just an observation."

"Well, in future, you will refrain from saying such things in my presence since it is completely untrue."

"Your defensiveness is most intriguing." Scranton took another sip of his drink. "I daresay I've never seen you defend a woman so passionately before. Not once."

Henry's chest rose and fell with the effort it took to draw breath. The comment had agitated him beyond reason and it had provoked him into showing his hand. "She matters to me."

"Duly noted." A glimmer of amusement filled Scranton's eyes before sliding into the background. "Word has it Tremaine is trying to stir up trouble for her. Considering your brother's association with the lady as well as your own newly established . . . friendship with her, I presume you're offering assistance?"

Henry stared at Scranton. The old man was as sharp as a wasp's stinger. "Of course." He narrowed his gaze. "How did you hear of it?"

"You know how it is. People see things. They talk. Nothing was certain until you just confirmed it." Scranton took a sip of his drink. His mouth moved as

if delighting in the champagne's flavor before returning to a more serious line. "As your grandfather, I feel
compelled to warn you."

"Really?"

"Taking on a duke is no laughing matter, Henry."
Realizing he'd spoken too loud, Scranton glanced
around before lowering his voice. "All he needs to do
is make a compelling argument in his favor and discredit a woman Society's already suspicious of. Tell
me, who's his barrister?"

Henry stuck his free hand in his pocket while
taking a fortifying swallow of his own drink. "Mr.
Hayes."

"Good God, that man never loses!"

"I'm aware, but the duchess has Steadford on her
side."

Scranton did not look remotely appeased. "If I
may offer a piece of advice, find something damning
on Tremaine. Quickly. And use it against him before
he has a chance to launch his own attack."

"I'm already working on it. No need to worry."

"Easy for you to say. I'm your grandfather and
the head of this family, of course I'm going to be
concerned about the possibility of having our name
dragged through the mud." He shook his head. "I
thought you and Tremaine used to be friends. Didn't
you know each other as boys?"

"That's a long time ago and a lot has happened
since," Henry told him gravely.

Scranton eyed him with the knowledge of a man
who did not need to inquire further. "Very well then.
I just hope she's worth it."

Henry smiled in spite of the worry he harbored
over not acquiring the evidence he needed to take
Tremaine down. "Indeed, I can assure you that she
most definitely is."

"**W**ould you think me too forward if I inquired about your circumstances, dear?" Lady Scranton asked.

Viola almost tripped in response to that question. "Um . . ."

"I've been curious about you ever since Florian first mentioned going to work in a woman's employ. It is most unusual, but at the same time intriguing. Your independence and accomplishments ought to serve as an inspiration to young women everywhere."

"Thank you, my lady."

"Oh, you might want to wait with that until I have finished prying." A mischievous smile pulled at the old woman's lips, and Viola could not help but respond with laughter. "It must have been terribly difficult for you, proving yourself to the men on whom you are forced to rely in order to run the hospital."

"Florian was tremendously helpful in that regard," Viola admitted as she thought back on the various committee members, physicians and surgeons who'd quit the moment they'd realized the ultimate person in charge was a woman only nineteen years of age. "Had it not been for the respect he has earned among his peers, I never would have gotten anywhere. Florian was the one who managed to convince the current staff to remain in my employ."

Lady Scranton stared at Viola with wide eyes. "This was just two years ago, was it not?"

"Indeed it was."

"So then, it is fair to deduce that you are currently one-and-twenty?"

Viola's lips quirked with amusement. "That is correct."

The countess shook her head as if trying to dislodge an obstruction in her brain. "Frankly, I do not know how you've managed, but I do commend you for it." She eyed her briefly before deciding to say, "You're still so young, though, and with the hospital running smoothly now, you could set your mind to other things."

"Like what?" Viola felt compelled to ask.

The lady tilted her head in quiet contemplation. "Have you not considered remarrying?"

Shaking off the discomfort the question instilled in her, Viola shook her head. They'd entered the bathing room, where a long mosaic-tiled pool awaited the first clients. "No, my lady. I have my independence now, the freedom to do as I please with my time and money without being subject to any man's will. Why on earth would I give that up?"

Lady Scranton took a deep breath. "When I married my husband, it was not out of need. I was an heiress with sufficient funds to enjoy a comfortable life without having to fall on any man's good graces. But, then I met Scranton and I fell in love."

"I suppose love would be a compelling reason for a woman to relinquish her independence if the sentiment were returned."

"Well yes, I suppose it would, but it was more than that for me. You see, I can think of no other person with whom I would rather spend each passing moment of every day. He is my fondest companion, the one person who knows me better than anyone else and with whom I have always felt truly at ease." Her eyes lit up like candles ignited at dusk. "There are many who find him too stern, but when we are alone together, there is laughter and banter. In my experience it is comforting to share life's moments with someone who truly understands and appreciates you for the person you are, no matter your flaws."

"The problem is, there is too much at stake," Viola murmured.

"You fear getting hurt." It was a quiet observation. Lady Scranton met Viola's gaze directly. "The thing about fear, however, is that it can only be defeated if you face it head-on, which is something I suspect you must be accustomed to doing by now. You cannot tell me you weren't afraid when your husband died and you set out to conquer the world of medicine all on your own?"

Viola blinked. "Of course I was, but love and marriage are different. They're . . ." *So much more terrifying.*

Lady Scranton made no attempt to fill in the rest of Viola's sentence when Viola failed to complete it.

Instead, she proceeded to walk the length of the pool. After going a few paces she glanced back at Viola and said, "Lowell is fortunate to know you."

The comment, following right on the heels of their discussion of marriage and love, caught Viola slightly off guard. It took her a moment to find her bearings enough to convey a truthful response. "Indeed, I feel it might be the other way around."

"Hmm." Lady Scranton reached the end of the pool and started walking back toward Viola. "He is a good boy, always has been in spite of all the rumors. Never put an ounce of weight in them myself, but Society thrives on gossip and chose him as a ready mark." She rolled her eyes. "Such is the world in which we live, as unfortunate as it may be. But there are benefits to our way of life as well, like not having to struggle in order to survive."

"I suppose that is true."

"Did he ever tell you how naughty he was as a child?"

Viola shook her head, her interest piquing. "No, but I am now hoping you will."

Lady Scranton grinned. "I would be delighted." She walked a few more steps until she'd returned to the spot where Viola waited. "He used to put jam in his brother's pockets, salt in the sugar bowl and grease on the door handles." She chuckled. "I once found a frog in the drawer of my escritoire. Jumped right out and into my lap when I opened it—almost stopped my heart!"

Viola grinned while imagining Henry's younger self running about causing trouble and smiling that mischievous smile of his when his subjects fell prey to his pranks. "I wish I could have seen that."

"Oh, it's more delightful to hear of it after the fact than to have actually been there when it happened." Lady Scranton's eyes shone with amusement. Affectionately, she added, "He was always such a happy child, full of laughter and joy. The man is a little more serious, which I suppose is to be expected, but at heart he is still the rascal he's always been, trying to have some fun." She eyed Viola. "My fondest wish is for him to meet the right woman with whom he can have that, the sort of woman who will be his friend, his confidante, his partner in all things that matter."

Unsure of how to respond, Viola turned and walked slowly toward the door of the room, waiting for Lady Scranton to fall into step beside her. "He is very lucky to have a grandmother who cares so much about him," she finally said while a series of strange sensations swirled through her body.

"And he is lucky to have you," the countess said. "Now, let us return to him and my husband before they come looking for us. I am sure Henry's already itching to find you considering how reluctant he was to let you leave his side. And before you protest, it was etched all over his face." She cleared her throat. "He is fond of you, Duchess. No doubt about that."

It was impossible for Viola to quiet her racing heart and her jangling nerves and the messy state her mind was in after having Henry's grandmother suggest she and Henry should marry. As they entered the foyer together, she drew a deep breath.

Two weeks ago when she and Henry had met for the very first time, she'd wanted nothing to do with him besides nursing him back to health. Then somehow, little by little, she'd ended up spending increasing amounts of time in his company and now, tonight, when he'd held her in his arms, her heart had felt as though it was blooming for the very first time, like a dormant bud bursting through the late winter snow to unfurl its delicate petals.

With a smile that weakened her knees and a gaze that seared her soul, accompanied by vast amounts of patience and understanding, he'd dismantled the wall surrounding her heart and become the person she longed for the most, missed the most and needed the most.

But marriage?

It terrified the hell out of her considering how fresh these feelings for him were. And it wasn't quite love. Not yet. But it would be soon, she believed, and that made her even more scared, because what if he didn't feel the same about her? She'd risked her heart once with detrimental results. What if that happened again?

It was a question that would have to wait to be answered, because as she and Lady Scranton approached Henry and his grandfather, Viola saw that Robert had joined them and that all three men's expressions were strained. Instinct urged Viola to turn around and run in the opposite direction. Instead she did what she'd done countless times before. She straightened her spine and squared her shoulders and allowed her feet to carry her forward.

"Your Grace," she said as soon as she reached Henry's side and could take some comfort in his closeness. "I did not expect to see you here this evening, since you were not invited."

"An oversight, I presume," Robert said with a smirk. He gave his attention to Lady Scranton and offered a half bow. "My lady."

Lady Scranton gave a swift nod of acknowledgment along with a clipped "Your Grace," before asking her husband to walk her into the dance room. The pair departed, leaving Henry and Viola alone with Robert.

"Why are you here?" Henry demanded.

Robert snatched up a glass of champagne from a passing tray and set it to his lips. "I've an interest," he said when he'd finished drinking. "A man ought to know what he stands to gain."

Every muscle in Viola's arms and shoulders expanded with a fierce urge to strike the smug look off his face. "You forget that this business is not mine alone. The Duke of Redding owns more than half since he made the larger investment."

Robert raised an eyebrow and for a brief second, it looked as though he was going to agree with her assessment on this and leave the rejuvenation center alone. But then he said, "In that case, I shall look forward to going into business with him."

Blood rushed to Viola's head, drowning out sound as her vision blurred and her limbs grew weak. Her hand reached for something firm to hold on to and she was grateful to find Henry's arm coming to her aid.

He steadied her quickly, ignoring Robert for a moment in order to ask if she was all right.

Robert snorted. "She is perfectly fine, Lowell. I

never saw a finer actress than her. Can't you see that it's all a show?"

"You ought to leave," Henry bit out.

"What I ought is—"

His words were cut off by the arrival of Gabriella and Amelia. They greeted Robert with the same degree of enthusiasm they might show a snake before offering to take Viola to the salon for some refreshment.

"You should go with them," Henry told her.

"This is my event," Viola said, rallying enough to stand her ground and show them her strength. "Ensuring it runs smoothly is my responsibility. I cannot allow you to handle all of my problems on my behalf, no matter how much I appreciate the offer."

"A problem?" Robert muttered. "You haven't seen half of it yet."

Viola ignored him and focused on Henry instead. Her head had started to hurt and in all honesty, she really wanted to turn her back on this discussion and let someone else deal with it for her, but that would only prove she was weak, in need of saving, a damsel in distress—the exact opposite of what she wanted to be.

Henry leaned in closer to her so he could whisper, "Robert is unpredictable. He may cause a scene, and if that happens, I think if would be wise of you to be as far away from it as possible, Viola. That does not mean you're running away or leaving me to fight your battles for you, it simply means you're being wise in protecting your own interests."

Even as anger raced through her, his words brushed over her skin with soothing strokes. He made her want so much she hardly knew where to begin with her list. "Very well," she agreed. "I will do as you suggest."

He inhaled deeply, and it occurred to Viola that her acquiescence in this matter signified more than she had expected it to. It suggested a partnership built on respect and trust and a shared understanding of mutual goals.

"Thank you," he murmured, the steely gaze he'd been giving Robert pushed aside to reflect his fondness for her.

Speechless, she nodded and allowed Gabriella and Viola to lead her away.

"Coward," she heard Robert shout in her wake.

"Don't listen to him," Gabriella said. "You're the bravest woman there is."

"And he knows fighting you won't be easy," Amelia added. "Least of all when you have Mr. Lowell by your side."

Viola knew there was truth to be found in those words. Without Henry, she wasn't sure what she'd have done. He didn't so much give her the strength she needed as show her how to use what she already had in her possession. His belief in her was undeniable and perhaps the most significant part of their relationship. He allowed her to be who she was and encouraged her to do so wholeheartedly. If anything would ever convince her to marry him, then that was it.

"Apologize," Henry growled while staring Robert down. Fury curled around every tendon, honing his muscles in preparation for battle. To hide it all beneath a calm exterior while Viola was present had been difficult, but now that she was gone, he felt no compulsion to pretend he would not savor punching Robert in the face.

"For what?" Robert asked as if he'd been dealt a great injustice.

"For showing up here uninvited, for ruining an otherwise pleasant evening and for calling the duchess a coward when you know damn well she's anything but."

"Devil take you, Lowell," Robert sneered. His posture turned rigid as if he too were preparing to fight. "You've let a woman, a charlatan of the first order, outfox you."

"Take that back right now or so help me God—"

"She's using you to her advantage. Don't you see?" Robert's eyes glinted like a raven's honing in on a piece of silver. "You and I were friends, so what better way to fight me than to get you on her side?"

"It's not like that."

"Isn't it?" They stared at each other for a long, drawn-out moment before Robert leaned back with a chuckle. "I pity you, Lowell. You're in love with a fucking whore!"

How Henry managed to stop his fist from making contact with Robert's face was something he would wonder over at great length later. What he did instead was grab the bastard by the arm and march him out of the building and away from anyone who might overhear the following words.

Chapter 18

"I see no other recourse than to meet with you to-morrow morning at dawn," Henry said.

"You're willing to risk your life for her?"

Henry refused to dignify his question with an answer. "Pick your weapon, *sir*."

Robert's face twisted with undeniable malice. "Pistols. So I can shoot you in the head!"

"Excellent choice," Henry murmured. "Best go find your second."

Robert glared at him for a long moment while the need to strike thickened between them. Henry bolstered himself in preparation for an attack while Robert's breaths came in small puffs. Eventually, he spun on his heel and walked away into the darkness.

"Six o'clock at Hackney Meadows. I'll bring the physician," Henry called after him.

He would also need a second, he realized, which meant he would have to speak to Yates. Returning inside, he went in search of the earl, whom he found lounging on one of the divans in the dance room. He was keeping company with Miss Harlow, who was presently laughing at something Yates was saying.

"I need to discuss something with you." Henry

cast a deliberate glance at Yates's companion and waited for the earl to excuse himself from her company and join Henry in a more private corner of the room. "Something's come up. An urgent matter with which I require your help."

Yates frowned. "You have my full attention, though I hope it is nothing too serious."

Henry drew a deep breath. "I've just called Tremaine out."

Yates's eyebrows lifted. "That is . . ." He stared at Henry. "Are you sure that is wise?"

"It is necessary."

"Will you tell me what he did?"

"He insulted the Duchess of Tremaine in the most despicable way."

Yates quietly nodded. "You fight to protect her honor."

Henry nodded. "She has become a close friend. I cannot let Robert speak ill of her."

"And if he apologizes?"

"He won't, but even if he did, I would not accept."

"Very well then," Yates said. "Just give me the hour and the location and I will be there to offer support."

"I appreciate that."

Henry shook his hand to confirm the deal before going in search of Viola. She would not understand or accept his decision. If anything, she would try to stop him, which meant that as far as this matter was concerned, she would have to be kept in the dark. And that meant he could not depart the party in haste or it would raise suspicion. He would stay until it was over, then stop by his club to update his will. He didn't expect to die tomorrow, but one had to prepare for the worst when meeting an adversary on the field of honor.

It was almost midnight by the time Viola arrived home. She let herself in quietly so as not to wake Diana or Harriet. Crossing to the small table in the foyer where an oil lamp had been left to provide a faint glow of light, she saw that a letter awaited.

Removing her gloves, she went to collect her spectacles from her study. Perching them on the bridge of her nose, she tore open the seal and read the letter with an increasing mixture of pure annoyance and dread.

> Dear Viola,
> I have been asked to attend an unexpected event tomorrow morning at Hackney Meadows. From what I gather, the preservation of your reputation is at stake, though I know little else. Mr. Lowell was rather vague when he asked for my assistance, but I do believe the location and the need for a physician says it all.
> Please know that I am betraying his trust by telling you this, but as you are my employer and friend, my loyalty in this particular instance is with you.
>
> Your humble servant,
> Mr. Tyler Haines

Clutching the letter so hard her nails drove into the palms of her hands, Viola stood as if frozen while trying to calm her nerves. It was a duel. It had to be, considering the part about preserving her reputation. And with Henry involved, she knew it had to be between him and Robert. He'd called Robert out without telling her!

To be sure, she read the letter again. There could be no misunderstanding. A duel was clearly in the making, and with rash-tempered men involved, she knew the only chance of stopping it was if she interfered. So she hurried back out to the foyer, snatched up her gloves and reticule, and exited her house. In the street, she hailed a hackney and directed it toward The Red Rose, hoping to God that Henry would be there, because calling on him at his home at this hour was out of the question.

She arrived at her destination ten minutes later, paid the driver and entered the club.

"Your Grace! What a wonderful surprise!"

She immediately recognized Henry's steward, Mr. Faulkner, and attempted a smile. It felt tight. "I came to see Mr. Lowell. Is he here by any chance?" she asked, getting straight to the point.

"He is in his office. I'll let him know you wish to see him." He departed down a corridor and was back again moments later. "Please come with me," he said, gesturing for her to follow.

She did, her gown swooshing around her feet as she walked. The door to Henry's office was opened by Mr. Faulkner, and Viola stepped in, her gaze landing on the man who made her heart race with wild abandon and her knees feel like wobbly jelly. The edge of his mouth lifted as he took her in, his eyes fixed on her person as if he could see every inch of the skin that lay hidden beneath her silk dress.

"That will be all, Mr. Faulkner," Henry murmured. He stood, not looking away from Viola for even one second.

"Very well."

She heard Mr. Faulkner's departing footsteps, and although her brain was telling her to move to the nearest chair, she remained where she was, utterly frozen. Because the force of Henry's gaze on her sent fiery embers racing along every limb. To her dismay, they instilled in her a sudden need to be touched.

Swallowing, she did her best to hide the effect beneath what she hoped was a blank expression. But when he grinned, she wasn't so sure she'd succeeded.

"You really do look incredible in that dress," he said, his voice a husky breath of air that seemed to caress her skin.

She shivered slightly and forced her feet into motion. "Thank you. I—" She cleared her throat and tried to recall her reason for coming. Oh right. The duel. Her jaw tightened and the heated effect he was having on her diminished enough to allow for coherent thought.

"I found a letter from Mr. Haines waiting for me when I got home. Your name was mentioned along with an early morning event at Hackney Meadows." She sat down in the nearest chair and gripped the armrest. "Please tell me you aren't planning a duel against Robert."

He held her gaze for what seemed an eternity before finally looking away. Moving slowly, he rounded the desk like a cat on the prowl. Viola's heart jumped a few times in her chest and a new sort of heat hugged her body. This time it was fueled by the knowledge that he was coming toward her, closing the distance and . . .

He moved the chair adjacent to hers, turning it slightly so it faced her. And then he was lowering himself down into it, his knee sliding briefly against her thigh as he did so. *Dear God!* It felt like the air had been sucked from the room. More so when he reached for her hand, peeled off her glove and pressed a kiss to her knuckles.

Heaven help her, she was literally pulsing with awareness and the scoundrel probably knew it, for he grinned like a boy causing mischief—as she imagined he'd done when his brother had found the jam in his pockets decades ago.

Pulling her hand out of his grasp, she deliberately frowned. "Well?"

He sighed and leaned back against his chair, bringing his knee more firmly against her leg. Surely he had to be aware of the contact, which could only mean that he'd chosen not to care. Viola glanced at the open door to his office and scooted back in her seat.

"You did not hear what he said about you, Viola."

"Whatever it was, it cannot be so grave."

"Letting it pass is not an option," he said by way of explanation. His eyes were now completely serious. "He needs a lesson. One that I am more than happy to provide."

"You do realize that Robert will most likely shoot to kill." She could picture Henry now, sprawled out on the dewy ground and spattered by crimson. A chill went through her, chasing away the heat he'd stirred.

"I expect him to since he told me he plans on aiming for my head."

Viola's stomach dropped. "Good heavens." The chance of possibly losing him was one she refused to face even as betrayal snuck its way into her heart. "I cannot believe you intended to hide this from me, that you pretended everything was fine earlier when we parted ways, even though it was far from it."

Straightening in his seat, he reached for her hand once more. He held it loosely between his own and proceeded to stroke his thumb across her palm, back and forth, so gently she almost begged for added pressure. "I'm sorry, Viola, but I knew you would not approve."

"And yet you chose to forge ahead anyway, heedless of my opinion on a matter that affects me directly."

"You're right." His voice was smooth and his touch

so wonderful it made her want to forget their argument so they could simply enjoy each other's company. "But I'm a man, Viola. Knowing what he once did to you, how he mistreated you, hurt you, and seeing him try to do it again . . ." His hand stilled and his brow knit. "It enrages me in a way that demands satisfaction."

She scarcely knew what to say except "Be that as it may, I cannot stand the idea of you risking your life over this. I want you to call it off."

"I cannot do that. It's a matter of honor now."

"That is ridiculous." When he drew back a little, she said, "I do not want to be treated like a weak-minded woman who needs to rely on a man when it comes to fighting my battles. I want to be able to handle my own problems and I certainly don't want you going behind my back and possibly getting killed!"

"What if I promise not to die?"

She stared at him. "No!"

His fingers tightened around her hand and then he smiled. "I like how agitated you are about all of this."

"What?" That made less sense than the duel. "Why?"

"Because it shows that you care."

"Of course I care!"

"About me," he clarified.

Viola caught her breath, then slowly exhaled it. He was right, of course, but because she still feared commitment and the surrender this would require, she tried to deny it by saying, "Mostly because of your irritating determination to take control of a situation that has absolutely nothing to do with you."

"You're wrong about that, Viola. It has everything to do with me." When she shook her head weakly, he smiled at her warmly. "I meant what I said when I told you I care for you, Viola, so turning my back on this . . . on you . . . is out of the question."

She stared at him. "How did it come to this?" The curiosity had been bobbing about her brain since earlier in the evening.

His fingers reached for a dislodged strand of her hair and tucked it carefully back into place. "You're an incredible woman, that's how. A man would have to be blind not to pay attention. And once he does, he has no choice but to realize that it will probably take him a lifetime of good deeds in order to deserve you."

Pushing back his chair, Henry went to the door and closed it. He then went back to his desk, opened a drawer and pulled out some paper and a pencil.

"I need you to understand something," he said as he returned to his chair. "No other woman is prettier than you, Viola. Not to me."

"But . . ." He had to be lying or at the very least embellishing the truth so he wouldn't hurt her. "I am so unbelievably dull! My coloring is all wrong and there isn't a single part of my appearance that has ever been coveted or considered fashionable."

"I disagree, but since that doesn't solve anything, I propose I show you how you look when seen through my eyes." He crossed one leg over the other and settled the paper in his lap where a thick atlas gave it support. "Will you allow it?"

Viola hesitated. He might as well have asked her to strip naked, she was so overcome by self-consciousness. "I know I'm not pretty," she said as if needing the reminder before she allowed herself to do something truly stupid, like imagine a drawing had the power to change her boring eyes, dull hair and pasty complexion.

"I think you should let me be the judge of that." Henry locked his gaze with hers. "You're obviously too objective."

"I do not think so."

He shrugged. "All right."

His capitulation threw her, because for some absurd reason, arguing helped. It served as a welcome distraction from the idea of him studying every imperfect line of her face for as long as it would take him to complete the sketch. Swallowing, she clasped her hands together in her lap. She'd never been a coward. This fear she felt right now was Robert's doing, and if she gave in to it, she'd be letting him win. So she tilted her chin up instead and said, "Very well. I will humor you."

For the next ten minutes Henry's pencil moved across the paper with swift and efficient strokes. His brow was knit in concentration, his eyes sharply focused and his mouth set in a flat line that conveyed how seriously he took the task of sketching Viola's likeness. Each time he looked at her, it was with an artist's critical eye, the expression so grave it tempted Viola to squirm in her seat. She resisted only because she didn't want him to know how nerve-wracking she found the experience.

"Do not move," Henry muttered. "I am almost done."

Viola held her breath and her pose until Henry sat back, shifted his gaze between Viola and the sketch, and finally smiled. "Perfect," he murmured.

Curiosity made her forget her nerves. She leaned forward. "Can I see?"

His eyes met hers and a brief moment of silence passed between them. Something brushed against her hand and she realized it was the paper on which he'd been drawing. He was holding it toward her.

Inhaling deeply, as if requiring the extra oxygen to steady herself, Viola fought past her tangled nerves and frenzied heartbeat and dropped her gaze.

Her breath caught, stuck somewhere in her throat because this . . . this woman gazing back at her had to be someone else. The eyes were intelligent and bright, the mouth curved as if seconds away from smiling and the nose a perfect complement to the other features. Even the spattering of freckles across her cheeks held appeal, adding charm and character in the most alluring way.

Tears started pressing against her eyes so she bit her lip and pushed them back. "I didn't think it possible, but you have actually made me look pretty."

"I only drew what was right before my eyes. What everyone else is too blind to see. Including you."

An incredulous bit of laughter slipped past her lips. Looking up, she saw that he hadn't moved, that his steady gaze was still on her, though it now held a very distinct edge of curiosity. Or perhaps expectation? She wasn't quite sure, but it did make her stomach dip and the paper between her fingers flutter.

He took the paper from her hand and set it aside on his desk. When he turned back to face her, he was somehow closer than before. His thigh settled firmly against her own and then his hand cupped her cheek.

"Do you have any idea how hard I struggle to resist you?" he asked.

She sucked in a breath, a little undone by his blatant manner and slightly unnerved by the heat in his eyes. This was Henry, she reminded herself. He was a good man, not the womanizing rake she'd initially labeled him as. He would not treat her as poorly as Robert once had. And yet the memory of that regrettable experience snaked its way through her and pushed aside any growing desire she had to be brave—to take the chance she had here right now for the sake of a kiss.

He must have noticed, because he instantly dropped his hand and leaned back, adding distance between them once more, and in that moment Viola hated what Robert had done to her more than ever before, because he'd stolen her courage and her ability to surrender to the one man she so desperately wanted.

Chapter 19

Judging from her wary expression and how readily she glanced away, Henry could tell the statement frightened her, but it was important for him to be honest—to make sure she knew how desirable he found her. Seeing her reaction, however, almost broke his heart, and he knew that additional words would have to be said.

"I will never act on my desire for you unless it is what you want, Viola. You have my word on that." Her cheeks turned a bright shade of pink, but he couldn't allow her embarrassment to deter him. It was vital she understood he was nothing like Robert. "We can go as slow as you like. Even if we kiss it doesn't mean anything else has to happen. I will make no demands of you. Do you understand that?"

She gave a vague nod. It wasn't enough.

"Viola. Please look at me." She raised her troubled gaze to his, and the struggle he saw in her eyes made him want to destroy the man who'd made her this way. "I cannot pretend I do not want you, because I do. In every conceivable way. But if we ever choose to share the same bed and make love to each other, it will be because you have decided to spend the rest of your life with me, for I would not go through with something like that unless I planned on spending the rest of my life with you."

Her eyes widened. "Henry . . ."

"I know you are not ready to think in those terms, but it is important to me that you know where I stand. My intentions toward you are honorable, Viola. I will never bed you and leave you and I will never trick you into submitting."

She sank back in her chair, and when he cupped her cheek again, she leaned into his warmth as if craving that extra support. "I'm not ready to contemplate marriage."

"Then don't." When she gazed back at him, he took her hands between his. "Know that you are in control, Viola. If you want to kiss me, please do. Because I can assure you I want that as well. But if you are not ready, then wait. I will not rush you in any way." He raised her hands to his lips and kissed her knuckles. "But just so you know, the fact that I am doing my best to behave doesn't mean I am not having scandalous thoughts."

Her breath hitched. "Really?"

He allowed a devilish smile to slide into place. "If you must know, they keep me up at night." Deliberately, his gaze dropped to the elegant line of her décolletage. "I cannot stop wondering what it would be like to peel your clothes from your body and run my hands over your skin." He imagined other things too—things that left him aching with need and desperate to feel her hands upon him. But he would not describe any of that right now because if he did he might lose control, and that would be really bad after promising her restraint.

So he straightened himself and released her hands while enjoying her dazed expression. Oh, he'd definitely given her something to think about later when she got home and climbed into bed. Again, not wise of him to allow his wicked mind to consider what *that* might lead to. Unless he wanted lust and desire to ruin everything.

Her eyes, burning bright with profound interest, pierced him until he could scarcely move. She studied him with the sort of sharpness that made him ache for her touch. "I should probably go," she said as if she'd somehow forgotten how she'd come to be in his office in the first place.

Henry nodded stiffly. "Probably." He waited for her to move, prepared to stand the moment she did.

Instead she remained where she was, watching, assessing, pondering something that made Henry's pulse leap with strange expectation. She was torturing him with her beauty, her closeness, her bloody décolletage which revealed far more than it ought. Christ, she was maddening and he needed her gone if he was to gather his wits and prepare for tomorrow.

Instead she leaned forward, affording him with the most perfect view of her breasts. He gripped the armrests and forced himself to stay still, breathe slowly, keep calm. "Viola," he murmured.

"The trouble is, I don't want to leave you," she said. "At least not yet. Not before doing this."

And then, to Henry's amazement and utter delight, she closed the distance between them and placed her lips against his.

It wasn't at all what she had been planning to do when she'd come to see him. The only thing on her mind had been making him give up the duel. But then he'd touched her and said things that filled her with want. And by God, she wanted. She wanted to know how he tasted and what he felt like beneath her own mouth. She wanted to kiss him so thoroughly that their kiss would be the only one she remembered. She wanted to mark him as hers and convey how she truly felt: that there was more between them than friendship alone and that if he survived the duel against Robert, they would need to discuss every facet.

For a second, he sat as if stunned, but then his lips moved against hers and a rough growl emerged as he started kissing her back. It was slow and gentle at first, and Viola took pleasure in growing accustomed to the feel of it. But as she pressed closer and their kiss grew deeper, his hand came around her waist, and before she knew what was happening, she was pulled straight onto his lap.

She gasped with surprise and Henry took advantage, claiming her mouth so fiercely it caused her to burn from within. More so when his hand began exploring her body with torturous slowness. Pressing into his sweet caress, she heard her own groan of pleasure like a stranger's wanton plea for more.

Henry bit her lip gently and abandoned her mouth, kissing his way along her jaw. "God, Viola." He nipped at her earlobe, and clusters of sparks raced straight to her core.

"Yes," she murmured while threading her fingers through his hair and arching against him so he could have better access.

To her dismay and thorough disappointment, he pressed his forehead against her neck and held her tightly against him, before loosening his hold and guiding her back to her seat. He stood and went to the sideboard to pour himself a drink while Viola struggled to catch her own breath.

"If I . . ." His voice was hoarse and his eyes bright with pure desire. He downed the contents of his glass and tried again. "If I kept on kissing you, we would have ended up on the floor with your skirts up around your waist and my . . ." He let the words fade but Viola got the picture. Right now, she wasn't sure that sounded all that bad. His shoulders seemed to harden as if under tremendous pressure. "I don't want us to be a quick tumble for each other. I want more than that, which is why I must ask you to leave now before I lose my resolve."

Viola was astounded, flattered and slightly disappointed, but she admired his ability to consider such things when all she wanted to do was feel and experience and show him how much he mattered to her. So she stood and smoothed the fabric of her gown with trembling hands.

Henry stared at her, nostrils flaring as he took in her appearance. She could only imagine what he saw after what they'd just shared. Her skin still felt flushed and her lips continued to tingle from where they'd connected with his.

"There is nothing I can do to dissuade you from going through with the duel, is there?" It was the only thing she could think to say for the sake of steadying herself just enough to quit his company and return to her home.

He came toward her, stopping only when he was directly before her. "No." Impulsively, he clasped her head between his hands and kissed her again with added fervor. It was quick but fierce and left no doubt in her mind that this point was not to be argued. As if to underscore what she already knew, he said, "This duel has to take place, Viola. I am sorry, but I will not call it off."

"Then I wish you success." She hesitated briefly

while holding his gaze. And then, before she could change her mind, she walked to the door, opened it wide, and exited into the hallway beyond.

The air was crisp against her face when Viola left her house to hail a hackney the next morning. Few people were about at this early hour, which made travel easy. She doubted Henry would want her attending the duel, but staying away and worrying over the outcome wasn't an option either. Especially not after the incredible kiss they'd shared the night before. They'd moved beyond the bounds of friendship within the blink of an eye, and were now joined together in a tightly wound knot of emotions that demanded she witness the events about to take place.

Arriving at Hackney Meadows, Viola climbed down from the carriage and paid the driver. She then straightened her spine and walked toward the men who were gathered some distance away. Robert was the first to notice her approach. He glared at her before turning aside and offering her his back.

Haines saw her next and hastened toward her. "You should not be here."

She raised a brow. "Is that why you left that *ambiguous* letter for me to find?"

"No." He frowned. "It was of course to alert you in the hope you might stop this madness before it got this far. But now we're here and the pistols have been examined. I fear there is no going back."

"You are right about that," Viola said as they came within hearing distance of Henry, who stood in close conversation with Yates. She raised her voice. "I only hope I shan't have to inform Florian of his brother's untimely death when he returns to England, for I daresay that would probably ruin the holiday he and his wife have had."

Henry turned toward her the moment he heard her speak, his eyes lit with appreciation before dimming beneath lowered eyebrows. "You should not be here," he said.

Viola snorted. "Haines said the exact same thing, yet here I am." She crossed her arms to ensure they knew she had no intention of leaving.

"What if he does actually kill me?" Henry jutted his chin in Robert's direction.

Viola flattened her lips. "Then I shall have 'Dead from unnecessary cause and too stubborn to listen to reason' engraved upon your headstone."

He stared at her and she felt the heat of it all the way to her toes. "I am serious, Viola."

"Yes. I know." She was trying to be strong for him, but fear filled her veins and her eyes were starting to sting. Squaring her shoulders and raising her chin, she aimed for an even tone and added, "But waiting however long it might take for word of what happened to reach me would likely put me in the hospital. So I am staying."

Sighing, he gave a slight nod. He did not touch her or look at her with any hint of desire. His emotions were restrained, his movements precise, but the words that followed were tender, in spite of the tension with which he spoke. "You mean the world to me, Viola. Don't ever doubt that."

"Shall we begin?" Yates asked.

Henry hesitated. He glanced at Viola and then looked at Robert. Indecision blanketed the sharp intensity of his gaze. "Will you apologize for the disparaging terms in which you referred to Her Grace last night?" he asked Robert.

"No." Robert's jaw was set in undeniable anger.

Henry stared back at him across the distance. "Are you absolutely certain?"

"You have the power to end this before either one of you gets hurt," Yates called.

"My words suit her to perfection," Robert spat. "I will not take them back."

Henry nodded. He met Viola's gaze. "I am sorry, but there's nothing else for it, I'm afraid." His eyes focused on Robert once more and he turned away from her then, his entire being fixed upon his opponent.

Viola's heart fluttered like a panicked bird against her chest. He'd tried to get out of it. Even though his pride demanded he face Robert, he'd made an attempt to avoid it, not for himself, but for her. The sting in her eyes worsened until she was forced to blink away tears.

"We should move over there," Haines said, and as reluctant as Viola was to listen, as much as she wanted to step between the two men now positioning themselves back to back, she knew she couldn't interfere any further.

Moving off to the side so they stood a good distance away, Viola watched with her heart in her throat as Yates started counting the paces. "One . . . two . . ." Her legs began shaking, and breathing became a difficult chore. It felt as though she was suffocating or drowning, she wasn't sure which, but the thought did strike her that it would be quite something if the duel was called off because she was too weak to endure it.

"Seven . . . eight . . ." Yates continued, his voice carrying loud and clear and bringing them all closer to the inevitable. "Nine . . . ten . . . Please turn!" Yates paused and Viola suddenly wanted to scream for him to continue so this awful nightmare could finally be over and . . . "Take aim and . . . fire!"

Shots exploded and both men went down so fast that

Viola could only stare in stark disbelief, as her brain refused to accept what she was seeing. *No*. The word was jammed in her throat. Somehow her feet started moving and then she was suddenly running while her heart thrashed wildly about in her chest. She skidded to a halt in the grass, landing on her knees beside Henry, whose hat had toppled from his head and . . .

A sob was wrenched from her throat and her hands patted frantically at his chest, his neck, his face, desperate to find sign of life.

"Viola." Yates's voice seemed to come from so far away. A pair of warm hands touched her shoulders, and through the tears she saw Haines checking Henry's body with much greater calm than she possessed at the moment. All Viola could look at was the bright crimson liquid trickling down the side of his head.

"There's so much blood." She could barely speak, the words trembling upon her lips while her body shook in absolute desperation.

"He's alive, Viola," Yates was saying, but then why was he lying so still? And what about all the blood?

"The lead ball penetrated his hat and grazed his scalp," Haines said. He produced a piece of linen from his bag, soaked it with gin and dabbed at Henry's wound. "See? The wound is shallow, Viola."

Haines pressed down on the wound to stanch the bleeding and Henry came to, sucking in a sharp breath between his teeth. "Christ almighty!"

Viola blew out a breath. "Don't move," she cautioned. "You were struck, though not too severely."

"But you did hit your head when you fell to the ground," Yates said. "You've been unconscious for about five minutes."

"And Tremaine?" Henry groaned.

"His second is helping him stand," Yates said. "I believe you struck his shoulder."

"If you hold this in place, I'll go take a look," Haines said. He waited for Viola to place her hand on the compress before getting up. "I'll be back in a moment."

Viola stared down at Henry, the relief she felt at knowing he lived so profound it stole her breath. Her hands still trembled and her heart continued to throb with the pain she'd endured when she'd thought she'd lost him. "You silly man," she choked while swiping a lock of his hair away from his eye. "Do you have any idea what you put me through just now?"

"It cannot be worse than what I put myself through," he muttered.

She scowled at him even as she smiled in response to his lopsided grin. "I'm going to fix you up really well so I can throttle you for taking years off my life."

"I cannot say I envy you, Lowell," Yates murmured at Viola's shoulder. "Facing death on the field of honor will likely have been a breeze by comparison."

Viola swatted him away and leaned slightly forward, so close she could see just a hint of gold in Henry's brown eyes. "Promise me you won't ever do something like this again."

"I did not expect Robert to hit me," he said, not giving her the assurance she needed. "He's never been a very good shot."

Viola shook her head. "You are unbelievable."

"Unbelievably handsome, I hope." And then, as if he hadn't annoyed her enough by getting shot and knocking himself unconscious, he waggled his eyebrows. And damn her if she didn't smile just a little bit more because of how charming he was even when he was lying on his back with blood smeared across his forehead.

Viola sighed. "We should probably get you back to the hospital."

"I agree," Haines said as he returned. "Tremaine has a lead ball stuck in his shoulder that needs to be extracted, while you, Lowell, could do with a thorough evaluation."

The grin on Henry's face left no doubt in Viola's mind about where his thoughts were straying. Of all the things to be contemplating in his current condition . . .

"And since Tremaine requires minor surgery and doesn't want you within a hundred yards of him," Haines said, addressing Viola, "I'm thinking that I'll take care of him while you take care of Lowell."

Viola wouldn't have it any other way. "I'm happy to."

Henry was starting to believe he had an uncanny ability to survive getting shot. When Elmwood had called him out last year, the earl had sprained his wrist on his way to the duel, then when Baron Highpool had tried to shoot him a little over two weeks earlier, he'd missed any vital organs, and now he was getting away with no more than an inconvenient headache.

"I think Tremaine might call me out again for refusing to die," Henry mused. Viola, who'd cleaned his wound again and applied a poultice, went absolutely rigid. Grabbing her hand, he pressed it gently against his cheek. "Perhaps I should apologize to him for still being alive."

She didn't laugh as he'd hoped she would. Instead her lips trembled and she suddenly turned her head away so he could not see her face.

With aching heart he drew her to him, aware that he'd put her through more than she deserved. As had Robert. Between the two of them it was no wonder

Viola wasn't racing toward the altar, eager to speak her vows. In her experience, men were selfish, boorish and possibly stupid.

"I am sorry I wasn't able to stop this from happening," he told her sincerely while stroking his hand down her back.

He felt the rise and fall of her breasts as she inhaled and exhaled against him. "I'm just glad you're not any worse off," she said after a moment had passed. And then, "I was so scared I thought I might kill you myself when I saw what had happened. To be honest, it was as if the world collapsed around me and I . . . I just couldn't breathe."

She leaned back a little in his embrace, just enough to meet his gaze, and the turbulence there completely undid him. Unable to resist, he dragged her mouth to his and kissed her as he had been dreaming of kissing her again since last night. This morning, when he'd made his way to Hackney Meadows, he'd carried with him the knowledge that if he died today, at least he would do so knowing what it was to be kissed by Viola—incomparable.

Her lips moved carefully over his, her body relaxing against him. "We must be careful," she murmured against his mouth.

"I'm fine," he assured her, and nipped at her lips just to prove it. "More so now that you're back in my arms."

She opened her mouth to respond, and he swallowed her words with his own, kissing her deeply, passionately and with the joy of knowing he was still alive to experience her warmth. Her breath brushed his skin as she moved to place a soft kiss on his cheek. Her brow pressed against his and for a long moment she stayed there, just breathing him in.

Eventually she swallowed and pulled away, her

shoulders setting as she started putting away her supplies. "You need to rest for a couple of days. Do not exert yourself and make sure you change your compress twice daily." Her cheeks were flushed and her voice slightly breathless. "I will send instructions home with you so your servants will know what to buy and how to prepare the poultice."

"Thank you, Viola." He watched as she moved about, busying herself with seemingly inane tasks. "We've kissed each other twice now," he felt compelled to point out just in case she hadn't noticed.

"Yes," she said as if responding to a mindless comment.

"This would suggest that you find me attractive." He grinned when she tripped over her own two feet. "It would also suggest that you like me, which makes me wonder if you might be more willing to consider marriage now than—"

"When I first met you?"

He gave her his most serious frown. "Well yes."

She stared at him so long he was tempted to grab her and kiss her again. Before he could do so, however, she said, "I worry I'm not a good match for you, Henry."

He shook his head, bewildered by such a concern. "You're a perfect match, Viola. We're both entrepreneurs, which means we share the same fundamental views on efficiency, spending, growing a business and finding the drive to turn dreams into brilliant successes. You ground me, while I remind you to have some fun, and when we're not together, I find myself anxiously awaiting the next time we meet."

Averting her gaze, she took a series of breaths as if needing the extra oxygen in order to process his words. Swallowing, she finally admitted. "I feel the same, but you're an earl's heir while I'm . . ."

"What?" he asked with incomprehension when she failed to continue.

"Not the sort of woman you ought to consider marrying."

"Why?"

She drew several quivering breaths before finally saying, "I'm illegitimate, Henry."

He frowned. "I suppose there are those who might not approve, but I'm not one of them, Viola. It's certainly not enough to deter me from seeking your hand. Not when my own brother was born on the wrong side of the blanket."

"And look what happened to him. He had to leave London because of the scandal."

"Yes, but he has since managed to return," Henry told her calmly. "More importantly, it did not change a thing between him and Juliette."

"No, but—"

"It doesn't alter my opinion of you or make me want you any less. Surely you must know that."

At least she nodded, which was something. "I do."

"But you worry what others will think if they ever find out?"

Another nod conveyed her answer. "I know I should have told Steadford, but . . ." She sighed. "My father revealed my illegitimacy to me on his deathbed. He claimed I deserved to know the truth about my birthright before he died, but he also insisted I keep the knowledge to myself. I feared revealing it might skew Steadford's opinion of me and cause him to stop helping me with the case."

Henry understood completely how misplaced fear could cause a person to keep his secrets close to his heart. For over ten years Florian had hidden the truth about his real father from Henry, afraid that Henry would look at him differently if he ever found out they were only half brothers.

"Very well. We'll keep this between the two of us as long as you can guarantee that there's no chance of Hayes finding out."

"He won't," Viola promised. "There's no record of it."

A moment of silence fell between them and Henry considered questioning her further. Since she hadn't mentioned her mother at all except in passing, he wondered who the woman might have been. In all likelihood, her father had had an affair and she wanted to protect his good name. And if that was the case, then Henry would allow her to do so with dignity. So he kept his question locked up inside as she led him out of the examination room and toward a front desk. There she quickly jotted down the items she'd mentioned for the poultice and handed it to him.

A carriage was called and Henry pocketed her note. "I will be in touch when I am fully recovered," he promised.

She smiled at that, and to his delight, her expression turned hopeful. "Get well soon, Henry. And if you start feeling dizzy or nauseous, I want you to send for me immediately."

He refrained from saying he might use that as an excuse to see her again. Instead he turned on his heels and walked out of St. Agatha's Hospital and into a welcome burst of sunshine.

Chapter 20

"How is the case progressing?" Henry asked Mr. Steadford a couple of days later. That morning, after issuing orders to his gardener about where to plant the rhododendron bushes and peonies he'd ordered, he'd decided to stop by the barrister for a quick update.

"Well, we've questioned the servants who used to be in Tremaine's employ and they had only favorable things to say about the duchess, while several were very critical of the new duke. My discussions with these people have, I believe, offered a degree of insight that ought to help us win this case."

Pleased to know there was hope on the horizon, Henry relaxed into his chair. "So what's the next step then?"

"Well, I have asked a clerk to investigate the claims you've made about Tremaine's past so I can discover exactly the sort of man he is. Speaking of which, I heard about the duel. Mr. Hayes notified me, adding that the case will be temporarily put on hold until Tremaine has fully recovered from the wound he received at your hand. So now I wish to ask you, sir, what the hell were you thinking?"

Henry winced and then he told Steadford about

the disparaging terms with which Tremaine had referred to Viola. "He insulted her most grievously and refused to apologize for it."

Mr. Steadford's eyes narrowed with interest. "I see." He reached for his quill and scribbled something on a piece of paper. "How interesting."

"I'm glad *you* think so," Henry told him dryly. He stood and prepared to leave. "How long do you think we have before we hear from Mr. Hayes again?"

"A couple of days, I should think."

Thanking Mr. Steadford, Henry exited the office and went to collect his carriage. "St. Agatha's Hospital," he told his driver. Because he'd suddenly had an idea and it involved not only Viola, but her beloved dog, Rex.

Returning to her office after a lengthy discussion with Gabriella over tea and biscuits, Viola paused in the doorway when she saw Henry there, studying her bookcase. Her heart made a funny little hop, skip and jump.

"I see there are other books here besides medical texts," he said with a glance in her direction.

She entered the room and came to see what he was looking at. "*Gulliver's Travels*. That was my father's. He used to read it to me when I was a child."

A glimmer of interest flickered behind his eyes. "And this?"

She couldn't help but smile as he pulled a box from a shelf and held it so they could both read what was printed on the lid. The New Game of Human Life. "Peter gave me that for my fifteenth birthday when he realized how fond I am of games." It had been a thoughtful gesture, which only increased the value of the gift.

"We have to play it one day." Henry lifted the lid and peeked inside. "It looks like it might be fun."

"Oh. It is. You have to use a teetotum to progress through life from year one to eighty-four." She returned the game to its designated spot. "It's a game of luck rather than skill, but I must admit I find it vastly entertaining."

He turned more fully toward her and smiled. "Speaking of entertaining, I want to propose an excursion."

"With me?" In spite of every reason she'd given herself to resist him, excitement bubbled in her veins. Scattered around her heart were the remnants of the wall she'd been building since the age of sixteen when Robert had hurt her. Henry had not only scaled it, he'd taken a hammer to it and knocked it down completely.

"Yes." He reached for her hand, and her insides started to fizz. "As it turns out, Robert's case against you has been put on hold."

"I know. Mr. Steadford informed me in a note he sent me this morning."

"Which allows for a little reprieve," Henry continued. "As I recall, you wish to visit the seaside. So I was thinking a day trip to Hastings might do some good." When she opened her mouth, he cut her off quickly by adding, "The beaches are long and wide—perfect for Rex to enjoy a good run—and we can even visit the ruins of Hastings Castle if you like. It's quite picturesque."

"I . . ." Viola paused. It was so incredibly tempting. "I really shouldn't," she forced herself to say. "I am a widow and you are a bachelor. If anyone finds out that we've gone on a day trip together, they'll assume that we're lovers."

His gaze darkened and his fingers tightened around hers, causing the most delightful tremor to rush down her spine. "I wouldn't mind that."

"Because you're a man." Her words scraped the air in an effort to gain a foothold. "Until a few days ago you were also a rake."

"Perhaps I ought to become one again." He stepped in close and her heart started racing. "Is it so terrible to want to escape with you to a place where we can be free from Society's rules for a while?"

"No. It sounds wonderful actually. I just don't want to give Hayes more ammunition."

He inhaled deeply and when he exhaled that breath, she felt it stir the hair at her temple. "You know, all of this could be solved if you simply agree to marry me."

Viola blinked. "Are you proposing?"

"No."

Oddly, her heart took a sudden nosedive. Which of course was ridiculous since her brain had yet to decide if marrying Henry was an option she truly wanted to consider. "Oh." God, she sounded stupid.

He didn't seem to notice, his eyes warming and his lips tilting until he was looking at her as if she held the key to eternal life. "I have my pride, Viola, so I am not going to ask you until I am certain of what your answer will be." Unsure of how to respond, she kept quiet, allowing him to add, "You must realize by now that I feel strongly about you, do you not?"

Her cheeks warmed as she dropped her gaze in a moment of pure self-consciousness. Tipping her chin back up with his fingers, he forced her to meet his challenging eyes. He raised an eyebrow and a single word crossed her lips. "Yes."

"And I like to think the sentiment is reciprocated." He dipped his head so they were only an inch apart. Just one tiny step and she'd be in his arms.

Her breath hitched and again she answered, "Yes," though the word now sounded sensual.

His eyes darkened and Viola's heart pounded against her chest. "God, I want to kiss you right now," he murmured, his voice so rough it raked her skin with hot little embers. A moment passed—the most torturous moment of Viola's life. She didn't care that the door to her office stood open or that anyone who happened to pass would witness the tension that hummed between her and Henry. All she wanted in that moment was his mouth against hers and . . .

He took a step back. "Unfortunately, I cannot do so here without risking an audience." He glanced over his shoulder at the door. "This is a busy place, and if someone were to find you in my arms like that, you would either have to face scandal or marry me right away. I do not want those to be your only choices, but if you come with me to Hastings . . ."

She bit her lip while trying to recall why she ought to say no.

"Did I mention that I'm making progress on my garden, by the way?"

"What?" Viola stared up at him in confusion. What on earth did this have to do with anything?

"I made a sketch for my gardener to follow. Poor fellow will be busy for the next month at least, replacing existing plants with new ones and putting in graveled walkways. Thanks to my books, I've managed to find a way of ensuring that there're always flowers present during spring and summer."

"It sounds as though it will be very pretty once it's done."

"I expect so. Now, about this excursion," he said, tossing her a boyish smile. "I can have a picnic basket prepared."

"You do realize I haven't agreed to come with you yet?"

He shrugged. "Semantics." When she rolled her eyes, he said, "It is just for the day, Viola, and somewhere far from here where no one will recognize either of us. If we leave early enough in the morning, there's not even a chance of us being seen. But of course, if the idea of being alone with me troubles you, we can ask the Huntleys or the Coventrys to chaperone."

Viola considered that as an option and then dismissed it again. She was a widow, after all, so would it really be so terrible if people saw them together and thought they were having an affair? Would it really give Hayes the added advantage? Perhaps she feared spending the day with Henry for a different reason entirely—because it made everything between them more serious somehow. It meant she would have to give their relationship some serious thought and decide if marrying him was a viable option for her. If it wasn't, she'd have to end things between them quickly.

The idea of giving him up, though, and going on without him, twisted her insides and stabbed at her heart. Suddenly everything came into focus with blinding clarity. She loved him. Living without him was no longer possible, so when he eventually asked, she would tell him yes without even blinking.

With this in mind, she smiled at him broadly while a new, more powerful sense of happiness clung to her heart. "There's no need for that," she said. "I am happy to spend the day with you alone."

His eyes brightened and he hesitated for a second, as if on the verge of kissing her after all. But then he said, "Is six o'clock too early for you to be ready?"

"I rise at five most mornings, so it suits me just fine."

He touched her shoulder with his hand, gave it a gentle squeeze and said, "I look forward to seeing you tomorrow then." His eyes held hers briefly and then he stepped away, bidding her a good day and leaving her with a flutter in her chest that remained for long moments after.

The time had come for her to reach for more than she'd ever thought possible—for more than she'd thought could be hers after everything that had happened. It was time for her to tell Henry the whole truth about herself and see where that led them. He'd already told her there was nothing she could say to alter the way he felt about her. Which meant it was time for her to be absolutely honest. Only then, when he knew all there was to know about her, could they truly have a chance at the happily-ever-after she'd started to dream of again.

Chapter 21

Joy had burst through Henry's veins when Viola had agreed to come with him to Hastings. Surprise and pleasure had followed when she'd told him that chaperones weren't required. Exiting his coach, he went to knock on her door.

It took only moments for it to open and reveal the woman who made his heart beat more wildly than ever before. She smiled at him through the purple light of dawn and bade him good morning.

He returned the greeting while she locked the door. Her hand reached toward him, and he saw she was offering him Rex's leash. "I think I should get inside the carriage first and then you can help Rex up afterward," she said.

Henry grabbed the knotted cord, waited for her to embark and then bent to pick Rex up. The dog struggled slightly against his grasp until he spotted Viola, upon which sight he leapt out of Henry's arms and straight in behind her. Laughing slightly on account of the obvious loyalty, Henry issued instructions to the driver and climbed up into the carriage as well before shutting the door.

They took off with a jolt, causing Rex to look up

in surprise. "I take it he's never ridden in a carriage before?" Henry asked. He'd deliberately taken the seat across from Viola, as was proper, even though he itched to be close enough to touch her.

But, considering the effect she had on him and the promise he'd made himself to stay on his best behavior, he knew more distance was required if he was to stop from being a scoundrel. They were after all in a closed carriage now. Together. Alone. If he kissed her his hands were bound to wander and . . .

She pushed her hood back with her fingers, and although she was cast in the shadows of early morning light, he could see she was looking straight at him, causing his pulse to leap with delight.

"No. This is the first time," she said, in answer to his question. Placing her hand on Rex's head, she gave the beast a few loving strokes before leaning back against the squabs. "Did you leave Newton at home by himself?"

"Yes. I'm not sure he would enjoy the sand or the water." Dropping a glance at Rex's big head, he added, "I'm also not sure Rex would like him very much."

She looked at him as if he had bats flying out of his ears. "Rex might be big, but he's got a lovely heart. He would never hurt Newton if that's what you're afraid of."

Henry considered the dog's wide jaw and the teeth protruding like stalactites from the roof of a cave. "Newton's entire body would fit in his mouth without much effort."

She frowned, but her eyes were dancing. "Perhaps we ought to arrange for the two to meet under more controlled conditions."

Henry smiled. "I like that idea." She smiled as well, and he found himself struggling to remain where he was—to not cross to her side of the carriage and kiss her with wild abandon. "I have a confession to make," he said instead. "I'm glad you decided to come alone even though I suggested a chaperone."

"So am I," she whispered, so softly he barely heard her, but her admission was like a balm to his soul and a spark to his desire.

"Really?"

"That surprises you?"

"Well yes. I know you fear inviting gossip and ruining your reputation."

She was quiet for a while, her body swaying ever so slightly in response to the carriage's jostling movements. "It occurred to me that spending the day alone with you was too appealing to be ignored, that any potential gossip about us would not damage my reputation more than the gossip about me being a social-climbing schemer already has."

"I think you're probably right."

"We'll see. Privacy has always mattered to me. I never liked being the center of attention, but after marrying Peter, all of that changed, and not in a good way." She clasped her hands in her lap. "The *ton* can be so unbearably vicious."

"Is that why you stayed away from social events?"

She shrugged one shoulder. "I had other priorities and little desire to meet the people who love to think the worst of me."

"The Huntleys got through it and so did my brother. If you want to, you can get through it as well."

"That's just it," she said. "I do not think I care to make the effort."

He wasn't sure he would either if he were in her shoes, because he could see the *ton* as she saw them, a group of arrogant judges perched upon pedestals and pointing fingers at those below. "I'm sorry I'm one of them," he said, wishing for the first time in his life that he was an ordinary man with no titles to inherit and no fortune to his name.

"You're not." Her words drifted toward him like mist carried forward on a breeze. "You are entirely different, Henry, which is one of the reasons why I like you as much as I do."

A powerful need for added closeness overcame him and he could resist no longer. He had to have her beside him, so he shifted sideways and held out his hand. "Come here, Viola."

Her lips parted and time seemed to slow to a halt until, to Henry's immense relief, she reached out across the space between them. The moment her fingers closed around his, he held her steady until she sank down beside him, at which point he wound his arm around her shoulders and pulled her snugly against him.

Her hand fell against his thigh and Henry went still. "Viola." He could scarcely utter a word on account of the pleasure, the need, the desire for more. She must have believed that he disapproved of her touching him so, for she started to pull away. "Don't move," he managed to say in what sounded more like a growl.

She froze, paused for a second and then relaxed back into his arms.

Henry took a deep breath and prayed for resilience. "I like your hand there," he muttered, because the last thing he wanted was to make her feel unsure. "It was just unexpected, that's all."

"I was trying to steady myself," she said.

Her fingers flexed against him as she repositioned her hand, causing flashes of heat to dart up his leg and straight to his groin. Caught between pain and pleasure, Henry closed his eyes and breathed in her scent. Lavender and starch as usual. Fresh and clean and incredibly enticing.

She shifted her weight, pulling slightly away. Henry opened his eyes and saw she was angled toward him, leaning forward, watching him closely. "May I kiss you?" she asked.

All hope of dampening his ardor evaporated in response to that simple question as need, urgent and fierce and full of devil-may-care intentions, assailed every cell in his body. "You don't ever have to ask for permission to do so, Viola."

Her gaze dropped to his lips and Henry held himself utterly still. Nothing existed for him in this moment except for Viola. It was as if his entire being hinged on what she did next.

Slowly, as if she'd learned the art of seduction from Aphrodite herself, she closed the distance between them and sighed against his mouth. Restraint abandoned Henry in a heartbeat and he crushed her to him, cradling her head in the palm of his hand while kissing her back. He no longer cared that his body responded the way it ought when she pressed her hand into his thigh or that she gasped when the blatant proof of his fierce desire brushed her wrist moments later.

He wanted her and he would not pretend otherwise. She was not an innocent, but a woman who knew what it was to be bedded. She was also a woman with professional knowledge of the human body, so rather than break the kiss and offer an apology, he kissed her with greater fervor, until nothing else existed besides her and the pleasure he felt from holding her close in his arms.

Her lips moved to place small sweet caresses against the edge of his mouth. Her breath tickled his jaw and her cheek came to rest against his. "This feels so right," she whispered. "More right than I ever imagined it would."

His heart swelled with contentment as he drew her head down to rest against his shoulder. "I hope this day lasts forever," he told her softly.

She snuggled closer, taking just as much comfort from him as he took from her. "Me too."

Savoring her warmth and closeness, Henry leaned back and stretched out his legs. When he felt her breaths ease and her body relax, he closed his eyes with a smile and allowed the gentle sway of the carriage to lull him to sleep as well.

She awoke as if called back to life from a faraway place. Something pressed against her arm. "Viola?" Henry's voice was gentle but firm. "We have arrived."

A wet tongue licked her hand and she opened her eyes to find Rex's head in her lap. Blinking, she realized she was half lying, half sitting in a somewhat awkward position and that Henry was leaning slightly against her.

"I'm awake," she murmured, and pushed her palm down on the bench in an effort to right her sprawling body. Except it wasn't the bench at all that she touched, but something else entirely—something that gave way beneath her weight in a way that made her think of kissing. She gasped and pulled away, aware that she'd placed her entire hand directly on Henry's thigh. Again.

He grinned, and she blushed while muttering an incoherent apology.

"I'm not sorry," he said. "Indeed, I enjoy nothing more than having your hands on me like that, Viola." And then, as if that wasn't the most inappropriate thing in the world for him to say, he exited the carriage and reached up toward her with unrepentant casualness. "Come on. I'll help you down."

Feeling as though he'd just lit a furnace inside her once more, she straightened her cloak and her gown, drew a deep breath and moved toward the door. Before she could manage to take his hand or place one foot on the step, he grabbed her by the waist and pulled her toward him.

"Henry!" She landed on her feet and with her breasts pressed right up against him. "You cannot—"

"There's no one else here, Viola." His arm wound around her waist and he held her to him until she was short of breath. Until she wanted to wrap her legs around him and— "The spot we're in is secluded and I sent the driver into town with a bit of spending money. He won't be back again until later this afternoon." Pulling her closer, he settled his cheek against hers and ran his fingertips down her back.

Her stomach tightened and awareness took hold, the promise of what this day might bring causing her body to tingle. She wanted to kiss him again, taste the flavor of hot morning coffee upon his tongue. But then he stepped away and took her by the hand. Pulling her along behind him, he led her past the crumbling stone walls of what she presumed had once been Hastings Castle. It was then that she noticed the way he was dressed in fawn-colored breeches, white shirt and a brown jacket fashioned from coarse-looking cotton. In the dim interior of the carriage, she hadn't paid attention. Her focus had been on the touch of his hands and the hard planes of his body pressing rigidly into hers.

Her skin heated with the reminder and it took her a moment to find her composure. "Where did you get your clothes?" she asked once this had been accomplished. She was curious how a man who dressed with impeccable taste, and always in a manner befitting his station, would have acquired such a plain-looking outfit.

He cast a look in her direction. "These are my work clothes," he said with a cheeky flash of humor in his eyes.

"Your work clothes?" He had to be joking.

"I do not wear fine linen or superfine wool when I'm helping my gardener pull unwanted plants from the ground." He drew her around a corner and stopped. "Now take a look at this."

Viola sucked in a breath as her vision filled with endless amounts of blue. Rex barked somewhere nearby and then raced past her, leaping down from the grassy hillock on which they stood and onto the beach below. A forceful breeze whipped at Viola, loosening strands of her hair and thrusting them out to the side. Above, birds flew in and out between the clouds, their cries mingling with the whoosh of waves breaking against the shore.

Henry tugged at her hand and held her steady while helping her down to the beach. A briny scent infused the air, along with something else she couldn't distinguish. Rex barked again and Viola looked in his direction, laughing when she saw how happy he was to be given this freedom to run and do as he pleased.

"What do you think?" Henry asked.

Overwhelmed with joy and deep appreciation for what he'd done for her and for Rex, Viola turned to meet his gaze, "It's wonderful," she said, speaking not only of the sea or the beach or the ruin, but of him as a person. "So much better than I ever imagined."

Tenderness lit his eyes, infusing her body with warmth as he raised his hand to her cheek. "All I want is for you to be happy."

The words, spoken with infinite longing, touched her soul with a new kind of hope. "There are still some things I must tell you," she said, because being honest was now of the utmost importance.

"I agree." His thumb stroked over her skin. "I would like to know who your mother was. Not because it will make any difference, but because I want to know all there is about you."

"I'm ready to tell you everything." Oh God, she loved the way his other hand pressed against her lower back. She swallowed, tried to focus.

"And I will listen to every word," he promised. Leaning into her, he whispered close to her ear, "But before we get to that, I think we ought to discard our shoes and stockings, or in my case my boots and hose, and enjoy the feel of the sand between our toes."

She turned to him with an impish grin that he'd later attempt to capture in a sketch. "Would that not be terribly indecent?"

"Do you fear I'll ravish you at the mere sight of your naked feet?" To his delight, she laughed. The sound was light and pretty. "Come now, Viola. You have not lived until you've dared a little indiscretion."

Rosy-cheeked and eyes aglow, she gave him a challenging look and then dropped to her bottom in the sand. "Very well." She tugged off one shoe and then the other. "I daresay you have convinced me."

He laughed more heartily than he had in a long time and lowered himself to the sand as well. Grabbing the heel of his boot, he tried to pry it off, but the damn thing was snug and difficult to budge. He glanced in Viola's direction just in time to watch her peel her stocking away from her foot. Dear God in heaven! She wriggled her toes, and Henry's mouth went dry. Perhaps the sight of her naked feet would lead to ravishment after all . . .

No.

He blinked and shook his head. Allowing his thoughts to stray in that direction would be unwise unless he meant to have her before they married. As it was, the kisses they'd shared so far had already tested him to the limit. But considering her past experience, he wanted there to be no doubt in her mind when he finally made love to her that he did so for the right reasons and not because he just needed fulfillment. He made another attempt at removing his boot and managed to get it off half the way.

"Would you like me to help?" she asked, and was suddenly on her feet, smiling down at him while grabbing hold of his leg. Holy hell! Henry's hands fell back, palms down in the sand, supporting himself as she tugged away as if what she was doing was perfectly normal and didn't cause sparks to lick their way through his taut body. And then the boot gave way and she disappeared from his view as she fell back with yet another laugh.

He laughed as well, more so when she popped back into view from behind his legs, waving his boot in her hand as if it were a prize she'd just won. "I did it," she said, and then tossed the boot aside so she could focus on the second one. It came off more easily and without her losing her balance. "There!" She handed it to him and raised a brow. "Aren't you going to take off your hose?"

Oh, right. He'd forgotten what he was supposed to be doing because of how mesmerized he was by her beauty. This was a livelier Viola than the one he knew in London. This version of her was unrestrained and devoid of any concern. Grateful to have been granted the opportunity to see her this way, he pulled off his hose and stood, curling his toes into the dry sand just as Rex ran by. The dog skidded to a halt and loped back toward Viola while wagging his tail. Henry watched as the pair walked toward the edge of the water.

"Oh dear God, this is cold," she squealed as she hiked up her gown without second thought and ran back to where he was standing.

Henry felt his heart double in size, and then, feeling playful and wanting to tease her, he grabbed her hand and ran forward, pulling her with him until they were both ankle-deep in the icy water. Her hand smacked his chest even as she hopped about laughing. Rex barked and ran farther out into the waves before circling back and rubbing his massive wet body against Henry's legs.

Unperturbed, Henry scrubbed his knuckles against the dog's head. The beast licked his hand before running back onto the shore. Turning, Henry guided Viola out of the water, releasing her hand so she could pick up her shoes and stockings.

"Are you hungry?" he asked, while grabbing his boots and hose. "We've a very full picnic basket waiting for us in the boot of the carriage."

"Sounds delicious." She called for Rex, who was busily sniffing about between seaweed and shells a short distance away. At the sound of her voice he came bounding toward them. "I don't suppose there's a treat for him too?"

Reaching down, Henry patted Rex's back and gave him a quick scratch behind one ear. "I had Cook chop up some beef and there's also a bone for him to enjoy when he's done."

"You truly are an amazing man."

He straightened himself and put his arm around her shoulders, pulling her close to his side. Together they started back toward the hillock. "And you are an amazing woman, which is yet another reason why we're perfect for each other."

When she didn't react, he knew her brain was working away at some issue. "Penny for your thoughts?" Lowering his arm, he took her by the hand so he could help her climb back up the slanted ground to the ruin.

She watched her feet as they went, careful not to trip over rocks or other uneven spots. "I feel as though we've reached a point where honesty is not only very important, but absolutely necessary. There are things I must say to you, Henry. Difficult things and—"

"Tell me about this point we have reached, Viola." He pulled her up beside him and met her troubled gaze. "I want to know how you feel. About me."

She glanced away, seeking refuge on the horizon. "It is difficult to describe."

"Is it really, or are you just afraid to?" He asked the question gently, hoping not to upset her, but he could tell by the tightening of her expression that it made her defensive.

"What do you want me to say?"

"The truth."

"As if it is so simple."

Blowing out a breath, he leaned forward and kissed her brow. "It should be, but if it isn't, then it must be because you're not sure."

"And you are?"

He didn't answer, because that would be unfair and because he didn't want her response to be influenced by what he said. But the truth was he loved her, and when she was ready to hear it, he would be ready to let her know.

"You're more than a friend to me, Henry." She was staring up at him now as if willing him to read her mind. "I don't know what the future holds for us, though, and I must confess that I'm scared; scared of entering into another marriage, scared of losing you if I don't and scared of losing myself either way. Most of all, I'm scared you might be wrong about your ability to accept me for who I truly am."

Sympathizing, Henry drew her into a tight embrace, offering comfort while hiding his growing alarm. He didn't want her to ruin what they had—what they were becoming—with words. He wanted to make her laugh some more and kiss away all her fears.

Instead he pulled back and did what she needed him to do. "Let us set up the picnic," he said, "and then you can tell me everything you need to while we eat."

Chapter 22

Even though this was what she had asked for, Viola's heart still shook with trepidation and her hands still trembled with the knowledge that she might never touch Henry again once he learned of her mother's identity. Part of her knew she was wrong to suppose that the good man she knew him to be would not accept her, but a dimmer, more cynical side, accustomed to Society's disapproval of those with blemished backgrounds, fueled her concern.

Because however normal he seemed, he was an aristocrat hoping to make her his wife. His opinion would be guided by this. What she said next might make him realize that her illegitimacy was one thing, her birthright quite another, which was why she'd hedged when he'd asked how she felt about him. To confess it before she knew he'd reciprocate, no matter what, was something she could not allow herself to do.

Staring down at the rich assortment of food on her plate, she found it impossible to eat. The spot where they sat was set in a corner of the old ruin, perfectly sheltered from the wind. It would have been wondrously romantic, with the wildflowers dotting the grass beneath and mossy shades of green adding color to the ancient stones.

"Remember that I am first and foremost your friend," Henry told her. He handed her a glass of wine. "For fortification."

She took a sip and then another, but couldn't really enjoy it. "What I am about to tell you could destroy my reputation forever." She swallowed, not daring to look at him as she spoke. "It is something not even Peter was made aware of, but the fact of the matter is that my mother was a courtesan and my father was not Jonathan Marsh."

He said nothing for a long, drawn-out moment. Eventually he asked, "Who was he then?"

She shook her head. "I do not know. A client of my mother's, I believe. According to my . . . to Marsh," she amended, "my mother didn't know his name or where to find him. When she went into labor with me, a friend of hers went to fetch Marsh. He helped with the delivery, and when my mother died shortly after I was born, he took me into his care and raised me as his own."

"And no one ever questioned your legitimacy?" He sounded genuinely confused. "They didn't wonder how an unmarried man came to be in possession of an infant?"

Viola shook her head. "Marsh didn't live in London back then. He lived in Paris, where he taught anatomy at the Sorbonne. After handing in his notice, he moved, returning to England as a widower whose experience and skill in the medical profession caught Tremaine's attention when he was looking to acquire a new physician. No one asked any questions, and if they did, Marsh either dissembled or lied."

Henry stared at her as if he found her story hard

to understand. "And nobody else knows about this? You are sure of that?"

"Marsh's insistence on secrecy makes it hard for me to imagine he would have shared the information with others, and I have never told anyone else. To be honest, I wasn't going to tell you either." She hazarded a glance in his direction. The sympathy there was like raindrops falling upon her parched soul. Encouraged, she straightened her spine and adjusted her position. "But I recently started to realize how serious things are getting between us and knew there was no other choice."

"You could still have kept it from me," he murmured. "Judging from what you have just told me, I never would have discovered the truth."

"But I would have known, Henry. I would have had to live with the guilt of keeping this from you, and that's not something that I'm prepared to do."

His hand came up to cup her cheek. "I'm sorry that this was so hard for you to confide. There's absolutely nothing for you to be ashamed of, no reason for me to think ill of you because of who your mother was or how you were conceived."

"I know, but people have been shunned for less." She pressed her cheek into the palm of his hand and savored the feel of his fingers stroking her skin. "I have always disagreed with Society's readiness to condemn a person for something that's not their fault."

"Is it strange that I am grateful to your mother for being the woman she was and selling an evening of pleasure to the man who fathered you?"

Viola smiled in response to the humor in his eyes. "Not at all, for I am grateful to her as well."

His expression grew pensive as he gazed back at her for a long, drawn-out moment before saying, "You're everything I've ever wanted, Viola. Don't ever doubt that again."

Undone by his honesty, his affection and his deep consideration, she allowed every reservation that bound her to melt away into nothing, because the truth was she needed him, more than she'd ever needed anyone else in her life. Holding his gaze, she let her hand seek out the nape of his neck and her fingers slide through his hair.

His eyes darkened as she raked the windblown locks. "I don't know what to say," she whispered, her body humming with increased awareness.

"Don't say anything then," he murmured. "Just show me how you feel."

Thunderous heartbeats echoed in her chest. She wanted to with the kind of desperation that threatened to kill her if she denied it. So she pulled his head closer, so close she could feel his breath stroking her jaw, and then closed the distance between them, settling her mouth against his.

Henry could not resist any longer. He reached out and grabbed her and pulled her up onto his lap. She gasped and he swallowed the sound with his mouth while holding her firmly in place. Drawing back slightly, he ran his thumb over her plump lower lip, dragging it down until her mouth opened. "Stay, just like that," he murmured, loving the heavy-lidded look on her face as he pressed her to him and slid his hand down from her face to her thigh, "so I can taste you."

She sucked in an audible breath and he smiled as he lowered his mouth over hers. She remained as he'd asked, granting him entry. When she whimpered slightly, he almost forgot himself as a new elemental power took over. She tasted so sweet, and the way she responded . . . Dear God, she was growing increasingly hard to resist. Especially now with her arms winding tight around his neck as if she were clinging to life itself. He could feel her heartbeat echoing through his chest as she pressed up against him.

If he wasn't mistaken, she wanted the same as he and with equal fervor. "Viola . . ." He breathed her name against the corner of her mouth before trailing a series of kisses along her jaw. "You can't possibly imagine what you do to me."

"I can feel it," she whispered, and he grinned close to her ear.

Finding her mouth once again, he kissed her as if it would never be enough, as if his life depended on this particular kiss. Her body leaned further into his embrace, seeking more, and when he lost his balance and fell back against the grass, she followed him down, landing against him with a gasp.

"Viola." Her name fell from his lips once more as he gazed up into her gorgeous face. She smiled in response and words failed him, the wonder of what was happening between them like a dream he feared waking up from. Unable to resist her beauty and completely unwilling to try, Henry brought her mouth back for more.

He wasn't sure how long he kissed her this time, but when she finally pulled away and leaned her forehead against his, his heart was calmer, his mind more at ease. "I think I could happily kiss you forever," he told her, and pressed his lips to her temple. "You taste divine, like fresh air and sea spray."

"So do you." She smiled a little before shyly adding, "This day together is—"

"Better than you expected it to be?" he asked while stroking her jaw in reverent adoration.

"Yes." She sighed and angled her head to grant better access.

He laughed into her cheek until she vibrated from head to toe. "Just imagine how good it will be when we finally make love."

"You speak of it as if it's an eventuality."

Rolling her onto her back, he gazed down at her without bothering to hide the hunger her kiss had evoked. "Coming here with me today, confiding your secrets and kissing me as you just did, says it all." Brushing a stray strand of hair from her cheek, he tucked the errant lock behind her ear. "You are mine, Viola." His lips brushed her forehead. "And I am never, ever letting you go."

Viola stared at the letter on her desk, sighing as she reread the missive from Mr. Steadford. Her stomach clenched. She'd been able to forget about Robert for a fleeting moment while she'd been away at Hastings and had hoped to continue doing so for a while longer. But that was not to be. She was back in London, where problems continued to plague her.

A solid knock at the door made her flinch. Looking up, she saw Henry standing in the doorway. A smile graced his lips and his eyes shone with pleasure. "Good morning," he said, stepping inside the office and crossing the floor to one of the empty chairs. His smile slipped slightly when he met her serious gaze. "Everything all right?"

"Robert and Hayes want to see me. I'm to meet with them at Tremaine House tomorrow together with Mr. Steadford, but the thought of having to go there again and face Robert's condescension is not something I relish." She set the letter down on her desk and removed her spectacles. Distressed and worried, she didn't even care that she'd been wearing them when Henry walked in. "Will you please come with me?"

"Of course," Henry said. He didn't sit but remained standing instead, one hand loosely resting against the chair's back. "I can also insist that we hold the meeting at my town house, if you prefer."

She nodded. "Yes. I think I would." Meeting with Robert on neutral ground, in a place where he had no authority, would make it easier for her to face him. "Thank you, Henry."

Rising, Viola rounded her desk. "Let's go and inform both Steadford and Hayes of the change." She collected her bonnet and spencer from a hook on the wall and stopped to think. "Unless, of course, you have other plans. I do not want to impose since—"

"Everything else can wait," he said. Taking her spencer out of her hands, he helped her put it on. He leaned in closer and whisper against her ear. "Helping you is the only thing that matters right now."

A shiver dove under her skin and she sucked in a breath, startled as always by the visceral effect he had on her. He didn't linger after he spoke but stepped toward the door, where he waited for her to gather her wits while regarding her with no small amount of mischief. She moved toward him and he, devil that he was, decided to add, "If I'm lucky, you'll thank me later with a kiss."

Unable to think, let alone speak after that had been said, she preceded him out of the hospital and toward his carriage. Once inside, she managed to wait until they were well under way before crossing to where he sat on the opposite bench and pressing her mouth to his. "I'm sorry," she muttered, breathless as he slid his mouth down her neck to the crook of her shoulder. "I don't want to wait until later."

He chuckled against her and playfully nipped her flesh with his teeth, sending hot little shivers straight into her belly. "Don't ever apologize for desiring me, Viola." His mouth found hers once again, kissing her until she felt light and restless and desperate for more. "It pleases me to no end, knowing that you do." Another kiss followed before he steered her back to the opposite bench. Eyes glowing, he regarded her while she straightened her clothes and her bonnet. "Lord help me, the things I want to do to you . . ." He grinned and shook his head while her entire face seemed to catch on fire.

The carriage drew to a halt, and Henry reached for the handle and opened the door. He helped her alight, and together they marched up the front steps of Mr. Steadford's place of business. But the barrister wasn't in, so they left a note with his secretary, informing Mr. Steadford of the proposed change in location and continued on to Mr. Hayes's office. A sharply dressed younger gentleman opened the door when they knocked. He took Henry's card and asked them to wait in the foyer, returning moments later to usher them through to Hayes's office.

Entering, they found the man they sought keeping company with another gentleman Henry didn't recognize.

"Good morning, Mr. Lowell," Hayes said. He nodded toward Viola. "Your Grace. Are you acquainted with the Honorable Mr. Justice Atkins? He and I were just discussing available court dates."

Henry addressed Atkins stiffly. "A pleasure to meet you, Judge."

Atkins gave Henry and Viola an assessing look. "Likewise."

"Turns out we might be able to settle this case quicker than I had expected," Hayes said with an eager look of anticipation. "Another case has been re-scheduled so there's an opening ten days from today."

"Ten days." Viola almost choked on the words as she spoke them. "But . . ."

"I sympathize with you, Duchess, truly I do," Hayes said.

Viola very much doubted it.

"What if we're not ready to go to court yet?" Henry asked.

"Unfortunately, once the case has been brought before a judge, *he* decides when to set the date," Atkins said. "The tenth of May suits well since we would otherwise have to wait at least a year."

A year sounded wonderful to Viola. She looked at Hayes, hoping to grasp just one straw. "You cannot possibly be ready to go to court after spending only a month gathering evidence."

He shrugged. "My clerks have been particularly efficient where you are concerned and . . . well . . . Tremaine has paid a steep price to expedite the matter."

"I was under the impression that he needed funds," Henry muttered with a jarring note of sarcasm.

Hayes chuckled. "Right you are, Mr. Lowell, but as it turns out, his stay in India wasn't wasted. He's still able to afford a comfortable lifestyle, though I daresay that the money he expects to make on selling your hospital, Duchess, will help him a great deal."

Viola bristled. "It will never be his."

Hayes smirked. "I think you'll realize how wrong you are about that when I present you with my findings tomorrow."

"About that," Henry said. "Her Grace prefers not to visit Tremaine House again so I would like to pro-pose we meet at my home instead."

Hayes seemed to consider. He glanced at Viola and

then back at Henry before saying, "As you wish. I see no reason to oppose."

Holding herself upright while the ground seemed to slip away beneath her feet, Viola glared at Hayes before turning to Atkins. "What do you stand to gain from all of this?"

"Viola," Henry cautioned.

"I don't like what you are implying," Atkins growled.

"I'm sorry," Viola said. "But who ever heard of a case progressing this fast?" She pointed an accusatory finger at the judge. "He's obviously been bought."

"I must caution you against accusing the man who'll be deciding your fate," Henry whispered.

"I think it is time for Her Grace to take her leave," Atkins said. "She's clearly overwrought."

"And understandably so," Henry clipped. "Tremaine has treated her abominably."

"That is a matter of opinion," Hayes said. "Furthermore, it is the word of a woman accused of manipulating an aging peer into marriage and stealing his fortune, against that of a duke. There's no doubt in my mind about who will win."

"We shall see about that," Viola told him even as her confidence buckled under his.

"Indeed we shall," Hayes agreed.

When he said nothing further, Viola walked out of the room without saying another word. Her hands were shaking when she stepped down onto the pavement, her bones chilled with wary apprehension. "I hate those men," she told Henry when he arrived at her side. "How can someone be so awful?"

Instead of responding, he offered her his arm and guided her toward the carriage, where he handed her up. When he climbed in after her and lowered himself to sit on the bench beside her, she took his hand and simply held it.

"Do you have any idea what information Hayes might have uncovered?" Henry quietly asked.

Viola swallowed and tried to stay calm. "I haven't a clue."

"There's no chance of him knowing you're not Marsh's daughter or that your mother was a courtesan?"

Shuddering, she shook her head. "No. I was born in France and Marsh did everything he could to protect me—to hide the truth of my birth. There are no records."

Henry was silent for a moment and then he drew a deep breath. "Good." He glanced out the window briefly before returning his attention to her. "Whatever happens, we'll get through it together."

As much as Viola appreciated him saying so and in spite of the fact that she knew he was helping because she mattered to him, she didn't feel right about all the trouble she'd caused him. "I'm sorry I got you involved in all of this."

"Don't be," he told her sincerely. "If it hadn't been for this case and your need for a good barrister, I might never have found an excuse to get to know you better. And that would have been a tragic shame."

"But my life is a mess, Henry. It is not exactly the sort of thing to tempt a man into forming a permanent attachment, and even if it were, you need a respectable wife by your side, not someone who's likely to cause a potential scandal."

His eyes searched her face in desperation. "Is that what you want, Viola?" he asked, focusing on the first part of what she'd just said. "A more permanent attachment?"

She turned more fully toward him and set her palm against his cheek. The carriage rocked side to side as it turned a corner. Looking back at the man who had come to mean so incredibly much to her lately, Viola searched her heart for the right thing to say. She wanted him desperately, but at the same time she needed to save him from the shame she might yet cause him if word got out about who she was.

"I don't know," she finally said, for she knew that if she said yes there would be no going back. He'd marry her in a heartbeat, trapping himself with a woman whose name was seconds away from being dragged through the mud. Again.

His eyes held hers for a long, difficult moment and then he kissed her, long and hard and without apology. "I meant what I said at Hastings," he told her when he drew back. Tipping her chin up with his fingers, he held her so he could stare down into her eyes, to the very depth of her soul. A smile tugged at his lips and she imagined he saw the truth that was written upon her heart. "I'm never letting you go, no matter how patient I must be or how long I have to wait for you to be ready."

Saying nothing, Viola tamped down the flare of excitement she felt in response to those words. Because she was more than ready. She just didn't want him to make a mistake that might end up destroying his life.

Chapter 23

When Viola arrived at Henry's house the next day, she was shown into the parlor, where a tea tray waited. Viola glanced around, appreciating the simple yet costly furnished space. No knickknacks cluttered the fireplace mantel or other available surfaces, but the sofas were clad in exquisite silk damask and the tables appeared to have been carved from rich mahogany.

"Good morning, Viola," Henry said as he entered the room. Dressed in a burgundy jacket and a pair of beige trousers, he was just as impeccably dressed as any duke might have been. But what flipped her stomach right onto its side was the fire in his eyes as he stepped toward her and reached for her hand. He raised it to his lips, his gaze fixed on hers as he brushed a kiss across her knuckles. And then, as if recognizing the sizzling effect he was having on her, the edge of his mouth hitched with mischief.

Viola just stood there, breathless and utterly incapable of movement. She swallowed, because heaven help her, she was having thoughts . . . thoughts that would only ever be realized if she agreed to be his wife. The temptation was great and he knew it, damn him. She could see in the glint of his eyes that he was being deliberately seductive and that it was working.

"Was the air very fresh on your way over?" he asked. His gaze lingered on her face and his hand continued holding hers for longer than what was deemed proper. When she failed to respond, he quietly murmured, "Because you look rather flushed. Delightfully so, I might add."

"It was, um . . . yes." The man had apparently made her stupid.

He leaned in closer, glanced hastily at the wide open door and then pulled her roughly into his arms, stealing her gasp of surprise with a bone-jarring kiss that weakened her knees and robbed her of all remaining thought.

When he set her aside moments later her head felt slightly unstable. Raising the tips of her fingers to her lips, she blinked as she looked up at Henry.

He grinned, the rascal. "Steadford confirmed that he will be joining us here, so he, Robert and Hayes are expected to arrive in roughly ten minutes. I could show you the automaton while we wait."

"Oh yes," Viola said. She'd been curious about the machine ever since Henry first mentioned owning it and followed him eagerly into his library. When they entered the room, a large ball of fur leapt onto the floor right in front of her feet, causing her to take a step back. "Oh!" She stared at the creature with wide-eyed dismay.

"My cat," Henry said with a wave of his hand. "I present to you Newton."

"He is very . . ." Viola struggled to find the right word.

"Fat," Henry supplied. He sighed while Viola watched Newton flop to the floor and sprawl out with lazy abandon. "My cook can't seem to resist him. I keep telling her she'll be the death of him one day but it's like talking to a brick wall."

Viola chuckled and bent to run her hand over Newton's fluffy coat. He purred with pleasure and turned to offer his belly.

"Enough of that, you scoundrel," Henry told Newton with notable humor in his voice.

"I think he likes me," Viola said.

"He's male," Henry said. "Of course he likes you."

Looking up, she became aware of the intensity with which Henry watched her. Heat fanned out across her shoulders, but then she spied the glass case they had come to see. Her temperature returned to normal while a new kind of excitement overcame her.

She leapt to her feet and hurried toward it. "Your automaton," she said, admiring the boy who held his quill in preparation for the next words he'd be asked to pen. "He's wonderful, Henry. Absolutely wonderful!"

Henry smiled with undeniable pleasure. "Just wait until you watch him write. It's quite a mechanical marvel."

"Do we have time for that now?" *Please say yes.*

"I—"

A loud banging sound came from the front of the house, causing Henry to frown. "I'm afraid not. It seems our guests have arrived." He led Viola quickly back to the parlor. When they entered the room, he gestured toward the sofa. "I think you should have a seat there at the end. It will offer you a regal appearance while preventing you from having to face Robert too closely."

Agreeing with him, Viola took the seat he indicated, arranged her skirts and folded her hands neatly in her lap. Back straight, she stared toward the parlor door while asking her nerves to be still.

Steadford entered shortly after, followed by Hayes and finally Robert, who glared at her as soon as she came into his line of vision. Greetings were made with clipped politeness and then Henry came to sit by her side before anyone else could do so. She breathed a sigh of relief and fought the urge to reach for his hand when Hayes placed a large pile of papers on the table before her.

"We are here today to share our findings with you so you may prepare for court," Hayes said. "The Duke of Tremaine will be seeking compensation from Her Grace, the Duchess of Tremaine, in the form of St. Agatha's hospital and her ownership in the rejuvenation center."

Viola blinked. "What about the money I haven't yet spent and the house I own?"

Hayes smiled. "The duke is not a monster, Duchess. He does not wish to turn you out of your home or take the few funds you have left. After all, you and his father were married, so you ought to be entitled to something."

"He knows going after my places of business is going to hurt me the most," she muttered while doing her best not to meet Robert's gaze.

"Indeed." Hayes stared at her for a second before repositioning himself in his seat and saying, "Judge Atkins has confirmed the tenth, so you'll probably receive a notice from him soon."

"You blindsided me with this, Hayes," Steadford grumbled. "And I don't take kindly to that so I ought to warn you that I have every intention of having that date postponed."

"You're welcome to try." Hayes held Steadford's gaze for a long uncomfortable moment before dropping it to the pile of papers on the table. Viola instinctively stiffened because she could sense, before anyone uttered another word, that what came next would not be good.

This feeling increased tenfold when Hayes smiled

and looked at her. "As I mentioned when last we met, my clerks have been very busy lately." Oh God. Her heart was pounding. More so when he slid a large leather-bound book out from under the papers and flipped it open. "This is the church record for St. Andrew's Holborn, years 1790 to 1800. The vicar there was kind enough to lend it to me so I can show you this very intriguing detail."

"I doubt it's anything we're not already aware of," Henry said. He gave Steadford a pointed look, and Viola realized he was trying to lessen the significance of Hayes's upcoming revelation.

Hayes hesitated and glanced at each of them in turn while Robert looked straight at Viola with predatory menace. "Here is Your Grace's name, Viola Elisabeth Marsh. And here, where your mother's name should be, it says Danielle Marsh. But an additional note has been added in the margin. See?"

Viola sucked in a breath as she stared down at the heavy scrawl. The word *bastard* was followed by a question mark. How Hayes had managed to find this she could not imagine. It made no sense. She'd been born in France, not England, but according to this . . . Dear God. Marsh must have had her christened after their arrival. He'd been a religious man so of course he would have. It made perfect sense even though she'd not thought to consider it before.

Unfortunately, his desire to do right by her had now done her harm.

Knowing her only resort was denial, she said, "There's obviously been a mistake since my parents are both listed."

"Indeed," Hayes murmured. He leafed through the pile of papers until he found the page he sought. Pulling it free, he leaned back in his seat. "What I have been able to piece together is that your mother and father were not married. I deduced this after a lengthy discussion with the clerk who filled out this record twenty-one years ago.

"He remembers Mr. Marsh and his infant daughter because of how unusual the whole situation seemed to him at the time. When he asked Mr. Marsh about the child's mother, Mr. Marsh could not provide a marital record. The clerk questioned him further and Mr. Marsh began dissembling, weaving a tale about a fire and how your unfortunate mother and the marital record had both been destroyed in it. Apparently, lying for the purpose of establishing legitimacy happens often, and one could not be named legitimate without proof. Which Marsh did not supply. His failure to offer any evidence of marriage leads me to believe that he knew exactly who your mother was and that he was trying to hide it."

"You're making a lot of assumptions without supporting any of them," Steadford drawled as if he'd lost interest in this conversation several minutes ago.

"I'm getting to that," Hayes said. The thrill of snaring his prey had brightened his eyes. "For you see, I've also managed to get my hands on this." He waved the piece of paper he held and smiled at Viola.

Her stomach lurched with the knowledge that whatever came next, she was not going to like it. "What is that?" she asked in a voice far braver than she actually felt.

"It's a record of Mr. Marsh's arrival in England on May 29, 1799. Accompanying him was his infant daughter, Viola Elisabeth Marsh." Hayes set the page aside and reached for another. "Discovering Mr. Marsh had lived abroad, my clerks tracked him to Paris, where he was highly respected as a professor at the Sorbonne."

"He was a skilled physician," Viola muttered while clutching the armrest beside her.

"And very dependable too, which apparently made his colleagues wonder about his sudden decision to quit his position and leave from one day to the next."

Viola shook her head. "Your Clerks cannot have discovered this. Paris is far. It's only three weeks since Tremaine hired you, and by the time you started investigating—"

"He had enough time," Henry told her. "Getting there and back would have taken no more than four days, plus whatever time was required for the interviews. In truth, a week would have been more than sufficient."

"One of my clerks made the trip," Mr. Hayes said, while hope began seeping out of Viola's body. He reached for the teapot and poured himself a cup. "Would anyone else like some?" When everyone shook their heads, Hayes set the pot aside with a shrug. "Apparently some of these men still work at the Sorbonne." He sipped his tea. "But most helpful of all was actually one of Mr. Marsh's former students, who now heads the same anatomy department Mr. Marsh used to teach. Turns out he was very eager to learn as much as he could from Mr. Marsh—so eager he asked Mr. Marsh if he could serve as his assistant when he tended to patients."

"Oh God," Viola whispered, so low only Henry would hear her. She knew what was coming now, what Hayes would say, and as much as she wanted to flee the room and pretend this wasn't happening, she straightened her spine and squared her shoulders.

"We'll get through this," Henry breathed in answer to her exclamation.

"Imagine my surprise when I learned that Mr. Marsh had helped a doxy deliver a child and then taken the child home with him after the woman died. The next day he was gone and, well, here we are."

"What an entertaining tale," Steadford said. His tone was tight and Viola knew then and there that he'd have some choice words to deal her later because she'd failed to mention this to him. "However, I am not sure what you hope to accomplish with it."

"She's the bastard daughter of a whore," Robert sneered, and Viola felt Henry stiffen. "My father obviously paid her so he could swive her."

Before she could stop him, Henry was out of his seat and hauling Robert to his feet by his shirtfront. "Apologize this instant, Tremaine."

"Why should I?" Robert asked with curling lip. "A woman who spreads her legs for the son before taking the father deserves no respect."

The punch landed against Robert's cheek so fast and with such force that the tea set rattled. "I'll bloody well kill you right now," Henry growled, while Steadford and Hayes both leapt to remove him from Robert's person.

Robert just laughed and threw back his head. "Oh, I see! You haven't had her yet, Lowell." Another punch landed in Robert's chest. "Best get a bank draft ready. Seems her price is going up by thousands of pounds per tup. Did I mention that with me it was free?"

"Shut up," Hayes demanded while pulling on Henry's arm.

Steadford tried to wedge himself between Henry and Robert. "This isn't helping, Lowell."

"She was so damn willing too," Robert added as Steadford and Hayes finally managed to pull the two men apart.

"Be quiet, damn you," Hayes fairly shouted.

Viola's blood had long since drained from her

body. She was cold inside and increasingly aware that nothing good would come of what happened here today.

He wanted to rip Robert's head off his shoulders and toss it across the room. Yes, it would be bloody, but at least then the man would cease talking. Even now while Hayes warned him to keep his mouth shut, Robert couldn't resist an additional jibe. "It's too late to save her, Lowell. I'm meeting with a couple of journalists later today."

Henry feared he was seconds away from grabbing his pistol. "I suggest you leave," he gritted out.

"Agreed," Hayes said. "We've shared everything we know and look forward to resolving this matter as quickly as possible. Good day." He grabbed Robert by the elbow and steered him out of the room.

"I knew there was something else," Steadford said. "Wish you would have apprised me of it beforehand, Your Grace."

"I'm sorry," Viola said. "I honestly didn't think it would be discovered or that it would matter."

Mr. Steadford nodded in understanding. "In future, please be aware that the truth does come out eventually. Especially when there's a hound on your heels." He turned to Henry. "I wouldn't have minded delivering a punch to that arrogant fop myself, but in this case, restraint is advisable. I hope you'll remember that when we meet him in court."

"Of course," Henry muttered. "I apologize for my behavior. I just—"

"Believe me, I know," Mr. Steadford said with a glance at Viola. "Is there anything else I ought to be made aware of at this point?"

"No," she said. "That is all there is."

"In that case—"

"Before you go," Henry said, "there is in fact something that I must tell you." He'd been holding off on mentioning Guthrie's visit and the information he had conveyed because he'd been waiting to have his own suspicions about Robert confirmed. As it stood, there was no evidence of any wrongdoing. "Carlton Guthrie came to call on me about a week ago." He told them both about the ensuing conversation and the letter Henry had taken upon himself to write.

"I can't believe you did not tell me," Viola said. She looked slightly hurt.

"I didn't want to get your hopes up about a solid defense until I had something concrete to offer."

"Without evidence it's just an accusation and a pretty outrageous one too," Steadford said. "Hayes will have it thrown out of court in no time at all and we'll just be left looking desperate."

"What if Guthrie testifies?" Viola asked.

"What reason is there to believe what he says over the word of a duke?" Steadford shook his head. "I'm afraid it won't work, but that doesn't mean there's no hope. Hayes isn't the only one with efficient clerks. Based on the information you provided me about Tremaine's character, Mr. Lowell, mine did some digging into his past. They found at least one person who can corroborate your story about the demimondaine and there are others who are willing to testify to his aggressive tendencies."

"Do you think that will be enough to discredit his claims about me taking advantage of his father?" Viola asked.

"Maybe. If he wasn't a duke it would help, but as he is one of the most powerful men in the country, I cannot say with certainty." He gave them each a final look. "I will wish you both a good day now. There is much for me to do in preparation for the battle lying ahead."

He strode away at a brisk pace, disappearing into the hallway beyond. As soon as he was gone, Henry turned to Viola, closed the space between them and pulled her roughly into his arms. "Are you all right?" He murmured the question against her head while reveling in the scent of her hair, the feel of her body, so familiar now, and the way she pressed her cheek against his shoulder in search of comfort.

"No. I don't think so. My life is unraveling, Henry, and there is nothing I can do but stand by and watch it happen."

He leaned back in order to meet her troubled gaze. "That's not true. We can still fight this."

"Really?" Her eyes pleaded for him to show her the way. "Steadford did not sound the least bit certain."

Henry had to agree with her there. His lack of confidence was not reassuring, but at least it was honest. "The odds aren't good, but that does not mean they're impossible, though I really do wish that we had more time. If I were to receive a response from the West Indies about Robert's wife, then——"

"There's every chance she died as Robert said she did. Knowing the truth might not help." With a heavy sigh, Viola stepped out of his arms and went to the window overlooking the garden. "This will be pretty once it is finished. What sort of tree is that over there?"

Disliking the space between them, he went to stand beside her. "Apple."

"That will be lovely in the autumn when it bears fruit. I like how neat and simple it is. Once the rhododendrons and peonies grow and begin producing flowers, the splashes of color will make your garden a lovely retreat."

"I'm considering a box over there to the left for some herbs and vegetables. What do you think?"

Her brow puckered slightly while she considered. "It could work, I think. Especially if it's right up against the garden wall so it doesn't take up too much space." They remained side by side looking out, until she suddenly glanced up at him, her eyes filled with question. "I was just wondering . . . That woman Mr. Guthrie mentioned . . . Do you know who she was?"

"Her name was Olivia Jones. Besides that, I've no idea."

"So you haven't made any inquiries?"

"No. Considering the source of the information I received, I dismissed it as inconclusive and chose to focus on the circumstances surrounding the death of Robert's wife. I believed I stood a better chance with that."

Viola stared back at him for a second. "I think you might be wrong."

"You heard Mr. Steadford, Viola. Guthrie won't work as a witness."

She smiled. "I know. But Olivia Jones must have a family, friends, people who might be able to offer some information about what happened to her. Reliable sources able to corroborate Guthrie's story."

The hope etched in every part of her expression made Henry wary. He didn't want to lead her toward disappointment. "I think it's a slim chance at best."

"Probably. But what's the alternative?"

Mr. Andrews stepped into the room before Henry could answer and announced the unexpected arrival of Henry's grandmother.

"I should probably go," Viola said, but was stopped from doing so by Lady Scranton herself.

Dressed in taffeta and lace, the old woman appeared in the doorway before Viola even managed to collect her reticule. The countess looked from Henry to Viola and back again. "What a pleasant surprise finding the two of you here together." She walked forward, skirts swishing.

"It's not what it looks like," Henry blurted before he could think to stop himself. Lady Scranton's face swiveled toward him, brows raised as if in challenge. "What I mean to say is that Her Grace is here for a very good reason."

"I'm sure she is," his grandmother said with no apparent attempt to hide her amusement.

Henry sighed. "We were discussing her case. Steadford just left," he muttered, and gestured toward the seating arrangement where Mr. Hayes's cup of tea still sat, mostly untouched. "Shall we?"

Lady Scranton nodded and moved toward the armchair. She lowered herself to the seat and waited expectantly for Henry and Viola to join her.

Viola hesitated. "I should probably—"

"Have a seat," Lady Scranton suggested.

Henry darted a look at Viola. She was eyeing the sofa with some uncertainty. Henry didn't blame her. There was no telling where this conversation with his grandmother was destined to lead.

A hint of a smile tugged at the countess's lips. She inclined her head. "I like you, Duchess, and I daresay my grandson likes you too. Please, join us for a moment. There is much I wish to discuss with you both."

Viola glanced between Lady Scranton and Henry before slowly edging her way toward the spot she'd vacated only a few minutes earlier. When she eventually lowered herself, it was to perch on the edge of the seat, like a bird prepared to take flight.

Henry sat down beside her.

"So," his grandmother said, "word has it that Tremaine is out for blood." She looked at each of them in turn. "According to your grandfather, it was the main topic of conversation last night at White's. A page in the betting book has even been dedicated to the outcome. People are staking money on who they believe will win."

"Good Lord," Viola muttered, and Henry immediately reached for her hand.

The gesture did not go unnoticed. His grandmother's eyes were filled with interest, but when she prepared to speak, he cut her off by saying, "Did Scranton say how word got out?"

"It was Tremaine's doing."

Viola sucked in a breath. "So he wasn't just talking about his upcoming meeting with journalists when he said it was too late to save my reputation. He wants to make a spectacle of me."

"Obviously," Lady Scranton agreed. "That man despises you or he would have kept the matter private."

"Articles will appear in tomorrow's papers," Henry muttered. "That is inevitable."

"My reputation will be in tatters before the hearing begins." She looked at Henry with the desperation of someone who feared her escape route had just been cut off. "Winning will take no effort at all for Tremaine and Hayes."

"As things stand at the moment," Lady Scranton said. She pushed Hayes's cup from earlier aside and reached for a clean one. "How about some tea?" When Viola and Henry both answered in the affirmative, she filled their cups and hers as well before taking a long sip. "Now, in my estimation, the best course of action for you right now, Viola, would be to marry Henry."

Viola sputtered before managing to say, "I beg your pardon?"

Lady Scranton pursed her lips. "Well. It would give you the advantage of being a Lowell and ensuring that you have the full strength of his entire family behind you," she said while Henry felt like protesting. Not because he disagreed, but because he didn't want anyone's interference when it came to his future with Viola. "As his wife, you would be a more difficult target."

"Because I and all my worldly possessions would belong to my husband," Viola said with a dull note that made Henry want to pick his grandmother up and carry her out of the house before she said something else to undermine his efforts of winning Viola.

Lady Scranton sighed. "Having seen the two of you together, it is clear to me that you care for each other."

Henry squeezed Viola's hand and addressed his grandmother. "Will you excuse us for a moment? I would like to speak with Her Grace alone."

"By all means," his grandmother said.

Henry stood and waited for Viola to do the same. She moved slowly, but her hand never left his as he led her from the parlor and back to his library. Entering the room, Henry glanced around to ensure that none of his servants was present before closing the door and turning to face Viola. His nerves jumped in response to her hesitant expression, and although this was not how he'd planned to propose, it was time for him to do so.

"She's right," he said, and took a step forward. Reaching up, he pushed a loose strand of hair from Viola's brow and tucked it behind her ear. His knuckles grazed her cheek as his hand fell away, stirring his senses on account of the sigh with which she responded. "As my wife—"

"Everything I own would belong to you."

"Not necessarily. I can have papers drafted granting you full control over everything you bring into our marriage."

Her eyes misted with wonder. "You would do that for me?"

He smiled. "I have no interest in acquiring your assets or in taking away your independence, Viola. All I want is you, the woman I've fallen in love with."

When she spoke again, her voice scraped her throat. "I love you too."

His heart swelled with joy. "So you'll marry me then?"

"Yes." She pressed her mouth to his, kissing him as if she meant to fuse herself to him forever.

He kissed her back with the desperation of a man who'd just been given carte blanche to ravish her completely. Except his grandmother was just down the hall, still waiting for them to return.

That put a damper on his passion.

He broke the kiss with reluctance and eased her away. Her breath was just as ragged as his, her eyes wonderfully dazed. "I cannot promise a positive outcome in court, but at least you will have my family's support. An earl and three dukes isn't so bad."

"I'd say it's quite good."

He cleared his throat and retreated a step to stop from dragging her back for additional kisses. There would be time for that later. "They'll show the world they accept you and I'll show the world that I love you. Together we'll fight the scandal that's bound to arise when Robert reveals your mother's identity to the papers."

Concern tightened her features. "Are you absolutely certain you want to face the consequences of marrying me?"

"I've never been more certain of anything else in my life, Viola." His voice was level and sure. "As my wife, your chance of winning the case will also improve. You'll be more than the woman accused of taking advantage of an old man on his deathbed. You'll be Mrs. Lowell, the future Viscountess Armswell, respected and adored by her husband and in-laws, which is bound to undermine Robert's claims about you. And if we can do that, the case might just fall apart."

"Do you honestly think so?"

"We would have to consult with Steadford to be certain, but I do believe it's our best chance. Either way, my feelings for you won't change. I want to marry you no matter what, Viola."

She smiled with adoration in her eyes, and it took every ounce of restraint on Henry's part to remain where he was. "We've a lot to do then, don't we?"

He grinned. Between investigating Olivia Jones's death and planning a hasty wedding, they would have time for little else in the coming week. "We should probably return to the parlor and inform my grandmother of our decision."

Viola turned toward the door but he stepped in front of her, blocking her path. He could not resist after all. "One more kiss."

Her willingness to accommodate him was evident in the haste with which she flung her arms around his neck and rose up to meet his mouth. Henry drew her against him, molding her perfectly against his solid frame. His back hit the door with a thud but he ignored it. All he could focus on at the moment were her lips, her scent, the feel of her fingers teasing his hair.

His hands trailed down her back, then lower until he could clasp her more firmly against him. A slew of wicked thoughts stirred his imaginings. God, how he wished they could simply surrender, right here, right now. The nearby sofa would do rather nicely because by all that was holy, he wanted Viola this instant.

Something soft moved against his leg. A sharp meow followed.

Viola grinned against his mouth. "I think Newton wants to remind us that this is not the proper time or place to get carried away."

Henry silently cursed the feline's unwelcome interruption, even though he supposed it had come at the right time. He glanced at the sofa on which he'd begun to imagine some rather scandalous things.

Right. Time to collect yourself and pretend you're not ready to chase every fantasy your brain has been contriving since the moment you first clapped eyes on this woman.

"Your grandmother is waiting for us," Viola added.

Bollocks!

Hadn't he just said as much seconds earlier? Yet somehow the kiss had made him forget. It had driven all thought from his mind and replaced it with one singular goal. "I think we need to acquire a special license posthaste," he muttered, while sending a quiet apology to his nether regions.

"I quite agree." Her eyes, he saw, were filled with a mixture of understanding, regret and desperate longing. "The sooner we do, the sooner we'll start doing . . . other things besides kissing."

Henry reached behind him and yanked the door open. "After you," he said. She chuckled low and sensually, and Henry prayed he'd have the strength to survive until their wedding night. He followed her out of the library and back to the parlor, his gaze feasting on the gentle sway of her hips as she moved.

Viola wanted him just as much as he wanted her, and he could not wait to make her his.

Chapter 24

"**Y**ou made the front page news," Diana told Viola the following morning. Standing in Viola's bedroom doorway, she wore an apologetic expression.

Viola stared at the dreaded paper in Diana's hand. "How bad is it?"

"Well, there's a caricature of you selling sexual favors to a long line of men, including your husband, Mr. Lowell and Tremaine." She held it up for Viola to see.

Viola sucked in a breath. "Dear God."

"I think you may be the center of attention for quite some time."

"Really?" Viola made no attempt to hide her sarcastic retort. She rubbed her hand over her face in frustration. "Henry has been ridiculed. Peter too, Lord rest his soul."

"You need to hold your head up high now. If you present yourself as weak, those who wish you ill will take advantage."

Viola nodded. "I'm not ashamed of who my mother was." She crossed the floor, accepting the paper from Diana. A quick glance at the caricature made her insides contract because of the effect it would have on

Henry, his family, the case. "She did what she had to in order to survive, just as you and Harriet once did."

"Neither one of us chose our path willingly. It might have been the same for your mother."

Viola considered her suggestion before saying, "It doesn't matter. She gave me life when she could have chosen not to. I will always be grateful for that." She gave the paper a final glance before tossing it onto her bed. "There's too much to do for me to worry about inevitable gossip." She grabbed her spencer and followed Diana out of the room. Henry would arrive soon. If she meant to have a slice of toast and a cup of tea before he did, the time to do so was now.

"Ignore them," Henry advised her an hour later when they alit from his coach on Bow Street and passersby stopped to stare.

She heard someone mutter, "Courtesan," and "Fallen woman," before she preceded Henry into the Bow Street office. The door closed behind them, silencing the crowd. Viola expelled a breath and glanced up at Henry. "I am trying."

He gave her a warm look of encouragement and stepped forward to address a man seated behind a wide desk. The man looked up. "How may I help you?"

"My name is Mr. Henry Lowell and this is the Duchess of Tremaine. We're here to open an investigation into the murder of a Miss Olivia Jones."

If their names meant anything to this man, he showed no indication of it as he stood, his expression a mask of complete inscrutability. "Wait here one moment please, while I confer with one of the officers." He departed through a doorway directly behind him.

"Have you ever dealt with the Bow Street office

before?" Viola asked Henry as she glanced around the reception. It was sparsely furnished with only the desk and a chair to go with it. A long case clock to Viola's left conveyed the passing of time.

"Last year, after helping Florian and Huntley save Juliette from Bartholomew, I informed the officers here of what had transpired so they could come to the scene and investigate. They brought the chief magistrate with them and showed extreme professionalism."

The man from earlier returned. "Officer Ericson says he would like to speak with you directly. If you'll please follow me."

Viola and Henry were shown into a tidy office that indicated Officer Ericson's preference for order. A young man with neatly combed brown hair, he stood as soon as they entered. "Your Grace." He offered Viola a stiff bow before turning to Henry. "Mr. Lowell. My secretary says you wish to investigate a murder." He extended his hand toward two vacant chairs and waited for Henry and Viola to sit before resuming his own.

"That is correct," Henry said. "The victim's name was Olivia Jones. She was stabbed to death in the St. Giles area five years ago."

Officer Ericson frowned. "Time destroys evidence. It won't be an easy investigation."

"We realize that," Viola said. She leaned forward slightly. "Is it possible her death was reported when it happened? Perhaps you have notes to look back on, an examination of her body or an interview with her family and friends?"

Officer Ericson regarded her with a shrewd gaze. "Can you offer any information about her, like age or appearance?"

"She would have been under the age of thirty, perhaps even twenty," Henry said. "We believe the Duke of Tremaine had a hand in her death so—"

"Hold on one minute." Officer Ericson looked at them each as though they were barking mad before pinning Viola with a discerning gaze. "Are we speaking of the man who's so intent on proving you to be a social-climbing charlatan that he's willing to drag you to court and have your husband's will contested?"

"You keep appraised of the news, I see."

"It is part of my job to do so." He stared straight back at her without flinching.

"We would not have come here unless we believed our suspicions about Tremaine to be accurate," Henry said.

Officer Ericson shook his head. "Do you have any idea how this will look if the papers get hold of it? You'll be accused of sullying a duke's reputation on top of everything else."

"That's a risk we're willing to take," Viola told him.

Officer Ericson hesitated briefly and then went to examine his bookcase. He pulled a large leather-bound volume from one of the shelves and dropped it on top of his desk. "Let me check my records." He leafed through the pages, pausing occasionally before continuing. Viola held her breath until he finally stopped. "Here it is. Olivia Jones's report. Her parents verified her identity. They came here to inquire about her when she went missing and were interviewed by Officer Jarvis." Ericson looked up. "He'll be in later in the day, so I'll be sure to have a word with him about this."

"I'll pay fifty pounds plus expenses for any information linking Tremaine to this crime," Henry said. He produced his calling card and handed it to Ericson. "I trust you'll keep us informed?"

Ericson nodded. "Of course. But I cannot guarantee the result you're hoping for. Not with a duke involved and not with the number of years that have transpired since this happened."

"Understood."

Viola and Henry took their leave. "You didn't tell him why you believe Tremaine might have killed Miss Jones," Viola said when they were back in the carriage.

"Neither did you." He reached for her hand and she twined her fingers with his.

"I wasn't sure if it would be helpful."

"Probably not. Carlton Guthrie is not a reliable source."

"But you believe him."

Henry kept quiet for a long while before saying, "When I consider Lady Beatrice's unlikely death, the way Robert has treated you, the ease with which he can fly into a rage and the demimondaine whose face I believe he once bruised, I am increasingly inclined to trust that what Guthrie says could be true."

Satisfied, Viola leaned her head against his shoulder. "Where are we off to now?" She'd failed to hear him give instructions to the driver after he handed her up into the carriage.

"To see the archbishop about a special license." When she tilted her chin up to meet his gaze, he captured her mouth in a tender kiss that made every tight muscle in Viola's body relax into supple languor. "After that," he added with a murmur, "we'll find a vicar with a minute to spare."

"**A**re you sure you want us there?" Harriet asked. She and Diana were helping Viola dress for her wedding which was to take place at St. George's in little more than an hour. "We're not very respectable."

"Nobody needs to know that save me and Henry." When she'd told him what her companions had once done for a living, she'd been prepared to fight his insistence that she distance herself from them completely.

Instead he'd been curious. Furthermore, he'd said he respected and admired her for choosing to help Diana and Harriet instead of turning her back on them. "Just be cautious," he'd advised. "Keeping their past a secret is in their best interest as well."

She'd agreed with him wholeheartedly.

"You are my friends," she said in response to Harriet's comment. "Celebrating the most important day of my life with you would mean a great deal."

"We shall miss you," Diana said as she placed the last pin in Viola's hair. Viola reached for her hand and gave it a squeeze. "We will see each other at the hospital every Monday when you host the women's support group and whenever you wish to visit for tea."

Viola stood so she could look at herself in the cheval glass. A smile tugged at her lips. The image reflected back at her was no longer of an unremarkable woman with dull eyes and lifeless hair. Right now, dressed for her wedding, she saw that she was really quite stunning.

Turning, she embraced both her friends. Once she was married, she would be going home with Henry, which meant these were her last moments in the house she had shared with them.

"Thank you, Viola, for all you have done for us," Harriet said.

Viola forced back the tears that threatened. "Indeed it is I who should thank you for advising me and listening to me when I needed it most."

"Even though we warned you against becoming involved with Mr. Lowell?" Diana asked with a smile.

Viola grinned. "You had my best interests at heart." She smoothed the white muslin of her wedding gown. It had been ordered two days earlier, immediately after they acquired the special license, and had been delivered by the modiste herself that very morning.

"We were wrong though, weren't we?" Harriet said.

"We all were," Viola agreed. Henry was not the scoundrel the rumors claimed him to be, but rather the most perfect man she had ever had the pleasure of knowing. Marrying him felt right and she looked forward to every second of it with fervor.

"**R**elax," Yates whispered in Henry's ear when he finally stood at the altar awaiting his bride.

Continuous tremors rolled through Henry, disturbing his nerves and making him restless. *Where was she?* He drew a deep breath and shifted his feet while making a desperate effort to maintain a calm appearance. According to Yates, he was apparently failing in that regard.

"I am trying," he muttered, to which Yates responded with a stifled bit of laughter.

And then the doors at the end of the aisle opened and Viola appeared, dressed in a simple white gown. She was holding a pretty bouquet of various flowers that Henry failed to register in detail because his eyes were fixed on her beautiful face. Swallowing, he clenched his hands and inhaled slowly to quiet the sudden urge he had to run toward her and carry her out the door so they wouldn't have to wait one additional second to begin their lives together.

But there was protocol for them to adhere to and of course the necessary service, which he did want to get through, though preferably at an increased pace if at all possible. Another deep breath had the blessed effect of slowing his heart ever so slightly, which allowed him to focus with greater ease on how lovely she truly looked with her rosy cheeks, her eyes glowing and her lips dimpling prettily at each corner as she smiled at no one but him.

Overcome by emotion, he felt the sting of tears press firmly against his eyes. Christ, she was perfect and she would be his and he knew . . . he simply knew without any shadow of a doubt that the rest of his life would be flawless from this day forward.

"I am the luckiest man in the world," he told her as soon as she reached him. Lifting her hand, he pressed a kiss to her knuckles and helped her turn so they could face the vicar together.

The rest happened in a blur and with only a slight awareness of reciting a few important lines that would bind him to Viola forever. Whatever they were, Henry didn't really care. He would have promised to walk through hellfire for her if that was what had to be done in order to make her his before God and the rest of the world. And then it was finally over, and for a startling second it was almost as if time drew to a halt, announcing the end of the life he had led before her and then ticking onward again with her as his wife.

Joy surged through him and he pulled her into his arms. "I love you, Mrs. Lowell." She answered with a wide smile meant exclusively for him and laughed as he bent to kiss her, sealing their union with every bit of passion he felt toward her, the most wonderful woman he'd ever known.

Viola was tempted to pinch herself to make sure she wasn't dreaming. Everything was perfect, especially

Henry, who hadn't stopped looking at her as though she were an angel descended from heaven to bestow a blessing on him. Incredibly, in spite of the swift wedding arrangements, Henry's mother and grandmother had managed to organize a lovely wedding breakfast at Scranton House. After almost four hours of eating and drinking with friends and family, Viola and Henry had finally managed to take their leave and head for Henry's more modest town house. Her own would remain in her possession for the benefit of Diana and Harriet and any other women who might one day need a place in which to recover from a difficult life.

Leaning into Henry, whose arm was wrapped firmly around her waist as they sat side by side in his carriage, Viola considered what was to come with a mixture of thrilling excitement and apprehension.

As if reading her mind, Henry dropped a kiss on her forehead. "Don't be nervous, my darling. I have every intention of ensuring that you enjoy all aspects of your wedding day and night to the fullest."

"I know," she said, taking comfort not only in his words but in the way her body instinctively clamored for his. And yet, "It is just . . ." She hesitated, unwilling to bring up the past and ruin the mood.

Turning slightly, he tipped her chin up so her gaze met his more directly. "You want this, Viola, but your previous experience has been unpleasant. I know this, so you mustn't fret. Our lovemaking will be entirely different because of the love we share and because I would never ever do anything to hurt you. Nor would I force you into something for which you're not ready. Just . . . try to put everything else out of your mind so all that remains is you and me and the pleasure we long to give and receive. Can you do that for me?"

She nodded, and his mouth met hers in a gentle caress that continued until the carriage jostled her toward him and she caught his shoulder for support. The impact forced her more firmly against him, and the deep rumbling growl he emitted in response sent waves of heat darting straight down her middle. His arms tightened and the kiss deepened, transforming into something else entirely, namely a primal urge to claim and be claimed in return.

"Dear God, we need to get out of this carriage," he murmured while scraping his teeth against a sensitive spot by her ear. "I cannot wait to fully seduce you."

Viola shivered in response and pressed herself further against him in a futile effort to relieve her response to his touch. "Are we almost there?"

He planted a row of scorching kisses along the length of her neck. "I hope so," he told her gruffly as she arched up against him. "Bloody hell."

Henry kissed her again as if he was starving and she was the nourishment he required to live. It was urgent and rough and unapologetic, and Viola cherished every wonderful second of it until they arrived at his house. Henry opened the door with an urgent thrust of his hand and leapt out so he could help her alight. He then escorted her up the front steps and into the foyer, where they were met by Rex, who proceeded to circle their legs and sniff at their feet. They'd given the servants the day off, so only the pets remained. Newton watched as if bored from his position at the top of the landing.

"Would you like some treats?" Henry asked. He approached a box on the hallway table and pushed back the lid. "I asked Cook to prepare something special for these two."

To Viola's relief, Rex and Newton had accepted each other almost immediately when they'd been introduced the previous evening. Rex had bounced back and forth a bit as if hoping to get a playful reaction out of Newton. When the cat had walked away without any sign of interest, the pair had both settled down for naps at opposite ends of the parlor.

"Sit," Henry ordered. When Rex complied, Henry offered him a large bone with meat still clinging to every side. Rex disappeared down the hallway with his prize.

Henry directed his attention toward Newton next. "How about you?" He waved a dried herring at the cat, who rose to his feet, stretched his back and proceeded to come down the stairs. Henry gave him his treat and the cat sauntered off to another part of the house.

Henry turned his full attention on Viola. "Mrs. Lowell," he said with a glint in his eyes. "The things I have planned . . ." He smirked, no doubt because he could tell she was struggling to remain upright.

"You did mention something about seduction," she said, her voice slightly thinner than she'd hoped.

Henry chuckled. "I did, didn't I? But before we get to that, I have a surprise for you."

"But . . ." She glanced toward the stairs.

He stepped toward her and offered his arm. "Consider this little detour of ours part of the lovemaking process." He leaned in, scraping his jaw against hers. "It will only help heighten the anticipation of what is to come—of you and I fully undressed in my bed."

"Good Lord," Viola squeaked as she let him escort her.

He drew her closer. "On the contrary, I have every intention of being rather bad."

Viola's stomach dipped and her heart took flight, pounding against her chest with increased frenzy. "I see," was all she could manage to say as visions of him and her in the most debauched embraces proceeded to clutter her brain.

Henry paused in the doorway to the library and stared down into her upturned face. A wolfish grin tugged at his lips. "Yes," he murmured, "I believe you do."

It took some effort to force her feet to cooperate and to follow him into the room. Was it hotter in here than in the rest of the house or was she simply having a blistering reaction to his words? Of course, he'd collected himself once again while she was left feeling as though she might suddenly combust.

But then she spied the glass case they were heading toward and she realized why they were there. So she could finally see how the automaton worked. She moved toward it, studying the figure more closely this time than when she'd last seen it. The detail on his face was impeccable.

Henry reached behind the case and wound a lever. A soft grinding of cogs and wheels accompanied the slow movement of the machine. Viola watched in fascinated silence as the automaton dipped his quill in his inkwell, repositioned himself and proceeded to write. The letters appeared to be neat, though perhaps a bit shaky at times, but overall, it looked as if they were written by a real live person as opposed to by a machine.

Squinting, she tried to discern the words, but they blurred just enough around the edges to make it impossible for her to do so effectively.

"These might help," Henry said, gently nudging her arm.

Viola glanced down at his hand and smiled. "Thank you," she said, accepting the spectacles and placing them carefully on the bridge of her nose.

"I have this relentless fantasy," Henry murmured

while sliding his arm around her shoulders, "of you wearing my shirt and spectacles and with your hair falling softly around your shoulders."

Viola's breath hitched and her skin tingled with awareness. "How am I to concentrate on anything when you continue to muddle my head?"

He grinned and stepped away, adding distance. "Forgive me, but you're a treat I'm having some trouble resisting."

Loving the effect she had on him, she gave him an adoring smile before returning her attention to the automaton's work. Words had started to emerge and Viola was eager to know what they said. She leaned forward and started to read.

You are my life, my world, my . . . The automaton scratched a few more letters . . . *everything.*

"I wanted it to write Shelley's latest poem for you, but I was limited to only forty characters."

Viola removed the spectacles with trembling fingers and turned to her husband, who was standing utterly still, his eyes fixed upon her with intense anticipation. Closing the distance between them, Viola pressed her mouth to his, kissing him with endless degrees of gratitude and affection. She was vaguely aware of tears clinging to her lashes, the joy thrumming through her so powerful it caused her to weep.

"I am so blessed to be married to you, Henry. You truly are the most incredible man I have ever known."

"You don't know the half of it yet," he told her, and swept her up into his arms.

She squealed with surprise and then laughed with delight as he carried her out the room. "But I'm about to show you," he promised in low, seductive tones.

Winding her arms around his neck, Viola held on tight as he marched toward the stairs and proceeded to climb. Gone was her earlier apprehension, replaced by wanton desire.

This was Henry, after all, a man who thought her the most beautiful woman in the world, even if no one else ever had. He loved her, and because of that, Viola knew deep in her heart that whatever passed between them was destined to be special.

Reaching the landing, Henry turned right and continued toward the door at the end. "I know we never discussed this," he said as they entered the bedchamber, "but I'm rather hoping you'll agree to sharing a room instead of sleeping apart. Of course, if you prefer, I've—"

"Yes," she said before he could finish. "The alternative never even crossed my mind, Henry. I've always imagined us sleeping together and . . ." She felt her cheeks warm beneath the heat of his gaze. "I like the idea of us spending as much time together as possible."

Setting her on her feet, he closed the door behind them, shutting them away in a lovely room decorated in creamy tones. A massive canopy bed occupied most of the space, dwarfing the armchairs that stood to one side and the dresser beneath the window.

Viola stared at the bed and tried to steady the rapid beats of her heart, but all effort to do so dissolved when she felt Henry's hands on her waist. He'd stepped up behind her, his chest pressed securely against her back.

"Viola," he murmured, and proceeded to place a series of kisses along her shoulder.

Sighing, she leaned into the caress and surrendered to his ministrations. His teeth nipped her skin and a frisson went through her, teasing her senses and making her restless.

Henry's hands left her waist and slid up her sides, exploring each curve until finally, when she feared she might die from her need to be touched more fully, he gave his attention to the buttons on her gown.

To her dismay, it felt as though his fingers trembled as he unhooked them, and when he pulled the gown down over her hips and asked her to step out of it, his voice shook.

On bended knee before her, he gazed up the length of her body as if she were Venus and he her mortal servant. Almost hesitantly, his fingers traced over one ankle and up the length of her leg. He paused when he reached the edge of her stocking, closed his eyes briefly as if in deep veneration and then peeled the silk slowly away.

Setting the flimsy stocking aside, he went to work on the next one until both legs were completely bare. "You have the most delicate ankles," he said as he brushed his thumb over her skin. "I noticed when we were at the beach and you hitched up your skirt to prevent the hem from getting wet." Stroking his way up her calf, he paused to toy with the edge of her chemise. "Since then I've had the most demanding need to uncover your knees . . ." He slid the chemise higher. "Your thighs . . ." His palms settled firmly against her as he rose, dragging the fine cotton upward. "Your belly and . . ." He swept the chemise up and over her head, pulling her stays off with it and leaving Viola completely naked. "Your breasts."

Viola sucked in a breath. She'd been so entranced by his touch she'd completely ignored his intention. For a second she stood as if frozen, but then she saw his expression and the way in which he was staring.

"Christ, Viola . . ." He spoke with sensual yearning and with so much desire that all inhibition she might have had ceased to exist at that exact moment.

Tentatively he reached out and touched her, the reverence in his gaze compelling her to be bold, to abandon restraint and to follow his lead. So she raised her hand and tugged at his knotted cravat and pulled until it was gone. Next came his jacket, which she pushed down over his arms. It was followed by his waistcoat, both items landing on the floor in quick succession. Eager to feel his skin against hers, she grabbed at his shirt and pushed it upward.

"I love your determination," he said with a grin as he helped her discard it. His mouth captured hers in the very next second as he pulled her to him so her heart met his. Running his hands over her hips, he wrought several sighs from her lips before lifting her slightly and setting her down on the bed.

Leaning back, Viola looked at the man she'd married and found herself staring in wonder. His chest was more defined than she remembered from when she'd helped Florian pull a lead ball from his shoulder. The scar was a redder hue than the rest of his skin and so small it was barely noticeable at all.

"You're the handsomest man I've ever seen," she told him honestly.

His chest rose and fell as he stared back at her, almost daring her to avert her gaze as his fingers dropped to the placket of his breeches. Diligently, he worked the fastenings to loosen the fabric until, with one swift movement, he pushed his breeches and smalls down over his hips, all the way to the floor, where they joined the rest of the discarded clothing.

Nothing in the world, not even a million pounds, could have made Viola tear her gaze away from her husband's splendor. "Oh my," she murmured as she took in the lean musculature of his legs and . . .

Swallowing, she scooted back on the bed. Because Henry Lowell was the very definition of masculine perfection.

"My experience isn't exactly—"

"Hush, Viola." He climbed onto the bed, and the mattress shifted beneath his weight. "None of that matters anymore, so please rid your mind of it if you can and focus on this instead." He bowed his head and licked his way along the entire length of her body with such thorough dedication that thinking of anything else became utterly impossible.

"The way you respond to my touch is thrilling," he whispered close to her ear while making her moan with the softest caress of his fingers.

"Henry." She drew him closer, spearing his hair with her fingers and needing . . . simply needing . . . something more.

His mouth met hers in a fierce caress as he settled between her thighs. And as he joined his body with hers, Viola welcomed the powerful sensation. Sharing herself with him so completely made her feel whole for the first time ever.

"I love you," he assured her, pausing for a moment to meet her gaze.

"As I love you," she replied, and then sighed as he started to move. This was the closest thing to perfection she'd ever experienced in her life. She clung to Henry and matched his movements, pushing herself toward the unknown until every sensation her body experienced collided and burst on a wave of euphoric pleasure. And as it did and she started to tumble, a guttural growl was wrenched from his throat right before he collapsed beside her.

Breathing heavily, he pulled her against him and simply held on. "You amaze me," he told her after a while. His fingers trailed along her hip, sparking a new desire. "You are far more passionate than I ever dared to imagine."

"I hope you don't mind," she said with a teasing lilt to her voice.

Without warning he rolled her toward him and kissed her deeply. "Not at all, my darling. It is yet another thing for me to love about you." A wicked gleam lit his eyes. "Because it makes me think you might enjoy this as well." Upon which he showed her precisely what he had in mind while she in turn wondered how she'd ever find the will to get out of bed again.

Chapter 25

∽◦∾

Unfortunately she was forced to do so when she and Henry awoke to the sound of loud banging. Groaning, Viola reached for Henry, who was already climbing out of bed.

"Must we respond?" she asked him while savoring the splendid view of his naked backside. They'd made love until dawn and she was both achy and exhausted, though in the best way possible.

"It might be important," he told her while throwing a shirt over his head. Another bang sounded and Henry put on his trousers and left the room without bothering to continue dressing.

Viola sighed. She desperately wanted him back in bed with her so they could explore each other further. But when he returned to the bedroom a few minutes later, his expression told her that this was unlikely to happen.

She sat up and pulled the sheets around herself. "Who was that?"

"Officer Ericson. He wants to give us an update." Henry came to sit on the edge of the bed. He took her hand in his. "I've admitted him to the library, so he's waiting for us to join him."

"Give me ten minutes to get myself ready," Viola said. She moved to get out of bed, but Henry held her in place.

Leaning toward her, he pressed his mouth to hers. "I should probably put on my hose and shoes as well," he murmured against her lips.

"And stop kissing me or we'll never get out of this room."

He released her with a grin and Viola went to gather her clothes.

"I hope you'll forgive the intrusion, Mrs. Lowell," Officer Ericson said when she and Henry arrived in the library.

"No need," Viola told him sincerely. "My husband and I are both anxious for any information you can provide. You did the right thing, coming here. Would you care for some tea or another refreshment?"

"No thank you. I do not wish to stay longer than necessary." He lowered himself back down to the armchair he'd risen from when she'd arrived. "Regarding Miss Olivia Jones. Both her parents confirmed that the man she was seeing was indeed the Duke of Tremaine, though he would have been the Marquess of Bremferrol back then."

"How can they be sure?" Henry asked.

"Because their daughter confided in them," Ericson said. "Apparently, Miss Jones's father was an accountant. He oversaw the current Duke of Tremaine's taxes for a brief period before he went abroad and made sure no monies were owed. He also assisted with keeping his accounts since, as I understand it, he does not have the same financial acumen his father did."

"So Robert met Miss Jones through her father," Viola said, relating all too well to the story Ericson was telling.

"She was the only one at home one day when Tremaine came to call. She invited him in, they started talking, flirtation most likely, occurred and . . . well . . ." Ericson scratched the back of his head. "At some point or other, Tremaine got Miss Jones with child and—"

"Good God!" Viola's hand had come up to cover her mouth in dismay. "All of this while he was engaged to another?"

Ericson cleared his throat. "Based on the timeline I have been able to piece together, it would seem that he had his affair with Miss Jones first and that she got in the way."

"He considered her an inconvenience," Henry bit out.

"According to Mrs. Jones, her daughter told her she meant to confront Tremaine. She wanted him to acknowledge the child once it was born and provide for it. Her mother warned her against doing so but Miss Jones was resolute."

"Do you know why she and Tremaine went into St. Giles?" Viola asked. It wasn't at all the sort of place where she believed any young woman would go without a really good reason.

"I have no idea," Ericson said, "but she was found near St. Giles-in-the-Fields."

Henry frowned. "The church?"

"All I know is that she told her mother that Tremaine had to take responsibility for his actions and that his title should not matter when it came to doing the right thing. Mrs. Jones believes her daughter meant to persuade him to marry her."

"Not an easy feat unless she planned to blackmail him," Henry said, while Viola just stood there still trying to come to terms with what Robert had done.

This could have been her after all. If he hadn't gotten betrothed immediately after their tryst, if she'd gotten pregnant, she might have suggested they marry. It would have been her dream at the time, a dangerous one that might have gotten her killed.

"It is possible," Ericson said, "but there is no evidence to suggest it besides the fact that the Joneses never saw their daughter alive again."

"They never confronted Tremaine about it?" Henry asked.

Ericson snorted. "What do you think?"

Viola flexed her fingers, allowing the movement to bring her back to her senses. "If we bring this before a judge, how good do you suppose our chances are of winning?"

"Slim to none," Ericson said. He looked at them both in turn. "I'm sorry, but there's no solid proof of Tremaine's guilt. Add to that the fact that he's a duke, and you're setting yourself up for failure by pursing this any further."

It wasn't what Viola had hoped to hear, but she had to accept the truth of the situation. Olivia Jones would not be avenged, her killer never brought to justice. There simply wasn't enough to go on.

"At least we tried," Henry said after Ericson was gone. He crossed the floor to where she still stood and pulled her into his arms. "I know you were hoping for justice, Viola."

"It isn't fair," she complained against his chest. Robert had taken at least two lives, possibly three, and it seemed he would get away with it. "What if he kills again?"

Henry leaned back and met her gaze. "Let's hope he doesn't have cause to." Dipping his head, he kissed her softly, slowly, with the sort of tenderness that made her focus on him alone. His hands pressed firmly against her back, imparting warmth and strength.

The day of the trial came more quickly than Viola would have liked. She shivered as she stepped outside with Henry and climbed into the carriage that would take them to the courthouse. Gray clouds the color of her eyes covered the sky. A light drizzle dampened the air. Since their wedding, they'd met with Steadford each day to discuss the case. During one such meeting, Henry had suggested that he could settle Viola's debt now that they were married.

"I cannot ask that of you," Viola had told him. "It's too much."

"There's no such thing as too much when it comes to protecting you," Henry had assured her. He'd looked her straight in the eye then and said, "I have the necessary funds, Viola. If you allow me, I might be able to make this entire case against you go away."

She'd eventually agreed because she'd sensed how important it was for Henry to protect her to the best of his abilities. So Steadford had taken the deal to Hayes, who'd passed it on to his client. But Robert had refused it. He only wanted the hospital and the rejuvenation center, since losing these was more likely to hurt Viola than a dent in Henry's coffers.

"We will get through this," Henry assured her as the carriage rolled toward the courthouse. "No matter what happens, we still have each other."

There was strength to be found in those words and in the kiss that followed. It helped expel some of the anxiety Viola harbored, allowing her to hold her head up high when they arrived at their destination and she was forced to face the waiting journalists.

"Is your second marriage as beneficial to you as your last?" one man asked as he fell into step beside her.

Henry wrapped his arm around Viola's shoulders and told the impertinent fellow to go to the devil.

"What do you stand to gain, Mrs. Lowell?" He shouted the question after them as they disappeared into the courthouse, where Viola was pleased to find the familiar faces of Henry's parents and grandparents, along with Huntley, Coventry, Amelia and Gabriella, waiting. All had come to offer their support and Viola quickly thanked them all for doing so. Mr. Steadford was there too, dressed in a long black gown and with a white powdered wig on top of his head.

"All the character witnesses I have invited to testify in your favor are here." He allowed a rare smile. "That in itself should suggest to the judge that you are not the woman Tremaine believes you to be."

"But will that be enough?" They'd been over this several times already in the last few days, and no matter how she tried to look at it, Viola could not find the assurance she needed. Especially since the nature of the dispute dismissed the need for a jury. Instead, they would have a bench trial in which the judge would make the final ruling.

"You know the answer to that," Mr. Steadford told her. "All I can promise is that I will do my best."

Viola could only hope that this would be enough. She accepted Henry's escort, and together they followed Mr. Steadford into the courtroom. Robert was already there, his expression hard and unsympathetic as he watched Viola and Henry take a seat on the opposite side of the room. Their friends and family sat down behind them while Mr. Steadford and Mr. Hayes claimed chairs facing the bench where Judge Atkins would eventually sit.

It felt like an eternity before he arrived, to the intonation of "All rise!" Those present shuffled to their feet while he strolled toward his designated spot as if he had all the time in the world. The wig he wore rippled over his shoulders, affording him with a rounded look that failed to flatter the stout build of his body. Viola much preferred the shorter ones worn by Steadford and Hayes.

Judge Atkins acknowledged the room with a nod before taking his seat. The rest of the room sat as well. Silence settled into the building's foundations. "This is not a criminal case," the judge began. "Nobody is on trial here today, though the basis for the Duke of Tremaine's contestation of his father's will can be found in his certainty that Mrs. Viola Lowell took advantage of an ailing man. Her character has been called into question, her motives and her right to the moneys she inherited from her former husband, equally so. Let us proceed therefore with you, Mr. Hayes, and see if we cannot come to a swift resolution."

Viola clutched Henry's hand. "The judge's intent to resolve this quickly concerns me."

"It is how things are done," Henry whispered. "Cases are bundled together and must therefore be processed efficiently. Judge Atkins will most likely hear five others before he returns home later today."

"But . . ." Viola had been told it would be like this but she'd imagined it to be an exaggeration. "To pass fair judgment in such short time doesn't seem possible."

"Just count yourself lucky that you're not on trial for murder."

Viola gaped at Henry, who gave her a pointed look before returning his attention to the middle of the courtroom, where Hayes was droning on about Viola's supposed aspirations, how her father had wanted to build a hospital and she'd done whatever it took to achieve his dream, even going so far as to lure a sick man into marriage.

It wasn't his dream alone, she wanted to scream. *It was Peter's as well.*

But if she fought back with the truth right now she would likely be asked to leave. So she sat in silence while Hayes declared that she'd tried to trap Robert first, and when that plan had failed she'd gone after his father. He spoke of her mother and suggested Viola had been born with a predisposition to whoring in much the same way that a lunatic might inherit his madness from a parent.

"Finally, I wish to present evidence of the former duke's declining mental health," Mr. Hayes said. "I have here records from his physician."

"And the physician himself?" Atkins asked.

"He is currently indisposed."

"The reason being?"

Mr. Hayes cleared his throat. "It is my understanding that he is currently serving a prison sentence for gross medical misconduct."

"I will take his records into consideration," Atkins said.

Viola took a deep breath and tried not to panic. Beside her, Henry sat perfectly still. His jaw was tight, his eyes sharply focused on Atkins and the barristers.

"Mr. Steadford," Atkins continued. "Have you anything to say?"

"Yes, Judge." Steadford stood, tall and steady, the only hope Viola had of winning. "Since we are deliberating as to whether or not Mrs. Lowell possessed the cunning and gall to do as Tremaine suggests and that her husband was not in his right state of mind when he willed her his fortune, I recommend an equally blunt assessment of the duke himself."

Murmurs shifted the air inside the courtroom. Robert glared at Viola with acute hatred in his eyes.

She did her best to ignore him, to focus on Henry's hand holding hers and on what Steadford meant to say next.

"To what end, Mr. Steadford?" Atkins asked.

"To suggest to you, Judge, that this case is nothing more than a spiteful vendetta orchestrated by Tremaine for the sole purpose of hurting Mrs. Lowell." Steadford paused before adding, "There are people here today who will tell you that he is the sort of man prone to beating a woman with whom he finds pleasure."

"Objection, Judge," Hayes shouted, but Atkins dismissed him with a wave of his hand, allowing Steadford to continue.

"I propose that Tremaine's jealousy, his inability to accept that his father cared more for Mrs. Lowell than for his own son, has prompted him to do what has never been done before," Steadford said while ignoring Hayes completely. He raised his voice while adding, "His greed and his hatred of Mrs. Lowell have fueled his attempt to ruin her reputation entirely, to take from her that which she has created—a hospital providing free treatment to needy families. Under Mrs. Lowell's management, St. Agatha's has become a medical institution from which much of London's population benefits. It has a higher survival rate than any other hospital in the land."

"That may well be, Mr. Steadford, but you are not here to dispute true ownership of St. Agatha's Hospital, but to determine whether or not the Fifth Duke of Tremaine's will ought to be dismissed on grounds of coercion."

"And I put it to you, Judge, that if it is, then Mrs. Lowell shall be forced to pay compensation. As you may be aware, Judge, Mr. Lowell has already offered to settle his wife's debt out of court, but the Duke of Tremaine has declined. Indeed, he is specifically ask-

ing for the hospital and her ownership in the rejuvenation center she recently opened." Mr. Steadford
glanced at Viola for a second before addressing Atkins
again. "Do you honestly believe either business would
be well served under someone else's direction?"

Atkins frowned. "I see the point you are trying to
make."

"Then let me remind you, Judge, that you have the
power to deny the Duke of Tremaine's request. You
can insist that he take the money Mr. Lowell is willing to give him instead, should Mrs. Lowell lose."

"Mr. Steadford," Atkins ground out, "I will consider your proposal if it becomes necessary for me
to do so. In the meantime I think the best way forward would be for me to examine the evidence put
before me. Can you prove to me that His Grace, the
Fifth Duke of Tremaine had all his wits about him at
the end of his life? Can you offer any compelling evidence to suggest that Mrs. Lowell did not persuade
him into changing his will at the final hour so she
could profit?"

Viola cringed and glanced around the room. It was
full of people who'd come to see this debacle play
out, many of whom were now watching her with
critical eyes.

"I have witnesses," Steadford said. "Servants in
the duke's employ who will testify to Mrs. Lowell's
kindness. They will tell you that Mrs. Lowell genuinely cared for the duke and that she nursed him herself toward the end. They will also inform you that
she and the Sixth Duke of Tremaine appeared to be
friends until he married and left the country."

"Supposition has no relevance here," Atkins said.
"As we all know, appearances can be misleading,
which is why I insist on fact. Have you any, Mr. Steadford?"

The barrister called his first witness, Peter's valet,

Mr. Weston. He was followed by Findlay and later by Mrs. Haroldson, the housekeeper. All attested to Viola's impeccable character and her loyalty toward Peter as he lay dying.

"Well, of course she sat at his bedside," Mr. Hayes said when Atkins allowed him to speak again. "She stood to earn twenty-three thousand pounds from doing so! People have been known to do a great deal more for less than that."

"I have to agree," Atkins said.

Viola's insides twisted and pulled. A shiver stole across her shoulders and breathing became more difficult than ever before.

"Remember," Henry whispered close to her ear, "no matter what happens, we have each other. We'll get through this, Viola. Fear not."

She closed her eyes and allowed Henry's words to soothe her.

Three men whom she did not recognize took the stand next. One claimed he'd been at the brothel when Tremaine had returned to exact his revenge on the demimondaine he'd quarreled with all those years ago. The other two had apparently seen Tremaine fly into fits of fury during his time at Cambridge when his grades failed to meet his expectations. According to one witness, he'd even thrown a book at one of his professors.

Once again, Hayes protested. "This is nothing but slander," he shouted, and unfortunately this time, the judge agreed.

"I find the notes made by Tremaine's physician more telling than any other evidence brought before me," Atkins said. "Whether or not Mrs. Lowell was fond of the duke has no bearing on the fact that he altered his will at a time when his mind was in rapid decline. As noted, he had started forgetting names,

roused the household in the middle of the night for
a game of charades, came down for breakfast one
morning in only his nightshirt . . . These are not the
actions of a rational man, and I must therefore con-
clude that bestowing his entire fortune on Mrs. Lowell
wasn't either."

Viola squeezed her eyes shut. If only she could fill
her ears with cotton as well so she did not have to hear
what the judge said next.

"By order of this court, the Fifth Duke of Tremaine's will shall revert back to the previous version.
If this names the Sixth Duke of Tremaine as his father's
sole heir, then Mrs. Lowell shall pay compensation by
signing over St. Agatha's hospital and her shares in the
rejuvenation center to the Duke of Tremaine. That is
all. I rest this case."

A bang punctuated Atkins's final word, causing
Viola to flinch. The gavel had fallen and with it, everything she'd worked so hard to accomplish was gone.
Slowly, she opened her eyes to see Robert looking her
way. He smirked and offered a bow before striding
out of the room with Hayes by his side.

"Did that really just happen?" Viola asked.

"I'm so sorry," Henry told her. "Atkins is clearly
on Robert's side or he would have forced him to accept a payment from me on your behalf."

She said nothing in response as he helped her rise.
Words failed her. It was like being held forcibly un-
derwater, unable to think as her body resigned itself
to drowning. When Henry's family took their leave
along with the Huntleys and Coventrys, she could
only nod her thanks and watch them walk away. Robert had won and she had lost. Dear God. He'd taken
what she'd feared losing the most—St. Agatha's.

"Are you having regrets?"

Viola blinked. "What?" She was in the carriage with

Henry but could not recall climbing in or taking off. She glanced out the window and recognized a building. They must have been driving for at least five minutes.

"Marrying me did not have the added benefit I had hoped for, Viola. I'm sorry."

She shook her head. "No. I have no regrets about that. Marrying you is the only good thing to come from all this."

The edge of his mouth lifted. "I'm glad you think so." He pulled her against him and pressed a tender kiss to the top of her head. "You are certainly the best thing that has ever happened to me."

"Will you help me forget this day, Henry?" She tipped her chin up and met his gaze.

Dark brown eyes heated with understanding. "When we get home, we'll lock ourselves away for the rest of the day," he promised while sliding his hand over her thigh. "I'll tend to you in ways that will rid your mind completely of this morning's events." He kissed the side of her neck and whispered against her skin, "All you will know is pleasure."

She arched against him with a throaty moan of approval. He had the skill to do as he promised and she could not wait for him to proceed.

Chapter 26

The first thing Henry did when they returned home was help Mr. Andrews prepare a bath for Viola. He'd sensed the tension tightening her muscles since she'd woken up that morning, and it had gotten visibly worse during the hearing. She needed to relax, so he helped her bathe and then asked his cook to prepare some food.

They ate both lunch and dinner in their bedchamber. In between meals, Henry helped distract Viola from her troubled thoughts in the best way possible. He hated seeing her hurt and upset and despised Robert for being the cause.

"I love you," Viola murmured as she sank back against the pillows with a sigh. Henry lifted his head from between her thighs and pressed a kiss to her hip. "The way you make me feel . . ." She watched from beneath lowered lashes as he moved up the length of her body. "Perhaps I ought to return the favor."

Henry froze. "Do you mean—"

"Yes." She gave him the coyest smile he'd ever seen. "I daresay you'll enjoy it."

"Of that I have no doubt." She gave him a nudge and he rolled over onto his back, allowing her to have her wicked way with him for a change. He'd fantasized about this for weeks, but it wasn't the sort of thing a gentleman broached with a lady.

To Henry's immense satisfaction, Viola approached the task with the same determination and diligence she applied to everything else in her life. Her focus was entirely on him and he, in turn, was in heaven.

He made love to her one more time before they both collapsed with unsteady limbs and the kind of languor that would not permit them to rise from the bed. Viola's breaths gentled and Henry realized she finally slept. She did not wake when he rose at seven, so he left her to sleep when he quit the room half an hour later, fully dressed and intent on checking up on The Red Rose.

"I told Mr. Faulkner I'd let myself in," a familiar voice said a short while later.

Henry looked up from the wine orders he'd been going over and instantly grinned upon seeing his brother. "Good God, it's great to see you again, Florian." He stood and rounded the desk to give his brother a rough embrace. "So much has happened while you've been away. I scarcely know where to begin."

"How about the part that involves you marrying Viola?" Florian's head tilted and a lopsided smile teased his lips while he studied Henry. "I stopped by Armswell House to announce my return and was rendered entirely speechless when Mama told me. Congratulations, by the way. I wish you every happiness in the world."

"Thank you, Florian. It's been a bit of a whirlwind romance, to be honest, but I know she and I are right for each other. I can feel it right here." He pressed his hand to his heart.

"Shall we drink to your wife?"

"Definitely." Henry turned to the sideboard and

prepared two glasses of brandy. He handed one to Florian and then proceeded to give his brother a detailed account of everything that had happened while he'd been away.

"And here I was, certain my experiences this past month would have outdone yours," Florian said. He sipped his drink with a solemn expression. "In all seriousness though, I'm sorry to hear of the difficulty Tremaine has put Viola through. It must have put a terrible strain on her, so thank you for helping her deal with it, Henry. I owe you a debt of gratitude."

"Not at all," Henry said. "If anything, I owe you one." When Florian frowned, he added, "If you'd remained here, then you would most likely have helped her instead and she and I wouldn't be where we are today."

"So there's a positive outcome in spite of a loathsome duke's interference."

"A very happy one," Henry said. He drank from his glass and studied his brother. "Now that Robert will be taking charge of the hospital, he may not want to keep you on."

"I may not choose to stay," Florian said. "It all depends on whether he sells it as you suggested he might. At least my shares in the rejuvenation center outnumbered Viola's," Florian said. "He'll never be able to trump my vote or make decisions without my authority."

"We must appreciate the small victories, Florian." Henry raised his glass to his brother and took a long sip of his brandy.

Henry spent the next few days either at home or at The Red Rose, though he kept his business to a minimum in favor of spending time with Viola. She'd taken to helping his gardener plant lavender next to the terrace. In spite of the old man's protestations, Viola claimed she enjoyed getting her hands dirty, and since Henry understood her, he refused to deny her the pleasure.

"I'm thinking of buying a jasmine and a trellis for it to climb on," she said to Henry when they arrived home a few days later after a lovely evening out with Florian and Juliette.

Henry escorted her up the steps to their home and started unlocking the door. "Don't you think that will look too busy?" He'd started the whole garden project because he wanted it to be simple.

"Not at all. I'll have it placed right against the house wall by the terrace. The scent will be divine during the summer."

Henry chuckled and pushed the door open. How could he deny her when the work gave her such joy? He helped her remove her bonnet and gloves before removing his own. A sharp noise coming from the library drew his attention. He glanced around. Where were Rex and Newton?

"Stay here," he cautioned Viola. "I just want to check something."

"You heard the noise too?"

Henry nodded. He went to his study first, collected the pistol he kept in his desk drawer and continued toward the hallway. His hand settled upon the door handle, fingers curling tightly around it. He paused to listen, his body poised for action while blood pumped rapidly through his veins. Intent on catching a potential intruder off guard, he shoved the door open and aimed his pistol at the first living thing he saw. And stilled.

"What the hell are you doing here?"

Guthrie raised both hands, one of which held a tumbler, in surrender. "Good evenin' to ye as well."

"Who's he?" Viola asked from behind Henry's shoulder. She'd come up behind him and was now considering their uninvited guest with interest.

Henry drew a sharp breath and lowered his pistol. "Carlton Guthrie."

Viola stared at the man before her. He'd risen when she'd appeared in the doorway, which meant he was not completely lacking in manners, even if he had broken into their home. His emerald green eyes sparkled in the golden glare of an oil lamp that stood on the table beside the chair in which he'd been sitting. They were intelligent eyes—the sort of eyes that saw everything and quickly analyzed the facts. If he'd been honest in his account of Olivia Jones's murder, Viola believed he provided Henry with very precise information.

She dropped her gaze to where Rex and Newton were napping. Both animals had obviously been pacified by something. The bowl next to where Newton slept had been licked completely clean. Traitors.

"How did you get in?" Henry asked.

Guthrie pursed his lips, drawing attention to the mustache right above them. It was ugly, Viola decided; too bristly and wide to be considered remotely flattering. It seemed to divide his face into two unequal parts and hid his upper lip completely from view.

"It goes without saying that I picked the lock," Guthrie said. "Oh, don't look so surprised, Lowell."

"I ought to fetch the authorities and have you arrested," Henry said, while Viola decided that upon closer inspection, Guthrie couldn't be over forty.

Indeed, she suspected he might only be in his mid-thirties, which was quite a bit younger than he appeared at first sight.

It was all because of that horrid mustache. "You really ought to shave that off," she said without thinking.

"What?" Both men asked as they turned their eyes on her.

"The mustache," she explained. "It doesn't suit you."

"Per'aps that's me intention," Guthrie drawled.

"I wonder if the chief magistrate is still awake," Henry said.

"Forget the magistrate, man, and ask yerself why I went to the trouble of waitin' fer ye to return home? If I'd come to rob ye I would 'ave been in an' out faster than a randy lad 'avin' 'is first tup."

"Guthrie." Henry's voice sliced the air in warning.

"Beg yer pardon, Mrs. Lowell. Me tongue's been tarnished by the gutter over the years. I 'ope ye'll forgive me." When she nodded, he glanced at Henry. "I've information that ought to be of some interest to ye."

"About Olivia Jones?" Henry entered the room, approached Guthrie and plucked his glass from his hand. Intrigued by the odd turn the evening had taken, Viola went to sit on a nearby sofa.

Guthrie sank back into his armchair and watched Henry refill his tumbler. "No." Henry poured another measure for himself. "This is about St. Agatha's Hospital."

"What about it?" Viola asked before Henry could manage to do so.

"Ye care about it a great deal, do ye not?" Guthrie's head was slightly tilted. He was studying her, assessing her, taking her measure with his emerald green eyes.

"Of course. I acquired the building, saw to the renovations, hired the staff . . . I ran the place methodically for two years, always ensuring that patients were given the best possible care even though they received it for free."

"Ye provided an incredible service fer the City of London. Before ye came along, many of those ye've helped would 'ave kept on sufferin', or worse. So I thank ye, Mrs. Lowell, fer takin' care o' the less fortunate."

Viola bowed her head to hide the emotion stirring her heart. "Thank you, Mr. Guthrie. It is kind of you to say so."

He was quiet for a moment and when Viola looked back up, she saw that Henry had returned Guthrie's tumbler to him and that he was having a drink. Henry took the vacant seat beside her on the sofa. "When I saw you last, you mentioned Tremaine's intention to sell the hospital if he acquired it. Is that why you're here?"

Guthrie narrowed his gaze. "In a manner o' speaking."

His eyes warmed and his lips drew into the sort of smile that convinced Viola he wasn't accustomed to looking happy. It was strained and looked rather awkward. "I've purchased St. Agatha's meself with the intention of 'avin' it returned to the rightful owner, which incidentally 'appens to be ye, Mrs. Lowell."

Viola's mouth fell open, and for a second all she could do was stare at the man sitting before her. "But why?" It was the first question that came to mind—a product of her complete and utter shock. "You don't even know me."

"I must confess I'm as stunned as my wife," Henry said. "One doesn't spend thousands of pounds on a building only to give it away to a stranger."

"'Ere's the thing of it though . . . Mrs. Lowell is

not a stranger. She is yer wife, Mr. Lowell, and Florian's employer too." Guthrie took another sip of his drink and smacked his lips together. "I despise injustice. Ye've proven yer worth since ye opened St. Agatha's two years ago, Mrs. Lowell. London needs ye. There's no doubt in me mind about that."

Viola could scarcely believe it. Her luck had turned in the most unexpected way possible. "Thank you, Mr. Guthrie." Her eyes misted with emotion and she struggled to stop her tears of joy from falling.

"Me pleasure." Guthrie's voice had softened to a gentler tone. He sat forward in his chair and reached inside his jacket to retrieve a folded bundle of papers. "I 'ad me solicitor prepare these. All ye need to do is sign an' St. Agatha's is yers once again."

Viola accepted his offering and studied the legal text with Henry. They both agreed that it looked highly professional, which was yet another surprise. She would not have expected it, but apparently Carlton Guthrie was more than what the rumors suggested, and if there was one thing she knew for certain, it was that rumors could be entirely wrong.

When Viola returned to St. Agatha's the following day, she was pleased to discover that nothing had changed during her absence. And with Florian back at work, things were once again running smoothly. In fact, it was as if the awful events of the past six and a half weeks had not taken place at all.

Arriving home after a busy day, she waited for Henry to return from his club. They'd gotten into the habit of having tea together in the parlor while discussing their day. After dinner they would retire to the library for a glass of port and a game of either cards, chess, or something else entirely. Tonight they were playing The New Game of Human Life and so far, Viola was winning.

She spun the teetotum and whooped when it landed on two before moving her mark to The Triflet at number nineteen. "I will pay one counter and advance to The Songster at number thirty-eight."

Henry studied the board. "If I can manage to get a five, I'll land on the Assiduous Youth, receive two counters from the pool and overtake you." He picked up the teetotum and spun the exact number required. Henry moved his counter and then looked at Viola. His eyes darkened and the edge of his mouth drew up in a roguish smile. "I do believe this deserves a reward," he murmured in that intoxicating voice that made heat flare up inside her.

"What about the game?"

"We'll continue it later." Rising from his chair, he rounded the table and held out his hand. Viola placed hers in his and allowed him to help her stand. "These last few weeks have been trying on you." He kissed her softly, gently, with all the tenderness in the world.

"For both of us," she said as soon as she was able to catch her breath.

"Perhaps we ought to consider getting away for a while." He planted a row of light kisses along her jaw. "Florian's account of Paris makes me want to see the city for myself."

It was tempting. "What about the hospital?" Viola breathlessly asked while he kissed a path down her neck and along her shoulder.

"Let my brother manage it for a while as you did while he was away." He pushed at her sleeve, revealing more skin, and placed a series of kisses against it.

A shudder went through her, straight to her belly, where it heated before sinking lower. "Perhaps we ought to venture upstairs?" His mouth was at her décolletage now, his intention to best her at The New Game of Life apparently forgotten for the moment.

"Too far," he murmured while going to work on the buttons at her back. "And besides, having you here on the sofa is a dream I'd like to realize sooner rather than later."

He tugged at her gown and it slipped from her shoulders. His hands swept over her curves, willing her to submit to his plan.

"The dining room is another place in which I hope to explore my craving for you," Henry told her later when they were both thoroughly sated. "The table there is exceptionally sturdy."

"You really are awful sometimes."

"Because I cannot resist my wife?"

She chuckled. "No. Because I fear I won't be able to think of anything else next time we have guests over for dinner."

Chapter 27

Paris exceeded Henry's expectations.

During their month-long stay, they lodged at the Pavillon de la Reine, a charming seventeenth-century building located in the Marais, within walking distance of the Notre Dame Cathedral. Twice they visited the Louvre in order to fully appreciate the vast collection of art it housed. They enjoyed a balloon ride over the Ranelagh Gardens and dined at a restaurant that floated on the Seine.

"Is it wrong of me not to want to go back to England?" Viola asked when their last day in Paris drew to a close.

"Not at all, my darling. We have had a wonderful time here together, but you know, there's no reason we can't come back here one day." His heart swelled as he wrapped his arms tighter around her waist. "I suspect our children will love it as much as we do."

Viola leaned into his embrace, cocooning him in her sweet perfume. Her courses had ceased while they'd been away and they now looked forward to a new chapter in their lives.

"You will make a superb father," she said. Turning in his arms, she rose up to meet his lips.

He kissed her back with overwhelming love and affection. "And you shall be the mother every child dreams of, Viola."

When they arrived in London after two long days of travel, Mr. Andrews was there to greet them. "Welcome back," he said as he helped them with their luggage. "I trust you had an enjoyable trip?"

Henry pulled off his gloves, dropped them into his hat and handed it over to Mr. Andrews, who nodded and smiled in response to what Viola told him.

Leaving them to their discussion, Henry went to his study to check on his correspondence. A pile of letters awaited, some of them invitations to various events and others notifications from Mr. Faulkner intended to keep Henry up to date. But one stood out from the rest because it was dated The Valley, June 10, 1820. Henry picked it up slowly. The London arrival mark had been stamped on the front three days earlier.

Breaking the seal, Henry unfolded the papers and read. His pulse quickened with every word his eyes absorbed until he reached the end. He drew a sharp breath. "Viola?" Crossing the floor he strode out into the hallway. "It's here," he told her, catching her on her way up the stairs. "Confirmation that Robert killed his wife."

She stared at him, her body poised between going up and coming down. She chose the latter, descending a step so they were at eye level. "Really?"

He held the letter up for her to see. "I think we've got enough evidence here to have him convicted of murder."

Officer Ericson's frown deepened as he scanned the letter Henry had handed him. He finally glanced up.

"Bollocks." He shifted his gaze to Viola. "I beg your pardon."

"No need," she muttered.

"It is just . . ." Ericson picked up the papers again and blew out an agonized breath. "Christ."

"I know," Henry said, agreeing with his verdict. Robert was a duke, after all. The last time one had been tried and sentenced to death was when the Duke of Norfolk had been found guilty of treason in 1572, which was quite some time ago.

"There's no real precedent for this sort of thing," Ericson said, mirroring Henry's thoughts, "but we are speaking of murder. At the very least, there ought to be a thorough investigation and a trial."

"Do you believe we've enough evidence to have him convicted?" Viola asked.

"The House of Lords will have to determine that, but Officer Marvis's letter to you is pretty damning. Considering his claim that Officer Hoff who was asked to look into Beatrice Cartwright's death was paid to list the cause as accidental, I don't believe that the duke will be acquitted."

"Especially since Officer Hoff has been under investigation for a while now, after inconsistencies began appearing in his reports," Viola pointed out.

"And then of course there's the snake Tremaine mentioned," Henry said. "According to Marvis, there are no venomous snakes in Anguilla, and Hoff's initial report suggested an accidental fall. But it's possible Tremaine didn't know this was deemed the cause of death. After all, he did leave almost immediately after the incident, which again doesn't fit exactly with what he told me."

"There are certainly inconsistencies," Ericson agreed, "and enough material to warrant a dialogue with Tremaine. I'll dispatch a couple of officers straight away and keep you posted." He picked the letter back up and shifted it slightly between his fingers. "May I keep this?"

Henry nodded. "Certainly."

Viola stood, as did Henry. "Thank you, Officer. We look forward to seeing justice served, not only on behalf of Beatrice Cartwright, but on behalf of Olivia Jones as well."

Ericson nodded, and Henry escorted Viola out of the building.

"I think that went rather well," Viola said as soon as they were back in the street.

"Agreed, but let's not get our hopes up until we're certain he'll face charges."

She nodded and accepted the arm he offered. The Red Rose wasn't far and neither was the rejuvenation center, so they decided to stop by both places to see how things were going before continuing on to Gunther's, where they stopped for an ice.

"Care for a game of cards?" Viola asked when they returned home that afternoon. They hadn't played since Paris when he'd beat her three times in a row. She was itching to have her revenge.

"All right. I'll have one of the maids bring up some tea," Henry said, already heading for the kitchen stairs. He rarely used the bellpull to summon the servants. In his opinion, it was more efficient for him to go to them instead of demanding they stop their chore, come upstairs to hear his request, only to return downstairs again to fulfill it.

Viola rather agreed. She went to retrieve a deck of playing cards along with the box filled with all the counters they used for betting. A knock at the front door made her still. She waited briefly to see if Mr. Andrews would come to answer it, but when he didn't, she supposed he must have gone out on an errand since he hadn't come to assist when she and Henry had returned home either.

Exiting the library, Viola went to open the door. As soon as it swung to one side, a boot lodged between the door and the frame. Then a gloved hand yanked the door out of her hands and opened it wide. She stumbled sideways, momentarily thrown off balance as Robert entered her home as if it were his.

"Henry!" She aimed for a steady timbre, calling out his name as she backed away in the direction of the stairwell leading to the kitchen. Instead it wobbled, betraying her fear.

"We need to have a little conversation," Robert said as he peeled off each of his gloves and shoved them carelessly into his jacket pocket. "I don't appreciate being slandered and accused of things I haven't done."

"Robert. Listen. I—"

"I'm the bloody Duke of Tremaine," he shouted, "and you shall call me Your Grace or so help me I'll—"

"What?" Viola asked as the door behind her burst open and Henry stepped into the hallway. "Kill me as well?"

Robert's lips flattened into a grim line. "You go too far," he said. "When I returned home half an hour ago I learned that the bloody Bow Street office is trying to bring me in for questioning. Findlay said it was in regards to my wife's death and Olivia Jones's murder, which leads me to suspect that you two decided to stir up things that don't concern you. You're the only people with any interest in causing me harm."

"You murdered those women," Viola announced.

Robert clenched his fists and advanced. Henry stepped in front of her, placing himself between her and Robert.

"I'll have you both charged with harassment," Robert said.

"A bit of a challenge for you, I'd think, considering you'll be swinging from a rope soon," Henry murmured.

"You bastard." Robert threw his fist into Henry's jaw, knocking him back into Viola. She stumbled slightly, but managed to regain her balance and add some distance between herself and the men who were now fighting like bare-knuckle boxers keen to draw blood.

"Stop it," she cried, but neither man listened.

"Get out of my house," Henry growled as he placed a sharp jab above Robert's right eye. The skin broke and blood trickled down the side of his face.

"Not until I've given you the thrashing you deserve." Robert rushed forward, jamming his head into Henry's abdomen, throwing him back.

Viola barely managed to get out of the way before they went down, landing with a thud on the floor. Robert leaned back and pinned Henry down with his body. A crack sounded as bone connected with bone, the knuckles on Robert's right hand reddening further with each successive strike to Henry's face.

"No!" Viola flung herself at him.

"Oh dear merciful God." The exclamation came from one of the maids who must have heard the ruckus and come to see what was going on.

"Go and fetch help," Viola yelled, and the maid quickly complied.

Viola latched on to Robert's shoulders with her hands, desperate to make him stop hitting Henry, but her weight was too slight and he easily pushed her aside.

Struggling to her feet, she made another attempt, pulling at his shoulders with all the strength she had in her. The effort allowed Henry to pull his hands free and place them around Robert's neck. Robert roared in frustration. His elbow came back, hitting Viola in the chest. She fell back onto her bottom.

A cry of outrage ricocheted off the walls. Viola

shifted her weight. She had to stand—had to help Henry. Her feet found the floor and she pushed herself up, ignoring the dull ache in her chest. Something silver gleamed in the afternoon light. It moved smoothly through the air, elegant but deadly.

Viola screamed as the blade went down with a clean stab to Henry's chest. His agony filled the air as Robert retrieved the blade. Everything slowed, the world fell away and all Viola could see was time running out—the last grains of sand spilling through the hourglass—taking her future with Henry with it.

Aware that she lacked the strength to overpower the madman before her, Viola sprinted toward Henry's study. She flung his desk drawer open and grabbed the pistol he kept there. Panting, she hurried back into the hallway, arriving just in time to see Robert prepare to stab Henry again.

Without hesitation, she aimed the pistol with trained precision and drew a deep breath, steadying herself so she would not tremble.

One shot. That was all she had. And she took it without even blinking as Robert's hand came down once more. He stiffened and the blade fell to the floor with a clatter as Robert slumped awkwardly to the side. He gasped as he rolled back against the wall, clutching at his chest while trying to rise.

Viola paid him no heed. She rushed toward Henry and tore his jacket and vest wide open. "You will survive this, my love," she croaked as she pulled at his bloodstained shirt with quivering hands.

Across from her, Robert leaned crookedly against the wall. His breaths were short and fast. "You've killed me." The words came haltingly from his throat.

Anger shoved pain and fear aside for a moment. "No, Robert. I'm not that kind." Henry's wound came into view and Viola's lips wobbled as hot tears welled behind her eyes. When she spoke to Robert again, her words broke apart in anguish. "I want you to survive this so you can face the condemnation of your peers in court."

He flung his arm out toward her as if to attack, but it was a futile attempt as strength failed him this time. Choking back her emotion, Viola reminded herself to stay calm. Panicking wouldn't help Henry right now, so she ripped his shirt with methodical movements, wiping the blood from his chest and adding pressure where it was needed.

"Viola." Her name was but a croak.

"Hush now, my love." She pressed one palm to his cheek. "You need to preserve your strength."

Seconds later, Viola heard voices and footsteps approaching and breathed a sigh of relief.

"Jesus," a man's voice exclaimed. He sounded vaguely familiar, and when she looked up, she recognized him as the Earl of Wilmington, one of St. Agatha's committee members. Another committee member, Baron Hawthorne, stood beside him.

"I brought the first men I could find," the maid said from somewhere near the front door.

"My husband is seriously injured," Viola informed them, even though the fact was blatantly obvious. "I need to get him to St. Agatha's right away."

"Fielding. Go call a carriage," Wilmington yelled to another gentleman who'd come with them. "Hawthorne. You're with me. Let's see to it that Lowell survives."

A hand caught Viola's elbow, urging her to rise. She resisted until she realized she was impeding all effort to help by being in the way. Wilmington and Hawthorne bent to pick Henry up. He groaned in response and Viola pushed her way forward again, doing her best to keep pressure on the wound as the men proceeded to carry him out of the house.

"Good God, what has happened?" Mr. Andrews exclaimed as he met them by the carriage Fielding had procured. He was carrying a couple of parcels, both clearly marked with labels from Henry's favorite tailor.

"The Duke of Tremaine tried to kill him," Viola explained while Henry was handed up into the carriage and placed upon one of the benches. "He's still inside and badly wounded. He'll need medical care as well."

"I'll see to it that he gets it," Mr. Andrews assured her.

"Why don't you and Hawthorne help him," Wilmington said to Fielding. "Make sure the authorities are made aware of what happened. I'll accompany Mrs. Lowell."

Hawthorne handed Viola up into the carriage. "We'll keep you posted." He closed the door behind her and the carriage took off.

Henry's body sprawled across the bench, blood pooling between Viola's fingers even as she attempted to staunch it. When the carriage lurched, Wilmington leapt forward to stop him from tumbling onto the floor.

"Thank you," she murmured. "For everything."

Wilmington gave a crisp nod. "I don't know him well, but the Earl of Yates is a mutual friend. From what I've heard, your husband is a very good man. I truly hope he survives this."

So did Viola, but there was no telling what sort of damage the blade had done inside Henry's body. His eyes were closed now, his lips slightly parted. Consumed by fear, she placed her palm above his mouth and prayed, not caring about the wet streaks dampening her cheeks when she felt air move across her skin. He was still breathing. Thank God.

When they arrived at the hospital moments later, Viola asked Wilmington to keep continued pressure on Henry's wound while she got out and proceeded to order people about. Within seconds, a stretcher arrived, carried by a pair of strong orderlies. They got Henry out of the carriage and moved him swiftly up the front steps of the building. Viola followed behind while Wilmington paid the coachman.

"Get him to one of the operating rooms," Viola commanded. "Where's Florian?"

"Right here!"

She turned and saw him running toward her, and the relief of seeing the one man capable of saving Henry made Viola's brief ability to stay strong crumble and fall. With a sob, she pointed in the direction the orderlies had gone while managing to say just one word. "Henry."

Florian left her where she stood and sprinted away, disappearing round a corner. Viola hurried after him with every intention of seeing to Henry's welfare. But when she entered the operating room and saw him lying on the table while Florian probed inside his chest, she wondered if she was up to it.

Florian heard her come in and glanced her way. "Are you sure you want to be here, Viola?"

She hesitated briefly, then nodded.

"I understand if this is too difficult for you."

"I'll be fine," she promised, and took a step forward.

He studied her briefly, then gave a firm nod. "You can take over from Haines after washing your hands."

Viola readied herself as she was accustomed to doing and relieved Haines of his duties. "How is he faring?" Viola asked while trying to think of Henry as just another patient. She had to detach herself as Florian had done if she was to be of use to him.

"His right lung has been punctured and blood is gathering in his pleural cavity."

"In other words, he might not survive this," Viola said with a voice that seemed to come from somewhere outside her own body.

"If we don't drain it, but at least he's unconscious for now. If he wakes up while we're working on him, we'll have to give him some morphine." Florian withdrew his fingers from inside Henry's chest and dropped the scalpel he was holding into a tray filled with gin. "I needed to increase the size of the wound, that's all."

That's all. That's all. Viola willed herself to focus, to not panic and do something stupid like start hitting Florian. He was the best physician there was. He knew what he was doing. She had to trust him.

"Attach the longest cannula you can find to the piston syringe and hand it to me."

Viola gave her attention to the surgical tray where tools were spread out. The tube he requested was curved, thinner at one end than at the other. She did as he asked and then helped hold the wound open while Florian slipped the cannula inside. He started sucking out liquid and then detached the syringe so it could drain freely into a small container.

"How does it look?" Viola asked.

Florian bent over the fluid and sniffed. "The color is good and there's no alarming smell to it, but our work would be easier if it were thinner. I need ginger extract and watered-down honey."

Locating the glass bottles containing the items, Viola prepared the solution Florian required and handed it to him. He pulled the tube from Henry's chest, rinsed it and the piston syringe with a hefty amount of gin, then filled the syringe with the solution and injected it into the wound. Henry groaned but remained completely still.

"Let's try again," Florian said after counting off a couple of minutes. He pulled back on the plunger, detached the syringe once more and allowed the wound to drain through the tube. "Much better. I'll make a counter incision in his back afterward and repeat the process just to make sure we've evacuated all the extravasated blood."

"And then?"

"Then we wait and see. Depending on how it heals, I may have to open the wounds back up and repeat the process."

Unable to think of such a possibility right now, Viola started readying the supplies that would soon be required, like compresses, bandages and the needle and waxed silk thread Florian would use for the sutures.

It took longer than Viola had hoped before Henry was stitched up and ready to be moved, or maybe time just worked differently when the life of a person one loved hung in the balance.

"Will you tell me what happened?" Florian asked as he and Viola followed the orderlies carrying Henry up to the room where he would be staying.

She gave him a quick outline of recent events and saw his expression darken. "Perhaps I ought to examine you next?"

"I'm fine," Viola assure him. "I wasn't struck too badly."

"Are you sure about that?"

"It doesn't even hurt anymore."

Florian nodded. "Let me ask if Robert's here as well then. I'll meet you upstairs in a minute." Florian left her, arriving as he'd promised almost immediately after Viola reached Henry's room.

"He's with Gilford," Florian said in reference to another surgeon in St. Agatha's employ. "Haines is attending."

"Do you know if the authorities have been notified of Robert's attempt to kill Henry?"

"Mr. Andrews was in the foyer. He and Hawthorne were keeping company with Wilmington and a Bow Street officer. I don't expect Robert to leave here a free man, Viola." He glanced at her over his shoulder. "Attempted murder carries the death sentence with it."

"I know." She went to stand on the opposite side of the bed. "He looks so peaceful right now."

"That will likely change when he wakes." Florian sighed. "I have to inform our parents and Mr. Faulkner too. I expect you'll be staying here with him?"

"Naturally."

Florian surveyed the room. "I'll have a cot brought in so you can lie down for a bit. Call for me when he wakes, all right?"

Viola appreciated him saying *when*, rather than *if*. "I'll do so right away."

He met her gaze just long enough to reveal his own pain before turning away and striding back out into the hallway. There was nothing left for him to do.

Chapter 28

He was back in a bloody hospital bed with aches and pains twisting beneath his ribs. Henry sucked in a breath and felt the tight pull of his wound as it stretched in response to the effort. Christ, this had to stop happening! His brain felt sluggish, so he couldn't quite remember . . . Oh yes . . . there it was . . . Robert's attack, the fighting that followed and the penetrating sharpness that sliced through his chest.

"Viola." He could scarcely hear his own voice. Trying again, he forced out a louder sound than before and was swiftly rewarded by the touch of her hand.

"I'm here," she whispered while carefully touching his cheek. It felt so wonderfully cool until her hand moved, settling more firmly against his forehead. "You're hot."

"Water," he managed. His throat felt much like Newton's tongue; prickly and rough.

A glass was held to his lips but swallowing the contents was a struggle when the effort of raising his head required the use of his muscles—muscles that presently screamed to be left alone.

It only got worse when Viola pressed down on his chest. "Hell and damnation," he cried through the pain.

"I'll be back in a second," she said as she left his side, heedless of his groans.

"Viola!" Her name sliced through his chest and he clutched at the sheets. She mustn't leave him. Not now. Not when he needed her most. "Viola!"

Viola skidded round a corner almost falling to her knees as she raced through the hallways, slamming doors open and nearly colliding with a couple of nurses. She didn't care. The only thing that mattered right now was Henry and saving his life.

She burst into Florian's office. He wasn't there. Dear God. She drew a deep breath and continued her search, storming into one operating room after another until she found him. "There's infection," she gasped. "He's burning up."

"Take over," Florian told the assisting surgeon and handed him his scalpel. He followed Viola from the room, quickening his pace until he jogged behind her. "Bring a syringe and some cannulas along with a discharge tube up to room twenty," he called to Emily as they passed her on the way.

Before they even arrived on his floor, Viola could hear creative expletives immediately followed by shouted groans and her name.

Florian swung a door open, bringing Henry's room into view. A couple of nurses had gathered in the doorway, most likely hoping to appease him somehow.

"Let us through," Florian said, and the nurses stepped aside. Three orderlies stood next to Henry's bed, attempting to hold him down. "Tilt his head back and open his mouth," Florian instructed while fetching a small glass bottle from a nearby cabinet. He poured a few drops into a clean glass, added a bit of water and set it to Henry's mouth.

Henry sputtered and twisted his head.

"Drink, damn you," Florian growled. "We're trying to save you not kill you."

Viola pushed her way past an orderly and leaned over Henry. "It's morphine, my love. It will help ease the pain."

"Viola?" Henry rasped.

His weak voice stabbed at her heart. "Yes. I'm right here. Now drink."

He breathed hard and low, wincing with each inhale, but he drank the liquid Florian offered and was soon allowed a reprieve from his pain.

When he slept, Florian pulled aside his bandages and studied his wounds. Both were swollen and red. "Has Emily arrived yet?"

"I'm right here, Florian." The orderlies stepped back, allowing her better access. In her hand, she held the syringe and the tubes Florian had requested.

"Here," Viola said, grabbing a surgical tray and setting it on the table beside Henry's bed.

Florian, who'd managed to procure a bottle of gin in the meantime, filled the tray with the watery liquid and asked Emily to place the syringe, cannulas and tubing inside. "I need a scalpel," he said, and Viola quickly produced one from a nearby drawer.

"Can you prepare some compresses?" she asked Emily as she handed Florian the scalpel. He disinfected this as well and then proceeded to cut away the sutures.

As soon as Henry's chest wound opened, pus oozed out. "Help me turn him onto his side," Florian said.

Viola grabbed Henry's shoulders and twisted them toward Florian while he adjusted Henry's position on the bed. Her husband was a large man, a heavy man, and he did not budge easily, but eventually, with a little extra help from one of the orderlies, they managed the feat.

"Prepare the syringe," Florian told Viola once Henry was in an acceptable position.

Emily returned with the compress Viola had requested and smoothed it out over Henry's forehead while Viola attached the long metal cannula to the end of the syringe and placed it in Florian's hand. Just like before, he inserted it into the wound and proceeded to suck out the liquid that had gathered there since the first surgery. A pale mixture of blood and pus flowed out, steadily filling a bowl that Emily was holding.

"Now for the back," Florian said. "How does it look?"

Viola gave the incision Florian had made earlier one look and shook her head. "Not good."

Together, they worked to open the wound. "This one's lower than the other," Florian pointed out. "We'll just insert a metal tube at an angle and let gravity do its work."

For the next two hours, they worked on evacuating the extravasated blood. Occasionally the fluid would stop flowing from the chest wound and Florian would once again apply the syringe. It was tedious work, but it was worth every second when the blood flowing out returned to a normal color.

"I just have to examine him now and make sure that the blood's not still pooling in the pleural cavity."

When he'd confirmed that it wasn't, he asked Viola to prepare a poultice of crushed onion and honey, just as she'd done weeks earlier when Henry had been shot. She dabbed it onto the wounds, which Florian preferred to leave open this time, added some cotton wadding and secured them with bandages.

"You did well," Florian told Viola as they stood side by side assessing their work. "I know it wasn't easy for you."

"It was a choice between standing idly by and doing whatever it takes to save the man I love," Viola said. Her heart still hurt and her soul dreaded the hours to come. There was a chance he wouldn't pull through this.

"You should sleep while he does," Florian said.

She gave him a quelling look. "You know that won't be possible." Not when Henry's condition had worsened during the nap she'd taken before. "I want to know the moment he wakes. I want to check on his fever through the night and make sure the compresses get changed regularly."

"One of the nurses could do that."

"That won't be necessary." Viola placed her hand against Henry's cheek and listened to the soft rolling snore suggestive of deep slumber. "I'll watch over him, Florian. I won't leave his side for a second."

Golden light spilled through the tall window at the end of the room when Henry opened his eyes once again. Just as before, a lifetime ago and yet somehow so recent, it shone at a woman's back, surrounding her in a halo of gold. Unlike the first time he'd seen her, however, he knew her name now.

"Viola." Her face was the loveliest there was, perfection itself with her pretty gray eyes and rose-colored lips. "I've missed you."

With tears rolling over her cheeks, she reached for his hand and bent to place a kiss on his lips. "Your fever has gone," she murmured softly, "and your wounds are healing. You will recover, Henry. You will be well again and . . ." Her voice broke and she bowed her head over their clasped hands, kissing his with sweet adoration. "I've never been so scared in my life." Her head came up and she met his gaze. "We need to keep you out of hospitals in the future. These past few days have put a terrible strain on my heart."

"Days?"

"It's been three since you were brought in." Her expression grew serious, transforming from the concerned wife to the diligent nurse. "How are you feeling?"

Henry gave his attention to his body and considered. "There's an ache in my chest and my back, but it's manageable." He frowned. "Why is there an ache in my back when I was stabbed in my chest?"

Viola explained while he listened, impressed by his brother's skill and Viola's ability to assist him. "I always knew you were more than a nurse," he told her. "You're irreplaceable, Viola, both to me and to Florian."

"I should let him know you're awake." She went to the doorway and called for a nurse to fetch him, then returned to Henry's bedside so she could give him another kiss.

"The medicine you administer is truly invigorating, Viola." He managed to wrap his arm around her waist while she leaned over him. "I hope you don't treat your other patients like this."

She grinned down at him with sparkling eyes. "You needn't worry. This particular remedy is reserved exclusively for you."

He kissed her again, but in his eagerness, he stretched his abdominal muscles, pulling at his wound, and was forced to fall back with a groan. "Maybe you can take pity on me for a while and not kiss me quite so passionately?"

"Of course. I'm sorry. I just . . . got carried away."

"I do tend to have that effect on you," he said with a smile. "But the effect you have on me is not very useful under the current circumstances."

She dropped her gaze to his lap. Her eyes widened. "But you're hurt and in great discomfort and . . ."

He chuckled. "My body doesn't seem to care about that. Or is it my brain? I'm not really sure at this point."

Thankfully, he'd managed to quell all hints of his ardor by the time his brother walked into the room. "Good to see you smiling," Florian said. "The last time you were awake you were cursing us all to high heaven."

"It must have been the pain talking. I'm sorry if I was rude or offended someone."

"Don't be. We're used to such experiences by now, though I'm not sure I've ever heard anyone yelling about King George's bollocks before."

Henry winced. "I can only hope word doesn't reach him."

"I've already spoken to the staff and they've assured me they'll hold their tongues, though I cannot vouch for the other patients." Humor flickered in his eyes and Henry knew his brother was having a bit of fun at his expense, the rascal. "You'll need to stay here a few more days, but after that you ought to be able to return home under Viola's supervision."

Henry reached for Florian's hand and clasped it tightly. "Thank you. I owe you my life."

"More than once now, I'd say. Any chance we can minimize your visits here in the future?"

"I'll see to it," Viola said.

"Good." Florian glanced at them each in turn. "I'll be back later in the day to check on you."

He started to leave but Henry stopped him with a quick question. "Is there any news about Robert?"

Florian turned back to face him. "The wound he sustained when your wife shot him has been treated by one of our surgeons. He's currently recuperating while under guard. Bow Street is waiting for my permission to have him discharged."

Henry looked at Viola. "You shot Robert?"

"Well, I wasn't going to watch him kill you," she said with exasperation.

"It was precisely done," Florian said. "She incapacitated him while ensuring he wouldn't expire by aiming at his pectoralis major, the muscle that reaches across the chest from the shoulder. It forced him to drop the blade and could make movement difficult for him in the future, though I daresay it will be a short future, all things considered. The officer I've spoken to says the information you gathered on Beatrice Cartwright's death and Robert's recent attempt on your life will surely condemn him."

"Is it strange that I find no pleasure in knowing that?" Henry asked after Florian was gone. He glanced at Viola. She gave his hand a squeeze while adding a wistful smile. "My conscience cannot align itself with seeing my school friend hanged even though I know the man he's become deserves it."

"I am equally torn and I think that's a good thing. It would be cause for concern if we were happy about it."

Henry agreed. To rejoice over Robert's fate would make them as callous and unfeeling as he was. Henry blew out a breath and settled back against his pillow. This conversation had depleted his energy. "Do you suppose some food might be possible?"

"Of course. Are you very hungry?"

"Ravenous."

She grinned and pressed a kiss to his forehead. "I'm pleased to hear it," she told him and went to make the request.

Viola was standing outside on the terrace overlooking the garden she and Henry had created when he came up behind her and wound his arm around her waist, pulling her into his warmth. Two months had passed since Robert had stabbed him and he'd managed to make a full recovery.

"This will look lovely next year when the plants are fuller and flowers start to bloom." Viola tilted her chin up, intending to look at him, but he pressed his cheek to hers, preventing her from doing so. A hint of afternoon stubble grazed her skin and a smile stretched her lips. She'd never been happier.

"Lady Beatrice's parents have come to call," Henry murmured. "They're waiting for us in the parlor."

Turning in his arms, Viola welcomed the kiss he gave her and let him escort her back inside. They entered the parlor together, greeting their guests just as a maid arrived with a tea tray. She set it on the sofa table and exited the room.

"We want to thank you," Lady Clarendon said. "What you've done—" Her voice cracked and her eyes grew suspiciously moist, prompting her to avert her gaze.

Her husband, the earl, placed an arm around her shoulders in a show of comfort. "Tremaine was sentenced an hour ago. He will be promptly stripped of his titles and locked away until his hanging."

"Did he confess?" Henry asked.

Lord Clarendon nodded. "He spoke of Beatrice and Miss Olivia Jones without remorse. Indeed, it appeared as though he failed to comprehend why anyone would fault him for what he had done. Especially in Miss Jones's case." The earl shook his head. "Frankly, I believe he's getting what he deserves."

Viola agreed even though it was difficult coming to

terms with the fact that a person she'd once shared the same roof with, played cards with, conversed with, would soon be executed for heinous crimes he'd committed. Or perhaps it was simply hard to accept how blind she had been. Her biggest regret would always be letting him use her affection for him against her. She glanced at Henry and was once again overwhelmed by the love she harbored toward him.

"I am just glad his father is not alive to witness his downfall," she said. "That would have been a shame."

Later, when they were once again alone together, Henry led her into the parlor where Rex and Newton were curled up together, side by side, near the fire. "I thought we might make another go of The New Game of Human Life." His words were light, but the wicked gleam in his eyes suggested seductive intentions.

"The last time we played we ended up on the sofa and forgot the game completely."

"You didn't seem to mind." He gave her a heated look and went to retrieve the game from a cabinet behind the sofa.

Embers sparked to life upon her skin. She stepped further into the room, drawn to him in a way she had long since stopped trying to resist. "That's not the point." Serving him the sharpest look she could manage, she said, "I am merely drawing attention to the coincidence. It was very convenient for you, considering you were losing."

Bent forward over the table and in the process of placing markers on the game board, Henry stilled. His eyes rose slowly toward hers and the edge of his mouth lifted into a roguish smile filled with pure masculine pride. "Winning is all about turning the situation to your advantage, Viola." Straightening, he came toward her and Viola's pulse quickened.

When he reached her, he wound one arm around her waist and pulled her securely against him. "Perhaps we should leave the game for later." He brought his free hand up to cradle the back of her head.

"Perhaps," was all she could say. Her limbs had gone week, her mind slightly drunk on the powerful sensations he wrought with his touch, and all she wanted right now was for him to kiss her.

And then he did, confirming the need he had for her in his life and a love that grew stronger with each passing day. He was her husband, the man she anticipated growing old with, soon to be the father of her child, and as Viola kissed him back, she savored the joy he'd brought to her life. It was greater than anything she'd ever known, indescribable in its perfection, its sweetness and its purity. Simply put, it was utterly divine.

Chapter 29

Snatching up his black beaver hat, Carlton Guthrie straightened the sleeves of his burgundy velvet tail-coat and exited The Black Swan where he'd made his home for the last fifteen years, ever since his falling out with Bartholomew. Pleased to know that particular man was now six feet under, Carlton smiled as he stepped down onto the packed dirt road and turned into the morning mist.

Not a single gaslight brightened this part of town, this poverty-stricken place where criminals made their beds. They were the forgotten, an afterthought of the City at large left mostly to their own devices. Passing a woman asleep in a doorway, he bent down and placed a pound in her hand.

She stirred, looked up and straightened slightly as soon as she saw him. Her gaze darted to the coin and her hand closed around it. "Thank ye, sir," she murmured, and Carlton tipped his hat before strolling onward.

Reaching a corner, he glanced up the street where a cart's creaking wheels were clanking along. This was his kingdom, the slum of St. Giles, and the place where he'd reinvented himself when his life had fallen apart.

The sound of the cart receded into the distance, most likely dragged off to market by someone hoping to sell their wares. It was time for that now at six in the morning. Other people were also starting to stir. He could hear the opening and closing of windows and doors as they woke to another day of hardship.

Walking on, Carlton strode through the mist while surveying the streets for signs of misconduct. Anyone had a right to live here. He didn't much care what crimes they committed, just as long as they did not target the other inhabitants of St. Giles, who were all under his protection.

He stopped again and tilted his head, alerted by a soft tapping noise. It sounded like feet hitting the ground at a frantic pace, and it seemed to be coming closer. Narrowing his gaze, he peered through the mist. If someone was being chased, he'd have to discern the reason for it, so he moved into the middle of the road, prepared to intercept the individual, when a bundle of white silk and lace topped by ribbons and tulle burst out of the ghostly haze and collided with his chest.

"What the devil?" It appeared to be covering a slender body now struggling frantically in his arms. "Be still, damn it! I've no intention to harm ye." *Yet.*

The silk and lace twisted, righting itself even as the ribbons and tulle got tangled in his hands. And then, from beneath the brim of a decorative bonnet, the prettiest pair of blue eyes he'd ever seen looked up and widened the moment they met his gaze.

"I know who you are," the woman, whoever she was, told him boldly. "You're the Scoundrel of St. Giles."

"At yer service," he said with a smirk while continuing to hold her. Not because he'd quit being a gentleman the day his father died, or because he wished to exert his power over her, but because there were very few pleasures to be had in this life and he'd once decided to savor each one. "And who, might I ask, are ye?"

She tilted her chin up a notch. "Lady Regina Berkly, if you please." She gave her arm a tug and he reluctantly released her. "And since you are here, I would like to enlist your help."

He didn't bother asking her why the hell she imagined he'd ever consider assisting a strange woman who looked like she'd exited a ballroom, taken a wrong turn and stepped straight into hell.

Instead he said, "With what?"

She squared her shoulders and tried to adjust the layers of fabric billowing around her. "With avoiding my wedding."

"You're"—he gave her a full perusal and acknowledged that the tulle now made sense—"a bride."

A firm nod confirmed this. "Forced into unhappy matrimony with the Marquess of Stokes."

Carlton considered his options for a moment and eventually asked, "Who are ye related to, exactly?"

"The Earl of Hedgewick is my father. My brother is—"

"Viscount Seabrook. Yes, I know."

She looked at him with some surprise but Carlton didn't bother explaining. He only smiled and offered his arm. "I'd be delighted to give ye sanctuary fer as long as ye need it, me lady. 'Tis the least I can do to ensure yer safety."

And to finish enacting the revenge that had thus far been twenty years in the making.

Author's Note

Dear Reader,

As with *The Illegitimate Duke*, this story required a great deal of medical research, especially pertaining to the early 1800s. For those of you who have not read that book, it is worth mentioning that Florian's insistence on handwashing is due to *Domestic Medicine* by William Buchan. This book is an excellent source on contagion attentiveness from the late 1700s onward. It proves that awareness of handwashing and general cleanliness in disease prevention existed even though it did not become a requirement for medical practitioners until much later. In fact, in spite of Buchan's book, which was originally published in 1771, Ignaz Semmelweis, a Hungarian physician, is credited with discovering the benefits of handwashing in 1847 when he noted a connection between physicians handling corpses, then delivering children without cleaning their hands first, and mothers contracting puerperal fever.

Not to diminish Semmelweis's findings, but

Buchan's were made almost eighty years earlier and would have been known to a well-read man like Florian and to Viola since she was in charge of managing the hospital.

Since some readers may protest to the use of morphine instead of laudanum, I'd like to point out that although morphine was not commercially used until the mid-1800s, a German pharmacist named Friedrich Wilhelm Sertürner had managed to isolate the crystalline compound from crude opium by 1816. During his experiments, he discovered that the pain-relief effect of this compound was ten times that of opium and named it morphine after Morpheus, the Greek god of dreams.

Considering how well traveled and open to new medicinal discoveries Florian was and his close working relationship with Viola, the two would have wasted no time in acquiring this new narcotic and administering it to their patients when performing surgeries.

Other historically accurate facts I've used to flesh out this story include the following:

✦ Pavillon de la Reine, the hotel in Paris where Henry and Viola stay. Built by King Henry IV of France in 1612, the hotel is named after Queen Anne of Austria, who once stayed there.

✦ The automaton. As noted in the story, Pierre Jaquet-Droz (1721–1790) was a Swiss watchmaker who built automatons to advertise his business, which also included the production of mechanical birds. His most notable works are *The Writer*, *The Musician*, and *The Draughtsman*. These mechanical wonders, so extraordinary for their time that some consider them the first computers, captured the interest of kings and emperors alike. For the purpose of this story, I chose to use *The Writer*, even though he was never sold at a market in Woolwich. Instead, he can be found at the Musée d'art et d'histoire (Museum of Art and History) in Neuchâtel, Switzerland, together with *The Musician* and *The Draughtsman*.

+ Berry Bros. & Rudd, the wine merchant used by Henry. This business was established as a grocer in 1698 at No. 3 St. James's Street by a widow with at least two daughters, though only her last name, Berry, is known. When her daughter Elizabeth and her husband inherited it, they began supplying the fashionable coffee houses of St. James's where their shop was located. They chose to advertise this, and to this day, Berry's continues to trade under the sign of the coffee mill. Eventually, Elizabeth's son and another family relation would begin focusing primarily on wine and spirits. Their success is evident in the fact that the business has survived for hundreds of years.

+ The New Game of Human Life. This game was published in England in 1790 by John Wallis and Elizabeth Newberry. It consists of a "board" created from sixteen pieces of paper mounted on linen, engraved with hand-colored images placed in eighty-eight squares. These squares are set in a flat spiral format going around the "board" with the rules engraved at the center. The rules and directions on how to play can be found online, which is how I wrote the scenes in which the game features as part of the story.

I hope you have enjoyed this romance. As you have probably guessed, Guthrie's story is next. I look forward to revealing how misunderstood this man really is and to giving him the happily-ever-after he truly deserves.

Until then, happy reading!

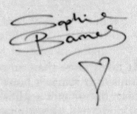

Acknowledgments

It takes more than an author to grasp an idea and transform it into a book. My name might be on the cover, but there's a whole team of spectacular people behind me, each with his or her own incredible skills and experience. Their faith in me and in my stories is invaluable, and since they do deserve to be recognized for their work, I'd like to take this opportunity to thank them all for their constant help and support.

To my editor extraordinaire, Nicole Fischer: your edits and advice have helped this story shine. Thank you so much for your insight and for believing in my ability to pull this off.

To my copy editor, Eleanor Mikucki; publicists Libby Collins, Pam Spengler-Jaffee, and Kayleigh Webb; marketing associate, Lauren Lauzon; and director of marketing, Angela Craft, thank you so much for all that you do and for offering guidance and support whenever it was needed.

I would also like to thank the amazing artist who created this book's stunning cover. Chris Cocozza has truly succeeded in capturing the mood of *The Infamous Duchess* and the way in which I envisioned both Henry and Viola looking—such a beautiful job!

To my fabulous beta readers, Dee Foster, Susan Lucas, Barb Hoffarth and Jacqueline Ang, whose insight has been tremendously helpful in strengthening the story, thank you so much!

Another big thank-you goes to Nancy Mayer for her assistance. Whenever I'm faced with a question regarding the Regency era that I can't answer on my own, I turn to Nancy for advice. Her help is invaluable.

My family and friends deserve my thanks as well, especially for reminding me to take a break occasionally, to step away from the computer and just unwind—I would be lost without you.

And to you, dear reader—thank you so much for taking the time to read this story. Your support is, as always, hugely appreciated!